Lynne Grah
has been a k
is very happi~~ly~~
w~~h~~o has learned to cook since she started to write!
Her five children keep her on her toes. She has a very
large dog who knocks everything over, a very small
terrier who barks a lot, and two cats. When time
allows, Lynne is a keen gardener.

About the Author

...ham was born in Northern Ireland and
...een romance reader since her teens. She
...ntly married to an understanding husband

Christmas with a Tycoon

LYNNE GRAHAM

MILLS & BOON

First Published in Great Britain 2018
By Mills & Boon, an imprint of HarperCollins *Publishers*
1 London Bridge Street, London, SE1 9GF

CHRISTMAS WITH A TYCOON © 2018 Harlequin Books S.A.

The Italian's Christmas Child © Lynne Graham 2016
The Greek's Christmas Bride © Lynne Graham 2016

ISBN: 978-0-263-26850-8

9-1118

MIX
Paper from
responsible sources
FSC® C007454

This book is produced from independently certified FSC™ paper to ensure responsible forest management.

For more information visit: www.harpercollins.co.uk/green

Printed and bound in Spain
by CPI, Barcelona

THE ITALIAN'S
CHRISTMAS CHILD

LYNNE GRAHAM

Christmas is one of my favourite times of year, it's about family and friends, so this is dedicated to you.

CHAPTER ONE

THE MOORLAND LANDSCAPE on Dartmoor was cold and crisp with ice. As the four-wheel drive turned off the road onto a rough lane, Vito saw the picturesque cottage sheltering behind winter-bare trees with graceful frosted branches. His lean, strong face grim with exhaustion, he got out of the car ahead of his driver, only tensing as he heard the sound of yet another text hitting his phone. Ignoring it, he walked into the property while the driver emptied the car.

Instant warmth greeted him and he raked a weary hand through the dense blue-black hair that the breeze had whipped across his brow. There was a welcome blaze in the brick inglenook fireplace and he fought the sense of relief threatening to engulf him. He was not a coward. He had not run away as his ex-fiancée had accused him of doing. He would have stood his ground and stayed in Florence had he not finally appreciated that the pursuit of the paparazzi and outrageous headlines were only being fuelled by his continuing presence.

He had grudgingly followed his best friend Apollo's advice and had removed himself from the scene, recognising that his mother had quite enough to deal with when her husband was in hospital following a serious heart attack without also having to suffer the embarrassment of her son's newly acquired notoriety. Undeniably, his friend had much more experience than Vito had of handling scandals and bad publicity. The Greek playboy had led a far less restricted life than Vito, who had known from an early age that he would become the next CEO of the Zaffari Bank. His grandfather had steeped him in the history and traditions of a family that could trace its beginnings back to the Middle Ages when the Zaffari name had stood shoulder to shoulder with words like *honour* and *principle*. No more, Vito reflected wryly. Now he would be famous for ever as the banker who had indulged in drugs and strippers.

Not his style, not his style at all, Vito ruminated ruefully, breaking free of his thoughts to lavishly tip his driver and thank him. When it came to the drug allegations, he could only suppress a groan. One of his closest friends at school had taken something that had killed him at a party and Vito had never been tempted by illegal substances. And the whores? In truth Vito could barely remember when he had last had sex. Although he had been engaged until a week earlier, Marzia had always been cool in that department.

'She's a lady to her backbone.' His grandfather had sighed approvingly, shortly before his passing. 'A Ravello with the right background and breeding. She will make a superb hostess and future mother for your children.'

Not now, though, Vito thought, glancing at his phone to discover that his ex had sent him yet another text. *Dio mio,* what did she want from him now? He had perfectly understood her decision to break off their engagement and he had wasted no time in putting the house she had been furnishing for their future occupation back on the market. That, however, had proved to be a move that had evidently rankled, even though he had assured Marzia that she was welcome to keep every stick of furniture in the place.

What about the Abriano painting? she'd texted.

He pointed out that his grandfather's engagement gift would have to be returned. It was worth millions—how much more compensation was he to pay in terms of damages? He had offered her the house but she had refused it.

But in spite of his generosity, he still felt guilty. He had messed up Marzia's life and embarrassed her. For probably the first time in his life he had wronged someone. On the spur of the moment he had made a decision that had hit Marzia very hard and even the sincerest apology could not lessen the impact of it. But he could not have told his former fiancée the truth because he could not have trusted her to keep it secret. And if the truth came out, his sacrifice would be pointless and it would plunge the only woman he had ever loved into gross humiliation and heartbreak. Vito had made a very tough choice and he was fully prepared to take the heat for it.

That, indeed, was why vanishing off-grid for a couple of weeks over Christmas *still* felt disturbingly gutless to Vito, whose natural instincts were pre-emptive and forceful.

'Ritchie's a lying, cheating scumbag!' Holly's flatmate and best friend, Pixie, ranted furiously down the phone.

Holly grimaced and pushed her hand through her

heavy mane of black curling hair, her big blue eyes red-rimmed and sad as she checked her watch to see that she was still safely within her lunch hour. 'You're not going to get any argument from me on that score,' she said ruefully.

'He's as bad as that last guy who borrowed all the money from you,' Pixie reminded her with a typical lack of tact. 'And the one before that who wanted to marry you so that you could act as a carer for his invalid mother!'

Wincing at her disheartening past history with men, Holly reflected that she could not have done worse in the dating stakes had she drawn up a specific list of selfish, dishonest losers. 'Let's not look back,' she urged, keen to move on to more positive subjects.

Pixie refused to cooperate, saying, 'So, what on earth are you planning to do now for your festive break with me, stuck in London and Ritchie out of the picture?'

A sudden grin lit Holly's oval face with surprising enthusiasm. 'I'm going to make Christmas for Sylvia instead!'

'But she's staying with her daughter in Yorkshire over the holiday...*isn't she*?'

'No, Alice had to cancel Sylvia at the last minute. Her house has been flooded by a burst pipe. Sylvia was horribly disappointed when she found out and then when I walked in on Ritchie with his floozy today, I realised that I could take two pieces of bad luck and make something good out of them...'

'I really hate it when you pick yourself up off the floor and come over all optimistic again.' Pixie sighed dramatically. 'Please tell me you at least *thumped* Ritchie...'

'I told him what I thought of him…briefly,' Holly qualified with her innate honesty, for really she had been too squeamish to linger in the presence of her half-naked boyfriend and the woman he had chosen to cheat on her with. 'So, is it all right for me to borrow your car to go to Sylvia's?'

'Of course it is. How else would you get there? But watch out: there's snow forecast—'

'They always like to talk about snow this close to Christmas,' Holly demurred, unimpressed by the threat. 'By the way, I'm taking our Christmas tree and orna-ments with me and I'd already bought and made all the trimmings for a festive lunch. I'm going to put on that Santa outfit you wore for the Christmas party at the salon last year. Sylvia loves a laugh. She'll appreciate it.'

'Sylvia will be over the moon when she finds you on the doorstep,' her friend predicted warmly. 'Between losing her husband and having to move because she couldn't manage the farmhouse alone any more, she's had a horrible year.'

Holly held firmly on to the inspiring prospect of her foster mother's happiness at her arrival while she finished her afternoon shift at the busy café where she worked. It was Christmas Eve and she adored the festive season, possibly because she had grown up mainly in foster care and had always been painfully conscious that she did not have a real family to share the experience with. In an effort to comfort her, Pixie had assured her that family Christmases could be a nightmare and that she was in love with an ideal of Christmas rather than the reality. But some day, somehow, Holly was deter-mined to turn fantasy into reality with a husband and children of her own. That was her dream and in spite of recent setbacks she understood that it was hanging on to her dream that essentially kept her going through more challenging times.

Both she and Pixie had been fostered by Sylvia Ware from the age of twelve and the older woman's warm acceptance and understanding had been far superior to the uncaring and occasionally neglectful homes Holly and Pixie had endured as younger children caught up in the care system. Holly had long regretted not paying more heed to Sylvia's lectures about studying harder at school. Over the years Holly had attended so many different schools and made so many moves that she had simply drifted through her education, accepting that she would always be behind in certain subjects. Now at almost twenty-four, Holly had redressed that adolescent mistake by attending night classes to achieve basic qualifications but the road ahead to further education seemed so long and complex that it daunted her and she had instead chosen to study for a qualification in interior design online.

'And what use is that to you?' Pixie, who was a hairdresser, had asked baldly.

'I'm really interested in it. I love looking at a room and thinking about how I can improve it.'

'But people from our sort of background don't get hired as interior designers,' Pixie had pointed out. 'I mean, we're just ordinary workers trying to pay our bills, not people with fancy careers.'

And Holly had to acknowledge as she donned her friend's Santa outfit that there *was* nothing fancy or impressive about her likely to combat that discouraging assurance. Fortunately the short dress had been far too generously sized on her infinitely more slender friend.

Pixie might envy Holly's curves but Pixie could eat whatever she liked and never put on a pound while Holly was engaged in a constant struggle to prevent her curves from taking over. Her golden skin tone hailed from an unknown father. He might or might not have been someone her erratic mother had met abroad. On the other hand he might simply have been a man who lived in the same street. Her only parent had told her so many lies that Holly had long accepted that the truth of her fatherhood would never be known.

At four feet ten inches tall, Holly, like her mother, lacked height. She pulled on warm black winter tights under the bright red satin and corseted dress. Thrusting her feet into cowboy boots rather than the heels Pixie had sported for her party a year earlier, Holly scowled at her gaudy, busty reflection in the mirror and jammed on the Santa hat in a defiant move. OK, she looked comical, she acknowledged, but her appearance would make Sylvia laugh and overlook the disappointment of not having her own daughters around her to celebrate Christmas Day with, and that was what was truly important.

Planning to spend the night on the sofa in Sylvia's tiny living area, she packed her rucksack and carefully placed what remained of the decorations and the food into a box heavy enough to make her stagger on her final trip to the car. *At least the food wouldn't be going to waste*, she thought with determined positivity, until a flashback of the ugly scene she had interrupted with Ritchie and the receptionist at his insurance office cut through her rebellious brain.

Her tummy rolled with nausea and her battered heart clenched. *In the middle of the day as well*, she thought with a shudder. She couldn't imagine even having sex, never mind going at it on a desk in broad daylight. Possibly she wasn't a very adventurous person. In fact both she and Pixie were probably pretty strait-laced. At twelve years old they had shuddered over the ugly chaos of broken relationships in their mothers' lives and had solemnly decided to swear off men altogether. Of course once puberty had kicked in, with all its attendant confusing hormones, that rule had failed. At fourteen they had ditched their embargo on men while deciding that sex was the real danger and best avoided outside a serious relationship. *A serious committed relationship.* Holly's eyes rolled at the memory of their mutual innocence. And so far neither she nor her friend had managed to have a serious committed relationship with a man.

All that considered thought about steering clear of sexual relationships hadn't done her many favours either, Holly reflected with helpless insecurity. There had been men she really liked who ran a mile from what they saw as her outdated expectations and then there had been the others who stayed around for a few weeks or months, eager to be the first into her bed. Had she only ever been a sexual challenge to Ritchie? How long, for instance, had he been messing around with other women?

'Did you expect me to wait for you for ever?' Ritchie had shouted back at her, blaming her for his betrayal because she had held back on having sex with him. 'What's so special about you?'

Holly flinched at that ugly recollection because she had always known that there was nothing particularly special about her.

It was snowing as she drove off in the battered little hatchback that Pixie had christened Clementine, and she groaned. She loved the look of snow but she didn't like to drive in it and she hated being cold. Thank goodness for the car, she acknowledged, as she rattled out of the small Devon town where she lived and worked.

Snow was falling fast by the time she reached Sylvia's home, which was dismayingly dark. Perhaps the older woman was out at a church service or visiting a neighbour. Jamming down her hat over the mass of hair fighting to escape its confines, Holly rapped on the door and waited, stamping her feet to keep warm. After a couple of minutes she knocked again and then she followed the communal path to the little house next door, which was brightly lit, and knocked there instead.

'I'm sorry to bother you but I wondered if you knew where Mrs Ware has gone and if she'll be home soon,' Holly asked with a friendly smile.

'Sylvia left this afternoon. I helped her pack—she was in such a tizzy because she wasn't expecting anyone,' the elderly little woman at the door told her.

Holly frowned, her heart sinking. 'So, she went to her daughter's after all, then?'

'Oh, no, it wasn't the daughter who came, it was her son. Big tall chap in a suit. He's taking her back to Bruges or Belgium or some place,' the neighbour told her less certainly.

'Brussels. That's where Stephen lives. Do you know how long she'll be away?'

'A couple of weeks at least, she seemed to think…'

As deflated as a pricked balloon, Holly walked back to her car.

'You watch yourself driving home,' the old lady called after her. 'There's to be heavy snow tonight.'

'Thanks, I will,' Holly promised, forcing a smile. 'Merry Christmas!'

And a very merry Christmas it was going to be on her own, she thought unhappily, annoyed to find that her eyes were prickling with tears. After all, Sylvia was going to have the best possible Christmas with her son and the grandchildren she rarely saw. Holly was really, really pleased that Stephen had swooped in from abroad to save the day. He and his wife were rare visitors but he had at least made the effort and now his mother wouldn't have to spend her first Christmas as a widow alone. Holly sniffed and blinked back the tears, scolding herself for being so selfish. She was young and healthy and employed. She had nothing to complain about, nothing at all.

Maybe she was simply missing Pixie, she reasoned, as she drove with care on the steep, icy road that climbed up over the moors. Pixie's kid brother was in some sort of trouble and Pixie had taken time off to go and stay with him and sort it out. It was probably financial trouble but Holly wouldn't ask any awkward questions or offer unwelcome advice because she didn't want to hurt her friend, who was deeply attached to her horribly self-centred sibling. Everyone had problems, she reminded herself doggedly, tensing as she felt the tyres of the car shift into a near skid on the slippery surface and slowing her speed even more. She had far fewer problems than most people and had no excuse whatsoever for feeling sorry for herself.

Ritchie? Well, that wasn't an excuse. So, she had got hurt but then Pixie would point out that she was too soft in that line, too prone to thinking well of people and being knocked back hard when they let her down. Pixie was more of a cynic, strong on distrust as a means of self-defence, except when it came to her own brother.

Holly peered out of the windscreen because visibility was fading fast with the wipers unable to keep up with the heavy snow. She wasn't the dramatic type, she assured herself, as the car coasted down a hill that seemed steeper than it had seemed when she drove over it earlier that evening, but the weather was foul and the light snowfall she had dimly expected now bore a closer resemblance to a blizzard.

And then without the smallest warning, and to the accompaniment of her strangled scream, the car glided in the most terrifying slow motion off the road into a ditch where it tilted over and wedged fast with a loud, nerve-racking crunch of metal. After switching off the engine, Holly breathed in slow and deep to calm herself. She was alive, no other car was involved and nobody was hurt. There was much to be thankful for, she told herself bracingly.

Sadly that was a conviction that took a beating once she climbed out with some difficulty, owing to the angle the car had crashed at, to inspect the damage. The side wing of Pixie's elderly vehicle was crushed up against a large rock, which had presumably been placed to mark the entrance to the lane. *My goodness, how much will the repairs cost?* was her first fearful thought. It was *her* responsibility, not Pixie's.

A spark of fear assailed her only after she had examined her surroundings. The road was deserted and lay under a covering of unbroken snow. It was a bad night and it was Christmas Eve and she didn't think there would be much passing traffic, if any. As she stood there nursing her mobile phone and wondering what she was going to do, Holly had never felt more lonely. She had no close friend she could ring and drag out in such dreadful weather on such a special night. No, she was on her own, sink or swim. Consternation gripped her when she couldn't get a signal on her phone to use it. Only then did she turn round to look again at the lane she stood beside and there, like a faint beacon in the darkness, she saw the lights of what could only be a house and relief filled her to overflowing. Hopefully it was occupied and the occupant had a landline she could use to call for a breakdown truck.

Vito was savouring a glass of award-winning wine and wondering what to do with the evening when the knocker on the door sounded. Taken aback, he frowned because he hadn't heard a car and there were no lights outside. Did the local caretaker live within walking distance? He peered out through the spyhole and saw a red-and-white Santa hat. Someone was definitely at the wrong house because Vito hated Christmas. He yanked open the door and enormous blue eyes like velvet pansies looked up at him. At first he thought his visitor was a child and then his eyes dropped and took in the swell of breasts visible between the parted edges of her coat and he registered that, although she might be very small, she was all woman.

Holly stared up in wonderment at the male who appeared in the doorway. He looked like every fantasy male she had ever dreamt about meeting all rolled into one spectacular package. In fact he was so gorgeous with his black hair, designer stubble and dark, deep-set, mysterious eyes that he made her teeth clench in dismay because he didn't look approachable or helpful or anything that might have encouraged her. That he wore a very formal dark business suit with a white shirt and natty gold tie didn't help to relax her either.

'If you're looking for a party, you're at the wrong house,' Vito told her loftily, recalling his friend's warnings about how sneaky the paparazzi could be. If he'd thought about that risk, he wouldn't have answered the door at all.

'I'm looking for a phone. Mine has no reception here and my car went off the road at the foot of your lane,' Holly explained in a rush. 'Do you have a landline?'

Exasperation flashed through Vito, who had far too much sensitive information on his cell phone to consider loaning it to anyone. 'This isn't my house. I'll look and see,' he fielded drily.

As he turned on his heel without inviting her in out of the heavily falling snow, Holly grimaced and shivered because she wasn't dressed for bad weather, having only thrown on a raincoat to cover her outfit because she had known she would be warm inside the car. *Not Mr Nice Guy, anyway*, she thought ruefully. She had recognised the impatience in those electrifyingly dark magnetic eyes, watched the flare of his nostrils and the tightening of his wide, sculpted mouth as he'd bit back a withering comment. She was good at reading faces, even gorgeous ones, she conceded, as she shifted her feet in a vain effort to heat the blood freezing in her veins. She didn't think she had ever seen a more handsome man, no, not even on a movie screen, but personality-wise she reckoned that there was a good chance that he was chillier than an icicle.

'There is a phone… You may step inside to use it,' he invited grudgingly, his foreign accent edging every syllable in a very attractive way.

Holly reddened with discomfiture, already well aware that she was not a welcome visitor. She dug out her phone to scroll through numbers for Pixie's car mechanic, Bill, who ran a breakdown service. As she did so, she missed seeing the step in front of her and tripped over it, falling forward with a force that would have knocked the breath from her body had not strong arms snapped out to catch her before she fell.

'Watch out…' Taken aback by a level of clumsiness utterly unknown to a male as surefooted as a cat, Vito virtually lifted her into the porch. As her hair briefly brushed his face he was engulfed by the scent of oranges, sweet and sun-warmed. But it was only by touching her and seeing her face below the lights that he registered that she was almost blue with cold. '*Maledizione*, you're freezing! Why didn't you tell me that?'

'It's enough of an imposition coming to the door—'

'Yes, I would surely have been happier to trip over your frozen corpse on my doorstep in the morning!' Vito fielded scathingly. 'You should've told me—'

'You've got eyes of your own and an off-putting manner. I don't like bothering people,' Holly said truthfully while she frantically rubbed her hands over her raincoat in an effort to get some feeling back into her fingers before she tried to work her phone again.

Vito gazed down at her from his height of six foot one. He was bemused by her criticism when he was trying to be pleasant and when he could not recall when a woman had last offered him a word of criticism. Even in the act of breaking their engagement, Marzia had contrived not to speak a word of condemnation. Either a woman of saintly tolerance or one who didn't give a damn who he might have slept with behind her back? It was a sobering thought.

An off-putting manner? Could that be true about him? His grandfather had taught him to maintain distance between himself and others and he had often thought that a useful gift when it came to commanding a large staff, none of whom dared to take liberties with their authoritarian CEO.

Thoroughly irritated by the thoughts awakened by his visitor and that unfamiliar self-questioning mode, he swiped the phone from between her shaking fingers and said firmly, 'Go and warm up first by the fire and then make the call.'

'Are you sure you don't mind?'

'I will contrive to bear it.'

Halfway towards the wonderful blaze of the log fire illuminating the dim interior, Holly spun round with a merriment in her eyes that lit up her whole face and she laughed. 'You're a sarky one, aren't you?'

In the firelight her eyes were bright as sapphires and that illuminating smile made the breath catch in his throat because it lent her incredible appeal. And Vito was not the sort of male who noticed women very often and when he did he usually swiftly stifled the impulse. But for a split second that playful tone and that radiant smile knocked him sideways and he found himself staring. He scanned the glorious dark hair that fell free of the Santa hat as she whipped it off, before lowering his appreciative gaze to the wonderfully generous thrust of her breasts above a neat little waist, right down to the hem of the shimmering dress that revealed slim knees and shapely calves incongruously encased in cowboy boots. He threw his shoulders back, bracing as the pulse at his groin beat out a different kind of tension.

Holly connected momentarily with eyes of gold semi-veiled by the lush black sweep of his lashes and something visceral tightened low in her pelvis as she let her attention linger on his lean, hard bone structure, which was stunningly hard and male from his level dark brows to his arrogant classic nose and his strong, sculpted jawline. Just looking at him sent the oddest flash of excitement through her and she reddened uneasily, and deliberately spun back to the fire to hold her hands out to the heat. So, he was very good-looking. That didn't mean she had to gape like an awestruck fan at a rock star, did it? She was only inside his house to use the phone, she reminded herself in embarrassment.

She flexed her fingers. 'Where did you put my phone?'

As she half turned it was settled neatly into her hand and she opened it and scrolled through the numbers. He handed her the handset of the house phone and she pressed out Bill's number, lifting it to her ear while carefully not glancing again in her host's direction.

Vito was engaged in subduing his sexual arousal and reeling in shock from the need to do so. What was he? A teenager again? She wasn't his type…if he had a type. The women in his life had invariably been tall, elegant blondes and she was very small, very curvy and very, *very* sexy, he conceded involuntarily as she moved about the room while she talked, her luxuriant hair rippling across her shoulders, her rounded hips swaying. She was apologising for disturbing someone on Christmas Eve and she apologised at great length instead of getting straight to the point of her problem with her car.

What were the chances that she was a particularly clever member of the paparazzi brigade? Vito had flown into the UK on a private plane to a private airfield and travelled to the cottage in a private car. Only Apollo and his mother, Concetta, knew where he was. But Apollo had warned him that the paps went to extraordinary lengths to steal photos and find stories they could sell. His perfect white teeth gritted. At the very least, he needed to check that there was a broken-down car at the foot of the lane.

'Boxing Day?' Holly was practically whispering in horror.

'And possibly only if the snowplough has been through ahead of me,' Bill told her apologetically. 'I'm working flat out tonight as it is. Where exactly is the car?'

The older man was local and, knowing the road well, was able to establish where she was. 'Aye, I know the house down there—foreign-owned holiday home as far as I know. And you're able to stay there?'

'Yes,' Holly said in as reassuring a tone as she could contrive while wondering if she was going to have to bed down in Pixie's car. 'Do you know anyone else I could ring?'

She tried the second number but there was no response at all. Swallowing hard, she set the digital phone down. 'I'll go back to the car now,' she told Vito squarely.

'I'll walk down with you… See if there's anything I can do—'

'Unless you have a tractor to haul it out of the ditch I shouldn't think so.' Holly buttoned her coat, tied the belt and braced herself to face the great outdoors again.

As she straightened her shoulders she looked round the room with belated admiration, suddenly noticing that the opulent décor was an amazing and highly effective marriage of traditional and contemporary styles. In spite of the ancient brick inglenook fireplace, the staircase had a glass surround and concealed lights. But she also noticed that there was one glaring omission: there were no festive decorations of any kind.

Vito yanked on his cashmere coat and scarf over the suit he still wore.

'If you don't have boots, I can't let you go down there with me… You'll get your shoes soaked,' Holly told him ruefully, glancing at the polished, city-type footwear he sported with his incredibly stylish suit, which moulded to his well-built, long-legged frame as though specifically tailored to do so.

Vito walked into the porch, which boasted a rack of boots, and, picking out a pair, donned them. Her pragmatism had secretly impressed him. Vito was extremely clever but, like many very clever people, he was not particularly practical and the challenges of rural living in bad weather lay far outside his comfort zone.

'My name is Holly,' she announced brightly on the porch.

'Vito…er… Vito Sorrentino,' Vito lied, employing his father's original surname.

His mother had been an only child, a daughter when his grandfather had longed for a son. At his grandfather's request, Vito's father had changed his name to Zaffari when he married Vito's mother to ensure that the family name would not die out. Ciccio Sorrentino had been content to surrender his name in return for the privilege of marrying a fabulously wealthy banking heiress. There was no good reason for Vito to take the risk of identifying himself to a stranger. Right now the name Zaffari was cannon fodder for the tabloids across Europe and the news of his disappearance and current location would be worth a great deal of money to a profiteer. And if there was one gift Vito had in spades it was the gilded art of making a profit and ensuring that nobody got to do it at his expense.

His grandfather would have turned in his grave at the mere threat of his grandson plunging the family name and the family bank into such a sleazy scandal. Vito, however, was rather less naive. Having attended a board meeting before his departure, Vito was aware that he could virtually do no wrong. All the Zaffari directors cared about was that their CEO continued to ensure that the Zaffari bank carried on being the most successful financial institution in Europe.

CHAPTER TWO

'YOU SAID THIS wasn't your house,' Holly reminded him through chattering teeth as they walked out into the teeth of a gale laced with snow.

'A friend loaned it to me for a break.'

'And you're staying here alone?'

'*Sì*...yes.'

'By choice...*alone*...at Christmas?' Holly framed incredulously.

'Why not?' Vito loathed Christmas but that was none of her business and he saw no need to reveal anything of a personal nature. His memories of Christmas were toxic. His parents, who rarely spent time together, had squabbled almost continuously through the festive break. His mother had made a real effort to hide that reality and make the season enjoyable, but Vito had always been far too intelligent even as a child not to understand what was happening around him. He had seen that his mother loved his father but that her love was not returned. He had watched her humiliate herself in an effort to smooth over Ciccio's bad moods and even worse temper. He had listened to her beg for five minutes of her husband's attention. He had eventually grasped that the ideal goal composed of marriage, family and respectability could be a very expensive shrine to worship at. Had he not been made aware that it was his inherent duty to carry on the family line, nothing would have persuaded Vito into matrimony.

He studied the old car in the ditch with an amount of satisfaction that bemused him. It was a shabby ancient wreck of a vehicle. It had to mean that Holly was not a plant, not a spy or a member of the paparazzi, but a genuine traveller in trouble. Not that that reality softened his irritation over the fact that he was now stuck with her for at least one night. He had listened to the phone call she had made. Short of it being a matter of life or death, nobody was willing to come out on such a night. Of course he could have thrown his wealth at the problem to take care of it but nothing would more surely advertise his presence than the hiring of a helicopter to remove his unwanted guest, and he was doubtful that even a helicopter could fly in such poor conditions.

'As you see…it's stuck,' Holly pointed out unnecessarily while patting the bonnet of the car as if it were a live entity in need of comfort. 'It's my friend's car and she's going to be really upset about this.'

'Accidents happen…particularly if you choose to drive without taking precautions on a road like this in this kind of weather.'

In disbelief, Holly rounded on him, twin spots of high colour sparking over her cheekbones. 'It wasn't snowing this bad when I left home! There were no precautions!'

'Let's get your stuff and head back to the house.'

Suppressing the anger his tactless comment had roused with some difficulty, Holly studied him in astonishment. 'You're inviting me back to the house? You don't need to. I can—'

'I'm a notoriously unsympathetic man but even I could not leave you to sleep in a car in a snowstorm on Christmas Eve!' Vito framed impatiently. 'Now, may we cut the conversation and head back to the heat? Or do you want to pat the car again?'

Face red now with mortification, Holly opened the boot and dug out her rucksack to swing it up onto her back.

The rucksack was almost as big as she was, Vito saw in disbelief. 'Let me take that.'

'No...I was hoping you'd take the box because it's heavier.'

Stubborn mouth flattening, Vito reached in with reluctance for the sizeable box and hefted it up with a curled lip. 'Do you really need the box as well?'

'Yes, it's got all my stuff in it...*please*,' Holly urged.

Her amazingly blue eyes looked up at him and he felt strangely disorientated. Her eyes were as translucent a blue as the Delft masterpieces his mother had conserved from his grandfather's world-famous collection. They trudged back up the lane with Vito maintaining a disgruntled silence as he carried the bulky carton.

'*Porca miseria!* What's in the box?'

'My Christmas decorations and some food.'

'Why are you driving round with Christmas decorations and food? Of course, you were heading to a party,' he reasoned for himself, thinking of what she wore.

'No, I wasn't. I intended to spend the night with my foster mother because I thought she was going to be on her own for Christmas. *But*...turns out her son came and collected her and she didn't know I was planning to surprise her, so when I went off the road I was driving home again.'

'Where's home?'

She named a town Vito had never heard of.

'Where are you from?'

'Florence…in Italy,' he explained succinctly.

'I do know where Florence is…it *is* famous,' Holly countered, glancing up at him while the snow drifted down steadily, quietly, cocooning them in the small space lit by his torch. 'So, you're Italian.'

'You do like to state the obvious, don't you?' Vito derided, stomping into the porch one step behind her.

'I hate that sarcasm of yours!' Holly fired back at him angrily, taking herself almost as much by surprise as she took him because she usually went out of her way to avoid conflict.

An elegant black brow raised, Vito removed the boots, hung his coat and scarf and then lifted the rucksack from her bent shoulders. 'What have you got in here? Rocks?'

'Food.'

'The kitchen here is packed with food.'

'Do you always know better than everyone else about everything?' Holly, whose besetting fault was untidiness, carefully hung her wet coat beside his to be polite.

'I very often *do* know better,' Vito answered without hesitation.

Holly spread a shaken glance over his lean, darkly handsome and wholly serious features and groaned out loud. 'No sense of humour either.'

'Knowing one's own strengths is not a flaw,' Vito informed her gently.

'But it is if you don't consider your faults—'

'And what are *your* faults?' Vito enquired saccharine smooth, as she headed for the fire like a homing pigeon and held her hands out to the heat.

Holly wrinkled her snub nose and thought hard. 'I'm untidy. An incurable optimist. Too much of a people-pleaser… That comes of all those years in foster care and trying to fit in to different families and different schools.' She angled her head to one side, brown hair lying in a silken mass against one creamy cheek as she pondered. In the red Santa get-up, she reminded him of a cheerful little robin he had once seen pacing on a fence. 'I'm too forgiving sometimes because I always want to think the best of people or give them a second chance. I get really cross if I run out of coffee but I don't like conflict and avoid it. I like to do things quickly but sometimes that means I don't do them well. I fuss about my weight but I *still* don't exercise…'

As Vito listened to that very frank résumé he almost laughed. There was something intensely sweet about that forthright honesty. 'Strengths?' he prompted, unable to resist the temptation.

'I'm honest, loyal, hardworking, punctual…I like to make the people I care about happy,' she confided. 'That's what put me on that road tonight.'

'Would you like a drink?' Vito enquired.

'Red wine, if you have it…' Moving away from the fire, Holly approached her rucksack. 'Is it all right if I put the food in the kitchen?'

She walked through the door he indicated and her eyebrows soared along with the ceiling. Beyond that door the cottage changed again. A big extension housed an ultra-modern kitchen diner with pale sparkling granite work surfaces and a fridge large enough to answer the storage needs of a restaurant. She opened it up. It was already generously packed with goodies, mainly of the luxury version of ready meals. She arranged her offerings on an empty shelf and then walked back into the main room to open the box and extract the food that remained.

Obviously, she was stuck here in a strange house with a strange man for one night at the very least, Holly reflected anxiously. A slight frisson of unease trickled down her spine. Vito hadn't done or said anything threatening, though, she reminded herself. Like her, he recognised practicalities. He was stuck with her because she had nowhere else to go and clearly he wasn't overjoyed by the situation. Neither one of them had a choice but to make the best of it.

'You brought a lot of food with you,' Vito remarked from behind her.

Holly flinched because she hadn't heard him approach and she whipped her head around. 'I assumed I would be providing a Christmas lunch for two people.'

Walking back out of the kitchen when she had finished, she found him frowning down at the tree ornaments visible in the box.

'What is all this stuff?' he asked incredulously.

Holly explained. 'Would it be all right if I put up my tree here? I mean, it is Christmas Eve and I won't get another opportunity for a year,' she pointed out. 'Christmas is special to me.'

Vito was still frowning. 'Not to me,' he admitted flatly, for he had only bad memories of the many disappointing Christmases he had endured as a child.

Flushing, Holly closed the box and pushed it over to the wall out of the way. 'That's not a problem. You're doing enough letting me stay here.'

Dio mio, he was relieved that she was only a passing stranger because her fondness for the sentimental trappings of the season set his teeth on edge. Of course she wanted to put up her Christmas tree! Anyone who travelled around wearing a Santa hat was likely to want a tree on display as well! He handed her a glass of wine, trying not to feel responsible for having doused her chirpy flow of chatter.

'I'm heading upstairs for a shower,' Vito told her, because even though he had worn the boots, his suit trousers were damp. 'Will you be all right down here on your own?'

'Of course… This is much better than sitting in a crashed car,' Holly assured him before adding more awkwardly, 'Do you have a sweater or anything I could borrow? I only have pyjamas and a dress with me. My foster mum's house is very warm so I didn't pack anything woolly.'

Vito had not a clue what was in his luggage because he hadn't packed his own case since he was a teenager at boarding school. 'I'll see what I've got.'

Through the glass barrier of the stairs, Holly watched his long, powerful legs disappear from view and a curious little frisson rippled through her tense body. She heaved a sigh. So, no Christmas tree. What possible objection could anyone have to a Christmas tree? Did Vito share Ebenezer Scrooge's loathing for the festive season? Reminding herself that she was *very* lucky not to be shivering in Pixie's car by the side of the road, she settled down on the shaggy rug by the hearth and simply luxuriated in the warmth emanating from the logs glowing in the fire.

Vito thought about Holly while he took a shower. It

was a major mistake. Within seconds of picturing her sexy little body he went hard as a rock, his body reacting with a randy enthusiasm that astonished him. For months, of course, his libido had very much taken a back seat to the eighteen-hour days he was working. This year the bank's revenues would, he reminded himself with pride, smash all previous records. He was doing what he had been raised to do and he was doing it extremely well, so why did he feel so empty, so joyless? Vito asked himself in exasperation.

Intellectually he understood that there was more to life than the pursuit of profit but realistically he was and always had been a workaholic. An image of Holly chattering by the fire assailed him. Holly with her wonderful curves and her weird tree in a box. She was unusual, not remotely like the sort of women Vito usually met, and her originality was a huge draw. He had no idea what she was likely to say next. She wasn't wearing make-up. She didn't fuss with her appearance. She said exactly what she thought and felt—she had no filter. Towelling off, he tried to stop thinking about Holly. Obviously she turned him on. Equally obviously he wasn't going to do anything about it.

Why the hell not? The words sounded in the back of his brain. That battered old car, everything about her spelled out the message that she came from a different world. Making any kind of a move would be taking advantage, he told himself grimly. Yet the instant he had seen Holly he had wanted her, *wanted* her with an intensity he hadn't felt around a woman since he was a careless teenager. It was the situation. He could relax with a woman who had neither a clue who he was nor any idea of the sleazy scandal currently clinging to his name. And why wouldn't he want her? After all, he was very probably sex-starved, he told himself impatiently as he tossed out the contents of one of his suitcases and then opened a second before finding a sweater he deemed suitable.

Holly watched Vito walk down the stairs with the fluid, silent grace of a panther. He had looked amazing in his elegant business suit, but in black designer jeans and a long-sleeved red cotton tee he was drop-dead gorgeous and, with those high cheekbones and that full masculine mouth, very much in the male-model category. She blinked and stared, feeling the colour rise in her cheeks, her self-consciousness taking over, for she had literally never ever been in the radius of such a very handsome male and it was just a little like bumping into a movie star without warning.

'Here… You can roll up the sleeves.' Vito tossed the sweater into her lap. 'If you want to freshen up, there's a shower room just before you enter the kitchen.'

Holly scrambled upright and grabbed her rucksack to take his advice. A little alone time to get her giddy head in order struck her as a very good idea. When she saw herself in the mirror in the shower room she was affronted by the wind-tousled explosion of her hair and the amount of cleavage she was showing in the Santa outfit. Stripping off, she went for a shower, exulting in the hot water and the famous-name shower gel on offer. Whoever owned the cottage had to be pretty comfortably off, she decided with a grimace, which probably meant that Vito was as well. He wore a very sleek gold-coloured watch and the fit of his suit had been perfection. But then what did she know about such trappings or the likely cost of them? Pixie would laugh to hear such musings when the closest Holly had ever got to even dating an office worker was Ritchie, the cheating insurance salesman.

She pulled on the blue sweater, which plunged low enough at the neck to reveal her bra. She yanked it at the back to raise it to a decent level at the front and knew she would have to remember to keep her shoulders back. She rolled up the sleeves and, since the sweater covered her to her knees, left off her tights. Her hair she rescued with a little diligent primping until it fell in loose waves round her shoulders. Frowning at her bunny slippers, she crammed them back in her rucksack, deciding that bare feet were preferable. Cosmetics-wise she was pretty much stuck with the minimal make-up she had packed for Sylvia's. Sighing, she used tinted moisturiser, subtle eyeliner and glossed her lips. Well, at short notice that was the best she could do. In any case it was only her pride that was prompting her to make the effort. After all, a male as sophisticated as Vito Sorrentino wouldn't look at her anyway, she thought with a squirming pang of guilty disappointment. Why on earth was she thinking about him that way?

And thinking about Vito that way put her back in mind of Ritchie, which was unfortunate. But it also reminded her that she hadn't taken her pill yet and she dug into her bag to remedy that, only to discover that she had left them at home. As to why a virgin was taking contraceptive precautions, she and Pixie both did on a 'better safe than sorry' basis. Both of their mothers had messed up their lives with early unplanned pregnancies and neither Holly nor Pixie wanted to run the same risk.

Of course a couple of years back Holly had had different and more romantic expectations. She had fondly imagined that she would eventually meet a man who would sweep her away on a tide of passion and she had believed that she had to protect herself in the face of such temptation. Sadly, nothing any boyfriend had yet made her feel could have fallen into a category that qualified as being *swept away*. Since then Holly had wondered if there was a distinct possibility that she herself simply wasn't a very passionate woman. Still, Holly reasoned wryly, there was nothing wrong with living in hope, was there?

Somehow Vito had been fully expecting Holly to reappear with a full face of make-up. Instead she appeared with her face rosy and apparently untouched, his sweater drooping round her in shapeless, bulky folds, her tiny feet bare. And Vito almost laughed out loud in appreciation and relief. What remained of his innate wariness was evaporating fast because no woman he had ever yet met could possibly have put less effort into trying to attract him than Holly. Before his engagement and even since it he had been targeted so often by predatory women that he had learned to be guarded in his behaviour around females, both inside and outside working hours. His rare smile flashed across his lean, strong face.

Holly collided involuntarily with molten gold eyes enhanced by thick black lashes and then that truly heart-stopping smile that illuminated his darkly handsome features, and her heart not only bounced in her chest but also skipped an entire beat in reaction. She came to an abrupt halt, her fingers dropping from her rucksack. 'Do you want me to make something to eat?' she offered shakily, struggling to catch her breath.

'No, thanks. I ate before you arrived,' Vito drawled

lazily, watching her shrug back the sweater so that it didn't slip too low at the front. No, she really *wasn't* trying to pull him and he was captivated as he so rarely was by a woman.

'Then you won't mind if *I* eat? I brought supper with me,' she explained, moving past him towards the kitchen.

She's not even going to try to entertain me, Vito reflected, positively rapt in admiration in receipt of that clear demonstration of indifference.

When had he become so arrogant that he expected every young woman he came into contact with to make a fuss of him and a play for him?

It wasn't arrogance, he reasoned squarely. He was as rich as Midas and well aware that that was the main reason for his universal appeal. He poured Holly a fresh glass of wine and carried it into the kitchen for her. She closed the oven, wool stretching to softly define her heart-shaped derrière.

'Do you have a boyfriend?' he heard himself enquire, seemingly before his brain had formed the question, while his attention was still lodged on the sweater that both concealed and revealed her lush curves.

'No. As of today I have an ex,' Holly told him. 'You?'

'I'm single.' Vito lounged back against the kitchen island, the fine fabric of his pants pulling taut to define long, muscular thighs *and*…the noticeable masculine bulge at his crotch. Heat surging into her cheeks, Holly dragged her straying attention off him and stared down at her wine. Since when had she looked at a man *there*? Her breath was snarled up in her throat and her entire body felt super sensitive.

'What happened today?' Vito probed.

'I caught Ritchie having sex with his receptionist on his lunch break,' Holly told him in a rush before she could think better of that humiliating admission. Unfortunately looking at Vito had wrecked her composure to such an extent that she barely knew what she was saying any more.

CHAPTER THREE

IN RECEIPT OF that startling confession, Vito had the most atrocious desire to laugh, but he didn't want to hurt Holly's feelings. Her cheeks had gone all pink again and her eyes were evasive as if that confession had simply slipped accidentally from her lips. He breathed in deep. 'Tough. What did you do?'

'Told him what I thought of him in one sentence, walked out again.' Holly tilted her chin, anger darkening her blue eyes as she remembered the scene she had interrupted. 'I hate liars and cheats.'

'I'm shockingly well behaved in that line. Too busy working,' Vito countered, relieved that she had not a clue about the scandal that had persuaded him to leave Florence and even less idea of who he was. In recent days he had been forced to spend way too much time in the company of people too polite to say what they thought but not too polite to stare at him and whisper. Anonymity suddenly had huge appeal. He finally felt that he could relax.

'So, why are you staying here all alone?' Holly asked, sipping her wine, grateful he had glossed over her gaffe about Ritchie without further comment.

'Burnout. I needed a break from work.' Vito gave

her the explanation he had already decided on in the shower. 'Obviously I wasn't expecting weather like this.'

He was unusually abstracted, however, ensnared by the manner in which the blue of his sweater lit up her luminous eyes. He was also wondering how she could possibly look almost irresistibly cute in an article of his clothing when the thick wool draped her tiny body like a blanket and only occasionally hinted at the treasures that lay beneath. What was the real secret of her appeal? he was asking himself in bewilderment, even though the secret was right in front of him. She had a wonderfully feminine shape, amazing eyes and a torrent of dark hair that tumbled round her shoulders in luxuriant loose curls. But what was most different about Holly was that she was genuine as so few people dared to be. She put on no show and said nothing for effect; indeed she followed a brand of candour that was blunt to the point of embarrassing.

'Why are you staring at me?' Holly asked baldly, straightening her spine and squaring her little shoulders for all the world as though she was bracing herself for him to say something critical.

'Am I?' Vito fielded, riveting dark eyes brimming with amusement as he straightened to leave the kitchen. 'Sorry... I didn't mean to make you uncomfortable.'

He was setting up a games console when Holly joined him with her plate of savoury snacks. 'I thought I'd have a game,' he told her, 'but perhaps you would rather watch TV—'

'No, what game is it?'

It was a war game Holly knew well. 'I'll play you,' she told him.

Vito shot her a startled glance. 'You play?'

'Of course I do. Every foster family had a console and you learned to play with the other kids to fit in,' she pointed out wryly.

'*Dio mio*...how many different families did you live with?'

'I never counted but there were a lot of them. I'd get settled somewhere and then someone somewhere would decide I should have another go at bonding with my mother, and I'd be shot back to her again for a few months.'

Vito was frowning as he set up the game. 'Your mother was still alive?'

'Just not a good parent. It never worked out with her,' Holly completed wryly, keen to gloss over the facts with as little detail as possible while she watched Vito, lean hips flexing down into powerful thighs as he bent down.

From her position kneeling on the floor, she could admire the fluidity of his long-fingered brown hands as he leant over the console. His every movement was incredibly graceful, she acknowledged. And when she glanced up at him she noticed the black density of his eyelashes and the definition that dark luxuriance lent to his already stunning dark eyes. Her nipples were tight little buds inside her bra and she felt hot.

'Your father?' Vito queried.

'I had no idea who my father was so he didn't come into the picture. But my mother still being around was the reason why I moved around so much, because she refused to allow me to be put up for adoption. Every time I went back to my mother and then had to leave her again to go back into care, I ended up with a new foster family.' Holly grimaced and shrugged. 'It was a messy way to grow up.'

Vito had always thought he had it rough with a tyrannical grandfather, warring parents and being an only child on whom huge expectations rested. But his glimpse at what lay on Holly's side of the fence sobered him and gave him an unsettling new perspective. He had always had security and he had always known he was loved. And although Holly had enjoyed neither advantage, she wasn't moaning about it, he thought with grudging appreciation.

As Vito lounged back on the sofa his six-pack abs rippled below the soft cotton stretched over his broad chest and Holly's mouth ran dry. He was amazingly beautifully built and the acknowledgement sent colour surging into her cheeks because she had never looked at a man's body and thought that before. But she couldn't take her eyes off him and it mortified her. It was as if she had been locked back into a teenager's body again because there was nothing sensible or controlled about what she was experiencing.

'We'll set the timer for a ten-minute challenge,' Vito told her lightly, doubting that she would last the game that long.

Fortunately, Holly didn't even have to think while she played him. In dark times the engrossing, mindless games had been her escape from the reality of a life that hurt too much. With the weapon she had picked she made kill after kill on screen and then the challenge was over and she had won.

'You're very fast,' Vito conceded with a slashing grin of appreciation, because once again he could not think of a single woman who, having chosen to play him, would not have then allowed him to win even though she was a better player. Of course that was a debatable point when he didn't actually know any other woman who could play.

'Lots of practice over the years,' Holly conceded, still recovering from the raw charisma of that wolfish grin that cracked right through his essential reserve. Gaming had relaxed him, warmed him up, melted that cool façade he wore to show the real man underneath. And now he didn't just strike her as heartbreakingly handsome, he was downright irresistible. She shifted uneasily in her seat, her body tense and so weirdly super sensitive that even her clothes seemed to chafe her tender skin.

'And the prize is…' Vito's attention locked like a missile to the soft pink fullness of her mouth and her nipples pinched into tight little points. 'You get to put your Christmas tree up.'

Holly sprang off the seat. 'Seriously?' she exclaimed in surprise.

'Seriously.' Vito focused on that sparkling smile and gritted his teeth in a conscious attempt to cool off and quell his hard-on. He didn't know what it was about her but one look from those melting blue eyes and he was hotter than hell. 'Go ahead…' He pinched one of the snacks on her plate by his feet. 'Any more of these?'

Holly laughed. 'I'll put more on before I get the tree sorted.'

Vito watched her rush about full of energy, and suppressed a rueful sigh. It didn't take a lot to make her happy. 'Why does Christmas mean so much to you?'

'I didn't have it when I was very small,' she admitted.

'How can you *not* have Christmas?'

'Mum didn't celebrate it. Well, not in the family sense. There was no tree, no present, nothing. She went out partying but I didn't know what the day was supposed to be until I went into care for the first time.'

Vito frowned. 'And how did that happen?'

Holly hesitated, eyes troubled as her oval face stiffened. 'You know, this is all very personal…'

'I'm curious…I've never met anyone who grew up in care before,' Vito told her truthfully, revelling in every fleeting expression that crossed her expressive little face. She was full to the brim with emotional responses. She was his exact opposite because she felt so much and showed even more. It shook him that he could find that ingenuousness so very appealing in a woman that he was challenged to look away from her.

Holly compressed her lips, those full pink lips with that dainty little cupid's bow that called to him on a far more primitive level. 'When I was six years old, Mum left me alone for three days over Christmas. I went to a neighbour because I was hungry and she called the police.'

Taken aback by that admission, Vito sat up very straight, dark-as-night eyes locked to her as she finished that little speech in an emotive surge. 'Your mother abandoned you?'

'Yes, but eventually she probably would have come back, as she'd done it before. I was put into a short-term foster home and the family gave me Christmas even though it was already over,' Holly told him with a fond smile of remembrance.

'And you've been making up for that loss ever since,' Vito said drily, shrugging off the pangs of sympathy assailing him, taking refuge in edgy cynicism instead. He didn't do emotion, avoiding such displays and feelings whenever he could because the memories of his mother's raw pain in the face of his father's rejections still disturbed him. As far as he was concerned, if you put your feelings out on display you were asking to be kicked in the teeth and it was not a risk he was prepared to take for anyone. Yet just looking at Holly he could tell that she had taken that same risk time and time again.

'Probably. As obsessions go, Christmas is a fairly harmless one,' Holly fielded before she got up to hurry into the kitchen and retrieve the snacks from the oven. After handing him the plate, she returned to winding the fairy lights round the small tree.

He watched the firelight flicker over her, illuminating a rounded cheekbone, a tempting stretch of gleaming thigh as she bent down, and the provocative rise of her curvy behind. 'How old are you, Holly?'

Holly attached an ornament to a branch and glanced over her shoulder at him. As soon as she collided with his spellbinding dark golden eyes, her heart raced, her mouth ran dry and her mind went blank. 'I'm twenty-four…tomorrow.'

Vito's gaze glittered in the firelight. 'It's both Christmas *and* your birthday.'

'Now it's your turn. Tell me about you,' Holly urged with unconcealed eagerness because everything about Vito Sorrentino made her insanely curious.

It should not have been an unexpected question but it hit Vito like a brick and he froze on the reality that having questioned her so thoroughly he could hardly refuse to respond in kind. He breathed in deep, squaring his broad shoulders, fighting his tension. 'I'm the only child of ill-matched parents. Holiday periods when my father was expected to play his part as a family man were always very stressful because he hated being forced to spend time with us. Christmas fell into that category.'

'Why haven't they separated?' He was so on edge talking about his family situation that it touched her heart. Such a beautiful man, so sophisticated and cool in comparison to her, so seemingly together and yet he too bore the damage of a wounding childhood. Holly was fascinated.

'My mother was raised to believe that divorce is wrong…and she loves my father. She's incredibly loyal to the people she loves.' Vito spoke very stiffly because he had never in his life before shared that much about his family dynamics. He had been taught to live by the same code of secretive silence and polite denial that his mother had always observed. Even if the roof was falling in, appearances still had to be conserved. Breaking that code of silence with an outsider filled him with discomfiture.

'That must've put a lot of pressure on you,' Holly remarked, soulful big blue eyes pinned to him with an amount of sympathy far beyond what he considered necessary.

And yet inexplicably there was something in Vito that was warmed by that show of support. He came up off the sofa as though she had yanked a chain attached to his body, and pulled her up into his arms, and in neither of those moves did he recognise conscious thought or decision. It was instinct, pure instinct to reach for Holly.

He tugged her close, long brown fingers flying up to tilt her chin, and gazed down into those inviting clear eyes of hers. A split second later, he kissed her.

In shock, Holly simply stood there, conflicting feelings pulling her in opposing directions. *Push him away, back off* now, one voice urged. *He finds me attractive, find out what it's like*, the other voice pleaded while she brimmed with secret pride. He touched her mouth slow and soft, nipping her lips lightly and teasingly, and she could hardly breathe. Her heart was thumping like a jackhammer inside her ribcage. His tongue eased apart the seam of her lips and flickered and a spasm of raw excitement thrilled down into her pelvis. With a hungry groan he tightened his arms round her.

Nothing had ever tasted as good as Vito's mouth on hers and she trembled in reaction, her whole body awakening. Her hands linked round his neck as the hard, demanding pressure of his mouth sent a delicious heat spiralling down through her. She felt wonderfully warm and safe for the first time ever. In that moment of security she rejoiced in the glorious feel of his mouth and the taste of the wine on his tongue. His fingers splayed to mould to her hips and trailed down the backs of her thighs. Tiny little shivers of response tugged at her as she felt a tightening sensation at her core and her breasts felt achingly full.

Vito lifted his dark head. Dark golden eyes sought hers. 'I want you,' he husked.

'I want you,' Holly framed shakily and it was the very first time she understood the need to say that to someone.

In all the years she had thought about having sex it had always been because sex was expected of her in a relationship, never because she herself was tempted. In the face of those expectations, her body had begun to seem like something to cede, and not fully her own. And that had been wrong, *so* wrong, she finally saw. It should be her choice and her choice alone. But she was learning that only now in Vito's arms and recognising the difference because she was finally experiencing a genuine desire for something more. And it was a heady feeling that left her bemused and giddy.

Staring up into Vito's dark, dangerous eyes, she stretched up on tiptoe to reach him, simply desperate to feel his beautiful mouth on hers again. And the sheer strength of that physical connection, the locking in of every simultaneous sensation that assailed her, only emphasised how right it felt to be with him that way.

This was what all the fuss was about, she thought joyously, the thrumming pulse of need that drove her, the tiny little tremors of desire making her tremble, the overwhelming yearning for the hard, muscular feel of his body against hers. And as one kiss led into another he drew her down onto the rug again and the heat of the fire on her skin burned no more fiercely than the raw hunger raging through her with spellbinding force.

With her willing collusion he extracted her from the sweater and released the catch on her bra. He studied the full globes he had bared with unhidden hunger. 'You have a totally amazing body, *gioia mia*.'

A deep flush lit Holly's cheeks and the colour spread because she was not relaxed about nudity. Yet there in the firelight with Vito looking at her as though he were unveiling a work of art, she was horribly self-conscious but she felt no shame or sense of inadequacy. Indeed, the more Vito looked, the more the pulse of heat humming between her thighs picked up tempo. Long fingers shaping the plump curves of her breasts, Vito flicked a tongue over a straining pink nipple and a hungry groan of appreciation was wrenched from him as he dallied there, toying with her sensitive flesh in a caress that made her hips squirm while a new sense of urgency gripped her.

'Kiss me,' she urged breathlessly as he tugged at the tender buds of her breasts and an arrow of burning heat pierced her feminine core, only increasing her agitation.

He crushed her ripe mouth beneath his again, his tongue plunging deep, and for a split second it satisfied the craving pulling at her, and then somehow even that wasn't enough any more. She shifted position restively, her legs sliding apart to let his hips slide between as she silently, instinctively sought more. Her hips rocked. She wanted and she *wanted*...

And then at last, as if he knew exactly what she needed, he smoothed his passage up a silken inner thigh and tugged off her panties. He stroked her, found the most needy place of all, and a current of almost unbearable excitement shot through Holly's veins. Suddenly in the hold of her own explosive response she was all heat and light and sensation. A long finger tested her slick, damp core and she whimpered, her teeth clenching, the ferocious need clawing cruelly at her as her spine arched, her body all too ready to take charge.

There was no room for thought in the passion that had swept her away in the way she had always dreamed. But it wasn't the same as her dream because what she was feeling was much more basic, much more wild and out of control than she had ever allowed herself to be. He moved to one side, yanking off his top, revealing an abdomen grooved with lean, hard muscle, and her hand slid greedily up over his chest, rejoicing in his sleek bronzed skin and the manner in which every muscle jerked taut the instant she touched him.

'I have no condoms,' Vito bit out in sudden frustration. 'But I had a health check a few weeks ago and I'm clean.'

'I'm on the pill,' Holly framed shakily, belatedly jolted into rational thought by the acknowledgement that she wasn't about to call a halt to their activities. And why was that? She had never wanted anything or anyone the way she wanted him and surely that was the way it was supposed to be? It felt right. *He* felt right.

Vito hauled in a shuddering breath of relief and came back down to her again, tasting her reddened mouth again with devouring appetite. Her hands smoothed over him, caressing every part of him she could reach from his wide brown shoulders to the satin-smooth expanse of his back. Desire drove her like an addictive drug. Beneath his touch she writhed, her reactions pitching her desire higher and higher until the mushroom of liquid-honey heat inside her flared up in ecstasy before spreading to every part of her. She gasped, shaken by an almost out-of-body feeling, her entire being singing with the potent rush of pleasure.

And then she felt him pushing at the heart of her, tilting her back for his entrance and she was wildly impatient, needing more, ready to try anything that he could give her. He filled her completely, thrusting deep with a slick, sure forcefulness that took her by surprise. The bite of pain was an equal surprise and she blinked back tears and sank her teeth into her lower lip, grateful that her face was against his shoulder where he couldn't see her reaction.

'You're incredibly wet and tight,' Vito growled in a roughened undertone. 'It's a hell of a turn-on, *gioia mia.*'

The pinch of discomfort evaporated as he moved

and she arched up to receive him. He vented a groan of all-male satisfaction as she joined in, no longer separate in thought and behaviour. That overpowering hunger kicked back in as his fluid, insistent thrusts filled her with renewed enthusiasm. In fact the wild, sweet rhythm of his sensual possession fired a blinding, pulsing excitement inside her. Locked with his, her body was snatched up into a passionate climax that flooded her with exquisite sensation.

Coiling back from her, Vito saw the blood on her thighs. '*Maledizione*…you're bleeding? Did I hurt you? Why didn't you stop me?'

Brutally summoned back to reality without warning, Holly snaked back from him and hugged her knees in sudden mortification. 'It's all right—'

'No, you being hurt is *not* all right in any way,' Vito shot back at her grimly.

Holly could feel a beetroot-red flush start at her toes and slowly burn up over her whole body. Lifting her head, she clashed reluctantly with glittering dark eyes of angry concern. 'I wasn't hurt…at least not the way you mean,' she explained grudgingly. 'I was a virgin… and obviously there was some physical evidence of it… which I wasn't expecting…'

'A virgin?' Vito exclaimed in raw disbelief. 'You were a *virgin*?'

Snatching up the sweater he had taken off her, Holly pulled it over her again, struggling to slide her arms back into the sleeves. 'Don't make such a big deal of it,' she urged while she was still safely submerged in the wool.

'It *is* a big deal!' Vito grated, springing upright to zip his trousers again and reach for his shirt.

Flushed and uncomfortable, Holly glanced at him

unwillingly. 'Maybe to me but I don't see why it should bother you!'

'Don't you indeed?' Vito riposted.

'No, I don't,' Holly countered on a rising note of anger because his reaction was the very last thing she had expected from him and the topic mortified her.

Dark eyes flashing gold, Vito studied her. 'You should've warned me. Why didn't you?'

Holly stood her ground, her vexation stifling her embarrassment. 'Because it was a private matter and none of your business.'

'Nothing of that nature stays private when you're having sex with someone!'

In discomfited retreat, Holly headed towards the shower room she had used earlier. 'Well, I'll take your word for that since it was my first experience.'

Vito was inflamed by her refusal to understand and chose to be blunt. 'I feel like I took advantage of you!' he admitted harshly.

Holly whirled back at the door. 'That's nonsense. I'm not a kid. My body, my choice.'

Vito snatched in a ragged breath, still reeling from the shock of her innocence. He hadn't told her who he was or indeed anything important about himself. She didn't, *couldn't* understand that in his position he was innately suspicious of anything as unexpected as their encounter and on top of it the very tardy revelation that she was a virgin. With his experience, that revelation had smacked of a possible sting of some kind and he had immediately wondered if she had some kind of hidden agenda. Now gazing into her troubled face, belatedly recognising the hurt and sadness there, he wanted to kick himself for treating her like some sort of scam artist.

'I'm sorry...' Vito breathed abruptly. 'I let my surprise push me into an overreaction, Holly. Of course, it's your choice...'

Some of her tension evaporated but her eyes remained guarded. 'I didn't even think of warning you. And if I *had* thought of it, I probably would've been too embarrassed to mention it.'

'I wrecked the moment,' Vito groaned in acknowledgement. He moved forward to close his arms round her and somehow, even after that uneasy exchange, it felt like the best thing in the world to Holly. Her stiffness slowly ebbing, she rested against him, drinking in the heat and the comfortingly hard, masculine contours of his lean, muscular body against hers. 'I also neglected to tell you that what we shared...it was amazing.'

'You're just saying that,' she mumbled.

'No. It *was* amazing, *cara mia*. Now let's go upstairs and shower,' Vito urged, easing her in a different direction, inexplicably keen to keep her close even though something in his brain was urging him to step back.

Amazing? Was that a polite lie? Just something a man said for the sake of it? He had flipped the situation on its head again and she didn't know how he had achieved that. She blinked in surprise as the lights illuminated a much bigger bedroom than she had expected, airily furnished in stylish tones of grey.

Vito pushed open the door of a very spacious en-suite. 'You first...unless you'd like company in the shower?'

Holly gave him a startled look. 'I don't think I'm ready for that yet.'

Vito laughed in appreciation and bent down to claim her swollen pink mouth with his own in a searing kiss that made every skin cell in her body sit up and take notice. 'I'll ask you again in the morning,' he warned her.

Holly's attention skated to the giant bed. 'We're going to share the bed?'

'There is only one bedroom here. I was planning to take the sofa.'

'No, I won't banish you to the sofa,' Holly breathed with a sudden grin as she slid past him into the en-suite while barely recognising her own thoughts or feelings. She only knew she didn't want him to sleep downstairs on the sofa and away from her. That felt wrong.

She stood in the shower feeling astonishingly light-hearted for a woman who had strayed from values that were as ingrained in her as her usual honesty. But making love with Vito had felt right and it was hard to credit that anything that had felt so natural and right could possibly be wrong. After all, they were both single and nobody was being hurt by their being together. What harm could it possibly do for her to go with the flow for a change in a relationship instead of trying to plan everything or wait for some extraordinary special sign? And why on earth was she feeling guilty about Ritchie when *he* had cheated on *her*?

It wasn't as though she had ever imagined that she was in love with Ritchie. She had only been seeing him for a few weeks and, even though he had been full of himself, he had been good company. Was what she felt with Vito a rebound attraction?

But how could it be? Ritchie couldn't be compared to Vito on any level. Vito utterly overshadowed his predecessor in every way. And just like her secret fantasy,

Vito had swept Holly away in the tide of passion she had always dreamt of experiencing. Of course, it wasn't going anywhere, she reminded herself staunchly, suppressing a pang of sorrow at that acknowledgement. There would be no ongoing relationship with Vito. She didn't need Vito to spell that out. What they had now was time out of time, separate from their normal lives and associations. Attraction had sparked purely because they were stuck together in a snowbound cottage, and she wasn't foolish enough to try and make more of it, was she?

She wrapped a towel round herself rather than put on his sweater again and crept out of the bathroom. Clad only in his jeans, which were unbuttoned at the waistband, Vito was towelling his hair dry. He tossed aside the towel, finger-combing his black hair carelessly off his brow. 'I used the shower downstairs.'

Holly hovered, suddenly awkward. 'I could have done that. This is your room, after all.'

Vito saw the wary uncertainty in her blue eyes and knew he had put it there. Holly was nothing at all like the women he was accustomed to meeting. Nevertheless he had initially judged her by the cynical standards formed by years of experience with such women. Yet he sensed that she would have been very shocked by the scandal that he had been forced to leave behind him. He had wounded her by questioning her innocence yet that same innocence of hers ironically drew him like a beacon. He crossed the room and closed both arms round her, responding to the inbuilt drive to bridge the gap between them. 'Tonight it's *our* room. Let's go to bed...' he urged.

And Holly thought about saying no and heading

down to the sofa. After all, she had broken her own rules and just because she had done that once didn't mean she had an automatic excuse to keep on doing it. Indeed, if having sex with Vito had been a mistake, she was honour-bound to choose the sofa over him.

But sleeping alone wasn't what she wanted and needed right then. She wanted to be with Vito. She wanted to make the most of the time they had together. She was even feeling sensible enough to know that it was fortunate that she wouldn't be with Vito for much longer, for she reckoned that given the opportunity she would fall for him like a ton of bricks. That, of course, would be totally, unforgivably stupid. And she might be a little sentimental, but stupid she was not.

She looked at Vito, even though she knew she really shouldn't, but there he was, etched in her head in an image that would burn for all time, she thought dizzily. He was beautiful, drop-dead beautiful and tonight...tonight he was all *hers*...

CHAPTER FOUR

At dawn, Holly sneaked out of bed and crept into the bathroom to freshen up. She grimaced at her reflection. Her hair was a mess. Her face reddened in places by Vito's stubble. Her mouth was very swollen and pink. And when she stepped into the shower she swallowed a groan because every muscle she possessed complained as if she had overdone it in a workout.

But no workout, she thought dizzily, could possibly have been more demanding than the stamina required for a night in bed with Vito Sorrentino. He was insatiable and he had made her the same way, she conceded in stupefaction. She felt as though she had changed dramatically in less than twelve hours. She had learned so much about herself and even more about sex. Her body ached in intimate places and a bemused smile tilted her lips as she emerged from the en-suite again.

Vito was sprawled across the bed, a glorious display of bronzed perfection. Luxuriant black lashes flickered as he focused on her. 'I wondered where you were,' he muttered.

'Bathroom,' she whispered, barely breathing as she slid back under the duvet.

Vito reached for her with a sleepy hand and pulled

her back against him. She shivered in contact with the raw heat and scent of him. 'Go back to sleep,' he told her thickly.

He wanted her again. What the hell was wrong with him? How could he want her again when he had already had her so many times? She had to be sore too, he reminded himself in exasperation. He was being a selfish bastard. As soon as he heard the deep, even tenor of her breathing sink into sleep, he eased out of the bed, went for a cold shower and got dressed.

Nothing in Vito's mental rule book covered what had happened the night before. He hadn't had a one-night stand in many years and none had been extraordinary on any level. Sex was sex, a temporary release and pleasure. He was practical about sex, cool about sex. His desire had never controlled him and he would never let it do so. But then he had never ever been intimate with a woman he wanted over and over again, and his voracious hunger for Holly even after having her downright unnerved him. What was wrong with him? Was he in some weird frame of mind after the trying ordeal of the publicity fallout he had endured over the past week? In his opinion it certainly wasn't normal to want a woman *that* much. It smacked of unbalance, of unhealthy obsession. It was fortunate that their time together had a built-in closing date, he told himself grimly.

Even so, it was Christmas Day as well as being Holly's birthday and it bothered him that he had nothing to give her. Vito was so accustomed to gift-giving and other people's high expectations of his gifts that he felt very uncomfortable in that situation. In an effort to make the day special for Holly he decided to make her breakfast in bed. He couldn't cook but how difficult could it be to make breakfast? He could manage orange juice and toast, couldn't he?

Holly was stunned when she blinked into drowsy wakefulness because Vito was sliding a tray of food on to her lap. She stared down in wonderment at the charred toast. 'You made me breakfast?'

'It's your birthday. It's not much but it's the best I can do.'

Holly tried not to look at him as though he were the eighth wonder of the world but that was certainly how he struck her at that moment because nobody had ever given Holly breakfast in bed before, no, not even when she was ill. It was a luxury she could barely even imagine and that Vito should have gone to that much effort to spoil her thrilled her. So, she didn't make a sound when her first sip of tea gave her a mouthful of the teabag that had not been removed and she munched through the charred toast without complaint. It was the thought that counted, after all, and that Vito *had* thought touched her heart. In addition, the effect of having Vito carelessly sprawled at the foot of the same bed sent her pulse rate rocketing. She remembered all the things they had done and tried desperately to feel guilty about them. But it didn't work. One look into those inky-black-lashed dark golden eyes of his and she was shot off to another planet.

'Thanks,' she said even though it took great effort to locate her voice.

'I'm not great in the kitchen. If it had only been for me I would have cooked one of the ready meals,' he admitted.

'It was very thoughtful of you.' Holly was registering how very lucky she was not to be facing roast meat for breakfast and she gratefully drank her orange juice, which was so cold it froze her teeth. As she drained the glass she pushed the tray away and he swept it up and put it on the floor.

He came back to the bed and moved towards her with the sinuous grace of a stalking cat and her mouth ran dry, her heartbeat racing. 'I was going to get up, organise lunch,' she framed shakily.

'Way too early for that, *bellezza mia*,' Vito husked, up close, his breath fanning her cheek and his luxuriant black hair brushing her chin as he bent his head to press his mouth to the pulse point below her ear.

And her whole body went into free fall as though he had hit a button. Breath fled her parted lips as she sank back into the pillows and gazed up at him with luminous blue eyes. 'Vito—'

He closed her mouth with the onslaught of his own. 'No, we don't talk,' he told her after kissing her breathless. 'We already know all we need to know about each other.'

'I don't even know what you do,' she began.

'I'm in business…and you?'

'Waitress…well, waitress with aspirations,' she adjusted jerkily when he tensed against her. 'I want to be an interior designer but it's more a dream than reality.'

'It takes work to turn dreams into reality.'

Holly smiled up at him. 'Vito… I've had to work hard for everything in life but sometimes getting a break relates more to resources and luck than slaving away.'

'This is getting way too serious,' Vito objected when he found himself on the brink of offering her advice.

Holly let her fingers drift up to brush his black hair off his brow, her attention locked to his lean, darkly handsome features even as her heart had sunk because she was scarily well attuned to his body language. 'Agreed. Let's stay away from the real world.'

His long, lean body relaxed against hers again and tears stung her eyes as she blinked against his shoulder. The news that she was a waitress had been too sharp a stab of reality for Vito, highlighting as it did the difference in their statuses. His clothing, even the variety and expense of the food in the refrigerator, not to mention the stylish opulence of her surroundings all told Holly that Vito inhabited a rather more privileged place in society than she did. And while here at the cottage without other people around, that difference didn't really matter. She knew it would matter very much outside these walls.

'I still want you,' Vito confided thickly, running the tip of his tongue along her collarbone.

Her tummy flipped, her feminine core clenched and she stiffened. Reality was intruding whether she wanted it to or not because she was too tender to engage again in the kind of intimacy he was probably envisaging. 'I can't,' she whispered tightly, a small hand smoothing down a denim-clad thigh, feeling the ripple of his muscles tightening in response.

'Maybe later,' Vito murmured sibilantly, fingers spearing into her hair to lift her mouth to his. 'But in the short term there are other things we can do, *gioia mia*.'

Holly laughed and buried her face in his shoulder. 'You're so shameless.'

'Why wouldn't I be? You've been brilliant. I can't understand why you were still untouched.'

'It was a promise I made to myself when I was very young…to wait. It just seemed sensible to wait until I was an adult and then…' Holly sighed. 'Somewhere

along the line it became a burden, a tripwire in relationships that held me back from who I could be.'

Vito gazed down at her with a frown of incomprehension. 'But why me? Why did you choose me?'

'Maybe it was because you let me put my Christmas
tree up,' she teased, because there were all too many
reasons why she had chosen him and very few she was
prepared to share. There was no safe way to tell a man
that he had been her fantasy without him getting the
wrong idea and assuming that she was feeling more
than she was supposed to feel in terms of attachment.

Her fingers slid up caressingly to the firm bulge at
his crotch and exerted gentle pressure and he groaned,
dark head falling back, wide sensual mouth tightening,
his broad chest vibrating against her. Holly leant over
him, staring down into lustrous eyes that glittered like
precious gold. 'Maybe it's because you act as though
I'm the most ravishing female you've ever met, even
though I'm perfectly ordinary. But perhaps that's your
true talent. Maybe you treat all women the same way.'

'No. I've never been with any woman the way I've
been with you…' Vito surveyed her with frowning
force, probing that statement, worrying about it because
it was true. He had never felt so comfortable with a
woman or so relaxed. He hadn't once thought about
work or about the shocking scandal he had left behind
him in Italy. Furthermore Holly was completely unique
on his terms because for the first time ever he was with
a woman who didn't know who he was, cherished no
financial expectations and in truth attached no undue
importance to him. He was Mr Anonymous with Holly
and he liked the freedom of that one hell of a lot.

Holly unzipped his jeans with a sense of adventure.

Her most driving need was to give him pleasure and she didn't understand it. Shouldn't she be more selfish? The catch in his breathing was followed by a long, unrestrained sound of rising hunger. She had distracted him with sex, she thought guiltily. She didn't want to talk about being a waitress, about any of the things that separated them as people in the outside world, and his unashamed sexual response to her gave her a shocking sense of power.

Heaven for Vito was the gentle friction of her mouth and the teasing, erotic stroke of her tiny fingers. His hand knotted in her hair and he trembled on the edge of release, gruffly warning her, but she didn't pull away. Then the sheer liberating wash of pleasure engulfed him and wiped him out.

Holly watched Vito sleep with a rueful grin. She went for another shower, donned the dress she had packed and dried her hair. Downstairs, she switched on the television and tuned it to a channel playing Christmas carols before going into the kitchen and beginning to organise the lunch she had prepared with such care. It shook her to acknowledge that she hadn't even known Vito Sorrentino existed the day before.

The shame and embarrassment she had fought off at dawn began to creep up again through the cracks in her composure. She had broken all her rules and for what? A one-night stand with a male she would probably never hear from or see again? How could she be proud of that? But would it have been any better to lose her virginity with a sleazy, cheating liar like Ritchie, who had pretended that she meant much more to him than she did?

She thought not. Anyway, it was too late for regrets, she reminded herself unhappily. What was done was done and it made more sense to move on from that point than to torture herself over what could not be changed. How much, though, had all the wine she had imbibed contributed to her recklessness? Her loss of inhibition? *Stop it, stop it*, she urged herself fiercely, *stop dwelling on it*.

Vito came down the stairs when she was setting the table. 'You should have wakened me.'

'You were up much earlier than I was,' she pointed out as she retrieved the starters from the kitchen. 'Hungry?'

Vito reached for her instead of a chair. 'Only for you.'

Her bright blue eyes danced with merriment. 'Now, where did you get that old chestnut from?'

In answer Vito bent his tousled dark head and kissed her and it was like an arrow of fire shooting through her body to the heart of her. She quivered, taken aback all over again by the explosive effect he had on her. His sensual mouth played with hers and tiny ripples of arousal coursed through her. Her breasts swelled, their buds tightening while heat and dampness gathered between her legs. It took enormous willpower but she made herself step back from him, almost careening into the table in her haste to break their connection. Suddenly feeling out of control with him seemed dangerous and it *was* dangerous, she told herself, if it made her act out of character. And whether she liked it or not, everything she had done with Vito was out of character for her.

'We should eat before the food gets cold,' she said prosaically.

'I'll open a bottle of wine.'

'This is an incredibly well-equipped house,' Holly

remarked as he poured the wine he had fetched from the temperature-controlled cabinet in the kitchen.

'The owner enjoys his comforts.'

'And he's your friend?'

'We went to school together.' A breathtaking smile of amused recollection curled Vito's mouth. 'He was a rebel and although he often got me into trouble he also taught me how to enjoy myself.'

'Pixie's like that. We're very close.' Holly lifted the plates and set out the main course.

'You're a good cook,' Vito commented.

'My foster mother, Sylvia, was a great teacher. Cooking relaxes me.'

'I eat out a lot. It saves time.'

'There's more to life than saving time. Life is there to be savoured,' Holly told him.

'I savour it at high speed.'

The meal was finished and Holly was clearing up when Vito stood up. 'I feel like some fresh air,' he told her. 'I'm going out for a walk.'

From the window, Holly watched him trudge down the lane in the snow. There was an odd tightness in her chest and a lump in her constricted throat. Vito had just rebelled against their enforced togetherness to embrace his own company. He hadn't invited her to join him on his walk, but why should he have? Out of politeness? They weren't a couple in the traditional sense and he didn't have to include her in everything. They were two people who had shared a bed for the night, two *very* different people. Maybe she talked too much, maybe he was tired of her company and looking forward to the prospect of some silence. It was not a confidence-boosting train of thought.

Vito ploughed up the steep gradient, his breath steaming on the icy air. He had needed a break, had been relieved when Holly hadn't asked if she could accompany him. A loner long accustomed to his own company, he had felt the walls closing in while he'd sat surrounded by all that cosy Christmas spirit.

And that really wasn't Holly's fault, Vito conceded wryly. Even her cheerful optimism could not combat the many years of bad Christmas memories that Vito harboured. Sadly the stresses and strains of the festive season were more likely to expose the cracks in an unhappy marriage. His mother's resolute enthusiasm had never contrived to melt his father's boredom and animosity at being forced into spending time with his family.

They had never been a family, Vito acknowledged heavily, not in the truest sense of the word. His father had never loved him, had never taken the smallest interest in him. In fact, if he was honest with himself, his father sincerely disliked him. From an early age Vito had been treated like the enemy, twinned in his father's mind with the autocratic father-in-law he fiercely resented.

'He's like a bloody calculator!' Ciccio had condemned with distaste when his five-year-old son's brilliance at maths was remarked on. 'He'll be as efficient as a cash machine—just like his grandfather.'

Only days earlier, Vito's relationship with his father had sunk to an all-time low when Ciccio had questioned his son's visit to the hospital where he was recovering from his heart attack. 'Are you here to crow over my downfall?' his father had asked nastily while his mother had tried to intervene. 'My sins have deservedly caught up with me? Is that what you think?'

And Vito had finally recognised that there was no relationship left to rescue with his father. Ciccio bitterly resented his son's freedom from all financial constraints yet the older man's wild extravagance and greed had forced Vito's grandfather to keep his son-in-law on a tight leash. There was nothing Vito could do to change those hard facts. Even worse, after his grandfather had died it had become Vito's duty to protect his mother's fortune from Ciccio's demands, scarcely a reality likely to improve a father and son relationship.

For the first time Vito wondered what sort of relationship he would have with his son if he ever had one. Momentarily he was chilled by the prospect because his family history offered no encouragement.

Holly had just finished clearing up the dishes when the knocker on the front door sounded loudly. She was stunned when she opened the door and found Bill, who ran the breakdown service, standing smiling on the doorstep.

'I need the keys for Clementine to get her loaded up.'

'But it's Christmas Day… I mean, I wasn't expecting—'

'I didn't want to raise your hopes last night but I knew I'd be coming up this way some time this afternoon. My uncle joins us for lunch and he owns a small-holding a few fields away. He has to get back to feed his stock, so I brought the truck when I left him at home.'

'Thank you so much,' Holly breathed, fighting her consternation with all her might while turning away to reach into the pocket of her coat where she had left the car keys. She passed the older man the keys. 'Do you need any help?'

He shook his head. 'I'll come back up for you when I'm done.'

'I'll get my stuff together.' With a weak smile and with every sensitive nerve twanging, Holly shut the door again and sped straight upstairs to gather her belongings. She dug her feet into her cowboy boots and thrust her toiletries and make-up bag back into her rucksack.

And throughout that exercise she wouldn't let herself even think that she could be foolish enough to be disappointed at being picked up and taken home. Clearly, it was time to *leave*. She had assumed that she would have one more night with Vito but fate had decreed otherwise. Possibly a quick, unexpected exit was the best way to part after such a night, she thought unhappily. There would be neither the time nor the opportunity for awkward exchanges. She closed her rucksack and checked the room one last time. Reminding herself that she still had to pack the Christmas tree, she went back down wondering anxiously if Vito would make it back before she had to leave.

She flipped open her cardboard box and stripped the tree of ornaments and lights, deftly packing it all away while refusing to think beyond the practical. She raced into the kitchen to dump the foil containers she had used to transport the meal, pausing only to lift a china jug and quickly wash it before placing it in the box. That was that then, all the evidence of her brief stopover removed, she conceded numbly.

She didn't want to go home, she didn't *want* to leave Vito, and the awareness of that stupid, hopeless sense of attachment to him crushed and panicked her. He would probably be relieved to find her gone and he would have cringed if he saw tears in her eyes. Men didn't like messy and there could be nothing more messy or embarrassing than a woman who got too involved and tried to cling after one night. *This one-night-and-walk-away stuff is what you signed up for,* Holly scolded herself angrily. There had been no promises and no mention of a future of any kind. She would leave with her head held high and no backward glances.

All the same, she thought hesitantly, if Vito wasn't coming back in time to see her leave, shouldn't she leave a note? She dug into her rucksack and tore a piece of paper out of a notebook and leant on the table. She thanked him for his hospitality and then hit a brick wall in the creative department. What else was there to say? What else *could* she reasonably say?

After much reflection she printed her mobile-phone number at the foot of the note. Why not? It wasn't as if she was asking him to phone her. She was simply giving him the opportunity to phone if he wanted to. Nothing wrong with that, was there? She left the note propped against the clock on the shelf inside the inglenook.

Holly wore a determined smile when Bill's truck backed into the drive. She had her box and her rucksack on the step beside her in a clear face-saving statement that she was eager to get going but there was still no sign of Vito. She climbed into the truck with a sense of regret but gradually reached the conclusion that possibly it was preferable to have parted from Vito without any awkward or embarrassing final conversation. This way, nobody had to pretend or say anything they didn't mean.

Vito strode into the cottage and grimaced at the silence. He strode up the stairs, calling Holly's name while wondering if she had gone for a bath. He studied the empty bathroom with a frown, noting that she had removed her possessions. Only when he went downstairs again did he notice that the Christmas decorations had disappeared along with her. The table was clear, the kitchen immaculate.

Vito was incredulous. Holly had done a runner and he had no idea how. He walked out onto the doorstep and belatedly registered that the old car no longer lay at the foot of the lane in the ditch. So much for his observation powers! He had been so deep in his thoughts that he hadn't even noticed that the car had gone. Holly had walked out on him. Well, that hadn't happened to him before, he acknowledged grimly, his ego stung by her sudden departure. All his life women had chased after Vito, attaching strings at the smallest excuse.

But would he have wanted her to *cling*? Vito winced, driven to reluctantly admit that perhaps in the circumstances her unannounced disappearance was for the best. After all, what would he have said to her in parting? Holly had distracted him from more important issues and disrupted his self-control. Now he had his own space back and the chance to get his head clear. And that was exactly what he should want...

'When you're finished throwing up you can do the test,' Pixie said drily from the bathroom doorway.

'I'm not doing the test,' Holly argued. 'I'm on the pill. I *can't* be pregnant—'

'You missed a couple of pills *and* you had a course of antibiotics when you had tonsillitis,' her friend and flatmate reminded her. 'You know that antibiotics can interfere with contraception—'

'Well, actually I *didn't* know.' Holly groaned as she

freshened up at the sink, frowning at her pale face and dark-circled eyes. She looked absolutely awful and she felt awful both inside and out.

'Even the pill has a failure rating. I don't know...I leave you alone for a few weeks and you go completely off the rails,' the tiny blonde lamented, studying Holly with deeply concerned eyes.

'I can't be pregnant,' Holly said again as she lifted the pregnancy testing kit and extracted the instructions.

'Well, you've missed two periods, you're throwing up like there's no tomorrow and you have sore boobs,' Pixie recounted ruefully. 'Maybe it's chickenpox or something.'

'All right, I'll do it!' Holly exclaimed in frustration. 'But there is no way, just no way on earth that I could be pregnant!'

Some minutes later she slumped down on the side of the bath. Pixie was right and she was wrong. The test showed a positive. The door opened slowly and she looked wordlessly up at her friend and burst into floods of tears.

'Remember how we used to say that the babies we had would be precious gifts?' Pixie breathed as she hugged her sobbing friend. 'Well, this baby is a gift and we *will* manage. We don't need a man to survive.'

'I can't even knit!' Holly wailed, unable to concentrate, unable to think beyond the sheer immensity of the challenges she was about to face.

'That's OK. You won't have time to knit,' her friend told her, deadpan.

Holly was remembering when she and Pixie had talked innocently about their ideal of motherhood. Both of them had been born unwanted and had suffered at the hands of neglectful mothers. They had sworn that they would love and protect their own babies no matter what.

And the vague circumstances suggested by 'no matter what' had actually happened now, Holly reflected heavily, her sense of regret at that truth all-encompassing. Her baby would not be entering the perfect world as she had dreamt. Her baby was unplanned, however, but *not* unwanted. She would love her child, fight to keep him or her safe and if she had to do it alone, and it looked as though she would, she *would* manage.

'If only Vito had phoned...' The lament escaped Holly's lips before she could bite it back and she flushed in embarrassment.

'He's long gone. In fact, the more I think about him,' Pixie mused tight-mouthed, 'the more suspicious I get about the father of your child. For all you know he could be a married man.'

'No!' Holly broke in, aghast at that suggestion.

'Well, what was Vito doing spending Christmas alone out in the middle of nowhere?' Pixie demanded. 'Maybe the wife or girlfriend threw him out and he had nowhere better to go?'

'Don't make me feel worse than I already do,' Holly pleaded. 'You're such a pessimist, Pixie. Just because he didn't want to see me again doesn't make him a bad person.'

'He got you drunk and somehow persuaded you into bed. Don't expect me to think nice things about him. He was a user.'

'I *wasn't* drunk.'

'Let's not rehash it again.' Her flatmate sighed, her piquant face thoughtful. 'Let's see if we can trace him online.'

And while Pixie did internet searches on several potential spellings of Vito's surname and came up with precisely nothing, Holly sat on the sofa hugging her still-flat stomach and fretting about the future. She had already secretly carried out all those searches weeks earlier on Vito and was too proud to admit to the fact, even to her friend.

'I can't find even a trace of a man in the right age group. The name could be a fake,' her friend opined.

'Why would he give me a fake name? That doesn't make sense.'

'Maybe he didn't want to be identified. I don't know...you tell me,' Pixie said very drily. 'Do you think that's a possibility?'

Holly reddened. Of course it was a possibility that Vito had not wanted to be identified. As to why, how could she know? The only thing she knew with certainty was that Vito had decided he didn't want to see her again. Had he felt otherwise, he would have used the phone number she had left him and called her. In the weeks of silence that had followed her departure from the cottage, she had often felt low. But that was foolish, wasn't it? Vito had clearly made the decision that he had no desire to see her again.

And why should she feel hurt by that? Yes, he had said that night with her was amazing but wasn't that par for the course? The sort of thing a man thought a woman expected him to say after sex? How could she have been naive enough to actually believe that Vito had truly believed they were something special together? And now that little bit of excitement was over. What was done was done and what was gone, like her innocence, was gone. Much as her tidy, organised life had gone along with it, she conceded unhappily, because, although she would embrace motherhood wholeheartedly, she knew it would be incredibly tough to raise a baby alone without falling into the poverty trap.

CHAPTER FIVE

Fourteen months later

HOLLY SUPPRESSED A groan as she straightened her aching back. She hated parcelling up the unsold newspapers at the end of her evening shift in the local supermarket but it also meant she would be going home soon and seeing Angelo snugly asleep in his cot.

Picturing her son's little smiling face made her heart swell inside her. There was nothing Holly wouldn't do for her baby. The minute she had laid eyes on Angelo after his premature birth she had adored him with a fierce, deep love that had shaken her to the roots.

Without Pixie's help she would have struggled to survive, but, fortunately for Holly, her friend had supported her from the start. When waitressing had become impossible, Holly had taken a course to become a registered childminder and now by day she looked after her baby and two other children at home. She also worked in the shop on a casual basis. If evening or weekend work came up and Pixie was free to babysit, Holly did a shift to earn some extra cash.

And it was right then when she was thinking about how much she was looking forward to supper and her bed that it happened: she looked down at the bundle of newspapers she was tying up and saw a photograph on the front page of a man who reminded her of Vito. She stopped dead and yanked out the paper to shake it open. It was a financial broadsheet that she would never normally have even glanced at and the picture showed a man standing behind a lectern, a man who bore a remarkable resemblance to the father of her son.

'Are you nearly done, Holly?' one of her co-workers asked from the doorway.

'Almost.' Her shoulders rigid with tension, Holly was frantically reading the italicised print below the photograph. Vittore Zaffari, not Sorrentino. It was a man who resembled Vito—that was all. Her shoulders dropped again but just as she was about to put the newspaper back in the pile she hesitated and then extracted that particular page. Folding it quickly, she dug it into the pocket of her overall and hurriedly finished setting out the newspapers for collection.

It was after midnight before Holly got the chance to check out Vittore Zaffari online. Holly had studied the photograph again and again. He looked like her Vito but the newsprint picture wasn't clear enough for her to be certain. But the instant she did a search on Vittore Zaffari the images came rolling in and she knew without a doubt that she had finally identified her child's father.

'*My word*,' Pixie groaned, performing her own search on her tablet. 'Now I know why he gave you a fake name and was hiding out on Dartmoor. He was involved in some drugs-and-sex orgy. Hold on while I get this document translated into English.'

'Drugs and sex?' Holly repeated sickly. '*Vito?* It can't be the same man!'

But it was. The photos proved that he was *her* Vito, not some strange lookalike character. Of course, he had never been hers even to begin with, Holly reminded herself doggedly. And it was two in the morning before the two women finished digging up unwelcome facts about Vito, the billionaire banker ditched by his fabulously beautiful blonde fiancée only days before Holly had met him.

'Of course, you don't need to concern yourself with any of that nonsense,' Pixie told her ruefully. 'All you want from him now is child support and he seems to be wealthy enough that I shouldn't think that that will be a big deal.'

Holly lay sleepless in her bed, tossing and turning and at the mercy of her emotions. Vito had lied to her by deliberately giving her a false name. He too had been on the rebound but he hadn't mentioned that either. How would he react when she told him that he was a father? And did she really want to expose her infant son to a drug-abusing, womanising father? The answer to that was a very firm no. No amount of money could make a parent who was a bad influence a good idea.

But that really wasn't for her to decide, she reasoned over breakfast while she spooned baby rice into Angelo, who had a very healthy appetite. She studied her son with his coal-black curls and sparkling brown eyes. He was a happy baby, who liked to laugh and play, and he was very affectionate. Vito had been much more reserved, slow to smile and only demonstrative in bed. Holly winced at that unwelcome recollection. Regardless, Vito had a right to know that he was a father and in the same way she had a right to his financial help. She had to stop considering their situation from the personal angle because that only muddied the waters and upset her.

Angelo was the main issue. Everything came back to her son. Set against Angelo's needs, her personal feelings had no relevance. She had to be practical for his benefit and concentrate on what *he* needed. And the truth was that financially she was really struggling to survive and her baby was having to do without all the extras that he might have enjoyed. That was wrong. Her son didn't deserve to suffer because she had made a bad choice.

On the other hand, if Vito truly was the sort of guy who got involved in sex-and-drug orgies, he wasn't at all the male she had believed him to be. How could she have been so wrong about a man? She had honestly believed that Vito was a decent guy.

Even so, he was still Angelo's father and that was important. She was very much aware of just how much she had longed to know who her own father was. There was no way she could subject Angelo to living in the same ignorance. Nor could she somehow magically estimate whether Vito would be a good or bad influence on his son. The bottom line was that Angelo had the right to know who his father was so that he did not grow up with the same uncertainty that Holly had been forced to live with.

Holly acknowledged the hurt she had felt when Vito failed to make use of her phone number and contact her. Naturally her pride had been wounded and she had been disappointed. No woman wanted to feel that forgettable, but Angelo's birth had cast a totally different light on her situation. She had to forget her resentment and hurt and move on while placing her son's needs first. That would be a tall order but she believed that she loved her son enough to do it. She had to face Vito in the flesh and tell him that he was a father.

One week later, Holly handed over her package to the receptionist on the top floor of the Zaffari Bank in London. 'It's for Mr Zaffari. I would like to see him.'

The elegant receptionist set the small parcel down on the desktop and reached for something out of view. 'Mr Zaffari's appointments are fully booked weeks in advance, Miss…er…?'

'Cleaver. I believe he will want to see me,' Holly completed quietly while she wondered if that could possibly be true. 'I'll just wait over there until he's free.'

'There's really no point in you waiting,' the receptionist declared curtly, rising from her chair as two security guards approached. 'Mr Zaffari doesn't see anyone without a prior appointment.'

Stubbornly ignoring that assurance, Holly walked over to the waiting area and sat down, tugging her stretchy skirt down over her thighs. It had taken massive organisation for Holly to make a day trip to London but she knew that if she wanted to confront Vito she had to take advantage of his current presence in the UK. Her internet snooping had revealed that he was giving a speech at some fancy banking dinner that very evening and was therefore highly likely to be at the Zaffari Bank HQ throughout the day. Pixie had taken a day off to look after Angelo, and the children Holly usually minded were with their grandparents instead.

Holly had made a very early start to her day and had been appalled by the price of the train fare. Pixie had urged her to dress up to see Vito but, beyond abandoning her usual jeans and putting on a skirt with the knee boots Pixie had given her for Christmas, Holly had made no special effort. Why? As she continually reminded herself, this wasn't a *personal* visit and she wasn't trying to impress Vito. She was here to tell him about Angelo and that was all. Her restive fingers fiddled with the zip on her boots while she watched the two security guards carrying off her parcel with the absurdly cautious air of men who feared they could be carrying a bomb. Did she look like a terrorist? Like some kind of a madwoman?

Vito was in a board meeting and when his PA entered and slid a small package in front of him, which had already been unwrapped, he frowned in incomprehension, but when he pulled back the paper and saw the Santa hat and the small sprig of holly, he simply froze and gave his PA a shaken nod of immediate acceptance. Interrupting the proceedings to voice his apologies, he stood up, his cool dark eyes veiled.

What the hell was Holly doing here at the bank? Why now? And how had she tracked him down?

Hearing about that night, Apollo had scoffed. *With all your options you settled for a stranger? Are you crazy? You're one of the most eligible bachelors in the world and you picked up some random woman? A waitress?* he had scoffed in a tone of posh disbelief.

In fact, Apollo's comments had annoyed Vito so much that he had fiercely regretted confiding in his friend. He had told himself that it was for the best that Holly had walked away without fanfare, freeing them both from the threat of an awkward parting. He had also reminded himself that attempting to repeat a highly enjoyable experience invariably led to disappointment.

With the information he had had he could have traced her but he had resisted the urge with every atom of discipline he possessed. Self-control was hugely important to Vito and Holly had obliterated his self-control. He remembered that he had acted oddly with her and that memory made him uncomfortable. Even so he still hadn't forgotten her. In fact he was eager to see her because his memories of her had lingered to the extent that he had become disturbingly indifferent to other women and more particular than ever in his choices. He *wanted* to see Holly in full daylight, shorn of the schmaltzy sparkle of the festive season. He was suddenly convinced that such a disillusionment would miraculously knock him back to normality.

But why the hell would Holly be seeking him out now so long after the event? And in person rather than more tactfully by phone? And how had she linked him to the Zaffari Bank? Black brows lowering over cold dark eyes suddenly glittering with suspicion, Vito strode back into his office to await his visitor without an appointment.

Holly smiled and stood up when the receptionist approached her. In spite of her apprehension, Vito *had* remembered her and she was relieved. The Santa hat had been designed to jog his memory. After all, a male who indulged in sex parties might well not recall one night with an ordinary woman from over a year earlier. When it came to a question of morals he was a total scumbag, Holly reminded herself doggedly while walking down the corridor after another woman—even more thin and elegant—had asked her to follow her. She wondered why the other people working there seemed to be peering out of their offices in her direction and staring.

Suddenly she wondered what she was doing. Did she really want a man of Vito's dissolute proclivities in her life and Angelo's? Common sense warned her not to make snap judgements and to give Vito a chance for Angelo's sake. Her son would want to know who his dad was. Hadn't she wondered all her life who had fathered her? Hadn't that made her insecure? Made her feel less of a person than others because she didn't know that most basic fact about herself? No, Angelo deserved access to the truth of his parentage right from the start and that was what Holly would ensure her son had, no matter how unpleasant seeing Vito again proved to be.

Vito was a total scumbag, Holly reminded herself afresh while wondering why she was experiencing the strangest sense of...*elation*. Why was her heart pounding and her adrenaline buzzing? Her guide opened a door and stood back for her to enter. My goodness, he had a big office, *typical scumbag office*, she rephrased mentally. She would not be impressed; she *refused* to be impressed. And then Vito strode in through a side door and she was paralysed to the carpet because he simply looked so drop-dead amazing that she could not believe that she had ever slept with him and that he was the father of her child.

Her mouth ran dry. She felt dizzy. Butterflies danced in her tummy as she focused on those lean, darkly handsome features, and she knew that Pixie would have kicked her hard. *Total scumbag*, she told herself, but her brain would not engage with that fact and was much more interested in opening a back catalogue on Vito's sheer perfection. *To look at—perfect to* look *at*, she rephrased doggedly, striving to get back to the scumbag awareness. *Drugs....sex with hookers*, she fired at herself in desperation.

'The hat and the holly were an original calling card,' Vito drawled, the dark, deep accent tautening every muscle in her already tense body. 'But I *did* remember your name. I didn't need the prompt.'

Holly turned the red-hot colour of a tomato because she hadn't expected him to grasp the reasoning behind her introduction that easily.

'It would have been much easier to phone me,' Vito assured her silkily.

'And how could I have done that without your phone number?' Holly asked stiffly, because she was determined to make no reference to the fact that she had left her phone number with him and that he had decided not to make use of it. Discussing that would be far, far too humiliating.

'Well, maybe you shouldn't have run out on me before I got back to the cottage that day.' Vito smiled suddenly, brilliantly. It almost stopped her heart dead in its tracks as she stared at him. But it had not sat well with Vito that a night he had considered exceptional should have meant so much less to her that she'd walked out without a backward glance. Her reappearance satisfied him. He now felt free to study her with acute appreciation. She was wearing the most ordinary garments: a sweater, a shortish skirt, a jacket and boots, all black and all unremarkable but the glorious hourglass curves he cherished could not be concealed. His dark eyes flamed gold over the swell of her breasts below the wool and the lush curve of her hips before flying up to her full pink mouth, little snub nose and huge blue eyes. Shorn of the schmaltz and the sparkle and in full daylight, Holly was passing the test he had expected her to fail and for the first time in Vito's life, failure actually tasted sweet. He shifted almost imperceptibly as the hot swell of an erection assailed him and he almost smiled at that as well because his diminished libido had seriously bothered him.

'How did you find out who I was?' Vito enquired.

'Yes, that's right…you *lied*. You gave me a false name,' Holly was prompted to recall as she struggled to fight free of the spell he cast over her just by being in the same room.

'It wasn't a false name. I didn't lie. I was christened Vittore Sorrentino Zaffari,' he told her, smooth as glass. 'Sorrentino was my father's surname.'

That smoothness set Holly's teeth on edge. 'You lied,' she said again. 'You deliberately misled me. What I don't understand is why you did that.'

'You must appreciate that I am very well known in the business world. I prefer to be discreet. You coming here today in such a manner…' Vito shifted fluid brown fingers in an expressive dismissive gesture. 'That *was* indiscreet.' From his inside pocket he withdrew a business card and presented it to her. 'My phone number.'

Holly put the card into her jacket pocket because she didn't know what else to do with it. Indiscreet? Coming to see him in the flesh was indiscreet?

Dark golden eyes fringed by inky black, unfairly long lashes surveyed her and her tummy flipped, her heart rate increasing. 'Holly…I have the feeling that you don't understand where I'm going with this but I must be frank. I like to keep my private life *private*. I certainly do not want it to intrude when I'm at the bank. My working hours are sacrosanct.'

My word, he was literally telling her off for approaching him at his place of work, for coming to see him where other people would see her and notice her. A sense of deep humiliation pierced Holly because it had taken so much courage for her to come and confront him with the news she had. His case was not helped by the reality that she had seen a photo of him and his ex-fiancée, Marzia, posing outside the Zaffari Bank in Florence. Evidently, Marzia had enjoyed such privileges because she was someone he was *proud* to be seen with in public. Holly just could not get over Vito's nerve in daring to talk to her like that. Did he really think she was the sort of woman who would let a man talk down to her?

Her blue eyes widened and raked over him but it was pointless to try and put him down that way because she couldn't see a single flaw in his appearance. His dark grey suit fitted him like a tailored glove, outlining his height, breadth and long, powerful legs. And looking at him inevitably sent shards of mortifying memory flying through her already blitzed brain. She knew what he looked like out of his suit, she knew what he *felt* like, she also knew how he looked and sounded when he… *No, don't go there*, she urged herself and plunged straight into punitive speech because he had to be punished for putting such inappropriate thoughts into her head.

'I can't believe you're talking down to me as if you're a superior being,' Holly bit out tightly. 'Why? Because you've got money and a big fancy office? Certainly not because you've been shopped for taking drugs and sleeping with hookers!'

There was a flash of bemused surprise in Vito's brilliant dark eyes before he responded. 'That was a case of misidentification. I was not the man involved.'

'Of course you're going to say that,' Holly retorted with a roll of her eyes. 'Of course you're going to deny it to me but, as I understand it, you never once denied it in public.'

'I had a good reason for that. I never respond to tabloid journalists and I was protecting my family,' Vito returned levelly. 'I assure you…on my honour…that I was not the man involved and that I profoundly disapprove of such activities.'

Holly remained unimpressed. How did she credit that he had honour? How was she supposed to believe him? He had been protecting his family by remaining silent? How did that work?

'I do believe it would be wiser to take this meeting out of my big fancy office to somewhere more comfortable,' Vito continued, his smooth diction acidic in tone. 'I have an apartment in London. My driver will take you and you can relax there until I can join you for lunch.'

Knocked right off balance by that suggestion coming at her out of nowhere, Holly actually found herself thinking about the offer of lunch. Telling him about Angelo in an office setting felt wrong to her as well, and then a little voice in the back of her brain that sounded alarmingly like Pixie told her to wise up and think about the invitation he had made. And at that point the coin finally dropped for Holly and she grasped how Vito had chosen to interpret her sudden reappearance in his life. She wanted to kick herself for not foreseeing that likelihood, but she wanted to kick him even harder for daring to think that he could have a chance with her again. Certainly not with what she now knew about his partying habits!

'I haven't come here for another hook-up,' Holly stated with an embarrassed force that made her voice rise slightly. Behind her mortification lurked a great well of burning resentment.

Did he really think that she was so desperate for sex that she would travel all the way to London for it? How dared he assume that she was that keen, that easy? Well, she certainly hadn't taught him that she was a big challenge the night they first met, Holly conceded grudgingly. *But, my goodness, that one night must have been as good on his terms as he had said it was if he was willing to do it again.* Or maybe he was simply a sex addict? Anything was possible. When Holly had snapped back at him about his money and his fancy office and his debauched partying, she had also picked up on his surprise. He had assumed she was a quiet, easy-going little mouse but Holly wasn't quiet when her temper was roused. And right now her temper was rising like lava in a volcano. The past fourteen months had been very challenging, and working all day after a sleepless night had become her new norm. Having no way of contacting her son's father, who had handicapped her by giving her a false name, had only added to her stress.

Vito tensed. 'I didn't say anything about that. No expectations…' he murmured silkily, lean brown hands sketching an eloquent arc in the air as if to nullify her suspicions.

'Of course you have expectations…but, in this case, I'm afraid it's not going to happen. You had your chance and you blew it!' Holly snapped back, striving to hang on to her temper.

His brows drew together. 'What's that supposed to mean?'

Holly rolled her eyes, her lush mouth compressed. 'A timely little reminder that if you had really *wanted* to see me again I did leave you my phone number.'

'No, you didn't,' Vito insisted.

Holly tensed even more, angry that she had let that reminder fall from her mouth. 'I left a note thanking you for your hospitality and I printed my phone number at the bottom of it.'

Vito groaned. 'I didn't find a note when you left. Where did you leave it?'

'On the shelf in the fireplace.' Holly shrugged dismissively, keen to drop the subject.

'If there was a note, I didn't see it,' Vito assured her.

But then he would say that, wouldn't he? Holly thought, unimpressed. Of course he had found the silly note she had left behind and he had done nothing with it. And in doing nothing he had taught her all she needed to know about how he saw her. She had gone over the events of that morning in her mind many, many times. She was convinced that Vito had gone out for a walk to get a break from her. For him the fun of togetherness had already worn thin. He had ignored her note most probably because he'd been relieved to find her already gone. He had seen that night as a casual one-night stand that he had no desire to repeat.

'Whatever. It's pointless to discuss it after the amount of time that has passed. But let me spell out one fact,' Holly urged thinly. 'I *didn't* come to see you today for anything…er…physical. I came to see you about something much *more* important.'

At her emphasis, Vito raised a level dark brow in cool query mode, his wide sensual mouth tightening with impatience. And she could feel the whole atmosphere turning steadily colder and less welcoming. Naturally. She had taken sex off the lunch table, as it were, and he was no longer interested in anything she might have to say to him. And why would he be interested? She was poor and he was rich. He was educated and she was more of a self-educated person, which meant that she had alarming gaps in her knowledge. He was hugely successful and a high achiever while she worked in dead-end jobs without a career ladder for advancement. It was incredible, she finally conceded, that they had ever got involved in the first place.

'More important?' Vito prompted, his irritation barely hidden.

Defiance and umbrage combined inside Holly. She had held on to her temper but it was a close-run battle. His assumption that she was approaching him for another sexual encounter had shocked her, possibly because she had persuaded herself that they had shared something more than sex. Now she saw her illusions for the pitiful lies that they were, lies she had told herself to bolster her sagging self-esteem while she was waddling round with a massive tummy.

'Yes, much more important,' she confirmed, lifting her chin and simply spilling out her announcement. 'I got pregnant that night we were together.'

Vito froze as if she had threatened to fling a grenade at him. He turned noticeably pale, his strong bone structure suddenly clearly etched below his skin by raw tension. 'You said you were on the pill—'

Holly wasn't in the mood to go into the intricacies of missed pills and antibiotic treatment. 'You must know that every form of contraception has a failure rate and I'm afraid there was a failure. I got pregnant but I had no way of contacting you, particularly not when you had given me a fake name.'

Vito was in shock. Indeed Vito could never recall being plunged into such a state of shock before. Everything he had assumed had been turned upside down and inside out with those simple words...*I got pregnant.*

'And do you usually reintroduce yourself with a very evocative Santa hat and a sprig of holly when this happens?' he heard himself snap without even mentally forming the words. 'Is this some sort of a scam?'

Holly's small shoulders pushed up, along with her chin. 'No, Angelo is not a scam, Vito. He was born eight months after that night.'

'You come here without a word of warning and throw this announcement at me like a challenge,' Vito ground out in condemnation, no fan of major surprises in his life, as yet not even capable of thinking of what she was telling him. The prospect of having a child had long struck him as a possibility as remote as the moon. He had known fatherhood was on the cards somewhere down the line if he married Marzia but he had also known that neither of them were in any hurry to start a family.

'No, I did not. If I challenged you it would be an awful lot tougher!' Holly shot back at him furiously. 'Tough was waitressing until I was eight months pregnant and being in labour for two days before I got a

C-section. Tough is working as a childminder and a shelf-stacker and never getting enough sleep. You wouldn't know tough if it leapt on you and bit you...because in your whole blasted spoilt-rotten life you have had *everything* handed to you on a plate!'

A dark line of colour had delineated Vito's high cheekbones as he viewed her in growing disbelief. 'That is enough.'

'No, it's not enough, and you do *not* tell me when enough is enough!' Holly fired back at him, while pointing at him with an angry finger.

'Ranting at me is not getting us anywhere.'

'I'm entitled to rant if I want to rant!' Holly launched back at him an octave higher, shaking with rage and the distress she was fighting off while wondering if Vito ever lost his temper, because he was still so very controlled. 'And I don't *want* to get anywhere with you. I'm done here. I've told you that you're a father and that's why I came to see you. I saw your photo in a newspaper, incidentally...a *lovely* way to identify the father of your child! But if you want to think Angelo's a scam, you're welcome.'

'Holly...'

Holly yanked open the door and marched down the corridor very fast because she could not wait to get out of the building. She could feel the tears building up and she didn't want them to fall in front of an audience. She ignored Vito's voice when he repeated her name and stabbed the lift button with frantic force.

'Holly...*come back here*!' Vito shouted without warning.

So taken aback was she by that sudden rise in volume from him that she spun round and looked at him. He was only halfway down the corridor, evidently having expected her to return at his urging, and if looks could kill she would have been lying dead at his feet. He did have a temper, though, she registered belatedly, and it made his dark eyes glitter like gold ingots and gave his lean, darkly beautiful features a hard, forbidding edge.

Horribly aware of the number of people openly staring, Holly turned back to the lift just as the doors opened. She dived in as fast as she could but not fast enough to prevent Vito from joining her.

'You should've come back to my office.'

In silence, Holly contemplated his polished shoes because the tears were even closer now and stinging her eyes like angry wasps.

'I have to look into this situation. I need your phone number and your address,' Vito breathed in a raw undertone.

'I wasn't expecting you to be so offensive—funny, how you get the wrong idea about people. I really didn't want to get pregnant, Vito, but I love my son and he is never ever going to hear me admit that because now that he's here he's the *best* thing that ever happened to me,' she bit out shakily, hurriedly stepping out of the lift.

'Phone number. Address,' Vito said again, closing a hand to a slight shoulder to prevent her from walking away through the crowded concourse.

With a heavy sigh, Holly dug into her bag and produced a notebook. He handed her a gold pen. She squinted down at the pen, dimly wondering if it was real gold, and then scolded herself for that stupid thought. She printed out the requested details and ripped out the sheet to hand it back to him. 'Look,' she muttered uncomfortably. 'There's no pressure on you here. If I'm honest I don't really want you in our lives. You're not the sort of man I want around my son.'

And having deprived Vito of breath and speech with that damning final indictment of his character, Holly disappeared into the crowds.

CHAPTER SIX

WELL, YOU MADE a real screw-up of that, Vito reflected
for the first time in his life. But Holly hadn't given him
the smallest preparation for what was to come, so it was
scarcely surprising that everything that could go wrong
had gone wrong. He didn't react well to surprises and
the delivery of the Santa hat and the holly had seemed
suggestively sexual. Was it any wonder he had got the
wrong idea? His hard mouth compressed while he wondered about that note she had mentioned. Had she left
a note? He had looked in all the obvious places. There
had been nothing on the table or the door, and what did
it matter now anyway?

What really mattered was that without the smallest
warning he was apparently a father...

That was a mind-blowing concept but Vito was
primarily ruled by his very shrewd brain and his first
call was to his lawyer, who within the hour put him into
contact with a London-based specialist in family law.
Once all his questions had been answered, Vito was
frowning at the realisation that he didn't really have
any rights over his own son. Only marriage granted
such legal rights. He didn't consult Apollo because he
knew that his friend would start talking about demand-

ing DNA tests but he and Apollo lived very different lives and Vito was confident that if Holly had given birth to a baby eight months after that night, it could only be his baby.

He didn't know how he felt about becoming a father, and after he had organised travel to Holly's home town for the following day and informed her by text of his planned visit, he phoned his mother to break the news.

Concetta Zaffari's delight at learning that she was a grandmother tumbled through her every word and then there were questions about Holly that Vito found hard to answer, and some he skipped altogether.

'*Obviously* you'll be getting married,' Concetta trilled cheerfully, and Vito laughed that his mother should even feel the need to say that. Of course they would be getting married. No Zaffari in history had had an illegitimate child and Vito had every intention of being a better parent than his own father had proved to be, although how to go about achieving that ambition he had no very clear idea.

Holly did not respond to Vito's text because it annoyed her. Why did he assume that she was free to drop everything to make herself and Angelo available at a time that suited him? She was working an early morning shift the next day because it was a Saturday and Pixie was taking care of Angelo for her.

As a result, when Vito arrived in his limousine, having been picked up from the helicopter ride that had brought him from London, he was taken aback to be met by Pixie and informed that his son was having a nap.

'Where's Holly?' he demanded, frowning down at

the diminutive blonde, whose facial expression tele-graphed her antagonism towards him.

'At work.'

'Where?'

'The supermarket fifty yards down the road,' Pixie advanced reluctantly. 'You can wait in your car. Her shift ends in an hour.'

Infuriated that Holly hadn't thought to warn him so that he could adjust his arrival time accordingly, Vito strode down the road. He was full of righteous indignation until he walked through the busy shop and caught a glimpse of Holly wheeling a trolley bigger than she was through the aisles and pausing to restock shelves. *Tough is working as a shelf-stacker and never getting enough sleep.* Abruptly, he spun on his heel and strode back out of the busy shop again, shamed by the reality that the mother of his child was being forced to work so hard to survive.

Vito would have argued that he had not been spoilt rotten, but he had been born rich and with a near-genius-level IQ, and phenomenal success in almost every field was a reward he took for granted. He had never had to struggle, never had to make the best of two bad choices, never had to do anything he didn't want to do and the sheer undeniable luxury of those realities about his life was finally sinking in on him. With uncharacteristic patience he directed his driver to take him away from the street of tiny terraced houses where Holly lived to a hotel, where he had lunch while imagining Holly going without food, which didn't im-prove his appetite.

'Vito came, then?' Holly exclaimed as she wriggled out of her overall.

Pixie nodded confirmation. 'Cheese toastie for lunch?'

'Lovely. I should've texted him to say that time didn't suit me. I don't know what it is about Vito but he makes me act completely out of character!' Holly declared guiltily.

'Take it from me, anything other than awe and flattery is probably good for Vito's character. At least he's interested in meeting his son,' Pixie said cheerfully. 'That's good news.'

Holly scoffed down the cheese toastie and touched up her make-up. She couldn't sit down, and she couldn't concentrate either. She wanted to stand at the window waiting for Vito like a kid watching out for Santa Claus arriving. Embarrassment gripped her then and she sat down, only to fly up again when Angelo cried as he wakened from his nap. Changing her son, she gave him a hug and he drank down some water to quench his thirst. It was cold in the small sitting room and she lit the fire to warm it up.

'I'm off out now,' Pixie told her while Holly was strapping a wriggling Angelo into his infant seat.

'But—'

'This is about you and him and Angelo and it's private. Give me a text when he's gone,' Pixie suggested.

Only minutes later the bell went and Holly's heartbeat leapt into her throat, convulsing it. She raced to the front door and then paused to compose herself for several seconds before opening it.

'Holly…' Vito pronounced softly, staring broodingly down at her from his great height. Sheathed in jeans and a sweater teamed with a buttery soft brown leather jacket, he totally took her breath away.

'Come in…' Her wary glance was ensnared by black-fringed dark golden eyes that sent her heart racing. 'Don't stare,' she scolded breathlessly.

'I find you very attractive. Naturally, I'm going to stare, *bellezza mia.*'

He hadn't found her attractive enough to use her phone number, Holly reminded herself ruefully. 'No, don't say insincere stuff like that. All we really have to do here is be polite to each other,' Holly told him in the small, confined hall as he came to a halt beside her.

'I can manage much more than polite,' Vito declared, his long brown fingers settling down onto her slight shoulders and feeling the rigid tension that now gripped her small frame. She had the most luscious mouth he had ever seen on a woman, pink and soft and succulent. His jeans tightened at his groin, his physical reaction instantaneous.

At his touch, Holly turned rigid with discomfiture. 'I meant friendly rather than—'

'*Maledizione!* You want me to be friendly when I can hardly keep my hands off you?' Vito shot at her with raw incredulity. 'I don't think I can manage that.'

'But you have to. I wouldn't be comfortable with anything else,' Holly told him earnestly, convinced that only disaster would follow if she allowed any further intimacy to complicate an already tense relationship.

'*Have* to?' Vito queried, a flash of glittering challenge entering his searching gaze as he stared down at her. 'Have you got someone else in your life…another man?'

Holly dealt him a startled glance. 'No… Why are you asking that?'

Without warning, Vito moved forward, pinning her up against the wall behind her. 'Because if there was

I'd probably want to kill him!' he muttered in a raw undertone.

In wonderment, Holly looked up into his lean, darkly beautiful face and then her view blurred as he hauled her up to his level and opened her mouth with the crushing demand of his own. He tasted so good, all minty and fresh, and the strength in the arms holding her felt even better. Every hard, angular line of his long, lean physique was pressed against her as he braced her hips against the wall. The passion of that hungry kiss threatened to consume her and the anomaly between the cool face he showed the world and the uncontrolled hotness hidden beneath electrified her. The piercing ache she had almost forgotten tugged cruelly in her pelvis as his tongue tangled with hers. His mouth was sublime, the feel of his unyielding muscles, hard against her softer curves, incredible. Insane chemistry...insane behaviour, she translated, pulling back from him with shell-shocked abruptness because she knew with shamed horror that all she really wanted to do with him at that moment was drag him upstairs to her bed to rediscover the amazing pleasure he could give her.

'No, this is not what you're here for...' she muttered in curt reminder, her spine stiff as she turned her back on him to walk into the small sitting room. 'You're here to meet Angelo and that's all.'

'You make it sound so simple when it's anything but simple,' Vito countered with a roughened edge to his voice because she had pushed him away and he had had to resist a powerful urge to turn caveman and yank her back to him.

'If we both make the effort, we can keep this simple and polite,' Holly stated with rigorous resolve.

'I have something I need to explain to you first…'
But by that point, Vito could see over the top of Holly's
head and his attention zeroed in so quickly on the child
in the infant seat that his voice literally trailed away.

And for Vito it was as though the rest of the world
vanished. He focused in amazement on the baby who
bore a remarkable resemblance to a framed photograph
Vito's mother had of her son at a similar age. Huge
brown eyes from below a mop of black curls inspected
him with sparkling curiosity. A chubby fist waved in the
air and suddenly Vito froze, out of his comfort zone and
hating it. He had never gone weak at the knees for pup-
pies or babies, had put that lack of a softer side down to
his grandfather's rigid discipline. But now he was looking at his son and seeing a baby with his own features in
miniature and he finally realised that the very thought
of fatherhood unnerved him. His own father had been
a hopeless parent. How much worse would he do with
Angelo when he had no idea even where to start?

Holly paused beside the child seat to say awkwardly,
'So…er…obviously this is Angelo. He's a little bored at
weekends because during the week I look after a pair
of toddlers and it's a lot livelier here.'

Vito tried to stand a little less stiffly but in truth he
felt much as if someone had swung open the door of a
lion's cage and left him to take his chances. 'Why did
you call him Angelo?'

'Because you're Italian,' Holly pointed out, wondering why he was questioning the obvious. 'I looked up
Italian names.'

Vito forced himself closer to the baby. His hands
weren't quite steady as he undid the belt strapping An-

gelo into his seat. As Vito lifted the baby, Angelo gave his father an anxious, startled appraisal.

'You're used to children,' Holly assumed, rather taken aback by that deceptively confident first move.

'No. I don't think I've ever been this close to a child before. There are none in the family and most of my friends are still single as well,' Vito told her abstractedly, wondering what he was supposed to do with the little boy now that he was holding him.

'Thank you for having him,' Vito breathed in a driven undertone. 'You could have made a different decision but you didn't.'

Nothing about this first meeting was going in any direction that Holly had foreseen. And she was even less ready to hear her baby's father thank her for not opting for a termination. Her eyes prickled with sudden emotion.

'I wanted him from the first, never had any doubts there,' she admitted gruffly. 'He's the only family I have…apart from my friend Pixie.'

As Angelo squirmed and wriggled, Vito lifted him higher and swung him round in aeroplane mode.

The baby's eyes grew huge and he let out a frightened howl before breaking down into red-faced, gulping sobs.

'Let me take him,' Holly urged in dismay as Vito lowered the squalling baby. 'He's not used to the rough stuff. There are no men in his life, really, just Pixie and me…'

Vito settled Angelo back into Holly's arms with more than a suggestion of haste and relief. 'Sorry, I upset him.'

'He needs time to get used to you,' Holly explained. 'I'll put him on the floor to play with his toys.'

Vito was tempted to back off entirely but that struck him as cowardly and he held his ground to crouch down on the rug. Finally recalling that he had brought a gift, he removed it from his pocket and tipped it out of a box. 'It's only a little toy.'

Holly winced as she noted a piece of the toy break off and fall. It had detachable tiny parts and was totally unsuitable for a baby. 'You can't give that to him,' she told Vito apologetically. 'He puts everything in his mouth and he could choke on those tiny pieces.'

In haste, Vito removed the toy and its parts again and grimaced. 'I didn't think. I really don't know anything about babies.'

Holly pulled over Angelo's toy box and extracted a red plastic truck that was a favourite. 'He likes this... Coffee?' she asked.

'Black, no sugar,' Vito murmured flatly, recognising that getting to know his son and learning how to play with him appeared to be even more challenging than he had feared.

Holly made coffee, acknowledging that she was simply delighted that Vito had had enough interest to come and meet Angelo. She could see how awkward he felt with their child and knew that if she didn't make Vito feel more comfortable he might not want to make another visit. Not that he had prepared very well for this first visit, she thought ruefully, wondering what he had thought a baby would do with a miniature brick action figure festooned in even tinier weapons.

When she returned with the coffee, Angelo was sucking on his little red truck and refusing to share the toy with his father. Holly got down on her knees beside them and, with his mother on hand, her son relaxed his grip on the truck and handed it to Vito. For an instant he looked as though he had no idea what to do with the toy and then some childhood memory of his own must have prompted him because he ran the toy across the rug making *vroom-vroom* noises and Angelo gave a little-boy shout of appreciation.

A little of Vito's tension ebbed in receipt of that favourable response. It shook him to appreciate that he had actually craved that first welcoming smile from his son. He wanted the little boy to recognise him as his father, he wanted him to like him and love him, but it was intimidating to appreciate that he hadn't the faintest idea how to go about achieving those things.

Holly parted her lips to say, 'When you first came in you said there was something that you needed to explain to me…?'

Vito's lean, strong profile clenched and he sprang upright. 'Yes. That sex-party scandal that made headlines,' he framed with palpable distaste. 'That wasn't me, it was my father, Ciccio.'

As she too stood up, Holly's mouth dropped open in shock. 'Your…*father*?'

'I didn't deny my involvement because I was trying to protect my mother from the humiliation of having her husband's habits exposed so publicly,' Vito explained grimly.

Holly dropped down on the edge of the sofa behind her. 'Oh, my goodness.'

'My mother could confirm the truth if you require further proof that I wasn't involved. What did happen that night was that I received a phone call in the early hours of the morning telling me that my father had fallen ill and needed urgent medical attention,' Vito told her, his delivery curt.

'The person calling refused to identify herself, and that should've been my warning. My mother was in Paris and I had to take charge. I wondered why my father had taken ill at an apartment owned by the bank but the minute I walked into it I could see what I was dealing with, and that I had been contacted like a clean-up crew in the hope of keeping the wild party under the radar.'

Holly nodded slowly, not really knowing what to say.

'My father had had a heart attack in the company of hookers and drugs,' Vito volunteered grimly. 'I had him collected by a private ambulance from the rear entrance and, having instructed a trusted aide to dispose of all evidence of the party, I intended to join my father at a clinic. Unfortunately the press were waiting outside when I left and I was mobbed. One of the hookers then sold her story, choosing to name me rather than my father even though I had never met her in my life. She probably lied because there was more of a story in my downfall than in that of a middle-aged married man with a taste for sleaze.'

'So you took the blame for your parents' sake?' Holly whispered in wonderment.

'My *mother's* sake,' Vito emphasised drily. 'But my mother worked out the truth for herself and she is currently divorcing my father. She looked after him until he had regained his health and then told him that she wanted a separation.'

'And how do you feel about that? I mean, their divorce means that your sacrifice was in vain.'

'I'm relieved that they've split up. I don't like my

father very much…well, not at all, really,' Vito admitted, his wide sensual mouth twisting. 'He's a greedy, dishonest man and my mother will have a better life without him.'

Utterly amazed by that flood of unrestrained candour from a male as reserved as Vito, Holly continued to scrutinise him with inquisitive blue eyes. 'Why are you telling me all this now?'

'You're family now in all but name,' Vito told her wryly. 'And I couldn't possibly allow you to continue to believe that I am not a fit person to be around my son.'

Holly fully understood that motivation and muttered, 'I'm sorry I misjudged you. I was naive to believe everything I read on the internet about you. I told you before that I don't know who my father is,' Holly admitted, wrinkling her nose. 'My mother gave me several different stories and I challenged her when I was sixteen to tell me the truth but she still wouldn't answer me. I honestly don't think she knows either. In those days she was fairly promiscuous. I've had no contact with her since then.'

'You've never had a father…much like me. Ciccio took no interest in me when I was a child and when I was an adult he only approached me if he wanted something,' he revealed, settling down with striking grace of movement into an armchair. 'My grandfather was my father figure but he was seventy when I was born and he had a Victorian outlook on childcare and education. It was far from ideal.'

Holly was fascinated by what she was learning about Vito's background, although she really wasn't sure why he was choosing to tell her so much. 'I think very few people have an ideal childhood,' she said ruefully.

'But wouldn't it be wonderful to give Angelo that ideal?' Vito pressed, black velvet lashes lifting on glittering gold as he studied her.

Her heart raced and her mouth ran dry. Hurriedly she dropped her gaze from his, only for her attention to fall to the tight inner seam of his jeans stretched along a powerful muscular thigh. Guilty heat surged through her and she shifted uneasily. 'And how could we give Angelo an ideal childhood?' she asked abstractedly.

'By getting married and giving our son a conventional start in life,' Vito spelt out with measured assurance. 'I'm not only here to meet Angelo, Holly...I'm here to ask you to be my wife.'

Disbelief roared through Holly. She blinked rapidly, doubting the evidence of her ears. He was proposing? He was actually proposing marriage to her because she had had his child?

Holly loosed an uneasy laugh and Vito frowned, because that was hardly the response he had envisaged. 'I think your grandfather's Victorian outlook is showing, Vito. We don't need to get married to give Angelo a decent upbringing.'

'How else can I be a proper father when I live in a different country?' Vito demanded with harsh bite. 'I really don't want to be only an occasional visitor in my son's life or the home he visits for a few weeks in summer when he's off school. That is not enough for me.'

Holly watched Vito lean down to lift Angelo, who was tugging at his shoelaces. He closed his arms tentatively round Angelo's small restive body and settled him down on a lean thigh. There was something incredibly sexy about his newly learned assurance with their son and her cheeks coloured at that seemingly tasteless reflection, but the smouldering edge of Vito's sexuality seemed to be assailing her every thought. 'Well, I can see that it would be difficult for you and far from ideal, but marriage…well, that's a whole different ball game,' she told him regretfully. 'I want to marry a man who loves me, not a man who accidentally got me pregnant and wants to do what he feels is the right thing by me.'

'I can't change how we conceived Angelo but with a little vision you should be able to see that where we started isn't where we have to end up,' Vito responded smoothly. 'I may not love you but I'm insanely attracted to you. I'm also ready to settle down.'

'Yes, you were engaged, weren't you?' Holly slotted in rather unkindly.

'That's not relevant here,' Vito informed her drily. 'Stay focused on what really matters.'

'Angelo,' Holly replied, with hot cheeks, while her brain trooped off in wild, unproductive circles.

He was asking her to marry him… He was actually asking her to marry him! How was she supposed to react to that when she had been astonished by his proposal?

'You should also consider the reality that eventually Angelo will be very rich, and growing up outside *my* world isn't the best preparation for that day,' Vito pointed out. 'I want to be his father. A father who is there for him when he needs me. A benefit neither you nor I enjoyed.'

He was making very valid points but Holly felt harassed and intimidated rather than grateful for his honesty. 'But marriage?' she reasoned. 'That's such a huge decision.'

'And a decision only you can make. But there would be other benefits for you,' Vito told her quietly. 'You could set up as an interior designer and live your dream with me.'

'You're starting to sound like a trained negotiator,' Holly cut in.

'I am a trained negotiator,' Vito conceded. 'But I want to give our son the very best start in life he can have, with a genuine family.'

And that was the real moment that Holly veered from consternation and fell deep into his honeytrap. Those emotive words, 'a genuine family', spoke to her on the deepest possible level and filled her head with happy images. That was a goal that she, and surprisingly Vito in spite of his privileged background, both shared, and that touched her. As she studied her son sitting peacefully in his father's arms her heart melted. She had felt ashamed of the lack of caution that had led to her pregnancy. She had been mortified that she had failed her own life goals and could not give her son the family security and the opportunities he deserved. But if she married Vito she would be able to put all her regrets behind her and *give* Angelo two parents and a stable home with every advantage.

'Even people in love find it hard to make marriage work,' Holly reminded him, fighting to resist the tempting images flooding her imagination, and to be sensible and cautious.

'We're not in love. Our odds of success may well be better because we have less exalted expectations,' Vito contended silkily. 'And our arrangement need not be viewed as a permanent trap either. In a few years, should one or both of us be unhappy, we can divorce.

All I'm asking you to do at this moment in time, Holly…
is give marriage a chance.'

He made it sound so reasonable, so very reasonable.
He was inviting her to *try* being married to him and
see if they could make it work. It was a very realistic
approach, guaranteed to make her feel that by trying
she would have nothing to lose. And she looked back
at him in silence with her heart hammering while he
raked an impatient hand through his cropped black hair.

'I'll think it over.' Holly fibbed, because she had already thought it over and really there was no contest
between what Vito was offering Angelo and what she
could hope to offer her son as a lone parent.

'Be more decisive, *bellezza mia*,' Vito urged. 'If you
marry me I will do everything within my power to
make you happy.'

Holly had known true happiness only a few times
in her life. One of those moments had been waking at
dawn enfolded in Vito's arms. Another had been the
first time she had seen her infant son. But just being
with Vito also made her happy and that worried her,
implying as it did that she was craving something more
than a very practical marriage based on their son's
needs. Should she listen to that voice of reason and
warning now? Stay on the sidelines where it was safe
rather than risk dipping her toes into the much more
complex demands of a marriage?

But at the baseline of her responses there was no
denying that she wanted Vito Zaffari with a bone-deep,
almost frighteningly strong yearning. How could she
possibly walk away from that? How could she stand
back and watch him take up with other women, as he
would, and know that she had given him that freedom?

And the answer was that she couldn't face that, would sooner take a risk on a marriage that might not work than surrender any hope of a deeper relationship with him.

Holly breathed in slow and deep and lifted her head high. 'All right. We'll get married…and see how it goes…'

And Vito smiled, that heart-stopping smile that always froze her in her tracks, and nothing he said after that point registered with her because she was washed away by sheer excitement and hope for the future.

Vito registered the stars in her eyes with satisfaction. Having been driven by the need to secure the best possible arrangement for his son's benefit, he had expended little thought on the actual reality of becoming a married man or a father. He wanted Holly and he wanted his son: that was all that mattered. And Holly would soon learn to fit into his world, he thought airily.

CHAPTER SEVEN

'SMILE!' PIXIE TOLD HOLLY. 'You look totally stupendous!'

Holly smiled to order and gripped her hands together tightly on her lap. The past four weeks had passed in a whirlwind of unfamiliar activity and changes. Now it was her wedding day and hopefully she would finally have time to draw a breath and start to relax. Only not when it was a wedding about to be attended by a lot of rich, important people, she reasoned nervously.

'How are you feeling?' she asked her best friend and bridesmaid, ruefully surveying Pixie's legs, which were both encased in plaster casts.

Her housemate had returned from a visit to her brother badly battered and bruised from a fall down the stairs, which had also broken both her legs. The extent of her injuries had appalled Holly and, although the bruising had faded, she couldn't help feeling that there was more amiss with her friend than she was letting on because Pixie's usual chirpiness and zest for life seemed to have faded away as well. And although she had gently questioned Pixie on several occasions, she could not work out if it was her own imagination in overdrive or if indeed there *was* some secret concern that Pixie wasn't yet willing to share with her.

Predictably, Pixie rolled her eyes. 'I keep on telling you I'm fine. I'll get these casts off in a couple of weeks and I'll get back to work and it'll be as if this never happened.'

'Hopefully you'll be able to come out to visit us in Italy in a few weeks' time.'

'That's doubtful.'

'Er…if it's money—'

'No, I'm not taking money off you!' Pixie told her fiercely. 'You may be marrying Mr Rich but that's not going to change anything between us.'

'All right.' Holly subsided to scrutinise the opulent diamond engagement ring on her finger. Vito wasn't the least bit romantic, she conceded ruefully, because he had sent the ring to her by special delivery rather than presenting her with it. That had been such a disappointment to her. It would have meant so much to Holly if Vito had made the effort to personally give her the ring.

'Let's simply be a normal couple from here on in,' Vito had urged, and seemingly the ring signified that normality he wanted even if it had not entailed him changing his ways.

She had wanted to ask if it was the same ring Marzia, his previous fiancée, had worn but had sealed her lips shut in case that question was tactless. And staging a potentially difficult conversation with a male she had barely seen since she had agreed to marry him had struck her as unwise.

'Of course I'm very busy now. How else could I take time off for the wedding?' Vito had enquired piously on the phone when she'd tried to tactfully suggest that he make more effort to spend some time with her and Angelo.

Vito hadn't even been able to make time for Angelo, whom he had only seen once since their agreement. Of course, to be fair, he *had* suggested that they move into his London apartment *before* the wedding and she had been ready to agree until she had heard from Pixie's brother and had realised that there was no way she could leave her injured friend to cope alone in a house with stairs. She had had to put Pixie first but Vito had not understood that. In fact Vito had called it a silly excuse that was dividing him from his son. After the wedding she needed to explain to Vito just how much of a debt she owed Pixie for her friend's support during her pregnancy and after Angelo's birth, and she needed to explain that she loved Pixie as much as she would have loved a sister. Although, never having had a sibling of his own, he might not even understand that.

And there were an awful lot of things that Vito didn't understand, Holly reflected ruefully. He had been thoroughly irritated when she'd insisted on continuing her childminding until her charges' parents had had time to make other arrangements for their care, but Holly would not have dreamt of letting anyone down, and took her responsibilities just as seriously as he took his own.

Furthermore, in every other way Vito had contrived to take over Holly and her son's lives. He had made decisions on their behalf that he had neglected to discuss with Holly. Maybe he thought she was too stupid and ignorant to make the right decisions, she thought unhappily.

First he had landed her with an Italian nanny, who had had to board at a hotel nearby because there were only two bedrooms in the house Pixie and Holly rented. London-born Lorenza was a darling and wonderful with Angelo, and Holly had needed outside help to cope with shopping for a wedding dress and such things, but she still would have preferred to play an active role in the hiring of a carer for her son.

Secondly, he had landed Holly with a horrible, pretentious fashion stylist who had wanted Holly to choose the biggest, splashiest and most expensive wedding gown ever made. Only sheer stubbornness had ensured that Holly actually got to wear her own choice of dress on her special day. And it was a very plain dress because Holly was convinced that she was too small and curvy to risk wearing anything more elaborate. She stroked the delicate edge of a lace sleeve with satisfaction. At least she had got her dream dress even if she hadn't got any input into any other details because Vito had placed all the organisation into the hands of a wedding planner, whom he had instructed *not* to consult his future wife.

In truth, Vito was extremely bossy and almost painfully insensitive sometimes. He had left it to his social secretary to tell Holly that she had a day at a grooming parlour booked for a makeover. Holly had been mortified, wondering whether Vito thought her ordinary ungroomed self was a mess and not up to his standards. Pixie had told her not to be so prickly and had asked her if she thought there was something immoral about manicures and waxing. And no, of course she didn't think that, it was just that she had wanted Vito to want her as she was, not be left feeling that only a very polished version of her could now be deemed acceptable. After all, she didn't have the security of knowing her bridegroom loved her, flaws and all, and that made a big difference to a woman's confidence, she reasoned worriedly.

'Will you stop it? And don't ask me what you're to stop!' Pixie said bluntly. 'You're worrying yourself sick about marrying Vito and it's crazy. You love him—'

'I don't love him,' Holly contradicted instantly. 'I like him. I'm very attracted to him.'

'You look him up online just to drool over his photos. If it's not love, it's a monster crush. So you might as well be married to him,' Pixie contended. 'Vito's all you think about. In fact watching you scares the hell out of me. I don't think I could bear to love anyone the way you love him, but with a little luck in time he may well return your feelings.'

'Do you think so?'

'I don't see why not,' Pixie responded thoughtfully. 'Vito's the caring type even if he hasn't yet learned to share. Why shouldn't he fall in love with you?'

But it wasn't love she felt, Holly told herself urgently. It was liking, attraction, respect, nothing more, nothing less. Loving Vito without being loved back would simply make her unhappy and she refused to be unhappy. No, she was a very hands-on person and she was going to make the most of what she *did* have with Vito and Angelo, not make the mistake of pining for what she couldn't have. After all, she could plainly see Vito in all his very good-looking and sophisticated glory and she knew she was only getting to marry him because some crazy fate had deposited her as a damsel in distress on his doorstep one Christmas Eve night.

Her foster mother, Sylvia, pushed Pixie down the aisle in her wheelchair while Holly walked to the altar, striving not to be intimidated by the sheer size of the church and the overwhelming number of unfamiliar faces crammed into it. Vito stood beside a guy with black shoulder-length hair and startling green eyes whom she recognised from online photographs as his best friend, Apollo Metraxis. Holly only looked at the bronzed Greek long enough to establish that he was giving her a distinctly cold appraisal before her attention switched quite naturally to Vito, who, unromantic or otherwise, was at least managing to smile that breathtaking smile of his.

Her heart bounced around in her chest to leave her breathless and when he closed his hand over hers at the altar she was conscious only of him and the officiating priest. She listened with quiet satisfaction to the words of the wedding ceremony, grinned when Angelo let out a little baby shout from his place on Lorenza's lap in a front pew and stared down all of a glow at the wedding band Vito threaded smoothly onto her finger. It was her wedding day and she was determined to enjoy it.

When they signed the register, she was introduced to a smiling older woman clad in a lilac suit and hat with diamonds sparkling at her throat.

'I'm Vito's *mamma*, Concetta,' the attractive brunette told her warmly. 'I've met my grandson. He *is* beautiful.'

Unsurprisingly, Holly was charmed by such fond appreciation of her son and her anxiety about how Vito's mother might feel about his sudden marriage dwindled accordingly. Concetta, it seemed, was willing to give her a fighting chance at acceptance. Vito's friend Apollo, however, could barely hide his hostility towards her and she wondered at it. Didn't he realise that this marriage was what Vito had wanted? Did he think she had somehow forced his friend into proposing? Holly's chin came up and her big blue eyes fired with resolution because she was happy to have become Vito's wife and Angelo's mother and she had no intention of pretending otherwise.

After some photos taken at the church they moved on to the hotel where the reception was being held. 'There are so many guests,' she commented with nervous jerkiness when they climbed out of the limo, an easier exercise than it might have been because Holly's closely fitted gown did not have a train.

'My family has a lot of friends but some guests are business acquaintances,' Vito admitted. 'You shouldn't be apprehensive. Invariably wedding guests are well-wishers.'

Apollo's name was on her lips but she compressed it. She didn't think much of the Greek for deciding he disliked her, sight unseen. What happened to giving a person a fair chance? But she refused to allow Apollo's brooding presence to cast a shadow over her day. And although Apollo was supposed to be Vito's best man, and Pixie the chief and only bridesmaid, Apollo snubbed Pixie as well. Of course, he had brought a partner with him, a fabulously beautiful blonde underwear model with legs that could rival a giraffe's and little desire to melt into the background.

As was becoming popular, the speeches were staged before the meal was served. Holly's foster mother, Sylvia, had insisted on saying a few words and they were kind, warming words that Holly very much appreciated. Concetta Zaffari had chosen not to speak and Vito's father had not been invited to the wedding. When Apollo stood up, Holly stiffened and the most excruciating experience of her life commenced with his speech. In a very amusing way Apollo began to tell the tale of the billionaire banker trapped by the snow and the waitress who had broken down at the foot of the lane. Holly felt humiliated, knowing that everyone who had seen Angelo and worked out her son's age was now aware that he had been conceived from a one-night stand.

Vito gripped her hand so hard it almost hurt and hissed in her ear, 'I did not know he was planning to tell our story!'

Holly said nothing. She wasn't capable of saying anything, meeting Pixie's compassionate gaze across the circular table, recognising Concetta Zaffari's compassion on her behalf in her gentle appraisal. She could feel her face getting hotter and hotter and pictured herself resembling a giant blushing tomato and it was a mercy when Apollo had concluded his maliciously polite speech, which had left her pierced by a dozen poisonous darts of condemnation. He had outed her as a slut at the very least and a gold-digger at worst because he had made it sound the most impossible coincidence that her car had gone off the road at that convenient point. But worst of all, he had not uttered a single lie.

'What a bastard!' Pixie said roundly when she had contrived to follow Holly into the palatial cloakroom. 'Vito's furious! He asked me to come and see that you were all right.'

'I shouldn't be ashamed of being a waitress or a woman who fell pregnant after a one-night stand,' Holly muttered apologetically. 'But somehow sitting there in front of all those richly dressed, bejewelled people I felt like rubbish.'

Sylvia joined them at that point and put her arms

around Holly. 'That young man's a rather nasty piece of work,' she opined ruefully. 'That was a very inappropriate speech, in the circumstances. Holly…sticks and stones may break your bones but words can never hurt you.'

'Not true.' Holly sighed, breathing in deep. 'But don't worry about me. I can handle it—'

'But you shouldn't have to on your wedding day, as I told your bridegroom,' Pixie framed angrily.

'No, no, let it go,' Holly urged ruefully. 'I've got over it already. I was being oversensitive.'

Her foster mother departed and Pixie said several rather unrepeatable things about Apollo Metraxis before the two women began to make their way back to the function room. And then suddenly Pixie stopped her wheelchair and shot out a hand to yank at Holly's wrist to urge her into the alcove in the corridor. She held a finger to her lips in the universal silencing motion and Holly frowned, wondering what on earth her friend was playing at.

And then she heard it, Apollo's unforgettable posh British accent honed by years of public schooling. 'No, as you know, he wouldn't listen to me. *No* DNA test, *no* pre-nup…get this? He *trusts* her. No, he's not an idiot. It's my bet he's playing a deeper game with this sham marriage. Maybe planning to go for full custody of his son once he has them in Italy. Vito's no fool. He simply plays his cards close to his chest.'

Holly turned deathly pale because there was not the smallest doubt that Apollo was talking about her and Angelo and Vito. For a split second she honestly wished she hadn't eavesdropped and she could see by her friend's expression that Pixie was now regretting the impulse as well because of what they had overheard. But without a word she planted firm hands on the handles of the wheelchair and moved her friend out of the alcove and back towards the function room.

But Holly was shattered inside and her expressive face was wooden and, after one glance at her, Vito whirled her onto the dance floor and closed his arms round her. Rage with Apollo was still simmering inside Vito like a cauldron. Well aware of his friend's attitude towards his marriage, Vito blamed himself for still including him in the event. He had naively assumed that, after meeting Holly, Apollo would realise how outrageous his cynical outlook was when it came to her. But his misplaced trust in the Greek billionaire had resulted in his bride's hurt on what he very well knew she believed should be a happy day. Even worse, he was still recovering from the unprecedented surge of raw protective reaction he had experienced during that speech. Any individual who wounded Holly should be his enemy, certainly not a trusted confidant of many years' standing.

'I'm sorry, really sorry about Apollo's speech,' he told her in a driven undertone. 'If I'd had the slightest idea what he was planning to say—'

'You should've kept your mouth shut about how we met,' Holly told him in an unforgiving tone. 'If you hadn't opened your big mouth, he wouldn't have known—'

'Holly...I didn't know that we were going to end up together—'

'No, that came right out of left field with Angelo, didn't it?' Holly agreed in a saccharine-sweet tone he had never heard from her before. 'Just boy talk, was it? The brunette slapper I pulled at Christmas?'

Dark colour rimming his high cheekbones, Vito gazed down at her with dark eyes blazing like golden flames. 'Are you seriously saying that you didn't tell Pixie about us?'

Hoist by her own petard, Holly reddened and compressed her lips.

'Thought so,' Vito said with satisfaction and she wanted to slap him very hard indeed. 'We both spoke out of turn but you have the kinder and wiser friend.'

'Yes,' Holly conceded gruffly, tears suddenly shining in her eyes.

'I have spoken to Apollo. If it's any consolation I wanted to punch him for the first time in our long friendship. He's a hothead with a very low opinion of marriage in general. His father married six times,' Vito explained ruefully. 'I know that doesn't take away the sting but, speaking for myself, I don't care how many people know how I met my very lovely, very sexy wife and acquired an even cuter baby. You're a Zaffari now. A Zaffari always holds his or her head high.'

'Is that so?' Holly's heavy heart was steadily lightening because it meant a lot that he was perceptive enough to understand how she felt and that he had made his friend aware that he was angry about that speech.

'Yes, *gioia mia*. We Zaffaris take ourselves very seriously and if one is lucky enough to find a waitress like you in the snow he's grateful for it, not suspicious. Apollo and I have a friendship based very much on the fact that we are opposites in character. He distrusts every woman he meets. He's always looking for a hidden agenda. It must be exhausting,' he said wryly.

Holly rested her brow against his shoulder as they slow-danced and she let the mortification and the anger seep slowly out of her again. It was being with Vito that was important, being with Vito and Angelo and becoming a family that really mattered. And in her heart of hearts she could not credit that Vito was planning a sham marriage purely to try and deprive her of their son. That accusation was hopefully the suggestion of a troubled, misogynistic mind, she reasoned hopefully.

'This is *your* jet…like really? *Your own jet?*' Holly carolled incredulously a few hours later when she scanned the ultra-opulent leather interior of the private jet.

'I travel a great deal. It's convenient,' Vito parried, amused by her wide, shaken eyes.

'As long as sleeping with the cabin crew isn't included,' Holly whispered, her attention resting on the more than usually attractive team overseeing the boarding of Lorenza and Angelo and all the baby equipment that accompanied her son. In consternation Holly realised that she had accidentally spoken that thought out loud.

Predominantly, Vito was shocked by the concept of having sex with anyone who worked for him and then he looked at his bride's burning face and he started to laugh with rare enjoyment. 'No, that sort of entertainment is probably more Apollo than me. Although I did take advantage of *you*.'

'No, you didn't,' she told him before she hurried forward to grasp her son, having missed him during her enforced break from him throughout the day.

'Older, wiser, plied an innocent with wine…' Vito traded, condemning himself for his crime for her ears alone. 'But if I had the chance to go back I would *still* do it again.'

Encountering a lingering sidewise glance from black-fringed dark golden eyes, Holly felt heat lick through her pelvis as she took a seat and cuddled Angelo. For possibly the first time since she had conceived she looked back at that night in the cottage without guilt and regret. No, on that score Vito had hit a bullseye. Given the chance, in spite of the moments of heartache and stress along the way, she would also still have done the same thing again.

And if Vito could be that honest, why shouldn't she match him? Tell him about the phone call she had over-heard Apollo making? She would pick her moment, she decided ruefully, and she would ask if he had ever thought of their marriage as a sham and if she had any-thing to worry about.

Angelo was asleep by the time they landed in Italy. Holly had freshened up, noting with disappointment that her outfit hadn't travelled very well. The fashion stylist had tried to persuade her to buy a whole host of clothes but with Vito already paying for the wedding and her gown she hadn't felt right about allowing him to pay for anything else before they were married. She had teamed an elegant navy-and-white skirt with a match-ing top but her get-up had creased horribly and looked as though she had worn it for a week rather than only a few hours. Straightening it as best she could, she won-dered if Vito would even notice.

Holly was enchanted by the wonderful scenery that enfolded as the four-wheel drive moved deeper into the countryside. Charming low hills rolled across a land-scape peacefully dotted with cypresses, serrated lines of fresh green vines and silvery olive groves. Medi-eval villages slumbered on hilltops while ancient bell towers soared into the cloudless blue sky. Occasionally she caught a glimpse of beautiful, weathered old farmhouses nestling among the greenery and the wild flowers and she wondered if Vito's home resembled them.

'There it is…the Castello Zaffari,' Vito announced with pride as the car began to climb a steep ribbon of road. Dead ahead Holly glimpsed a building so vast it covered the whole hilltop like a village while elaborate gardens decorated the slopes below it. She froze, convinced that that could not possibly be his home because it was a palace, not a mere dwelling. A giant domed portico denoted the front entrance where the car came to a halt.

'Is this it? Is this where you live?' Holly asked in a small voice, wondering crazily if she could hide in the car and refuse to emerge until he admitted that the palace wasn't really his and he had only been joking. It *had* to be a joke, she thought fearfully, because no ordinary woman could possibly learn to live in the midst of such medieval splendour.

Vito picked up on the edge in her voice and frowned at her. 'Yes. What's wrong?'

'Nothing,' she said hurriedly as she took Angelo to allow the nanny to climb out.

'Don't you like it?'

'Of course I like it,' Holly lied in a rush, utterly overpowered by the huge building as she accompanied Vito into a massive marble-floored hall studded with matching lines of columns. 'But you could've at least hinted that you lived like royalty.'

'I don't,' Vito incised in firm rebuttal. 'I live in a historic building that has belonged to my family for centuries. I live a very average, normal life here…'

Please tell me he didn't say that, Holly argued with herself as they rounded the gigantic centrepiece of a winding stone staircase and were faced with a long assembled row of what could only have been house-hold staff all dressed up in uniform as though they had strayed off the set for *Downton Abbey. Average? Normal?* On what planet was Vito living?

Sick with the nervous unease of someone totally out of their comfort zone, Holly fixed a smile to her stiff face while Vito conducted introductions. There was a great deal of billing and cooing over Angelo and Vito's own former nanny, Serafina, surged forward to take the baby. Apart from her, Silvestro was the head honcho in the household and little giggly Natalia, it turned out, was Holly's English-speaking maid. With great difficulty Holly kept her face straight at the prospect of having a maid and watched while the two nannies carried Angelo off upstairs.

'Natalia will show you to our room,' Vito informed her at the foot of the stairs and then he paused, a frown etching between his level brows, his dark eyes semi-concealed by his ridiculous lashes as he murmured, 'I should have asked you—do you object to sharing a room?'

The planet he was on was definitely far, far from the moon, Holly thought crazily as she raised her brows. 'Where else would I sleep?'

'Obviously you could have your own room,' Vito told her valiantly.

And Holly almost burst out laughing because Vito was being his extraordinarily polite self and going against his own instincts. She could see it in the tension etched in his lean, darkly handsome face, hear it in the edge roughening his dark, deep drawl. He really, *really* didn't want her to choose a separate bedroom and she wondered why on earth he had made the offer. 'No…' Holly reached for his clenched hand. 'You're not getting rid of me that easily,' she teased.

Vito laughed and smiled almost simultaneously and all the tension vanished. *Silly, silly man*, she thought warmly as she followed Natalia up the stairs. Why had he even given her a choice? Separate bedrooms? Was that how husband and wife normally lived in such a gigantic house? How his parents and grandparents had lived? Well, from here on in Vito was going to have to learn how a normal, average couple lived, and having shared a bed with him once had only made her all the keener to repeat the experience, she acknowledged, her colour rising. But there was just no way of denying that the most unbearable hunger clenched her deep down inside when she looked at Vito.

Months had passed since that night in the cottage but she had learned a lot about herself after that first educational experience. Other men hadn't tempted her the way Vito had and she had always assumed that that'd meant she wasn't a very sensual person. Vito, however, had unleashed her newly discovered appetite for intimacy and taught her differently. He was definitely the right man for her. She could only hope that she would prove to be the right woman for him.

Natalia opened the doors of what had to be the most drop-dead ugly bedroom Holly had ever seen. It was truly hideous. Heavy dark drapes shut out most of the light and made the vast room gloomy. A material that looked and felt like dark red leather covered the walls and every other surface from the high, elaborately moulded and domed ceiling to the furniture, which was heavily gilded in gold. Holly swallowed hard. It looked as though it hadn't been decorated in at least a hundred years and it was very possible that the weird paper was antique like the furniture.

Well, Holly thought as her maid cast open the doors to show her around what appeared to be an entire suite of rooms for their use, she might be keen to share a bedroom with Vito but he might have to move the location of the shared bedroom to make her happy. Natalia beamed and showed her into a large room walled with closets, which she swept open to display the contents.

'Who does all this belong to?' Holly asked, recoiling while wondering if all the garment-bag-enclosed items of clothing had been left behind by Vito's former fiancée, Marzia.

'Is *your* gift…is *new*,' the brunette stressed while showing off a still-attached label to what appeared to be a hand-embroidered ballgown of such over-the-top glamour that it took Holly's breath away.

A gift that could only be from Vito. The gift of an entire wardrobe of clothes? Holly fingered through drawers packed with lingerie and nightwear in little decorative bags and stared at the racks of shoes and accessories Natalia was eager for her to see and appreciate. It was a mind-blowing collection and it was just way too much altogether for Holly, after the wedding, the massive palace Vito lived in and his revealing query about whether or not she was willing to share a bedroom with him. What on earth? What on earth kind of marriage was she in that he had told her so little about his life and yet bought her so much? Did he think flashing around his money made up for his failure to explain all the other stuff?

Catching a glimpse of her creased and tousled reflection in one of the many mirrors in the dressing room, Holly almost groaned. She didn't want to get tricked out in fancy clothes, she simply wanted comfort, and as Natalia opened Holly's single case on the now seemingly pitiful assortment of clothing that had been her lot pre-Vito, Holly bent down to scoop out her one extravagance: a shimmering maxi dress with an iridescent sheen that skimmed her every curve with a flattering fit. She was relieved to see that while the bedroom belonged to a bygone age, the en-suite bathroom, while palatial, was contemporary. Stepping into a wonderful walled rain-forest shower, she rinsed away the tired stickiness of travel and tried to let her anxieties float off down the drain with the soapy water.

A marriage was what you made of it and she had no intention of underestimating the challenge ahead. They had married for Angelo's benefit but their son could only enjoy a happy home life if his parents established a good relationship. Holly's childhood had been damaged by her mother's neglect and self-indulgence, Vito's by his father's indifference. He should've warned her about the giant historic house and the extravagant new wardrobe, but she could no more shout at him for being richer and more pedigreed than she had estimated than she could shout at him for his unvarnished generosity.

Dressed, her black hair tumbling freely round her shoulders, Holly explored the connecting rooms Natalia had briefly walked her through earlier. A door stood ajar on the balcony that led off the sitting room and she strolled out, watching the sun go down over the stunning landscape and the manicured gardens below and slowly veil them in peach, gold and terracotta splendour. Sounds in the room she had vacated alerted her to the arrival of a trolley, and the rattle of cutlery fired her appetite and drew her back indoors.

Vito was framed by a doorway at the far end of the room, his suit abandoned in favour of jeans and a white shirt open at his strong brown throat. Her tummy was awash with butterflies as she instinctively drew in a deep breath and savoured her view of him. He stood there, so tall and dark and devastatingly handsome, watching her with the assessing eyes of a hawk.

Vito finally tore his gaze from his bride's opulent curves, that were so wonderfully enhanced by the fine fabric of her dress, but the words he had been about to speak had vanished from his brain. Holly, he acknowledged simply, was an incredibly sexy woman. Innate sensuality threaded her every movement. It was there in her light gliding walk, the feminine sway of her hips, the swell of her breasts as she straightened her spine and angled her head back to expose her throat.

He had expected Apollo to recognise the sheer depth of Holly's natural appeal, but he couldn't be sorry that his friend's distrust had blinded him because when Vito had seen some of his guests look at his bride with lustful intent, it had annoyed the hell out of him. And that new possessive, jealously protective streak about what was *his* disturbed Vito, who was immensely suspicious of emotional promptings. He had always chosen women who brought out the rational side of his nature but Holly incited much more primal urges.

Vito's butler, Silvestro, moved forward to pour the

wine with a flourish and light the candles on the circular table. Holly tasted the wine with an appreciative sip.

'It's an award-winning Brunello my grandfather laid down years ago. This is a special occasion,' Vito pointed out as he dropped lithely down into his seat and shook out his napkin.

'I cut my teeth on wines that tasted like vinegar.' Holly sighed. 'I'm not much of a drinker.'

'Why would you be if it tasted that bad?' Vito asked with amusement.

'Why didn't you warn me that you lived in a vast house your family have owned for centuries?' Holly asked quietly.

'It didn't occur to me,' Vito admitted with a frown.

'This place was a shock…as was the new wardrobe.'

'You were supposed to shop for clothes at the same time as you chose your wedding dress but the stylist said you weren't interested. So I took care of it for you.'

'Thank you, I suppose…'

As Silvestro left the room, having drawn the trolley close to enable them to serve themselves, Holly embarked on the tiny delicate parcels on her plate. They were exquisitely displayed, and the oriental flavours tasted phenomenal. The courses that followed were even better. Holly had never eaten such fabulous food before.

'Who does the cooking here?' she asked.

'I have a very well-paid chef on staff. When I'm staying at one of my other properties he travels ahead of me.'

Bemused by the concept of a mobile personal chef, Holly blinked. 'You have *other* properties?'

'Here I have the apartment in Florence and a villa

on the shores of Lugano in Switzerland. Those were inherited. But I also own property in the countries I visit most frequently,' Vito admitted.

Holly was frowning. 'What's wrong with hotels?'

'I don't like them. I like quiet and privacy, particularly when I'm working,' Vito advanced smoothly. 'It's my sole extravagance.'

'When I called you a spoilt-rotten rich boy I wasn't far off the mark,' Holly dared.

'Had you ever met my grandfather you would never have awarded me that label. He was a rigid disciplinarian with a punitive approach. He thought my mother was too soft with me.' A rueful smile brought a gentler than usual curve to Vito's wide sensual lips. 'He was probably right.'

'Your grandfather sounds very judgemental. I don't think I would've liked him very much.'

'He was a dinosaur but a well-intentioned one. Since he passed away two years ago, however, I have instigated many changes.'

Holly dealt him a sidewise glance and whispered conspiratorially, 'Our bedroom is a complete horror.'

A flashing grin illuminated Vito's lean, dark features. 'Really?'

'Very dark and depressing.'

'I think I've only been in that room once in my life.'

Her brow furrowed. 'You mean it wasn't yours?'

'No, it's simply the main bedroom in the house and Silvestro has been trying to move me in there ever since my grandfather departed,' Vito confided with amusement. 'But I always resist change and I need the allure of a wife there to entice me.'

Holly compressed her lips as she sipped her wine. 'I

have no allure,' she told him, wrinkling her snub nose in embarrassment.

Vito laughed, lounging back in his chair to study her with gleaming dark golden eyes. 'Being unaware of it doesn't mean you don't have it. In fact that very lack of awareness is incredibly appealing.'

'I should check on Angelo.'

'No, not tonight, *bella mia*,' Angelo intoned as he sprang upright to reach for her hands and raise her slowly from her seat. 'Tonight is ours. Angelo has two nannies and an entire household devoted to his needs. After all, he is the first child in the Zaffari family for a generation, and as such more precious than diamonds to our staff.'

Her throat tightened as he looked down at her with glittering golden eyes fringed by ridiculously long lashes. Suddenly she couldn't breathe or move. 'Er... what are we standing here for?'

'I want to see this horror of a bedroom,' Vito said thickly and then he lowered his head and sealed his mouth to hers with hungry, driving urgency.

Like a flamethrower on a bale of hay his passion ignited hers with instantaneous effect. Her arms closed round him, her small hands roving up over his strong, muscular back to cling to his shoulders. His tongue slid moistly between her lips and an erotic thrill engulfed her in dizzy anticipation. Her nipples prickled into tingling tightness while damp heat surged between her legs. She pressed her thighs together, struggling to get a grip on herself but still wanting him so much it almost hurt...

CHAPTER EIGHT

HAULING HOLLY UP into his arms, Vito carried her into the bedroom and settled her on the foot of the bed to remove her shoes.

'I didn't appreciate how dark it was in here,' Vito admitted as he switched on the bedside lamps. 'Or how hideous. My grandfather liked grand and theatrical.' He sighed.

Holly scrambled back against the headboard and studied him with starry eyes. He stood half in shadow, half in light, and the hard, sculpted planes and hollows of his lean, strong face were beautiful. She marvelled at the fate that had brought two such different people together and rejoiced in it too. Liking, respect, attraction, she listed with resolution inside her head, buttoning down the stronger feelings battling to emerge, denying them.

'Did your parents occupy separate bedrooms?' she asked curiously.

'It was always the norm in this household. I didn't want it for us.' Vito came down on the bed beside her. 'If you only knew how much I've longed for this moment. I wanted you with me in London *before* the wedding.'

'But it couldn't be done. I had responsibilities I couldn't turn my back on.' Holly sighed.

'I could've made arrangements to free you of those duties.'

'Not when they're dependent on friendship, loyalty, and consideration for other people,' Holly disagreed gently, lifting a hand to follow the course of his jutting lower lip and note the stubborn angle of his strong jawline. 'You can't rearrange the world only to suit you.'

'*Sì*...yes, I can,' Vito declared without shame.

'But that's *so* selfish—'

'I will not apologise for being selfish when it comes to your needs and Angelo's.' Vito marvelled at her inability to appreciate that he would always place their needs over the needs of others. What was wrong with that? It was true that it took a certain amount of ruthlessness and arrogance, but he had fought hard in life for every single achievement and saw nothing wrong with an approach that maximised the good things for his family and minimised the bad. The way he saw it, if you made enough effort happiness could be balanced as smoothly as a profit-and-loss column.

With his strong white teeth he nipped playfully at the reproving fingertip rapping his chin.

Holly startled and then giggled and sighed. 'What am I going to do with you?'

'Anything you want... I'm up for *anything*.' Vito savoured her, his dark golden eyes holding hers with explicit need for a heartbeat. He pushed her back against the pillows and then his mouth claimed hers with hungry, delicious force.

Heat unfurled in her pelvis. Her heart raced and the tension went out of her only to be replaced by a new kind of tension that shimmied through her bloodstream like an aphrodisiac and made her heart race. Her breath came in quick, shallow gasps between kisses, each leading into the next until he rolled back and, having established that there was no helpful zip, he gathered the hem of her dress in his hands and tugged it up over her body and over her head to pitch it aside.

'That's better,' he growled, pausing to admire the picture she made in her pretty bridal lace lingerie.

'Except you're still wearing far too many clothes,' Holly objected, embarking on his shirt buttons.

Vito yanked off his shirt without ceremony, kicked off his shoes, peeled off his socks, only to halt there, his long, lean frame trembling while Holly's hands roamed over the hills and valleys of his hard, muscular abdomen. Her reverent fingers took a detour to follow the furrow of dark hair vanishing below the waistband of his jeans.

'I missed you,' she said truthfully. 'I missed *this…*'

Unfreezing, lean dark features rigid with control, he unsnapped his jeans and vaulted off the bed to take them off. 'It was the best night of my life, *bellezza mia.*'

And yet he still hadn't made any mention of seeing her again that night or the following morning. That still stung and Holly said nothing. Had he really not seen her note? Could she believe that?

'That note I left at the cottage for you—' she began breathlessly.

'I didn't see it.'

'Would you have phoned if you'd had my number?' she prompted in a reckless rush.

'I don't know,' Vito responded quietly. 'Certainly I would've been tempted, but on another level I distrust anything that tempts me.'

His honesty cut through her. Even if he had found the

note, he wouldn't have phoned her, she decided painfully. He would have written off their night of passion as a once-in-a-lifetime experience and left it behind. That hurt, but there was nothing she could do about it. She wanted to know who else had since shared his bed but it wasn't a question to be asked on their wedding night even though her heart cried out for reassurance. It would be an unfair question when he had not owed her loyalty. Of course there had been other women in the months they had been apart. That was yet another pain she had to bear.

'I've never wanted a woman the way I want you,' Vito told her thickly.

He flung a handful of condoms down by the bed and stripped naked without inhibition while she watched.

Pink washed Holly's face because he was fully aroused and ready.

'I couldn't get enough of you that night and that unnerved me,' he framed abruptly. 'You were a very unexpected discovery.'

He reached for her again, deftly skimming off her bra and panties, twisting his hips away when she tried to touch him. 'No... If you touch me, you'll wreck me. I'm on a hair trigger after months of abstinence,' he growled, lean brown hands roving over the full curves of her breasts, lingering over her pink pointed nipples to tug and tease until little sounds she couldn't silence broke from between her lips.

Vito flung back the sheet and settled her beneath him to pay serious attention to her swollen mouth and the glorious swell of her breasts.

'Months of abstinence?' Holly encouraged helplessly, her breath tripping in her throat as he sucked on a protruding bud while long, skilled fingers stroked her thigh.

'I'm not an easy lay,' he told her. 'I'm very, very fussy.'

'Nothing wrong with that,' Holly framed in ragged reassurance, all the feeling in her body seemingly centred between her thighs where she was scarily desperate for him to touch her.

And then he did and she gasped and her eyes closed and the fire at the heart of her grew hotter still, hips shifting up and from side to side, the drumbeat of need awakened and throbbing and thrumming through every skin cell. Vito shifted down the bed and parted her thighs. He knew exactly what he was doing. She had discovered that the night Angelo was conceived.

He teased her with the tip of his tongue, slow and then quicker until she could no longer stay silent and whimpers and gasps were wrenched from her. A long sure finger stroked through her wet folds and she quivered, every nerve ending jumping to readiness as the excitement crept higher.

At the height of her climax she cried out his name, lost in the convulsive spasms of erotic pleasure. She was so lost in that pleasure that she struggled to remember what day it was and even where she was. Her lashes flickered when she heard him tear open a condom. As he returned to her she wrapped both arms round him possessively, her body temporarily sated.

He pushed her back and drove into her with a guttural groan of satisfaction. 'Like wet satin,' he bit out appreciatively.

Hunger sizzled through her as his bold shaft stretched her and sank deep. Suddenly she was sensually awake again, her body primed as he angled his lean hips to ensure that she received the maximum enjoyment. His hunger for her was unhidden, his strokes were hard and fast, tormentingly strong. The ache low in her body pinged and climbed in intensity. She wanted, oh, *how* she wanted, craved, needed and longed for that maddening pulse of yearning to be answered, overwhelmed. And then her spine was arching and her body jerking and the waves of hot, drenching pleasure were like a shooting star flaming through her and setting her on fire with the wondrous release from her own body.

'Sexiest, most amazing woman ever...and *mine*,' Vito husked in her ear, his weight heavy on her as he rolled over and pulled her down on top of him. 'That's the most important fact. You're mine, *gioia mia*.'

'Are you mine too?' Holly whispered dizzily.

'*Sì...*'

'Is sex always this good?'

'Not even half the time. We have our own unique variety of fireworks.'

Holly rested her cheek on a damp bronzed shoulder, her body replete. He smelled so good she drank him in like a drug. She liked being his. She liked that possessive note she heard edging his dark drawl because it made her feel less like Angelo's mother and more like Vito's wife, valued, needed and wanted on her own account. Long fingers traced the path of her spine as he shifted position.

'I have an impossibly fast recovery time with you,' Vito husked, sliding her back onto the sheet on her front, lingering on the soft full curves of her behind.

He reached for another condom. Holly didn't even lift her head. She was still in that place somewhere between total satiation and awareness, shifting obediently as he eased a pillow below her hips, raising her, rearranging her to his satisfaction. And then she felt him rigid and full at her entrance where she was now tender and swollen. He drove in hard and she came suddenly fully awake, eyes wide, throat catching on a breath, heart hotwired back into pounding. He buried himself deep and it felt so good she moaned.

'I like the little sounds you make.' He ground into her with power and energy and a spontaneous combustion of heat surged at the apex of her body.

Excitement crowned with her every cry and snatched breath. She couldn't breathe against the onslaught of raw, surging excitement. With every savage thrust he owned her in a way she had never thought to be owned and she gave herself up to the rise of the hot, pulsing pleasure. The excitement crested with white-hot energy and the sweet waves of deep, quivering pleasure consumed her. Winded, she slumped back down into the pillows.

'Shower time,' Vito told her, lifting her out of bed. 'You're not allowed to go to sleep yet.'

'You and your son have a lot in common.'

'We're both very attached to you?' Vito urged her into the shower.

'You don't sleep at night,' she contradicted. 'Although I have to admit that you're more fun than he is in the middle of the night. Angelo gets grouchy when he's teething.'

'I won't get grouchy with you in my bed,' Vito assured her, leaning back against the tiled wall, lean, bronzed and muscular, a study in male perfection.

Holly was like an energy drink, releasing his tension, refreshing him, leaving him feeling amazingly relaxed. Vito had never done relaxed and wasn't quite sure how to handle it. It was a great deal easier simply to concentrate on working off that surplus energy in bed.

Even with the honeyed ache of sex and satiation Holly wanted to put her hands all over him and explore him with the freedom she had restrained on their first night together. She was so comfortable with him, so indescribably comfortable it almost spooked her. 'I can sleep standing up,' she warned him, resting her damp head down on a strong brown shoulder.

'I have to work tomorrow, *bellezza mia*. Make the most of *now*,' Vito murmured huskily, gathering her close.

Her eyes opened very wide on the tiled wall. He had to work the day after their wedding? Was there some crisis on?

'No. I just like to work,' Vito confided lazily, as if there were nothing the slightest bit strange about his desire to act as though the day after their wedding were just like any other day.

'Are you taking *any* time off?' It was a loaded question but she tried to make it sound casual and unconcerned and then held her breath.

'I'll be home every night...you can bet on that,' Vito growled, nipping at the sensitive flesh below her ear until she shivered helplessly against him and his big hands rose to cup and massage her breasts. 'I'll be keeping you very much occupied.'

Sex, she thought dully. Nothing wrong with his enthusiasm in that department but was that really all he was interested in, all he had ever been interested in? Or simply all she had to offer? Her teeth gritted. What did she have to offer in the intellect category? No, she was never going to be his equal there. Were they going to be one of those couples who never interacted except when their child was around? Would she chatter on relentlessly about Angelo and only ever really get Vito's attention in bed? It sounded a sad and desperate role to her but what was she going to do about it? She couldn't *make* him want more or force him to see her in a different light, could she?

A sham marriage? That overheard phone call returned to haunt her. How hard could it be for Vito to fake being genuinely married when all he intended to do was have sex with her? A chill trickled through her tummy and made her tense. Suddenly fears that she had earlier dismissed were becoming a source of genuine concern. Why had she so easily believed that Apollo was talking nonsense about Vito's intentions? Apollo Metraxis had known Vito since childhood. Apollo probably knew Vito a great deal better than she did and if he suspected that Vito had only married her to gain custody of his son, shouldn't she be sincerely scared?

When she wakened it was still dark, with only the faintest glimmer of light showing behind the curtains. She was deliciously comfortable. Vito had both arms wrapped round her and she was snuggled up to him, secure in the warmth and the wonderfully familiar scent of his skin. He was stroking her hip bone and she stretched in a helpless little movement.

'I want you, *tesoro mia*.'

Her eyes flew wide as he shifted against her back, letting her feel the hard swell of him. *'Again?'*

His sensual mouth pressed into the sensitive skin of her throat. 'Don't move. I'll do all the work.'

And he did, repositioning her, gently rousing her

from her drowsiness and then sinking into her with exquisite precision. She heard herself gasp and then moan and the sweet swell of pleasure surged up and overpowered all her anxious thoughts. Excitement took hold and she trembled with need as his smooth thrusts rocked her sensitised body. She couldn't fight her responses or the uncontrollable wave of ecstatic sensation that swept her to an explosive climax.

'What a wonderful way to wake up,' Vito groaned into her tumbled hair. 'I never dreamt that having a wife could be so much fun. Are you joining me for breakfast?'

Behind her hair, Holly rolled her eyes. She was married to one of those horrid people who came alive around dawn and acted as though it were late morning. Either she stayed in bed and saw very little of him or she changed herself to fit. She lay listening to the shower running and watched him emerge swathed in a towel, the long, lean length of his unspeakably beautiful body mostly exposed. Her mouth ran dry as he disappeared into the dressing room and opened another door. Closet doors were rammed back, drawers opened and closed. She scrambled out of bed and ran for the shower before she could be tempted to backtrack and fall back asleep. Dabbing on minimal make-up, she brushed her hair and extracted some of her new clothes to wear because a pair of jeans and a washed-out cotton top didn't seem quite sufficient for the grandeur of the Castello Zaffari.

Clad in beautifully tailored chinos and a filmy blouse in autumn shades, she slotted her feet into canvas shoes and went out to join Vito. He looked as he had the day she had confronted him at the Zaffari Bank: cool, sophisticated, remote, very much the banker. And at the

same time he contrived to look amazing whether he
was slotting cufflinks into his cuffs or brushing his
cropped black hair.

'Who wears cufflinks these days?' Holly prompted.

Vito shrugged. 'We all use them at the bank.'

'Not at the cutting edge of fashion, then,' she mocked,
although his dark suit was incredibly well tailored to
lovingly shape wide shoulders, a broad chest, narrow
hips and long, powerful legs. Just looking at him, she
wanted to touch him.

'Breakfast,' he reminded her, heading for the door.

The *castello* was silent until they reached the ground
floor where vague signs of industry could be heard
somewhere in the distance. Silvestro entered the hall
and looked taken aback to see them. He burst into Italian and Vito responded with quiet amusement.

'Why does everybody think I should be staying home
today?' he quipped, leading the way into a sunlit dining room.

'Maybe...because you should be?' Holly dared. 'Just
married and all that...'

Silvestro fussed round the table making unnecessary adjustments while Vito translated all the many
options Holly could choose for breakfast. As the older
man sped off Vito lifted one of the financial newspapers piled at his end of the table and began to read it
and Holly wondered whether she should have stayed in
bed. She wanted to go and see if Angelo was awake but
she didn't want to leave Vito lest he leave for the bank
while she was gone.

She had already decided to confront Vito about that
phone call she had overheard Apollo making but she had
intended to pick and choose the right moment, which

might well have been while they were still wrapped round each other in bed. But something about the way Vito lifted that newspaper after dragging her downstairs awakened her temper.

'I overheard Apollo talking on the phone to someone at our reception yesterday.'

Vito lowered the newspaper and frowned at her. 'Overheard?' he questioned.

Below the onslaught of his dark glittering gaze, Holly went pink. 'Well, eavesdropped...I suppose.'

'Are you in the habit of listening in on other people's phone calls?'

'That's not really relevant here,' Holly fudged in desperation, feeling like a child being called to account for misbehaviour. 'Apollo was so obviously talking about us...about our marriage. He was saying that you hadn't had a DNA test with Angelo and that there had been no pre-nup—'

'You're trying to shock me with facts?'

Holly scrambled out of her seat and squared her small shoulders. 'Apollo was sneering about his belief that you trust me.'

'Obviously I won't be trusting you in the vicinity of confidential phone calls,' Vito pronounced, deadpan.

Somehow the confrontation was not proceeding in any expected direction and Holly was stung into anger. 'Apollo thinks our marriage is a sham!'

Vito elevated an ebony brow. 'I think the only two people who can comment on that probability are the two of us.'

'Apollo seemed to believe that you had only married me to get me to move to Italy. He thinks you're planning to go to court and try to claim full custody of our son.'

'I'm not sure whether to be more offended by my friend's low take on my morals or by my wife's,' Vito imparted very softly, marvelling that she could have placed credence in such an unrealistic plot, which smacked very much of Apollo's sensational outlook on life. 'Do you think I would do that to you and Angelo?'

'That's not the point,' Holly protested.

'It is exactly the point,' Vito incised with ruthless bite. 'Why else are you challenging me with this nonsense?'

As Silvestro reappeared with a tray Holly sank back down into her seat. She was angry and mortified at the same time but clung to the comforting fact that Vito had called her concerns 'nonsense'. While food was being laid on the table, Holly studied her pale pink nails and suspected that one day she might possibly throw a coffee pot at Vito for his sarcastic cool.

'To clarify matters,' Vito mused as Silvestro retreated, 'Apollo was most probably talking to a mutual friend called Jeremy, who happens to be a lawyer trained in family law. Although it is ridiculously unnecessary, Apollo tries to protect me from the gold-diggers of this world. If it is any consolation he was no keener on Marzia. He would never marry without a pre-nuptial agreement in place. I deemed it unnecessary because I would not marry a woman I couldn't trust. You're being naive and insecure.'

Holly bridled at that blunt speech. 'I don't see how.'

With precise movements that set her teeth on edge, Vito poured a cup of black coffee. 'I would not deprive my son of his mother. I was sent to boarding school abroad at the age of seven, Holly. I was incredibly homesick and unhappy. Do you honestly think I would subject Angelo to anything similar?'

Holly studied her cup of tea with wooden resolve. Her face was so hot she could feel her ears heating up in concert. No, she could not see him planning to do anything that would damage their son. Boarding school abroad at the tender age of seven? That was brutal, she thought helplessly.

'I *love* my son. I will try hard never to hurt him and I know how much he needs his mother,' Vito framed with measured cool. 'I am also an honourable man. I am not deceitful in personal relationships. I married you in good faith. If eavesdropping on Apollo can rouse your suspicions to this level, what are our prospects for the future? Trust has to work both ways to be effective.'

Holly swallowed hard. Vito was annoyed with her for doubting him and for paying heed to a stupid phone call she shouldn't have been listening to in the first place. She wasn't sure she could blame him for that. On the other hand his determination to head to the bank the day after their wedding was hardly likely to boost her confidence in his attitude towards either her or their marriage.

How much did Vito value her? Just how unimportant was she in his desire for a marriage that would not interfere in his inflexible daily schedule? To thrive, all relationships needed compromise, commitment and the luxury of time spent together. Didn't he appreciate that? And if he didn't, was she clever enough to teach him that she could offer him something more worthwhile than sex? That was a tall order.

Vito rose from his chair and studied her in brooding silence. 'By the way, we're dining out this evening with friends.'

Holly looked up in surprise. 'What friends?'

'Apollo and his girlfriend and Jeremy Morris and his wife. They're currently staying on Apollo's yacht with him.'

The prospect of spending an evening in Apollo Metraxis's radius appealed about as much to Holly as a public whipping. She frowned, studying Vito with incredulous eyes. 'Knowing how I feel about Apollo, why would you arrange something like that?'

Vito compressed his stubborn mouth. 'He's a close friend. He made a mistake. You need to get over it.'

Temper threw colour into Holly's cheeks. 'Do I, indeed?'

Vito gazed expectantly back at her. 'I want it all smoothed over and forgotten…'

'Right, so that's me got my orders, then.' Holly lifted her chin.

'It's not an order, Holly, it's advice. I'm not dropping a lifelong friend because you don't like him.'

'And isn't there some excuse for that dislike?'

'Apollo didn't tell any lies about how we met. Remember that,' Vito retorted with succinct bite.

A painful flush illuminated Holly's face.

'Why shouldn't we have a night out?' Vito fired at her in exasperation. 'I thought you would enjoy getting dressed up and socialising—most women do.'

'That's not my world,' Holly breathed in taut objection.

'It is *now*,' Vito pointed out without hesitation, his impatience unconcealed. 'You need to make an effort to fit in. Why do you think I bought you all those clothes? I want you to have the expensive trappings and to *enjoy* having them.'

As Vito strode out Holly held her breath, feeling a

little like someone trying to fight off a panic attack. He had voiced truths she didn't really want to face. This was his world and, in marrying him, she had become part of that world. He saw no reason why his life shouldn't continue the way it always had and he was making no allowances for Holly's insecurities. No, it was her job to swallow her ire with Apollo and be nice. Well, that certainly put her in her place, didn't it? Vito's long-standing friendship with the Greek billionaire meant more to him than his wife's loss of face at her own wedding. Just as work still meant more to him than settling into marriage and fatherhood. Vito, she recognised painfully, was highly resistant to change of any kind...

CHAPTER NINE

AFTER LUNCH THE same day, Holly lifted Angelo out of the high chair in the dining room and walked outside to settle the baby on a rug already spread across the grass. Her son beamed as she arranged several toys within his reach, enjoying the change of scene.

'Tea,' Silvestro pronounced with decision, having followed her, and he sped off again. Holly made no comment, having already learned that Silvestro liked to foresee needs and fulfil them before anyone could make a request and, truthfully, she did fancy a cup of tea.

She cuddled Angelo and studied the bird's-eye view of the gardens spread out below in an embroidered carpet of multi-hued greens with occasional splashes of colourful spring flowers. Daily life at the Castello Zaffari promised to be pretty much idyllic, she reflected ruefully, feeling ashamed of her negative thoughts earlier in the day when Vito had left her to go to work.

Here she was on a permanent holiday in a virtual palace where she ate fabulous food and was waited on hand and foot. She had beautiful clothes, an incredibly handsome, sexy husband and a very cute baby. What was she complaining about? For the first time ever since Angelo's birth she also had free time to spend with her son. As for the dinner outing? That was a minor hiccup and, having examined her new wardrobe, she had decided to follow the 'little black dress rule' rather than risk being over-or underdressed for the occasion.

A woman in a sunhat with a basket over her arm walked up a gravelled path towards her. Holly tensed, recognising her mother-in-law, Concetta Zaffari.

'Are you on your own?' the small brunette asked. 'I thought I had seen Vito's car drive past earlier but I assumed I was mistaken.'

'No, you weren't mistaken. He's at the bank,' Holly confirmed, as the older woman settled down beside her to make immediate overtures to Angelo.

'Today? My son went into work *today*?' his mother exclaimed in dismay.

Holly gave a rueful nod.

'He should be here with you,' Concetta told her, surprising her.

The rattle of china and the sound of footsteps approaching prompted Holly to scramble upright again. She handed Angelo to Concetta, who was extending her arms hopefully and chattering in Italian baby talk. The two women sat down by the wrought iron table in the shade while Silvestro poured the tea. He had magically contrived to anticipate the arrival of Vito's mother because he had brought an extra cup and a plate of tiny English biscuits.

'A honeymoon isn't negotiable. It should be a given,' Concetta pronounced without hesitation.

'If Vito wants to work, well, then he wants to work,' Holly parried, tactfully non-committal.

'You and this darling little boy are Vito's family

and you must ensure that my son puts you first,' Vito's mother countered. 'That is very important.'

Holly breathed in deep. 'Vito loves to work. I don't feel I have the right to ask him to change something so basic about himself.'

'Priorities have to change once you're married and a parent. As for having the right…' The older woman sipped her tea thoughtfully. 'I will be open with you. I saw your distress after Apollo made that unsuitable speech at the wedding yesterday.'

Holly winced. 'I was more embarrassed than distressed…I think.'

'But why should you be embarrassed by this gorgeous little boy?' Concetta demanded. 'Let me tell you something… When I married Vito's father, Ciccio, thirty-odd years ago, I was already pregnant…'

Holly's blue eyes widened in surprise at that frank admission.

Concetta compressed her lips. 'My father would never have allowed me to marry a man like Ciccio in any other circumstances. He knew that Ciccio was a fortune hunter but I was too naive to see the obvious. I was eighteen and in love for the first time. Ciccio was in his thirties.'

'That's a big age gap,' Holly remarked carefully.

'I was an heiress. Ciccio targeted me like a duck on a shooting range,' the brunette declared with a wry twist of her lips, 'and I paid a steep price for being young and silly. He was unfaithful from the outset but I closed my eyes to it because while my father was alive divorce seemed out of the question. Only when Ciccio dragged our son's reputation down into the dirt with his own did I finally see the light.'

'The scandal in the newspapers?' Holly slotted in with a frown, fascinated by the elegant brunette's candour.

'I could not forgive Ciccio for saving himself at Vito's expense.'

'Vito wanted to protect you.'

'That hurt,' Concetta confided tautly. 'It hurt me even more to see Vito falsely accused and slandered but it also let me see that he was an adult able to handle the breakdown of his parents' marriage. Now I'm making my middle-aged fresh start.'

'It's never too late,' Holly said warmly, noticing how Angelo's sparkling dark eyes matched his father's and his grandmother's.

Concetta confided that she regularly took the flowers from the garden at the *castello* as arranging them was her hobby. Holly admitted that she had never arranged a flower in her life and urged the older woman to keep on helping herself. Vito's mother promised to continue doing the flowers for the house and the two women parted on comfortable, friendly terms.

Holly spent what remained of the day doing her hair and her nails and refusing to think about the evening ahead. Thinking about it wasn't going to change anything. Apollo was Vito's friend and he thought highly of him, she reminded herself. Unfortunately it didn't ease the sting of the reality that her husband seemed to rate Apollo more highly than he rated his wife.

Vito collected her in a limo. He wore a sleek dinner jacket. 'I used my apartment to change,' he admitted, smiling as she climbed into the car. 'You look very elegant.'

But as soon as Holly arrived at the restaurant and saw the other two women she realised she had got it wrong in the frock department because she had played it too safe. Apollo's girlfriend, Jenna, wore a taupe silk dress that plunged at both back and front and was slit to the thigh, while Jeremy's wife, Celia, wore a short fitted scarlet dress that showed off her very shapely legs. Holly immediately felt frumpy and dumpy in her unexciting outfit, wishing that at the very least she had chosen to wear something that displayed a bit of cleavage.

While the men talked, Celia shot inquiries at Holly and it was no surprise to discover that the highly educated and inquisitive redhead was a criminal lawyer. Having her background and educational deficiencies winkled out and exposed made Holly feel very uncomfortable but her attempts to block Celia's questions were unsuccessful and she was forced to half turn away and chat to Jenna to escape the interrogation. Jenna, however, talked only about spa days and exclusive resorts.

'You've never been on a ski slope?' she remarked in loud disbelief.

'I'll teach Holly to ski,' Vito sliced in, smooth as glass.

Holly paled because the idea of racing down a snowy hill at breakneck speed made her feel more scared than exhilarated. As the entire conversation round the table turned to ski resorts and talk of everyone's 'best ever runs', she was excluded by her unfamiliarity with the sport. Jenna's chatter about hot yoga classes and meditation were matched by Celia's talk about the benefits of an organic, *natural* diet, ensuring that Holly felt more and more out of her depth. She was also bored stiff.

'How do you feel about yachting?' Apollo asked smoothly across the table, his green eyes hard and mocking. 'Do you get seasick?'

'I've never been on a yacht, so I wouldn't know. I'm fine on a fishing boat or a ferry, though,' she added with sudden amusement at the amount of sheer privilege inherent in such a conversational topic.

'Who took you fishing?' Vito asked her abruptly.

'Someone way before your time,' Holly murmured, unwilling to admit in such exclusive company that it had been a rowing-boat experience with a teenaged boyfriend.

'Way to go, Holly! Keep him wondering.' Celia laughed appreciatively.

Her mobile phone vibrated in her bag and she pulled it out. 'Excuse me. I have to take this,' she said apologetically, and rose from the table to walk out to the foyer.

It was Lorenza phoning to tell her that Angelo had finally settled after a restless evening. Aware that her son was teething, Holly had asked the nanny to keep her posted. On the way back to the table she called into the cloakroom. She was in a cubicle when she heard Jenna and Celia come in.

'What on earth does a guy like Vito see in a woman like her?' Jenna was demanding thinly. 'She's like a little brown sparrow beside him.'

Angry resentment hurtled through Holly and in the strangest way it set her free to be herself.

'Jeremy thinks Vito must have had a pre-nup written up by another lawyer,' Celia commented. 'There's no way Vito hasn't safeguarded himself.'

Emerging, Holly washed her hands and glanced at the aghast pair of women frozen by the sinks. 'At least I've got a wedding ring on my finger,' she pointed out to Jenna. 'You have to be at least number one hundred in Apollo's long line of companions.'

'We had no idea you were in here,' Celia began sharply, defensively.

'Ah, Celia,' Holly pronounced gently, flicking the tall redhead a calm appraisal in turn. 'I can assure you that there is no pre-nup. My husband *trusts* me.'

And with that ringing assurance, Holly turned on her heel, head held high, and walked back out to the table. And she might resemble a little brown sparrow, she thought with spirit, but she was married to a guy who found little brown sparrows the ultimate in sex appeal. Amused by the level of her own annoyance, Holly returned to her seat and in a break in the conversation addressed Apollo. 'So where's the best place for me to learn to ski?' she asked playfully.

Vito dealt her a bemused look and watched her begin to smile at Apollo's very detailed response because Apollo took his sports very seriously.

A deep sense of calm had settled over Holly. She was still furious with Vito for subjecting her to such an evening with very little warning but, having stood up for herself and spoken up in her own defence, she felt much more comfortable. After all, she could be herself anywhere and in any company. The only person able to make her feel out of her depth was herself and she was determined not to let those insecurities control her reactions again. So, she was more accustomed to stacking shelves in a shop and occasional trips to the cinema but she could do spa days and skiing and yachting trips if she wanted to. It was Vito's world but that wedding ring on her finger confirmed that now it was her world as well and she needed to remember that.

She would have to adapt. But Vito had to learn to adapt too, she reflected grimly. He had told her over the breakfast table that she had to trust him, but so far he had done little to earn that trust. And so far, Holly had been the one to make all the changes. She had given up her home, her country, her friends, and her entire life to come to Italy and make a family with Vito. True, it was a gilded life but that didn't lessen the sacrifices she had made on her son's behalf. When was Vito planning to become a family man, who put his wife and his child first?

'You've been very quiet,' Vito remarked as Holly started up the stairs.

'I want to check on Angelo.'

'There is no need.'

'There is every need. I'm his mother,' Holly declared shortly. 'It's immaterial how efficient or kind your staff are, Vito. At the end of the day they are only employees and none of them will ever love Angelo the way I do. Don't ever try to come between me and my son!'

In silence, Holly went up to the nursery, tiptoeing across the floor to gaze down at the slumbering shape of her little boy lying snug in his cot. Smiling, she left the nursery again.

'I wouldn't try to come between you,' Vito swore.

Holly ignored him and went down to their bedroom, kicking off her shoes before stalking into the bathroom.

'Holly...' Vito breathed warningly from the doorway.

'I'm not speaking to you. You have a choice,' Holly cautioned him thinly. 'Either we have silence or we have it out. *Choose.*'

Vito groaned. 'That's not much of a choice.'

'It's the only one you're going to get and probably more than you deserve.' Holly dabbed impatiently at her eyes with a cotton pad and eye-make-up remover.

'Have it out, I suppose,' Vito pronounced very drily.

Holly tilted her chin. 'You had no business forcing me out to that dinner tonight because I wasn't ready for it. I was uncomfortable, of course I was. Two days ago I was living in an ordinary world with ordinary jobs and meeting ordinary people and now I'm in this *weird* new environment,' she framed between compressed lips. 'And I know everyone seems to think I'm in clover and it *is* wonderful not to have to worry about money any more, but it's strange and it's going to take me time to get used to it. You haven't given me any time. You expect *me* to make all the changes...'

Vito had paled. 'You're making valid points. I'm not a patient man.'

'And you don't always live up to your promises either. You said you'd do everything within your power to make me happy,' Holly reminded him doggedly. 'Then you go back to work within a day of the wedding even though you have a son you barely know and a wife you don't know much better. If you want me to trust you, you have to show me that you value me and Angelo, that we're not just new possessions to be slotted into your busy life and expected not to make any waves. You have to give us your time, Vito, take us places, show us around our new home.'

Holly was challenging him and he hadn't expected that from her. She had thrown his words about trust back at him. And she was also telling him that he was already failing dismally in the successful husband stakes. He had married her one day and walked away the next, acting as though a wedding ring were more than sufficient proof of his commitment.

And had Holly been Marzia it *would* have been sufficient. Marzia had wanted that ring and his lifestyle. She would have thrown a party to show off the *castello* and she would have invited all the most important socially connected people to act as her admiring audience. She would have spent half the day at a beauty salon and the other half shopping for couture garments designed to impress. Vito had lost count of the number of times he had returned to the town house he had once shared with Marzia only to discover that they were hosting a dinner when he was longing for a quiet evening. Marzia had been easily bored and had needed others to keep her entertained. Holly, in comparison, asked for and expected very little. In fact she was asking for something she shouldn't have had to ask for, he acknowledged with a grim look in his dark, unusually thoughtful gaze.

Family came first...*always*. Even his workaholic grandfather had never put the bank before his family. What had he been thinking of when he'd left Holly and Angelo to amuse themselves? They needed him and he hadn't spared them a thought.

'And tonight?' Vito prompted.

'It was bearable. I heard Celia and Jenna bitching about me but I stood up for myself and I couldn't care less about their opinions. But I would've been more equipped to enjoy myself and relax if I'd had more time to prepare.'

'I screwed up,' Vito acknowledged broodingly.

'Yes,' Holly agreed, sliding into bed while he still hovered. 'And sometimes I'll screw up. That's life.'

'I'm not used to screwing up,' Vito told her.

'Then you'll try harder not to make the same mistakes again,' Holly riposted sleepily.

* * *

Holly slept in the following morning. She woke with a start, showered and pulled on jeans to pelt upstairs and spend some time with Angelo. In surprise she stilled in the doorway of the nursery bathroom when she saw Vito kneeling down by the side of the bath and engaged in dive-bombing plastic boats for Angelo's amusement. She had simply assumed that Vito had gone into the bank as usual but it was clear that at some stage, even though he had dressed for work, he had changed his mind. His jacket and tie were hooked on the radiator, his shirtsleeves rolled up.

'Vito…'

Raking damp, tousled black hair off his brow, Vito turned his head and flashed her a heart-stopping grin. 'Angelo emptied his cereal bowl over his head at breakfast and I decided I should stay home.'

Holly moved forward. 'I can see that…'

'I'm very set in my ways but I believe I can adapt,' he told her, laughing as Angelo smacked the water with a tiny fist and splashed both of them.

'He'll grow up so fast your head will spin. You won't ever get this time back with him.' She sighed. 'I didn't want you to miss out and then live to regret it.'

'You spoke up and that was the right thing to do. I respect your honesty. Parenting is a whole new ball game and I still have to get my head around it,' Vito confided, snatching down a towel and spreading it on the floor before lifting Angelo's squirming little body out of the bath and laying him down.

'How to get yourself soaked!' Holly groaned.

'I'm already drenched to the skin,' Vito riposted with quiet pride. 'Angelo and I have had a lot of fun.'

The nursery was empty and Holly rustled around gathering the necessities. 'What have you done with the nanny posse?' she asked curiously.

'I told them to take a few hours off. Being so new to this I didn't want an audience.'

Holly dried Angelo and deftly dressed him. Vito unbuttoned his wet shirt, the parted edges revealing a bronzed sliver of muscular torso. Together they walked downstairs.

'Do you have any photographs of when you were pregnant?' Vito asked, startling her into turning wide blue eyes onto his lean, dark face.

'I don't think so…I wasn't feeling very photogenic at the time. Why?'

'I'm sorry I missed all that. Something else I can't get back,' Vito conceded gravely. 'I really would have liked to have seen you when you were carrying our child.'

Regret assailed her, for she would have loved to have had his support during those dark days of worry and exhaustion. She had struggled to stay employed and earning for as long as possible so as not to be a burden on Pixie.

'As for that challenge you offered me,' Vito mused, walking back to their bedroom to change. 'Draw up a list of places you would like to go.'

'No lists. I'm phobic about lists,' she told him truthfully. 'Let's be relaxed about what we do and where we go. No itineraries laid out in stone. Are you taking time off?'

'Of course. But I'll catch up with my email in the evenings,' he warned her. 'I can't completely switch off.'

'That's OK,' she hastened to tell him. 'But you may be bored.'

'Not a chance, *gioia mia*,' Vito riposted as he cast off his wet shirt. 'You and Angelo will keep me fully occupied from dawn to dusk and beyond.'

'And beyond' was very much in Holly's mind as she studied his muscular brown torso, a tiny burst of heat pulsing between her thighs. It was the desire she never really lost around Vito. Her colour heightened. She was so pleased, so relieved that he had listened to her, but there was a fear deep down inside her that she would not have enough to offer to satisfy him outside working hours.

'When was the last time you saw your mother?' Vito asked lazily as they lay in bed six weeks later.

Holly stretched somnolent limbs still heavy with pleasure and rolled her head round to face him, bright blue eyes troubled. 'I was sixteen. It wasn't the nicest experience.'

'I can deal with not nice,' Vito volunteered, closing an arm round her slight shoulders to draw her comfortingly close.

Holly felt gloriously relaxed and shockingly happy. With every day that passed she was increasingly convinced that Vito was the man of her dreams. He was everything she had ever wanted, everything she had ever dreamt of. But even better, he had proved that he was capable of change.

Six weeks ago, she had reminded Vito that he had to learn how to be part of a family instead of an independent operator seeing life only from a work-orientated point of view. He had started out wanting to make up lists and tick off boxes as if that were the only route to success. He had a maddening desire to know in advance exactly what he would be doing every hour of every day and had only slowly learned to take each day as it came.

Holly had spent several days creating a mood board of her ideas on how to redecorate their hideous bedroom. While she was doing that, Vito had learned how to entertain Angelo. Settling on a colour palate of soothing grey enlivened with spicy tangerine accents, Holly had ordered the required products and utilised a local company to do the actual work. Throughout the entire process, Vito had shown depressingly little curiosity, merely agreeing that it was many years since the *castello* had been decorated and that, as his mother had never had any interest in revitalising the interior, he was sure there was plenty of scope for Holly to express her talents.

Leaving the work team to handle the decorating project, Holly and Vito had taken their son to stay on the shores of Lake Lugano. Vito's family had bought a Swiss villa because, like Zurich and Geneva, Lugano was a major financial centre. Over the generations the Zaffari bankers had found the shores of the lake a convenient business location to stash the family while they worked.

At the villa they had thrown open the shutters on the magnificent lake views and enjoyed long lazy meals on the sun-dappled *loggia*. By day they had explored the water in a private boat, stopping off to ramble around the picturesque little villages on the rugged shoreline. Some evenings they had sat on the lake terrace drinking garnet-coloured Brunello di Montalcino wine while they watched the boats sailing by with twinkling lights. Other nights they had strolled round the cobbled lanes in Lugano to pick a quiet restaurant for dinner, but none

had yet lived up to the perfection on a plate offered by
Vito's personal chef.

They had visited the Zoo al Maglio, where Angelo
had been enchanted by the antics of the monkeys and
had struggled fiercely to copy them. They had caught
the funicular railway to the top of Monte San Salvatore
to enjoy the alpine scenery and on the way back they
had stopped off at a chocolate factory, where a peckish
Holly had eaten her weight in chocolate and had sworn
never to eat it again while Vito teased her about how
much he adored her curves.

There had been shopping trips as well, to the designer boutiques on the Via Nassa, where Holly had
become bored because her new wardrobe was so ex-
pansive she saw no reason to add to it. She had much
preferred the bustling liveliness of the farmers' market
in the Piazza Riforma, from which she had returned
home carrying armfuls of the flowers she couldn't resist. Discovering that arranging them was more of an
art than a matter of simply stuffing them in a big vase,
she had resolved to ask her mother-in-law for some tips.

'Your mother…' Vito reminded her. 'Are you going
to sleep?'

'No. It's only two o'clock in the afternoon.' But in
truth she was already smothering a yawn because their
post-lunch nap had turned into a sex-fest. 'Mum…' she
reminded herself. 'It was the last time I ever lived with
her. I thought she wanted me back because I was no
longer a child who needed looking after twenty-four-
seven. I thought she finally wanted to get to know her
daughter. But I got it all wrong—'

'How…?' Vito asked, long fingers inscribing a soothing pattern on her hip bone.

'Mum was living with a guy who owned a little su-permarket. She asked me to help out in the shop...' Holly's voice trailed away ruefully. 'It was a crucial school year with exams and I didn't want to miss classes but she insisted she couldn't cope and I fell for it—'

'And...?' Vito prompted when she fell silent again.

'It turned out that she only wanted me working in the shop to save *her* having to do it and they weren't even paying me minimum wage. I was just cheap labour to please her boyfriend and give her a break.' Holly sighed. 'I missed so much school that social services took me back into care. Of course I failed half my exams as well. I haven't seen her since. I realised that she was never going to be the mother I wanted her to be and I had to accept that. She wasn't the maternal type—'

'And yet you're so different with Angelo.'

'And if you compare your relationship with your fa-ther, aren't you different with Angelo too? We both want to give our son what we didn't have ourselves,' Holly murmured, rejoicing in the heat and strength of his long, lean length next to hers. 'Why didn't you in-vite your father to our wedding?'

'I thought it would be too awkward for my mother and our guests, particularly when Ciccio is fighting for a bigger divorce settlement because he stands to lose a lot of things that he's always taken for granted.'

'Concetta seems quite happy...well, for someone going through a divorce, that is,' Holly qualified rue-fully.

'With my father gone she has a lot less stress in her life and for the first time she has her independence without the restriction of either a father or a husband. She loves her new home and the freedom she has there.'

'It's a new life for her,' Holly mused drowsily, thinking that her own new life was still in the honeymoon period and wouldn't really officially start until they returned to the *castello* the following day and embarked on a more normal routine.

'I didn't realise that marrying you would be a new beginning for me as well,' Vito admitted thoughtfully, acknowledging that he had not fully thought through the ramifications of marrying and becoming a parent. He had plunged into matrimony, dimly expecting life to go on as it always had only to learn that change was inevitable.

'Do you have regrets?' she whispered fearfully. 'Do you sometimes wish you were still single and unencumbered? I suppose you must.'

'I have no regrets when I'm in bed with you...not a single one.' Vito gazed down at her with dancing dark golden eyes alive with wolfish amusement. '*Sì*, I knew you'd be annoyed by that point but, *Dio mio*...at least I'm honest!'

And as his eyes laughed down at her, her heart swelled inside her and she knew, just *knew* in her very soul that she loved Vito. She loved him the way she had tried not to love him. She had tried so hard to protect herself from feeling more for Vito than he felt for her because that was the hard lesson she had learned in loving her unresponsive mother. You couldn't *make* a person care for you; you couldn't force those feelings.

In any case, it had crossed her mind more than once that Vito's emotions might be quite unavailable in the love category. Holly had met Vito on the rebound, shortly after his fiancée had ditched him. That Christmas theirs had been a classic rebound attraction. Was

Vito still in love with Marzia? Had he tried to return to the beautiful blonde during the fourteen months he and Holly had been apart? Had he mourned the loss of Marzia once he'd decided that he had to marry Holly for his son's sake? And how, when he never ever so much as mentioned the woman, could Holly possibly ask him to tell her honestly how he currently felt about Marzia?

She couldn't ask because she didn't think she could bear to live with the wrong answer.

CHAPTER TEN

Two weeks later, Holly shuffled the messy pile of financial publications that Vito always left in his wake and lifted the other, more gossipy newspapers out to peruse. She flicked through the pages, thrilled when she was able to translate the occasional word of Italian.

Her knowledge of the language was slowly growing. She could manage simple interactions with their staff and greetings. Hopefully once she started proper Italian lessons with a local teacher later in the week her grasp of Italian would grow in leaps and bounds. After all, both her son and her husband would speak the language and she was determined not to be the odd one out. Vito's desire that their son should grow up bilingual was more likely to be successful if she learned Italian as well.

Abandoning the papers, she selected a magazine, flipping through glossy photographs of Italian celebrities she mostly didn't recognise until one picture in particular stopped her dead in her tracks. It was a photo of Marzia wearing the most fabulous sparkling ballgown with Vito by her side. She frowned and stared down at it with such intensity that she literally saw spots appear in front of her eyes. She struggled to translate the blurb beneath the picture. It appeared to be recent and it had been taken at some party. The previous week, Vito had spent two nights at his Florence apartment because he had said he was working late. Well, the first time he had been working late, the second time he had actually said that he had to attend a very boring dinner, which invariably would drag on into the early hours...

For dinner, read dinner *dance*, she reflected unhappily. Her entire attention was welded to the photo. Vito and Marzia had been captured at what appeared to be a formal dance with their arms in the air as if their hands had just parted from a clasp. Both of them were smiling. And my goodness, didn't Marzia look ravishing? Not a blonde hair out of place. Holly's fingers crept up to finger through her own tumbled mane. She studied Marzia's perfectly made-up face and thought about her own careless beauty routine, which often consisted of little more than eyeliner, blush and lip gloss. Looking at that gorgeous dress, she glanced down at her own casual silky tee and skirt and low-heeled sandals. She was dressed very nicely indeed in expensive garments but there wasn't even a hint of glamour or sequinned sparkle in her appearance.

Maybe it had only been one dance that Marzia and Vito had shared. And of course they had been photographed for such a potentially awkward moment between former partners was always of interest to others. And they were smiling and happy together. Why not? Her heart had shrunk into a tight, threatened lump inside her chest and her tummy felt as though it were filled with concrete. Vito had spent a couple of years with Marzia. They knew each other well and why should they be enemies? There was no reason why they shouldn't dance together and treat each other like old friends, was there?

Vito hadn't broken any rules. He hadn't told her any lies. All right, he hadn't mentioned the dancing or seeing Marzia, but then he never mentioned his ex, a reality that had made it very difficult for Holly to tackle the subject. Wasn't Vito entitled to his privacy in relation to past relationships? In any case he was not the kind of man who would comfortably open up about previous lovers. Her eyes stung with tears because trying to be reasonable and take a sensible overview was such a challenge for her at that moment.

At the heart of her reaction, Holly registered, was Marzia's sheer glamour and her own sense of inadequacy. Holly didn't do glamour, had never even tried. The closest she had ever got to glamour was a Santa outfit. But what if that kind of gloss, *Marzia's* gloss, was what Vito really liked and admired?

Obviously she had to confront him about the photo and there would probably be a perfectly reasonable explanation about why he had said nothing…

'I knew you would make a fuss,' Vito would be able to point out quite rightly.

She was a jealous cow and he probably sensed that. Although she had never been competitive with other women, having a rival that beautiful and sophisticated could only be hurtful and intimidating. She loved Vito so much and was painfully aware that he did not love her. In addition, she was always guiltily conscious that she had won her wedding ring purely by default. Vito had married her because she was the mother of his son.

Mother of his son, Holly repeated inwardly. Not a very sexy label, certainly not very glamorous. But it didn't have to be that way, she reasoned ruefully. She could walk that extra mile, she could make the effort and dress up too. But she needed the excuse of an occasion, didn't she? Well, at least to begin with... On her passage across the hall, she spoke to Silvestro and told him that she would like a special romantic meal to be served for dinner.

Silvestro positively glowed with approval and she went upstairs to go through her new wardrobe and select the fanciest dress she owned. In the oddest way she would have liked to put on a Santa outfit for Vito again but it wouldn't work out of season. She would tackle Vito the moment he came home. She wouldn't give him time to regroup and come up with evasions or excuses. What she wanted most of all was honesty. He needed to tell her how he truly felt about Marzia and they would proceed from that point.

Did he still have feelings for the beautiful blonde? How would she cope if he admitted that? Well, she would have to cope. Her life, Vito's and Angelo's were inextricably bound to the stability of their marriage. Would he want a separation? A divorce? Her brain was making giant leaps into disaster zones and she told herself off for the catastrophic effect that photo had had on her imagination and her confidence. Since when had she chosen to lie down and die rather than fight?

From the dressing room she extracted the hand-embroidered full-length dress, which glittered with sparkling beads below the lights. It definitely belonged in the glamour category.

Vito knew something strange was afoot the instant he walked into the hall of the *castello* and Silvestro gave him a huge smile. Silvestro had the face of a sad sheep-dog and was not prone to smiling.

'The *signora* is on the way downstairs...' he was informed.

Vito blinked and then he saw Holly as he had only seen her on their wedding day, and quite naturally he stared. She drifted down the staircase in a fantastic dress that seemed to float airily round her hourglass curves. It was the sort of gown a woman wore to a ball and Vito suffered a stark instant of very male panic. Why was she all dressed up? What had he forgotten? Were they supposed to be going out somewhere? What special date had slipped past him unnoticed?

Silvestro spread wide the dining-room door and Vito saw the table set in a pool of candlelight and flowers and thought...what the hell? He spun back as Holly drew level with him, her blue eyes bright but her small face oddly tight and expressionless. A pang ran through Vito's long, lean frame because he was accustomed to his wife greeting him at the end of the day as though he had been absent for a week...and in truth he thoroughly enjoyed the wholehearted affection she showered on both him and his son.

'You look magnificent, *bellezza mia*,' Vito declared, while frantically wondering what occasion he had overlooked and how he could possibly cover up that reality rather than hurt Holly's feelings by admitting his ignorance.

She was so vulnerable sometimes. He saw that sensitivity in her and marvelled that she retained it even after all the disappointments life had faced her with. His primary role was to protect Holly from hurt and disillusionment. He didn't want her to lose her innocence. He didn't want her to turn cynical or bitter. But most of all he never ever wanted to be the man who disillusioned her.

'Glad you like the dress,' Holly said a tad woodenly. 'Shall we sit down?'

'I'm no match for your elegance without a shower and a change of clothes,' Vito pointed out with a slight line dividing his black brows into the beginnings of a frown because her odd behaviour was frustrating him.

'Please sit down. We'll have a drink,' Holly suggested, because she had laid that photo of Marzia and him at his place at the table and she was keen for him to see it before she lost her nerve at confronting him in what was starting to feel a little like a badly planned head-on collision.

Maybe she should have been less confrontational and given him warning. Only not if the price of that was Vito coming up with a polite story that went nowhere near the actual truth. She didn't believe he would lie to her but he wouldn't want to upset her and he would pick and choose words to persuade her in a devious way that her concerns were nonsensical.

Vito was on the edge of arguing until he glimpsed the photo, and its appearance was so unexpected that it stupefied him. He stared down at the photo of himself dancing with Marzia in wonderment while Silvestro poured his wine. Why were they apparently celebrating this inappropriate photograph with rose petals scattered across the table and the finest wine? His frown of incomprehension deepened.

'What is this?' he demanded with an abruptness that startled Holly as he swept up the photo.

Consternation gripped Holly because he didn't sound

puzzled, he sounded downright angry. 'I wanted to ask you to explain that picture,' she muttered warily.

'So you set me up with some sort of a romantic dinner and tell me I can't have a shower? And sit me down with a photo of my ex?' Vito exclaimed incredulously. 'This is more than a little weird, Holly!'

Legs turning wobbly as she encountered scorching dark golden eyes of enquiry, Holly dropped reluctantly down into her chair. 'I'm sorry. I just wanted to get it over with and I wanted you to say exactly what's on your mind.'

'Weird!' Vito repeated with an emphatic lack of inhibition, crumpling the photo into a ball of crushed paper and firing it into the fire burning merrily across the room. 'Where did you get that photograph from and when did you see it?'

Holly sketched out the details, her heart beating very fast. She hadn't expected to feel guilty but now she did because taking Vito by surprise had only annoyed him.

'Today?' Vito stressed in astonishment. 'But that photo is at least three years old!'

'Three years old…' Holly's voice trailed off as she studied him in disbelief.

'It was taken at our engagement party. Why on earth would it be printed again now?' he questioned.

Holly scrambled out of her seat and pelted off to find the magazine she had cut the photo from. Reappearing, she planted it into Vito's outstretched hand while Silvestro struggled to set out the first course of the meal.

'Per l'amor di Dio…' Vito groaned. 'You need to learn to read Italian!'

'It's not going to happen overnight,' she grumbled.

'That photo was quite cleverly utilised to symbolise

the fact that I have now cut my ties to the Ravello Investment Bank,' Vito framed in flat explanation. 'Note the way our hands are pictured apart...'

'What does the Ravello Bank have to do with anything? What ties?'

'Marzia is a Ravello,' Vito informed her drily. 'When we got engaged I agreed to act as an investment adviser to the Ravello Bank. When Marzia ditched me her father begged me to retain the position as Ravello was going through a crisis and my resignation would have created talk and blighted their prospects even more.'

Holly blinked. She had become very pale. 'I had no idea you had any business links to Marzia and her family.'

'As of yesterday I *don't*. I resigned the position and they have hired the man I recommended to take my place. Once you and I were married it no longer felt appropriate for Marzia's family and mine to retain that business link,' Vito pointed out wryly.

Holly had been blindsided by an element of Vito's former relationship with Marzia that she could not have known about. A business connection, *not* a personal one. 'You know, I assumed that that was a recent picture of you with Marzia,' Holly confided. 'I thought that dinner you mentioned last week must have been a dinner dance.'

'Had it been I would have taken you with me or bowed out early to get home to you. As it was I was landed with a group of visiting government representatives, whose company I found as exciting as watching paint dry,' Vito told her drily and pushed back his chair. 'May I have my shower now?'

'No, we can't just abandon dinner!' Holly breathed

in dismay. 'Not when Francisco has gone to so much trouble to make us a memorable meal.'

'So, you've been down to the kitchen and have finally met our chef?' Vito gathered in some amusement.

'Yes, he's a real charmer, isn't he?'

'I'm sure he can reheat the food,' Vito pronounced impatiently.

'But we haven't finished talking yet,' Holly protested, all her expectations thrown by Vito's eminently down-to-earth explanation of that photo and its meaning.

'Why are you dressed as though you're about to attend a costume ball?' Vito shot at her.

Holly went red. 'I wanted to show you that if I made the effort I could polish up and look all glam like Marzia.'

Vito groaned out loud. 'You look amazing but I don't want you to look all glam like Marzia.'

'But you bought me all those fancy clothes...'

'Only to cover every possible occasion. And when would you have bothered going shopping?' Vito enquired drily. 'You hate shopping for clothes.'

Holly compressed her lips. 'You don't like me glammed up? Or you don't want me copying Marzia?'

'Both,' Vito told her levelly as he signalled Silvestro and rose from his chair again. 'I like you just to be yourself. You're never fake. I *hate* fake. But why did you think I would be out dancing any place with Marzia?'

'What are you doing?' Holly gasped as he scooped her bodily out of her seat.

'I'm going for my after-work shower and you're either coming in with me, which would sacrifice all the effort you have gone to, or you're waiting in bed for me,' Vito informed her cheerfully.

'I thought you still cared for Marzia,' Holly finally confessed on the way up the stairs. 'I thought you might still love her.'

Vito grunted with effort as he reached the landing. 'I can carry you upstairs but I can't talk while I'm doing it,' he confided. 'I never loved Marzia.'

'But you got engaged to her... You *lived* with her!'

'Yes, and what an eye-opening experience that was!' Vito admitted, thrusting wide the door of their bedroom. 'I asked her to marry me in the first place because she was everything my grandfather told me I should look for in a wife. I wasn't in love with her and when we lived together I discovered that we had nothing in common. I don't want to dance the night away as if I'm still in my twenties but Marzia does. She has to have other people around all the time. She likes to shop every day and will avoid any activity that wrecks her hair... up to and including a walk on a windy day and sex.'

'Oh...' Open-mouthed and taken aback by that information, Holly fell very still as Vito ran down the zip on her dress.

'I was relieved when she ditched me. Not very gallant but it's the truth. We weren't suited.'

'Was my ring...? I've always wanted to ask,' Holly interrupted, extending her ring finger. 'Was it Marzia's before you gave it to me?'

An ebony brow shot up. 'Are you joking? Marzia didn't return her engagement ring and even if she had I hope I would've had more class than to ask you to wear it.'

'You *never* loved her?' Holly was challenged to credit that fact because it ran contrary to everything she had assumed about his engagement.

'When I met Marzia, I had never been in love in my life,' Vito admitted ruefully. 'I got burned young watching my mother trying to persuade my father to love her. I spent my twenties waiting to fall in love, convinced someone special would eventually appear. But it didn't happen and I was convinced it never would. I decided I was probably too practical to fall in love. That's why I got engaged to Marzia the week after my thirtieth birthday. At the time she looked like the best bet I had. Similar banking family and background.'

'My word…that sounds almost…almost callous,' Holly murmured in shock. 'Like choosing the best offer at the supermarket.'

'If it's any consolation I'm pretty sure Marzia settled for me because I'm extremely wealthy.'

Vito yanked loose his tie and shed his jacket. Holly's dress slid down her shoulders and for an instant she stopped its downward progress and then she let it go and shimmied out of it. In many ways she was still in shock from Vito's honesty. He had never fallen in love? Not even with the gorgeous Marzia, who by all accounts had irritated him in spite of her pedigreed background and family. She swallowed hard, trying not to wonder how much she irritated him.

'You're definitely not joining me in the shower,' Vito breathed in a roughened undertone as he took in the coffee-coloured silk lingerie she sported below the dress that had tumbled round her feet. 'You can't deprive me of the fun of taking those off.'

His shirt fell on the floor and she lifted it and the trousers that were abandoned just as untidily to drape them on a chair along with her dress. Sharing a bedroom with a male as organised as Vito had made her clean up her bad habits. Vito had paused to rifle through his jacket and he strode back to her to stuff a jewellery case unceremoniously into her hand. 'I saw it online, thought you'd like it.'

'Oh...' Holly flipped open the case on a diamond-studded bracelet with a delicate little Christmas tree charm attached. 'Oh, that's very pretty.'

'It's very *you*, isn't it?' Vito remarked smugly.

'Why didn't you give it to me downstairs over dinner?' Holly exclaimed, struggling to attach it to her wrist until he stepped forward to clasp it for her.

'I forgot about it. You swanning down to greet me dressed like Marie Antoinette put it right out of my mind.'

'And then you just virtually threw it at me,' Holly lamented. 'There's a more personal way of giving a gift.'

'You mean romantic.' Vito sighed as he strode into the en-suite bathroom, still characteristically set on having his shower. 'Shouldn't the thought *behind* the gift count more?'

Holly thought about that and then walked to the bathroom doorway to sigh. 'You're right. I'm sorry. It's a cute, thoughtful present and I love it. Thank you.'

'My thank you was your face. It lit up like a child's when you saw the Christmas tree,' Vito confided with amusement before he turned the water on.

Holly kicked off her shoes, stared down appreciatively at the bracelet encircling her wrist and lay down on the bed. He had never loved Marzia. Marzia was wiped from Holly's standard stock of worries for ever. Marzia was the past—a past Vito neither missed nor wanted to revisit. That, she decided, was a very encouraging discovery.

All of a sudden hiding her love, being so painfully careful not to let those words escape in moments of joy, seemed almost mean and dishonest. Vito loved Angelo so freely. She witnessed that every day. Her husband hadn't even had to try to love his son and Angelo loved his father back. Perhaps in time Vito could come to love her too, she reflected hopefully. When he had told her that he much preferred her to just be herself around him without the fancy clothes or any airs her heart had taken wings. He liked her as she was. Wasn't that wonderful?

Vito strode out of the en suite, still towelling dry his hair. 'We'll have a very special Christmas this year. For the first time I'll happily celebrate the season. That's the effect you and Angelo have had on my Scrooge-like outlook.'

'I'm grateful because I will always love Christmas.'

'Because that's how we met,' Vito reasoned. 'And I've never forgotten how appealing you looked dressing that little tree at the cottage.'

'Is that so? And yet you made me fight for the opportunity,' Holly reminded him.

'You gave me a fresh look at the world and it's never been the same since,' Vito intoned very seriously as he settled down on the bed beside her and closed her into his arms.

'Meaning?'

'Remember I said I went through my twenties waiting for someone special to appear?'

Holly nodded and rubbed her cheek against a damp bronzed shoulder.

'And then she came along when I was thirty-one years old and, unfortunately, incredibly wary and set in my ways.'

Her brow furrowed because she thought she had missed a line somewhere. '*Who* came along?'

'You did,' Vito pointed out gently. 'And I wasn't waiting or looking for love any more, and my practical engagement had gone belly-up. So, when you appeared and you made me feel strange I didn't recognise that it was special. The sex was incredible but I was blind to the fact that everything else was incredible too.'

'I made you feel…*strange*?' Holly exclaimed in dismay.

'Confused, unsure of myself. I behaved differently with you, I *felt* more with you…and it troubled me. So, like an idiot, I walked away from what I didn't understand,' he completed.

'I wish you'd found my note,' Holly lamented.

'When you walked out first, I told myself that was for the best, that we could never work in the real world. But we *do* work,' Vito told her with quiet satisfaction. 'We work like a dream on every level and I have never been as happy as I am now…'

Holly was thinking about what he had said and a spark of excitement lit inside her.

'If you and Angelo hadn't found me again, where would I be now? The heart and soul of my world was the Zaffari Bank but the bank wasn't enough to satisfy me.'

'Are you trying to tell me that you fell for me that night?' Holly whispered shakily.

'Well, if you have to ask, obviously I'm not doing a very good job of the telling.' Vito groaned. 'What you made me feel unnerved me. I wouldn't even let myself try to trace you because I was too proud. If you didn't want me I wasn't going to chase after you. I tried very hard to forget that night. I even tried to sleep with other women.'

'And how did that go?' Holly broke in to demand.

'It didn't. I made excuses to myself that I was stressed, overtired. I had endless fantasies about you.'

'Me…the temptress,' Holly framed blissfully. 'Who would ever have thought it?'

'You're the love of my life…the *only* love I have ever had,' Vito husked, clamping her to his long, powerful length with strong arms. 'And I fell hard. I fell *so* hard I can't imagine ever living without you and our son. You have brought passion and fun into my daily life and I never had either before.'

'I love you too,' Holly muttered almost shyly.

Vito smiled down at her with burnished golden eyes and her heart skipped a beat. He kissed her with hot, hungry fervour and she ran out of breath. He lifted his tousled dark head and murmured, 'I have one special request. Would you consider having another child?'

'Another?' Holly gasped in astonishment.

'Not immediately,' Vito hastened to assure her. 'I want to share your next pregnancy, *be* there when my child is born, and experience everything I missed out on with our son. If you employ an assistant, even if you get pregnant I don't see why you shouldn't still be able to concentrate on your interior design plan.'

Holly smiled at that prospect. Her very successful bedroom project had quickly spread to include other major rooms at the *castello*. She had had the adjoining reception room done in toning colours before moving on to attack the scarlet Victorian dining room. At present she was well aware that the *castello* was large enough to offer her the chance to utilise her talents and gain proper experience before she considered moving on to tackle outside projects.

'I'll think about another baby,' she told him thoughtfully. 'I would prefer Angelo not to be an only child.'

Vito stared down at her as she gazed up at him with starry eyes. *He loves me, he loves me, he* loves *me,* she was thinking on a happy high. She ran an appreciative hand up over a long, muscular, hair-roughened thigh and sensible conversation ceased around that point. Vito told her he loved her. Holly told him she loved him too. No sooner had they exchanged those sentiments than they both succumbed to an overwhelming desire to dispel the tension with the passion they shared.

Long after, Vito lay studying Holly as she slept, marvelling at how happy he felt. He wondered if he could persuade her into another sexy Santa outfit at Christmas and wondered if it would be a little pushy to buy one for her. Pushiness came so naturally to him that he soon convinced himself that his laid-back bride would simply laugh.

He curved an arm round her slight body.

'Love you...' Holly mumbled automatically.

Vito smiled. 'Love you. You're my happy-ever-after, *amata mia.*'

EPILOGUE

VITO STRODE THROUGH the door and was immediately engulfed in the flying energy of his son, who flung himself at his knees in a classic tackle. Angelo started chattering in a hail of words, only a handful of which were in distinguishable Italian and occasional ones were in English. *Mamma* figured a lot. *Nonna*, as he called his grandmother Concetta, figured too. If Angelo was to be believed, he, his mother and his grandmother had spent the afternoon feeding a dinosaur. A very small dinosaur was waved in Vito's general direction and comprehension set in as he crouched down to dutifully admire the toy.

A giant Christmas tree adorned the hall. It was festooned with ornaments and lights. There were no gifts heaped below the branches because Angelo loved to rip off wrapping paper. Silvestro had been heard to tell a tenant that the Zaffaris were having 'an English Christmas', and Vito's chef, Francisco, had been feeding them turkey for weeks as he fine-tuned his recipes to provide them with an English banquet on Christmas Day. In respect of the Italian traditions, Angelo would receive *la calza*—a stocking full of sweets. The red-suited Babbo Natale would obviously visit on Christmas Eve, but the kind-hearted Italian witch La Befana, who searched for the Christ child in all the houses, would visit at Epiphany with more gifts.

Vito breathed in deep as he saw a small figure clad in white-fur-trimmed scarlet appear at the top of the stairs. 'You're not wearing your hat,' he complained.

Holly stopped midway and jammed it on over her mane of hair and made a face at him. 'Satisfied now?'

Vito angled a lazy, sexy smile at her. 'Don't I have to wait until bedtime for that?'

'Maybe I'll suggest an early night.' Holly remained anchored two steps up so that she was almost level with him.

Vito took the invitation, leaning down to claim that lush pink mouth that he still fantasised about and curving his hands to the swell of her hips to lift her up into his arms. Her hands locked round his neck with satisfying possessiveness and held him fast. He could feel the slight bump of the baby she was carrying against his stomach and he smiled as he lifted his head again.

'I love you,' he groaned.

'Love you madly.' Holly felt ridiculously intoxicated and happy. One kiss from Vito could do that, two were irresistible, and three would only end with her dragging him up the stairs. Evidently falling pregnant sooner than they had expected had done nothing to cool her husband's desire for her and that truly did make her feel as alluring as some legendary temptress. That was very welcome to a woman who was five months pregnant and subject to all the usual aches and complaints of her condition.

Her redecoration schemes at the *castello* had led to an approach from an exclusive interiors magazine, which had taken a whole host of photos. The glossy photo spread and the accompanying article had ensured that within days of the magazine going on sale, Holly was inundated with exciting offers of design work.

This, however, was their first family Christmas and she was revelling in every detail because Vito had really thrown himself into the spirit of the holidays and she didn't think it was solely because he had become a father. She reckoned he had put his sour childhood memories of Christmas behind him. His mother, recently divorced, was joining their festivities and hugely excited about the second grandchild on the way.

'Please tell me turkey isn't on the menu again tonight,' Vito murmured.

'No, we're having steak. I told Francisco I fancied steak,' she admitted.

'When are our guests arriving?' Vito prompted.

'Well, they were supposed to be here for dinner but Apollo's social secretary rang to say they would be late. Why does he need a social secretary?'

'He's always got hundreds of invitations and he's never at home.' Vito paused. 'I appreciate you being willing to give him another chance.'

Holly gave him a soothing smile that concealed her tension. It was past time to forgive and forget—she knew that. After all, Apollo was Vito's closest friend, but Holly had only seen him twice since their wedding. And when she had made the mistake of voicing her opinion on what he considered to be his private business it had been awkward as hell. But she was madly curious to see who he was bringing with him as a guest. Another leggy underwear model? Or his *wife*?

That, Holly supposed, would be another story…

* * * * *

THE GREEK'S
CHRISTMAS BRIDE

LYNNE GRAHAM

I do enjoy an alpha male, but none of them are a match for my husband. This one is for you

PROLOGUE

THE MALE VOICES drifted in from the balcony while Holly hovered, waiting uneasily for the right moment to join the conversation. That was a challenge when she knew she was never particularly welcome in Apollo's radius.

But there wasn't much she could do about that when she was married to Vito, Apollo's best friend. Only recently had she come to appreciate just how close the two men were and how often they talked no matter where they were in the world. Friends from a childhood spent at boarding school, they were as close as brothers and Apollo had distrusted Holly from the outset because she was a poor woman marrying a very rich man. Aware of that fact, she had offered to stay home instead of attending the funeral of Apollo's father but Vito had been shocked at that suggestion.

So far, their visit to the privately owned island of Nexos and the Metraxis compound had been anything but pleasant. The funeral had been massive. Every one of Apollo's former stepmothers and their children had attended. Earlier today the reading of the will had taken place and Apollo had stormed out in a passion, having learned that he needed a wife to inherit the vast empire he had been running for several years on his ailing father's behalf. Vito had shared only that bare detail with his wife, clearly uncomfortable at divulging even that much. But as virtually anybody who knew Apollo also knew of his aversion to matrimony, it was obvious that his father's last will and testament had put him between a rock and a hard place.

'So, you pick one of your women and marry her,' Vito breathed, sounding not at all like the loving husband Holly knew and adored. '*Dio mio*, there's a long enough list. You marry her, stay married as long as you can bear it, and—'

'And how am I going to get rid of her again?' Apollo growled. 'Women cling to me like superglue. How am I going to trust her to keep her mouth shut? If word escapes that it's a fake marriage, the stepfamilies will go to court and try and take my inheritance off me. If you tell a woman you don't want her, she's insulted and she wants revenge.'

'That's why you need to *hire* a wife as if you're interviewing one for a job. You need a woman with no personal axe to grind. Considering your popularity with the opposite sex and your bad reputation, finding her could be a challenge.'

Reckoning that it was now or never, Holly stepped out onto the terrace. 'Hiring a wife sounds like the best idea,' she opined nervously.

Even sheathed in an elegant dark suit, Apollo Metraxis looked every inch the bad boy he was. With shoulder-length black hair, startling green eyes and an elaborate dragon tattoo peeping out of a white shirt cuff, Apollo was volatile, unconventional and arrogant, the direct opposite of Holly's conservative husband.

'I don't believe you were invited to join this conversation,' Apollo countered very drily.

'Three heads are better than two,' Holly parried, forcing herself down stiffly into a seat.

Apollo elevated a sardonic brow. 'You think so?'

Holly refused to be excluded. 'Stop dramatising yourself—'

'Holly!' Vito interrupted sharply.

'Well, Apollo can't help himself. He's always doing it,' Holly argued. 'Not every woman is going to cling to you like superglue!'

'Name me one who won't,' Apollo invited.

Holly blinked and thought very hard because Apollo was universally acknowledged to be a gorgeous, super-wealthy stud and nine out of ten women followed him round a room with hungry eyes. 'Well, my friend Pixie for a start,' she pronounced with satisfaction. 'She can't stand you and if she can't, there's got to be others.'

A very faint flush accentuated Apollo's supermodel cheekbones.

'Pixie wouldn't quite meet the parameters of what is required,' Vito interposed hastily, meeting his friend's appalled gaze in a look of mutual understanding because he had not told his wife the exact terms of the will. Ignorant as Holly was of those terms, she could not know how impossible her suggestion was.

Apollo was outraged by the reference to Holly's friend, Pixie, who was a hairdresser and poor as a peasant. Apollo already knew everything there was to know about Holly and Pixie because he had had the two women thoroughly investigated as soon as Holly appeared out of nowhere to announce that she had given birth to Vito's son, Angelo. Apollo had been appalled by Pixie's grubby criminal background and the debts her unsavoury brother had accrued and which she for some strange reason had chosen to take on as her own. Those debts had resulted in her brother's punishment beating and her attempt to interfere with that had put Pixie in a wheelchair with two broken legs.

Was it any wonder that when her friend had such a bad background he had instinctively distrusted Holly and marvelled at his friend's eagerness to marry the mother of his child? Indeed Apollo had been waiting on the sidelines ever since for Pixie to try and take advantage of her friendship with Holly by approaching her friend for financial help. To date, however, she had not done so and Apollo had been relieved for he had no desire to interfere again, knowing how much that would be resented. And thanks to his ungenerous attitude at their wedding, Holly already resented Apollo quite enough.

Pixie Robinson, Apollo thought again in wonderment as Vito and Holly retreated indoors to change for dinner. He was unlikely to forget the tiny doll-like blonde in the wheelchair at Vito's wedding. She had given Apollo nothing but dirty looks throughout the day and had really irritated him. Holly was insane. Of course she was biased, Pixie being her best friend and all that, but even so, could she really imagine Apollo marrying Pixie and them producing an heir together? Apollo almost shuddered before he reminded himself that Holly didn't know about that most outrageous demand in his father's will.

He had seriously underestimated the older man, Apollo conceded angrily. Vassilis Metraxis had always had a bee in his bonnet about the continuation of the family name, hence his six marriages and unsuccessful attempts to have another child. At thirty, Apollo was an only child. His father had urged his son to marry many times and Apollo had been blunt and honest about his resolve to remain single and childless. In spite of the depredations of the manipulative, grasping stepmothers and the greedy stepchildren that had come with those marriages, Apollo had always enjoyed a relatively close and loving relationship with his father. For that reason, the terms of Vassilis's will had come as a very nasty shock.

According to the will, Apollo was to continue running his father's empire and enjoying his possessions but that state of affairs was guaranteed to continue only for the next five years. Within that period Apollo had to legally marry and produce a child if he wanted to retain his inheritance. If he failed on either count, the Metraxis wealth would be shared out amongst his father's ex-wives and former stepchildren even though they had all been richly rewarded while his father was still alive.

Apollo could not credit that his father had been so foolish as to try and blackmail his son from beyond the grave. And yet wasn't it proving most effective? Rigid with tension as he made that sudden leap in understanding, Apollo stood on the terrace looking out to sea and watching the stormy waves batter the cliffs. His grandfather had bought the island of Nexos and built the villa for family use. Every Metraxis since then had been buried in the little graveyard down by the village church, including Apollo's mother, who had died in childbirth.

The island was Apollo's home, the only real home he had ever known, and he was disconcerted to realise that he literally could not *bear* the idea of his home being sold off, which would mean that he could never visit it or his memories again. He was discovering way too late to change anything that he was far more attached to the family name and the family property than he had ever dreamt. He had fought the prospect of marriage, habitually mocking the institution and rubbishing his father's unsuccessful attempts to recreate a normal family circle. He had sworn that he would never father a child, for as a child Apollo had suffered a great deal and he had genuinely believed that it would be wrong to subject any child to what he had endured. Yet from beyond the grave his father had contrived to call his bluff...

For when it came down to it, Apollo could not contemplate losing the world he took for granted even though he knew that fighting to retain it would be a hellish struggle. A struggle against his own volatile inclinations and his innate love of freedom, a struggle against being *forced* to live with a woman, *forced* to have sex with her, *forced* to have a child he didn't want.

And how best could he achieve that? Unfortunately, Vito was right: Apollo needed to hire a woman, one who was willing to marry him solely for money. But how could he trust such a woman not to go to the media to spill all or to confide his secrets in the wrong person? He would need a *hold* on the woman he married, some sort of a hold that meant she needed him as much as he needed her and would have good reason to follow any rules he laid down.

Although he would never consider her as a possibility, he *needed* a woman like Pixie Robinson. In her case he could have bought up her brother's debt and used it to put pressure on her, thereby ensuring that it was in her best interests to keep her mouth shut and give him exactly what he needed to retain his family empire. How was he supposed to find another woman in that kind of situation?

Of course, had he trusted women generally, he might have been less cautious. But Apollo, his cynical distrust honed over no fewer than six stepmothers and countless lovers, had never trusted a woman in his life. In fact trust was a real issue for him.

His first stepmother had sent him off to boarding school at the age of four. His second stepmother had beaten him bloody. His third had seduced him. His fourth stepmother had had his beloved dog put down. His fifth stepmother had tried to foist another man's child on his father.

Add in the innumerable women whom Apollo had bedded over the years. Beautiful, sexually adventurous women and gold-diggers, who had endeavoured to enrich themselves as much as possible during their brief affairs with him. He had never known any other kind of woman, couldn't quite believe that any other type existed. Holly was different though, he acknowledged grudgingly. He could see that she adored Vito and their child. So, there was another category out there: women who *loved*. Not that he would be looking for one of those. Love would trap him, inhibit him and suffocate him with the dos and don'ts he despised. He suppressed a shudder. Life was too short to make such a mistake.

But in the short term he still needed a wife. A wife he could *control* was the only sort of wife he would be able to tolerate. He thought about Pixie again. Pixie and her weak, feckless brother's financial problems. She had to be pretty stupid, he reflected helplessly, to mess up her life by taking on her sibling's problems. Why would you do that? Never having had a brother or a sister, Apollo was mystified by the concept of such thankless sacrifice. But just how far would Pixie Robinson go to save her brother's skin?

It amused Apollo to know so much more than Holly did about her best friend's problems. It amused him even more that Holly had cheerfully assured him that Pixie couldn't stand him. Holly had to be blind. Obviously Holly hadn't noticed that, in spite of the dirty looks, Pixie had covertly watched Apollo's every move at her friend's wedding.

The beginnings of a smile softened the hard line of

Apollo's wide sensual mouth. Maybe he should take a closer look at the miniature blonde and work out whether or not she could be of use to him…what did he have to lose?

CHAPTER ONE

'Morning, Hector,' Pixie mumbled as she woke up with a tousled bundle of terrier plastered to her ribs.

Smothering a yawn, she steeled herself to get up and out. She got out of bed to head to the bathroom she shared with the other tenants on the same floor before returning washed and dressed to snap a leash on Hector's faded red collar and take her pet out for his morning walk.

Hector trotted along the road, little round eyes reflecting anxiety. He flinched when he noticed another dog across the street. Hector was scared of just about everything life threw at him. People, other animals, traffic and loud noises all made the whites of his eyes gleam with an edge of panic. Calm and untroubled the rest of the time, he was very quiet and had never been known to bark.

'Probably learned not to as a puppy,' the vet next door to the hair salon had opined when Pixie had asked. 'He's scared of attracting attention to himself in any way. Abuse does that to an animal. But in spite of his injuries he's young and healthy and should have a long life ahead of him.'

Pixie still marvelled at the fact that regardless of her own problems she had chosen to adopt Hector. But then, Pixie had triumphed over adversity many times in life and so had the little terrier. Hector had repaid her generosity a thousand times over. He comforted her and warmed her heart with his shy little ways and eccentricities. He had filled some of the giant hole that had opened up in Pixie's world when Holly and Angelo had moved to Italy.

She had lost her best friend to marriage and motherhood but their friendship had been more damaged by the secrets Pixie had been forced to keep. There was no way she could tell Holly about her brother Patrick's gambling debts without Holly offering to settle those debts for them. Holly was very generous but Patrick was not Holly or Vito's responsibility, he was Pixie's and had been since the day of their mother's death.

'Promise me you'll look after your little brother,' Margery Robinson had pleaded. 'Always do your best for Patrick, Pixie. He's a gentle soul and he's the only family you have left.'

But looking after Patrick had been near impossible when the siblings had invariably ended up living in different foster homes. During the important teenaged years, Pixie had only met up with her brother a handful of times and until she'd finished training and achieved independence her bond with her kid brother had been limited by time, distance and a shortage of money. Once she was working she had tried to change all that by regularly visiting Patrick in London.

Initially Patrick had done well. He was an electrician working for a big construction firm. He had found a girlfriend and settled down. But he had also got involved in high-stake card games and had lost a lot of money to a very dangerous man. Pixie had duly cut down her own expenses, moving out of the comfortable terraced house she had once shared with Holly into a much cheaper bedsit. Every week she sent as much money as she could afford to Patrick to help him pay off his debts but as interest was added that debt just seemed to be getting bigger and if he missed a payment he would be beaten up… or worse. Pixie genuinely feared that her brother's debts would get him killed.

Pixie still came out in a cold sweat remembering the night the debt collectors had arrived when she had been visiting her brother. Two big brutish men had come to the door of Patrick's flat to demand money. Threatening to kill him, they had beaten him up when he was unable to pay his dues. Attempting to intervene in the ensuing struggle, Pixie had fallen down the stairs and broken both her legs. The consequences of that accident had been horrendous because Pixie had been unable to work and had been forced to claim benefits during her recovery. Now, six months on, she was just beginning to get back to normal but unhappily there seemed to be no light gleaming at the end of the tunnel because Patrick's debt situation seemed insurmountable and his life was still definitely at risk. The man he owed wasn't the type to wait indefinitely for settlement. He would want his pound of flesh or he would want to make an example of her brother to intimidate his other debtors.

Settling Hector into his basket, Pixie set off down the street to the hair salon. She missed her car but selling Clementine had been her first sacrifice because she had no real need for personal transport in the small Devon town where she could walk most places. She would return home to take Hector out for a walk during her lunch break and grab a sandwich at the same time.

Entering the salon, she exchanged greetings with her co-workers and her boss, Sally. After hurriedly stowing her bag in her staff locker she caught a glimpse of herself in a mirror and winced. It had been a while since she had looked her best. When had she got so boring? She was only twenty-three years old. Unfortunately cutting costs had entailed wearing her clothes for longer and her jeans and black top had seen better days. She had good skin and didn't wear much make-up but she always wore loads of grey eyeliner because black liner was too stark against the blonde hair that fell simply to just below her shoulders. She had left behind her more adventurous days of playing with different styles and colours because she had soon come to appreciate that most of her clients had conservative tastes and were nervous of a hairdresser who had done anything eye-catching to her own hair.

She cleaned up after her third client had departed. She regretted the reality that yet another junior had walked out, leaving the stylists to deal with answering the phone, washing hair and sweeping up. She checked the appointment book for her next booking and, unusually, she didn't recognise the name. It was a guy though and she was surprised he hadn't asked for the only male stylist in the salon. And then, without the smallest warning, Apollo Metraxis walked in and as every female jaw literally dropped in wonderment and silence spread like the plague he strode up to Pixie and announced, 'I'm your twelve o'clock appointment.'

Pixie gaped at him, not quite sure it could actually be him in the flesh. 'What the heck are you doing here? Has something happened to Holly or Vito?' she demanded apprehensively.

'I need a trim,' Apollo announced levelly, perfectly comfortable with the fact that he was the cynosure of every eye in the place. Clad in a black biker jacket, tight jeans and boots, he seemed impossibly tall as he towered over her, bright green eyes strikingly noticeable in his lean bronzed face.

'Holly? Vito? Angelo?' Pixie pressed with staccato effect, her attention glued to his broad chest and the tee shirt plastered to his six-pack abs.

'As far as I know they're all well,' Apollo retorted impatiently.

But that still didn't explain what a Greek billionaire was doing walking into a high-street hair salon in a small country town where as far as she was aware he knew nobody. And she couldn't be counted because he had never spoken to her, never even so much as glanced at her on the day of Holly's wedding. The memory rankled because she was only human, whether she liked it or not. After trying to ruin Holly's wedding for her by making an embarrassing speech in his role of best man, he had royally ignored Pixie as if she was beneath his lofty notice.

'I'm afraid I have another appointment.'

'That's me. *John Smith?* Didn't you smell a rat?' he mocked.

In actuality the only thing Pixie could smell that close to Apollo was Apollo and the alluring scent of some no doubt very expensive citrusy designer cologne.

'Let me take your jacket,' she said jerkily, struggling to regain her composure and behave normally.

He shrugged it off, more powerful muscles bunching and flexing with his every movement. He exposed the bare arm with the intricate dragon tattoo that had made her stare at her friend's wedding. Then she hurriedly turned away and hung the heavy leather jacket on the coat stand beside the reception desk.

'Come over to the sinks,' Pixie urged, alarmingly short of breath at the prospect of laying actual hands on him.

Apollo stared down at her. She was even smaller than he had expected, barely reaching his chest and very delicate in build. He had seen boards with more curves. But she had amazing eyes, a light grey that glittered like stolen starlight in her expressive face. She had an undistinguished button nose and a full rosebud mouth while her flawless skin had the translucent glow of the finest porcelain. She was much more natural than the women he was accustomed to. Definitely no breast enhancements, no fake tan and even her mouth appeared to be all her own.

As he sat down Pixie whisked a cape round him and then a towel, determined not to be intimidated by him. 'So, what on earth are you doing here?'

'You'll never guess,' Apollo intoned, tilting his head back for her.

Pixie ran the water while noting that he had the most magnificent head of hair. Layers and layers of luxuriant blue-black glossy strands. His mocking response tightened her mouth and frustration gripped her. 'When did you last see our mutual friends?' she asked instead.

'At my father's funeral last week,' Apollo advanced.

Pixie stiffened. 'I'm sorry for your loss,' she said immediately.

'Why should you be sorry?' Apollo asked with unsettling derision. 'You didn't know him and you don't know me.'

Her teeth gritted at that scornful dismissal as she shampooed his hair. 'It's just what people say to show sympathy.'

'*Are* you sympathetic?'

Pixie was tempted to drench him with the shower head she was using. Her teeth ground together even tighter. 'I'm sympathetic to anyone who's lost a family member.'

'He was dying for a long time,' Apollo admitted flatly. 'It wasn't unexpected.'

His outrageously long fringe of black lashes flicked down over his striking eyes and she got on with her job on automatic pilot while her mind seethed with questions. What did he want with her? Was it foolish of her to think that his descent on the place where she worked had to relate to her personally? Yet how could it relate to her? Outside her ties to Holly and Vito, there was no possible connection.

'Tell me about you,' Apollo invited, disconcerting her.

'Why would I?'

'Because I asked…because it's polite?' he prompted, his posh British upper-class accent smooth as glass.

'Let's talk about you instead,' she suggested. 'What are you doing in England?'

'A little business, a little socialising. Visiting friends,' he responded carelessly.

She applied conditioner and embarked on a head massage with tautly nervous fingers. A second after she began she realised she had not asked him if he wanted one but she kept going all the same, desperate to take charge of the encounter and keep busy.

Apollo relaxed while lazily wondering if she did any other kind of massage. The file hadn't shed much light on her sex life or her habits but then two broken legs had kept her close to home for months. As her slender fingers moved rhythmically across his skull he pictured her administering to him buck naked and the sudden tightening at his groin warned him to give it a rest.

Irritated by the effect she was having on his highly tense body, Apollo thought about how much he needed sex to wind down. His last liaison had ended before his father's funeral and he had not been with anyone since then. Unlike Vito, Apollo never went without sex. A couple of weeks was a very long time for him. Had he found Pixie unattractive, he would've backed off straight away; however that wasn't the case. But—*Diavole!*—she was teeny, tiny as a doll and he was a big guy in every way. She rinsed his hair and towelled him dry while he thought about her hands on his body and that ripe bee-stung mouth taking him to climax. It was a relief to move and settle down in another chair.

'What do you want done?' she asked him after she had combed his hair.

He almost told her because he was all revved up and ready to go and he had never before reacted to a woman with such unsophisticated schoolboyish enthusiasm. 'A trim...but leave it long,' he warned her while he wondered what the secret of her attraction was.

Novelty value? He was tall and he generally went for tall, curvy blondes. But possibly he had got bored with a steady diet of women so similar they had become almost interchangeable. Vito had raved about how down-to-earth and unspoilt Holly was but Apollo was a great deal less high flown in his expectations. If Pixie pleased him in bed, he would count her a prize. If she got pregnant quickly he would treat her like a princess. If she gave him a child, she would live like a lottery winner. Apollo believed in only rewarding results.

Of course, she might turn him down. A woman had never turned him down before but he knew there had to be a first time and it was not as though he were in the habit of asking women to have a child with him. And if he spilled all to Pixie then he would be vulnerable because she might choose to share his secrets with the media for a handsome price and that would scupper his plans. So, however she reacted, he would be stuck having to pay her to keep quiet and that reality and the risk involved annoyed him.

Momentarily, Pixie stepped away to right the swaying coat stand, knocked off balance by an elderly woman. In the mirror, Apollo watched as Pixie bent down to pick up and hang the coats that had fallen and he was riveted by a glimpse of her curvy little rump before she straightened and returned to his side.

Her scissors went snip-snip. She was confident with what she did and every so often her fingers would smooth through his hair in a gesture almost like a caress. He glanced at her from below his lashes, wondering if it was a come-on, but her heart-shaped face was intent on her task, her eyes veiled, her mouth a tense line. It didn't stop Apollo imagining those touchy-feely hands roaming freely over him. In fact the more he thought about that, the hotter he got.

When she wielded the drier over him, Apollo tried to take it off her. He usually dried his own hair and then damped it down again to make it presentable but Pixie swore she would do nothing fancy and withheld the drier, determined to personally tame his messy mane.

Until she had had the experience of cutting Apollo's hair it had never crossed Pixie's mind that her job could be an unsettlingly intimate one. But touching Apollo's surprisingly silky hair disturbed her, making her aware of him on a level she was very uncomfortable with. He smelled so damned good she wanted to sniff him in like an intoxicating draught of sunshine. Wide shoulders flexed as he settled back in the chair and she sucked in a slow steadying breath. She had never been so on edge with a customer in her life. Her nipples were tight inside her bra and she felt embarrassingly damp between her thighs.

No, she absolutely was *not* attracted to Apollo. It was simply that he made her very nervous. The guy was a literal celebrity, an international playboy adored by the media for his jet-set womanising lifestyle. Any normal woman would feel overwhelmed by his sudden appearance. It was like having a lion walk into the room, she reflected wildly. You couldn't stop staring, you couldn't do less than admire his animal beauty and magnificence but not far underneath lurked a ferocious fear of what he might do next.

Apollo sprang upright and Pixie hastened to retrieve his jacket and hand it to him. He stilled at the reception desk and dug inside it while she waited for him to pay. He frowned, black brows pleating, and stared at her. 'My wallet's gone,' he told her.

'Oh, dear…' Pixie muttered blankly.

His green eyes narrowed to shards of emerald cutting glass ready to draw blood. 'Did you take it?'

'Did I take your wallet?' In the wake of that echo of an answer, Pixie's mouth dropped open in shock because her brain was telling her that he could not possibly have accused her of stealing from him.

'You're the only person who touched my jacket,' Apollo condemned loud enough to turn heads nearby. 'Give it back and I'll take no action.'

'You've got to be out of your mind to think that I would *steal* from you!' Pixie exclaimed, stricken, as her boss, Sally, came rushing across the salon.

'I want the police called,' he informed the older woman grimly.

The dizziness of shock engulfed Pixie and she turned pale as death. She couldn't credit that Apollo was accusing her of theft in public. In fact her first thought was insane because she found herself wondering if he had come to the salon deliberately to set her up for such an accusation. All he had to do would be to leave his wallet behind and then accuse her of stealing from him. And who would believe her word against the word of someone of his wealth and importance?

Her stomach heaved and with a muffled groan she fled to the cloakroom to lose her breakfast. Apollo was subjecting her to her worst possible nightmare. Pixie had always had a pronounced horror of theft and dishonesty. Her father had been a serial burglar, in and out of prison all his life. Her mother had been a professional shoplifter, who stole to order. If Pixie had stumbled across a purse lying on the ground she would have walked past it, too terrified to pick it up and hand it in in case someone accused her of trying to steal it. It was a hangover from her shame-filled childhood and she had never yet contrived to overcome her greatest fear.

CHAPTER TWO

THE POLICEMAN WHO arrived was familiar—a middle-aged man who patrolled the streets of the small town. Pixie had seen him around but had never spoken to him because she gave the police a wide berth. Acquainted with most of the local traders, however, he was on comfortable terms with her boss, Sally.

By the time Apollo had been asked to give his name and details he was beginning to wonder if it had been a mistake to call in officialdom. He didn't want to be identified. He didn't want to risk the media getting involved. And if she *had* taken his wallet wasn't it really only the sort of behaviour he had expected from Pixie Robinson? She was desperate for money and he was well aware of the fact that his wallet would offer a bigger haul than most. The constable viewed him in astonishment when he admitted how much cash he had been carrying.

Pixie gave her name and address in a voice that trembled in spite of her attempt to keep it level. Sick with nerves, she shifted from one foot onto the other and then back again, unable to stay still, unable to meet anyone's eyes lest they recognise the panic consuming her. Perspiration beaded her short upper lip as the police officer asked her what had happened from the moment of Apollo's arrival. While she spoke she couldn't help noticing Apollo lounging back in an attitude of extravagant relaxation against the edge of the desk and occasionally glancing at his gold watch as though he had somewhere more important to be.

She had never been violent but Apollo filled her with vicious and aggressive reactions. How could he be so hateful and Vito still be friends with him? She had known Apollo wasn't a nice person on the day of Holly's wedding when his speech had made it obvious that Holly and Vito's son had been conceived from a one-night stand. Since then she had read more about him online. He was a womaniser who essentially didn't like women. She had recognised that reality straight off. His affairs never lasted longer than a couple of weeks. He got bored very quickly, never committed, indeed never got involved beyond the most superficial level.

'Don't forget to mention that you went back to the coat stand when the old lady knocked some of the coats to the floor,' Apollo reminded her in a languorous drawl.

'And you're suggesting that that's when I took your wallet?' Pixie snapped, studying him with eyes bright silver with loathing.

'Could it have fallen out of the jacket?' the police officer asked hopefully, tugging a couple of chairs out from the wall to glance behind them. 'Have you looked under the desk?'

'Not very likely,' Apollo traded levelly. 'Is no one going to search this woman? Her bag even?'

'Let's not jump to conclusions, Mr Metraxis,' the policeman countered quellingly as he lifted the rubbish bin.

Apollo raised an unimpressed brow. He was so judgemental and so confident that he was right, Pixie thought in consternation. He was absolutely convinced that she had stolen his wallet and it would take an earthquake to shift him. Her stomach lurched again and she crossed her arms defensively, the sick dizziness of fear assailing her once more. She didn't have his wallet but mud would stick. By tea time everyone local would know that the blonde stylist at Sally's had been accused of theft. At the very least she could lose her job. She wasn't so senior or talented that Sally would risk losing clients to her nearest competitor.

The policeman lifted the newspaper lying in the bin and, with an exclamation, he reached beneath it and lifted out a brown hide wallet. 'Is this it?'

Visibly surprised, Apollo extended his hand. 'Yes...'

'When the coat stand tipped, your wallet must've fallen out into the bin,' Sally suggested with a bright smile of relief at that sensible explanation.

'Or Pixie *hid* it in the bin to retrieve at a more convenient time,' Apollo murmured.

'This situation need not have arisen had a proper search been conducted before I was called in,' the policeman remarked. 'You were very quick to make an accusation, Mr Metraxis.'

Impervious to the hint of censure, Apollo angled his arrogant dark head back. 'I'm still not convinced my wallet ended up in the bin by accident,' he admitted. 'Pixie has a criminal background.'

Pixie froze in shocked mortification. How did Apollo Metraxis know that about her? That was private, that was her past and she had left it behind her a long time ago. 'But *not* a criminal record!' she flung back curtly, watching Apollo settle a bank note down on the desk and Sally hastily passing him his change.

'We shouldn't be discussing such things in public,' the policeman said drily and took his leave.

'Take the rest of the day off, Pixie,' Sally urged uncomfortably. 'I'm sorry I was so quick to call the police... but—'

'It's OK,' Pixie said chokily, well aware that her employer's business mantra was that the customer was always right and such an accusation had required immediate serious attention.

It was over. A faint shudder racked Pixie's slender frame. The nightmare was truly *over*. Apollo had his wallet back even though he still couldn't quite bring himself to accept that she hadn't stolen it and hidden it in the rubbish bin. But it *was* over and the policeman had departed satisfied. The fierce tension that had held Pixie still left her in a sudden rush and she could feel herself crumpling like rice paper inside and out as a belated surge of tears washed the backs of her eyelids.

'Excuse me,' she mumbled and fled to the back room to pull herself together and collect her bag.

She sniffed and wiped her eyes, knowing she was messing up her eyeliner and not even caring. She wanted to go home and hug Hector. Pulling on her jacket, she walked back through the salon, trying not to be self-conscious about the fact that the customers who had witnessed the little drama were all staring at her. A couple who knew her called out encouraging things but Pixie's entire attention was welded to the very tall male she could see waiting outside on the pavement. Why was Apollo still hanging around?

Of course, he wanted to apologise, she assumed. Why else would he be waiting? She stalked out of the door.

'Pixie?'

'You bastard!' she hissed at him in a raw undertone. 'Leave me alone!'

'I came here to speak to you—'

'Well, you've spoken to me and now you can…' Pixie swore at him, colliding with his scorching green eyes and almost reeling back from the anger she saw there.

'Get in the car. I'll take you home,' he said curtly.

Pixie swore at him again and, with a spluttering Greek curse and before she could even guess his intention, Apollo stooped and snatched her off her feet to carry her across the street.

Pixie thumped him so hard with her clenched fist, she hurt her knuckles.

'You're a violent little thing, aren't you?' Apollo framed rawly as he stuffed her in the back seat of the waiting limo.

'Let me out of this car!' Pixie gasped, flinging herself at the door on the opposite side as he slid in beside her.

'I'm taking you home,' Apollo countered, rubbing his cheekbone where it was turning slightly pink from her punch.

'I hope you get a black eye!' Pixie spat. 'Stop the car… let me out! This is kidnapping!'

'Do you really want to walk down the street with your make-up smeared all over your face?'

'Yes, if the alternative is getting a lift from you!'

But the limousine was already turning a corner to draw up outside the shabby building where she lived, so the argument was academic. As the doors unlocked, Pixie leapt out onto the pavement.

She might be petite in appearance but she was wiry and strong, Apollo acknowledged, and, not only did she know how to land a good punch, she also moved like greased lightning. He climbed out of the car at a more relaxed pace.

Breathing rapidly, Pixie paused in the hall with the door she had unlocked ajar. 'How did you know that about my background?'

'I'll tell you if you invite me in.'

'Why would I invite you in? I don't like you.'

'You know I can only be here to see you and you have to be curious,' Apollo responded with confidence.

'I can live with being curious,' Pixie told him, stepping into her room and starting to snap the door shut.

'But evidently you don't think you can live without your foolish little brother…do you?' Apollo drawled and the door stopped an inch off closing and slowing opened up again.

'What do you know about Patrick?' Pixie asked angrily.

Apollo strode in. 'I know everything there is to know about you, your brother, your background and your friend Holly. I had you both privately investigated when Holly first appeared out of nowhere with baby Angelo.'

Pixie studied him in shock and backed away several feet, which took her to the side of her bed. Even with the bed pushed up against one wall it was a small room. She had sold off much of the surplus stuff she had gathered up over the years before moving in. 'Why would you have us both investigated?' she exclaimed.

'I'm more cautious than Vito. I wanted to know who he was dealing with so that if necessary I could advise and protect him,' Apollo retorted with a slight shrug of a broad shoulder as he peered into a dark corner where something pale with glimmering eyes was trying to shrink into the wall.

'Just ignore Hector. Visitors, particularly male ones, freak him out,' Pixie told him thinly. 'I should think that Vito is old enough to protect himself.'

'Vito doesn't know much about the dark side of life.'

It was no surprise that Apollo considered himself superior in that regard, Pixie conceded. From childhood, scandal had illuminated Apollo's life to the outside world: his family's wealth, his father's many marriages to beautiful women half his age, the break-ups, the divorces and the court battles that had followed. Apollo's whole life had been lived in a histrionic headline-grabbing storm of publicity.

And there he stood in her little room, the perfect figurehead for a Greek billionaire, a living legend of a playboy with a yacht known to attract an exceptional number of gorgeous half-naked women. It seemed unfair that a male with such wealth and possessed of such undoubted intelligence should also have been blessed with such intense good looks. Apollo, like his namesake the sun god, was breathtakingly handsome. And he had undeniably taken Pixie's breath away the first time she'd seen him at Holly's wedding.

Apollo might be a toxic personality but when he was around he would always be the centre of attention. He had sleek dark brows, glorious green eyes, a classic nose and a stubborn, wilful mouth that could only be described as sensual. His sex appeal was electrifying and it was a sex appeal that Pixie would very much have liked to be impervious to. Sadly, however, she was a normal living, breathing woman with the usual healthy dose of hormones. And that was all it was...the breathlessness, the crazy race of her heartbeat, the tight fullness of her breasts and that strange squirmy, sensitive feeling low in her pelvis. It was all hormonal and as reflexive and trivial in Apollo's radius as her liking for chocolate, not something she needed to beat herself up about.

A faint little pleading whine emanated from the shadows and recalled Pixie to rationality. As she realised she had been standing dumbly gaping at Apollo while she thought about him an angry flush crept up her face. In a sudden move, she reached for Hector's leash. 'Look, I don't know what you're doing here but right now I have to take my dog out for a walk.'

Apollo watched her drag…literally *drag*…a tattered-looking and clearly terrified little dog out of the corner to clip it onto a leash and lift it into her arms, where she rubbed her chin over the crown of its head and muttered soothingly to it as if it were a baby.

'I have to talk to you. I'll come with you.'

'I don't want you with me and if you have to talk to me about anything I have to say that accusing me of theft and utterly humiliating me where I work wasn't a good opening.'

'I know how desperate you must be for money. That's why I assumed—'

Pixie spun angrily, her little pearly teeth gripped tightly together. 'That's why it doesn't pay to *assume* anything about someone you don't know!'

'Are you always this argumentative? This ready to take offence?'

'Only around you,' Pixie told him truthfully. 'Look, you can wait here while I'm out. I'll be about fifteen minutes,' she said briskly and walked out of the door.

Two steps along the pavement she couldn't quite believe she had had the nerve. After all, the way he talked he knew about Patrick's gambling debts and the threat against his continuing health. She broke out in a cold sweat just thinking about that reality because she really did love her little brother. Patrick didn't have a bad bone in his body. He had made a mistake. He had tried too hard to be one of the boys when he took up playing cards and instead of stopping the habit when he lost money he had gone on gambling in the foolish belief that he could not continue on a losing streak for ever. By the time he had realised his mistake, he had built up a huge debt. But Patrick was working very hard to try and stay on top of that debt. He was an electrician during the day and a bartender at night.

Apollo had dangled a carrot and that she could have walked away even temporarily from the vaguest possibility of help for Patrick shook Pixie. But *was* Apollo offering to help them? No, that was highly unlikely. Why would he help them? He wasn't the benevolent, sympathetic type. Yet why had he come to the salon in the first place and sought her out personally? And then accused her of theft? Her head aching with pointless conjecture, she sighed. Apollo was very complicated. He was also unreadable and impulsive. There was no way she could guess what he had in mind before he chose to tell her.

Apollo examined the grim little room and vented a curse. Women did not as a rule walk out on him, no, not even briefly. But Pixie was headstrong and defiant. Not exactly submissive wife material, a little voice pointed out in his head but he ignored it. He trailed a finger along the worn paperback books on the shelf above the bed and pulled out one to see what she liked to read. It was informative: a pirate in top boots wielding a sword. A reluctant grin of amusement slashed Apollo's lean, darkly handsome features. Just as a book should never be judged by its cover, neither apparently should Pixie be. She was a closet romantic with a taste for the colourful.

Registering that he was hungry, he dug out his cell phone to order lunch for the two of them.

Walking back into her room, Pixie unclipped Hector's leash and watched her pet race under the bed to hide.

Apollo was sprawled in the room's single armchair, long, muscular, jeans-clad legs spread apart, his black hair feathering round his lean strong face, accentuating the brilliance of eyes that burned like emerald fire. 'Does your dog always behave like that?' he demanded, frowning.

'Yes. He's scared of everything but he's most afraid of men. He was ill-treated,' she murmured wryly. 'So, tell me why you're here.'

'You're in a bind and I am as well. I think it's possible that we could work out something that settles both our problems,' Apollo advanced guardedly.

Her smooth brow indented. 'I don't know what you're talking about.'

'For starters, I will *pay* you if necessary to keep quiet about what I am about to tell you because it's highly confidential information,' Apollo volunteered.

Faint colour rose over Pixie's cheekbones. 'I don't need to be paid to keep your secrets. In spite of what you appear to think, I'm not that malicious or grasping.'

'No, but you are in need of money and the press put a high value on stories about me,' Apollo pointed out, compressing his lips. 'You *could* sell the story.'

'Has that happened to you before? Someone selling a story about you?' she shot at him with sudden curiosity.

'At least half a dozen times. Employees, exes…' Apollo leant back into the chair, his strong jaw line taut, dark stubble highlighting his full sculptured mouth. 'That's the world I live in. That's why I have a carload of bodyguards follow me everywhere I go.'

Pixie had noticed the sleek and expensive car parked across the street and a man in a suit leaning against the bonnet while he talked into an earpiece and her grey eyes widened in wonderment. 'You don't trust anybody, do you?'

'I trust Vito. I trusted my father as well but he let me

down many times over the years and not least with the terms of his will.'

Belatedly, Pixie recalled the recent death of his parent and the reference to the older man's will made her suspect that they were finally approaching the crux of the matter that had put Apollo 'in a bind'. It was, however, hard for her to credit that anything could trap Apollo Metraxis in a tight corner. He was a force of nature and very rich. He had choices most people never even got to dream of having and he had always had them.

'I have no idea where you're going with this,' she muttered uncomfortably. 'I can't even begin to imagine any set of circumstances where you and I could somehow settle our…er…problems. Are you asking me for some sort of favour or something?'

'I don't ask people for favours. I *pay* them to do things for me.'

'So there's something that you *think* I could do for you that you'd be willing to pay for…is that right?' Pixie pressed in frustration as a knock sounded on the door.

Apollo sprang upright, all leaping energy and strength, startling her into backing away several steps. He didn't want to get to the point, she registered in wonderment. He was skating along the edge of what he wanted to ask her, reluctant to give her that much information.

And Pixie understood that feeling very well. Trust had never come easily to her either. She loved Holly and her brother and Holly's baby and would have done anything for them. Once won, her loyalty was unshakeable and it had caused her a great deal of pain in recent months that she had had to step back from her friendship with Holly because it was simply impossible to be honest about the reasons why she had been more distant and why she had yet to visit Holly and Vito in Italy. Holly would be determined to help and there was no way Pixie could allow herself to take advantage of Holly's newfound wealth and still look herself in the face. Instead she was dealing with her problems as she always did…*alone*.

She stared in disbelief as a procession of covered dishes were brought in by suited men and piled up on her battered coffee table along with cutlery and napkins and even wine and glasses. 'For goodness' sake, what on earth is all this?' she framed, wide-eyed.

'Lunch,' Apollo explained, whipping off covers as his men trooped back out again. 'I'm starving. Help yourself.'

He whipped off the final cover. 'That's for the dog.'

'The *dog*?' Pixie gasped.

'I like animals, probably more than I like people,' Apollo admitted truthfully.

Pixie lifted the plate of meat and biscuit and sniffed it. It smelled a great deal better than Hector's usual food did and she slid it under the side of the bed. Hector was no slowcoach when it came to tucking in and he began chomping on the offering almost immediately.

'Where did you get the food from?' she asked.

'I think it's from the hotel round the corner. There's not much choice round here.'

Pixie nodded slowly and reached for a plate. Apollo did not live like an ordinary person. He got hungry, he phoned his bodyguards and they fetched a choice of foods at an undoubtedly very stiff price. She helped herself to the fish dish.

'Are you going to tell me what's put you in a bind yet?' she enquired ruefully.

'I can't inherit my father's estate without first getting married,' Apollo breathed in a driven undertone. 'He knew how I felt about marriage. After all, it didn't make him very happy. He was married six times in total. My mother died in childbirth but he had to divorce the five wives that followed her.'

Pixie listened with huge eyes. 'A bit like Henry VIII with his six wives,' she mumbled helplessly.

'My father didn't execute any of his, although had he had the power I suspect he would have exercised the right with at least two of them,' Apollo derided.

'And you're *still* an only child? Why would he try to *force* you to marry?'

'He didn't want the family name to die out.'

'But to prevent that from happening...you'd have to have a child,' Pixie pointed out with a frown.

'Yes. He stitched me up every way there is. My legal team say the will is valid as he was in sound mind when he had it drawn up. I also have a five-year window of opportunity to carry out his wishes and inherit, which is deemed reasonable,' Apollo ground out between gritted white teeth. '*Thee mou*...how can anyone call any of it *reasonable*? It's insane!'

'It's...it's...er...unusual,' Pixie selected uncertainly. 'But I suppose a rich, powerful man like your father thought he had the right to do whatever he liked with his own estate.'

'*Ne*...yes,' Apollo conceded gruffly in Greek. 'But I have been running my father's business empire for many years now and his will feels like a *betrayal*.'

'I can understand that,' Pixie said thoughtfully. 'You trusted him. I used to believe my father when he told me he'd never go back into prison but he didn't even try to go straight and keep his promise. My mother was the same. She said she would stop stealing and she didn't. The only thing that finally stopped her was ill health.'

Apollo studied her in astonishment, not knowing whether or not to be offended that she had compared his much-respected and law-abiding father to a couple of career criminals.

Enjoying her delicious fish, Pixie was deep in thought and surprised that she could relax to that extent in Apollo's volatile radius. 'I get your predicament,' she confided. 'But the terms of the will must be public property, and they aren't confidential, so what—?'

'I have decided that I must meet the terms,' Apollo incised grimly. 'I am not prepared to lose the home and the business empire that three generations of my family built up from nothing.'

'Attachment meets practicality,' Pixie quipped. 'I still don't understand what any of this has to do with me.'

Apollo set down his plate and lifted his wine glass. 'I intend to meet the demands of the will on my *own* terms,' he told her with emphasis, his remarkable green eyes glittering below black curling lashes. 'I don't want a wife. I will hire a woman to marry me and have my child. We will then separate and divorce and my life will return to normal again.'

'And what about the child?' Pixie prompted with a frown of dismay. 'What will happen to the child in all this?'

'The child will remain with its mother and I will attempt to be an occasional father to the best of my ability. My goal is to negotiate a civilised and workable arrangement with the woman of my choice.'

'Well, good luck with that ambition,' Pixie muttered, tucking into her meal with appetite while sitting cross-legged on the floor beside the coffee table because there was only one chair and predictably Apollo had not offered it to her. 'It sounds like a very tall order to me... and anything but practical. What woman wants to marry and have a child and then be divorced?'

'A woman I have paid well to marry and divorce me,' Apollo said drily. 'I don't want to end up with one who will cling.'

Pixie rolled her eyes and laughed. 'When a woman knows she's not wanted, she's rarely clingy.'

'Then you'd be surprised to learn how hard I find it to prise myself free of even the shortest liaison. Women who become accustomed to my lifestyle don't want to give it up.'

Pixie set down her plate and lifted the wine glass he had filled. 'You do indeed have a problem,' she commented with a certain amount of amusement at his predicament. 'But I really don't understand why you're confiding in me of all people!'

'Are you always this slow on the uptake?'

Her smooth brow indented as she sipped her wine and looked up at him enquiringly from below her spidery lashes. 'What do you mean?'

She had beautiful eyes, Apollo acknowledged in surprise, eyes of a luminous clear grey that shone like polished silver in certain lights. 'What do you think I'm doing here with you?' he prompted huskily.

Green eyes met bemused grey and an arrow of forbidden heat shot to the heart of Pixie. She froze into uneasy stillness, her heart banging inside her chest like a panic button that had been stabbed because all of a sudden she felt vulnerable...vulnerable and...*needy*, the very worst word in her vocabulary when it related to a man.

'I believe that for the right price *you* could be the woman I marry and divorce,' Apollo spelt out smoothly. 'I would get a wife, who knows and accepts that the marriage is a temporary arrangement, and you would get your brother off the hook and a much more comfortable and secure life afterwards.'

As Pixie's throat convulsed, her wine went down the wrong way and she set the glass down on the low table with a jarring snap as she went off into a coughing, choking fit. He was thinking of her? *Her?* Her and him, the ultimate mismatch? The woman he had accused of being a thief? Was he certifiably insane? Or simply madly eccentric?

As Pixie's arms convulsed, her drink went down the wrong way and quickly the glass over. Choking as she coughed and gasped for breath, she scrambled off the bed with the wine glass still in her hand and rushed to the bathroom. There she got control of the coughing and rinsed her mouth with water taken from her cupped hand.

CHAPTER THREE

SPLUTTERING AND GASPING for breath, Pixie waved a silencing hand and rushed out of her room to the bathroom. There she got control of the coughing and rinsed her mouth with water taken from her cupped hand. In the mirror over the sink she saw her sad, watering panda eyes and groaned out loud. She looked dreadful. Her eyeliner was rubbed all round her eyes and there was even a smear across one cheek. She did her best with what little there was in the bathroom to tidy herself up.

Apollo Metraxis was offering to rescue Patrick from the debts he was drowning in if she married him in a pretend marriage. *And* had a child with him. *Don't forget the child,* she told herself while she clutched the sink to keep herself upright. She was blown away entirely by the crazy prospect of having a child with Apollo, having sex with Apollo… Swallowing hard, she breathed in deep. It was the most insane idea she had ever heard and she couldn't work out how or why he had decided to approach her with it.

Was he nuts? Temporarily off his rocker after the death of his father? Grounded again, she returned to her room and stared at him.

'That has to be the most ridiculous idea I've ever heard and I can't believe you're serious. I mean…' Pixie paused '…you don't even know me.'

'I'm not suggesting a normal marriage. I know what I need to know about you.'

'Little more than an hour ago you accused me of stealing your wallet!' Pixie fired back at him unimpressed.

'Because I know how desperate you have to be for money. You know that if your brother fails to make a payment or doesn't pay what he's supposed to pay his life could be on the line. He owes that money to a thug, who rules with fear and intimidation,' Apollo countered levelly. 'He could choose to make an example of your brother to deter others from making the same mistake.'

Apollo did indeed know exactly how precarious her brother's position was. Her tummy churned sickly at his confirmation that Patrick's creditor was a violent man because regardless of the beating Patrick had received she had hoped that that was the worst that would be done to him. She paled. 'But that still doesn't explain why you would approach someone like me!' she gasped.

'I told you that I prefer to choose a woman I can pay to marry me. I also want to be in control of the whole arrangement and the way I would set this up would mean that you *had* to follow the rules until our arrangement ends. That feels safer to me. It wouldn't be in your interests or your brother's to cross me or to admit to anyone that our marriage was phony,' he pointed out with assurance. 'Were you to admit that to the wrong person I could be challenged in a courtroom and I could lose my father's estate for ever. If you did betray me, you would be breaking the terms of our agreement and you would land you and your brother straight back into the same trouble that you're in right now.'

It was quite a speech, a sobering and intimidating speech that told her a lot she would rather not have known about exactly how Apollo's mind worked. He wanted a woman over whom he had total control, a woman who had to strictly adhere to his conditions or lose all benefits from the arrangement.

'I hear what you're saying,' Pixie breathed tautly, 'but I think it's twisted. You want a wife you can blackmail into doing what you want her to do, someone powerless. I could not be that woman.'

'Oh, don't underestimate yourself. I think you're gutsy enough to take me on,' Apollo told her with grudging amusement in his gaze. 'Did you or did you not grasp the fact that I am offering to save you and your brother from the consequences of his stupidity?'

Pixie reddened. Silence fell. In the interim, Apollo made use of his cell phone and spoke in what she assumed was rapid Greek.

'You're serious about this…?' she almost whispered in sheer bewilderment. 'But you said you need to have a child as well, and—'

'If you fail to conceive the marriage would end in divorce within eighteen months. I can't afford to waste more time than that,' Apollo imparted without hesitation. 'However, you would still get the same financial payoff. In that way, whether you have a child or not, you would still benefit from a debt-free future. '

A knock came on the door again. This time it was Pixie who rushed to answer it because she desperately needed a breathing space to get her thoughts in order and was thinking of diving for the bathroom again. Two men entered and deftly cleared away the dishes, leaving behind only the wine and the glasses.

'There's no way on earth I could go to bed with you!' Pixie spluttered out bluntly without meaning to as soon as the door had shut on the men's exit.

Apollo studied her in open astonishment and then he

flung his handsome dark head back and roared with un-
fettered amusement. In fact he laughed so hard he almost
tipped the chair back while she stared at him in disbelief.

'I really don't understand how you can find that so
funny,' Pixie snapped when he had regained control
of himself. 'You're talking about me having sex with a
stranger and that may be something you do on a fairly
regular basis but it's not something I would do! You're
also talking about having an awful lot of sex,' she told
him half an octave higher, her voice thinning with extreme stress and embarrassment. 'Because it could take
months and months to conceive a child. I couldn't do
it. There's absolutely no way I could do that with you!'

'You sound a little hysterical and I'm surprised,'
Apollo admitted. 'Holly's the starry-eyed type but you
struck me as more sensible. Marry me and try to have
a child and you won't be struggling in a dump like this
to save your brother and make a decent life. All the bad
things will go away… I can make that happen. You won't
get a better offer.'

Mortification had claimed Pixie because she knew she
had sounded panic-stricken. Face hot, she retreated to the
bed and sank down on the edge of the mattress. In truth
the thought of having sex with Apollo drove every sensible thought from her mind and only provoked a giant
'no' from every corner of her being. A long, *long* time
ago she had promised herself that sex would only ever
be combined with love in her life. She hadn't saved her
virginity simply to throw it away in some immoral arrangement with Apollo Metraxis intended to conceive a
child and moreover a child he didn't *really* want.

Apollo studied her in frustration. He didn't understand
what was wrong. A woman had never found him unattractive before. He knew she didn't like him but he didn't

consider liking necessary to a successful sexual liaison. Sex was like food in Apollo's life, something he enjoyed on a frequent basis and wasted little time thinking about. He was amazed that she had concentrated her objections on the need for a sexual relationship. Head down bent, she sat on the side of the bed in a rigid position with one arm stretched down in an unavailing attempt to lure the terrified dog out from underneath the bed. But the dog was too wary of Apollo's presence to emerge. He could see its beady little eyes gleaming watchfully from deep under the mattress.

'Tell me what the problem is…' he invited impatiently.

'I don't want to have a baby with someone who doesn't love me or my child,' Pixie muttered in a rush. 'That's way too like what I had growing up with the parents from hell!'

Apollo was taken aback. 'I don't want a woman who loves me because she might well want to stay married to me and I will want my freedom back as soon as I have fulfilled the terms of the will. Rejecting a wife who loved me could well lead to her breaking our agreement and telling someone that the marriage was a fake created to circumvent the will and allow me to inherit. And speaking for myself, I can't put love on the table for *any* woman. But, I *would* hope and expect to love my child.'

That admission soothed only one of Pixie's concerns because her brain could not surmount the unimaginable challenge of going to bed with Apollo again and again and *again*. A trickle of heat sidled through her slender frame as she lifted her head a few inches higher and focussed on her tormentor. He was gorgeous and he knew it but that did not mean he would be kind or considerate in bed. What did she feel like? A medieval maiden being auctioned off for a good price? That was nonsense because the choice, the decision was hers alone. And women had been marrying men for reasons far removed from love for centuries. Some women married to have children, some for money, some for security and some to please their families. She was making too much of a fuss over the sexual component. Sex was a physical pastime, not a mental one.

So, did that mean that she was actually considering Apollo's ridiculous proposition? She took a mental look at her life as it was. She was drowning in her brother's debt. She didn't have a life. She couldn't *afford* to have a life. She went to work, she came home, ate as cheaply as she could and saved every possible penny. Aside from Hector, whom she adored, it was a pretty miserable life for a young woman but sixth sense warned her that Apollo, if displeased, probably had the power to make even the life of a rich wife a great deal *more* miserable. Even so, when Holly visited the UK, Pixie went to meet her and they would have a meal and a couple of drinks and for a few sunny hours Pixie would forget her worries and enjoy being with her friend again. If she married Apollo, she would surely see much more of Holly, wouldn't she?

But then nothing could make marrying Apollo for money the right or decent thing to do, she reasoned unhappily. It would be akin to renting out her womb. And although she loved children and very much missed her friend Holly's adorable son, Angelo, from when they had both lived with her, she had never planned to have a child so young or to raise one alone. To plan to do that would be wrong, she thought with a shudder of distaste. And Apollo had also reminded her that circumventing his father's will would be breaking the law and she refused to be involved in anything of that nature.

'I can't believe you are willing to go to such lengths

just for money…but then I've never had enough money to miss,' Pixie admitted wryly. 'I guess it's different for you.'

'I'm already a very rich man in my own right,' Apollo contradicted drily. 'But there is more to this than money. There is my family home on the island where all my relatives are buried. There are the businesses originally founded by my grandfather and my great-grandfather, the very roots of my family. It took my father's death for me to appreciate that I'm much more attached to those roots than I was ever willing to admit even to myself.'

His obvious sincerity disconcerted Pixie. She understood that he had taken those things for granted until he was forced to confront the threat of losing them.

'Lying and pretending wouldn't come naturally to me,' she told him flatly. 'And faking the marriage would also be breaking the law, which I couldn't do. I don't even have a traffic violation on my record,' she told him truthfully. 'Because of my experiences growing up I won't do anything that breaks the law.'

'But we would be faithfully following the terms of the will, which specifies that I must marry and produce a child—boy or girl—within the space of five years. My intent to eventually go for a divorce is not barred by the will. If the marriage is consummated and we have a child it will be, to all intents and purposes, a *normal* legal marriage,' Apollo told her forcefully.

Pixie hovered, her small heart-shaped face pale and stiff. 'I don't want to be involved. I realise that you think I'm an easy mark but I couldn't do it. I won't discuss this with anyone either. I should think anyone I told would threaten to lock me up and throw away the key because they'd think I was crazy!'

Apollo rose slowly to his feet, dominating the room

with his height and breadth. 'You're not thinking this through.' Reaching into his pocket, he withdrew a card and set it down on the table. 'My private number if you change your mind.'

'I'm not going to change my mind,' Pixie told him stonily.

Apollo said nothing. He paused at the door, looking at that soft ripe mouth of hers, his body hardening in response to the imagery flashing through his inventive mind. 'It would've been good in bed. I find you surprisingly attractive.'

'Can't say the same,' Pixie retorted as she yanked open the door with a shaking hand. 'I don't like you. You're arrogant and insensitive and completely ruthless when it comes to getting what you want.'

'But I still make you hot, which infuriates you,' Apollo murmured huskily. 'You're not very good at faking disinterest.'

Her grey eyes sparkled with anger. 'You're not irresistible, Apollo!'

He lifted a lean-fingered hand and tilted up her chin. 'Are you sure of that?' he asked thickly, a Greek accent he rarely revealed roughening and lowering his dark drawl to a pitch that vibrated like a storm warning down her stiff spine.

'One hundred per cent certain,' she was mumbling as his breath fanned her cheek and the scent of him flared her nostrils and her mouth ran dry while her heartbeat raced into the danger zone.

'I bet I could get you to break the law,' Apollo murmured soft and low, all untamed masculinity and dominance. 'I bet I could get you to do just about anything I wanted you to. I even bet that I could make you *enjoy* breaking the rules…'

Her knees were trembling, her feet welded to the floor by the mesmeric effect of those stunning green eyes firing down into her own. 'You'd like to think so.'

Her pupils were fully dilated, her breathing was audible. Her nipples were making tiny indentations in her top and Apollo was hard as a rock. He bent his head a fraction more and traced her stubborn little mouth with his. She jerked almost off balance and his arms snapped round her to steady her. She couldn't breathe then for excitement. It was the most extraordinary sensation. Suddenly she wanted what she hadn't wanted until that moment. She wanted to stretch up on tiptoe and claim the kiss he had teased her with and refused to give.

Apollo bit out a laugh, perceptive eyes mocking her. 'Stubborn and proud. That's dangerous in my vicinity because I'm stubborn and proud as hell too. We'd clash but we'd also have fireworks, not something I usually look for with a woman but I'd make an exception for you, *koukla mou*. I would enjoy making you eat every word of your defiance and your denial...'

Her blood ran cold in her veins because she believed him. Below the bed Hector uttered a soft little growl that she had never heard from him before.

Apollo laughed again with genuine appreciation. 'Aw, stop kidding yourself, dog! You're not going to attack. You're too scared even to come out from under the bed. What do you call him?' he asked, disconcerting her with that sudden change of subject.

'Hector.'

'Hector was a Trojan prince and a great army commander in Greek mythology. Did you know that?' he enquired lazily as he strolled out of the door.

'No, I didn't. I just thought the name suited him,' she mumbled weakly.

She didn't breathe again until she had closed the door and she rested back against it with eyes shut and the strangest sense of disappointment filtering through her. In the most disturbing way Apollo Metraxis had energised her. The threat gone, Hector scampered joyously out from below the bed and danced at her feet. She lifted him up, stroking what remained of his ragged little ears, and cuddled him. 'A Trojan prince, not just an ordinary dog, Hector. I named you well,' she whispered, burying her face in his tousled fur, feeling her lips tingle as she thought of that almost-but-not-quite kiss that had left her foolishly, mindlessly craving more.

Patrick Skyped her that evening, his thin face worn, eyes shadowed. 'I've got bad news,' he told her heavily. 'Maria's pregnant and she's not well.'

'Pregnant?' Pixie gasped in dismay.

Patrick grimaced. 'It wasn't planned but we want the baby. We've been together three years now,' he reminded his sister with a weak attempt at a smile. 'I just wish the pregnancy wasn't making her so ill because she can't stand on her feet all day in a shop in her current condition. I'm never here, I'm always working…who's going to look after her?'

'Give her my congratulations,' Pixie urged, concealing her feelings because she very well knew that her brother's pregnant partner could bring his entire debt repayment scheme tumbling down round their ears because it was a struggle for him to make his monthly payment as it was.

Her brother's blue eyes glittered. 'I hate asking but could you manage anything extra this month?'

'I'll see what I can do,' Pixie said thickly, not wanting him to realise that she could see the tears in his eyes.

A few minutes later the call was complete and Pixie felt as though she had received a punch in the stomach.

Patrick and Maria's financial situation was as fragile as a house built of cards. If one card fell, they would all fall. She groaned out loud. She couldn't afford to give Patrick any more money and she should have admitted that upfront. Unfortunately her panic-induced thoughts had flown straight to Apollo because she wanted her little brother to stay alive and in one piece and if he couldn't keep up those payments, he could well pay with his life.

Patrick was under threat and now there was Maria and a new baby on the way to consider as well, Pixie reflected wretchedly. How could she ignore their plight? How could she turn her back on them when Apollo had made it clear that if she did as he asked he would make all the bad things go away? And suddenly she was just desperate for those bad things to go away and for life to return to normal again.

Apollo as saviour? That concept didn't work. Apollo was more into helping himself than other people. In fact Pixie and her brother were more like chess pieces to be moved strategically on Apollo's master board. The human cost, the rights and wrongs and emotions didn't come into it for Apollo and how much simpler that must make his life, she thought enviously. She lifted the card and snatched up her phone.

I will be your Baby Mama if you settle my brother's debts, she texted with a sinking heart.

Ideals, she was learning, wouldn't be any comfort if her brother or Maria or the baby got hurt or were left alone in the world. Apollo had found her price and she felt humiliated, and even worse manipulated, for he had made her crave his mouth that afternoon and the memory of that unnerved her. It was one thing to defy Apollo, another thing entirely to contemplate being married to him and wholly within his power.

You won't regret it. We'll talk business the next time we meet.

Business, *not* marriage, she reflected uneasily, but maybe that was the right way to look at it, as an arrangement rather than a relationship. As a deal between two people rather than the intimacy normal between a married couple. He wouldn't really be her husband and she wouldn't really be his wife. Mostly they would be faking it…wouldn't they? Would that make it easier to bear?

CHAPTER FOUR

'IT'S QUITE SIMPLE,' Apollo murmured in a cold, dangerous tone. 'You pack up you and your dog and you'll be
picked up this evening.'

'I can't just walk out on my job, and I'm supposed to
give notice when I move out.'

'My staff will organise everything of that nature for
you. You don't need to worry. I want you in London with
me tonight, so that we can get on with the preparations.'

'What preparations?'

'You'll have to sign legal papers, see a doctor, buy
clothes. There must be a dozen entries on the to-do list
I've had drawn up for you. You're going to be very busy.'

Pixie thought about her brother and briefly closed her
eyes, digging deep for composure. She had just put her
life and her free will in Apollo's hands and the pressure
was on *her* now. 'Where will I be staying?'

'At my apartment. It'll be more discreet than a hotel
would be and I won't be there for most of the week. I'll
be working in Athens.'

'OK.' Pixie forced herself to agree because she knew it
was only the first step in another hundred or more steps
when she would have to obediently fall in with Apollo's
wishes. Dear heaven, had she ever hated a man so much?

Vito was one of the very few men Pixie had learned

to trust. She could see his love for her friend, Holly, every time he looked at his wife and his feelings for his son were equally obvious. But Pixie had had few such role models while she was growing up. Her own father had frequently resorted to domestic violence when he was drunk. He had beaten her mother and Pixie as well, calling her 'a mouthy little cow' for trying to interfere. When he wasn't in prison serving time for his burglaries, he had often taken his bad moods out on his family. Pixie had never had Holly's cosy, idealistic images of family life because she had experienced family life in the raw. Her father had married her mother when she fell pregnant but she had never seen any love or affection between them. Patrick had been born within a year of his sister's birth and her mother had found it a challenge to cope with two young kids.

By the time Pixie was eight years old, both children had been placed in a council run children's home because her mother had finally been imprisoned for her incessant shoplifting. Social workers had taken a very dim view of a mother trying to teach her children to steal. The council home and the various foster homes that followed had occasionally contained men with sexual designs on their charges. Pixie had been very young when she first learned to fear the opposite sex and the fact that she went on looking like a much younger child due to her lack of adolescent development had ensured that she had to remain on her guard around such men for years longer than most.

The foster home that had become the first real *home* for Pixie had been Sylvia and Maurice Ware's and she had gone to them when she was twelve. The semi-retired farmer and his wife had had a spacious farmhouse in the Devonshire countryside and they had been

devoted guardians to the often traumatised children who
had come to live with them. Now Maurice was dead, the
farmhouse sold and Sylvia lived in sheltered accommo-
dation but Pixie had never forgotten the debt she owed to
the older couple for the love, kindness and understanding they had shown her. And it was in their home that
she had met Holly and their friendship had been forged,
even though Pixie was eighteen months younger.

Her possessions fitted into her one suitcase and a box
she begged off the local corner shop. She left an apolo-
getic message on her employer Sally's answering machine. What else could she do with Apollo calling all the
shots? But being forced into such dangerous life changes
genuinely frightened her. What would she do if Apollo
decided that she wasn't suitable to be his wife after all?
Where would she go? How would she find another job?
She didn't trust Apollo and she didn't want to end up on
the street, homeless and unemployed, particularly not
with Hector to worry about.

A limousine arrived to collect her. The driver came to
the door and carried out her luggage and then produced
a pet carrier, which Hector refused to enter. Pixie protested and promised that the little dog would be quiet
and well-behaved if he was allowed to travel on her lap.
She climbed into the opulent car with an engulfing sense
of detached disbelief. She'd had glimpses of Holly and
Vito's wealth, had attended their wedding, had seen impressive photos of their Italian home, but Holly didn't
wear much jewellery or particularly fancy clothes and,
essentially, she hadn't *changed*. It was surprisingly easy
to meet up with Holly and forget that she was the wife
of a very rich man.

The luxurious interior of the limousine fascinated
Pixie. It had a television and a phone and a bar. It was a

long drive but there were regular stops to exercise Hector and an evening meal stop for Pixie at a very swanky hotel. It was only there that she noticed another car was accompanying them because it was one of the men in it who escorted her into the fancy dining room and urged her to choose whatever she liked from the menu. Pixie was so horrified by the prices on the menu and so scared that the bill would be handed to her at the end of the meal that even though she was starving she only dared to have soup, which came with a roll. Of course no one presented her with a bill. The big beefy bodyguard or whatever he was appeared to be there to take care of such necessities while Hector waited in the car.

By the time they finally arrived in London, Pixie was exhausted and living on her nerves. It was after ten in the evening and it was dark and, with Hector cradled in her arms, she left the limo in the underground car park and walked into a lift with the big beefy guy and his mate towering over her.

'What're your names?' she asked nervously.

'Theo and Dmitri, Miss Robinson. You're not really supposed to notice us,' Theo told her gently. 'We're here to take care of you but we're staff.'

It was yet another strong message that Apollo lived in a different world because Pixie could not imagine ever ignoring anyone in such a way. But at that moment she reminded herself that she had more pressing concerns. Would she see Apollo this evening? The lift stopped directly into a massive apartment foyer and she realised that it had to be a private lift only used by him and his employees.

A small, portly older man in a jacket approached her. 'I'm Manfred, Miss Robinson. I look after the apartment. Let me show you to your room.'

Pixie followed him across the foyer towards a corridor and on the way past saw into a large reception room where she glimpsed a lithe blonde beauty standing talking with a drink in her hand. One of Apollo's women? Probably, she thought. He always seemed to have a woman on the go. She would have to ask him what he planned to do after their marriage if they got that far because no way was she prepared to sleep with a man sleeping with other women at the same time. That wasn't negotiable yet the picture of a quiet, clean-living version of Apollo married refused to gel.

'This is the garden room,' Manfred announced grandly, walking across a big, lushly appointed bedroom to indicate the patio doors. He buzzed them open to show her the outside space. 'Perfect for the little dog…'

'Yes,' Pixie agreed in wonderment. Stepping out, she noticed that part of the roof garden was neatly and clearly temporarily fenced off, presumably to prevent Hector straying into the glimmering blue pool that lay beyond it.

'Can I get you any refreshments?' he asked cheerfully.

'I wouldn't say no to some sandwiches,' Pixie muttered apologetically.

Pixie unpacked while Hector explored the new environment and his own first private outside space. In one corner of the room sat a fur-lined pet bed with a roof. Hector sniffed all round it, finally decided it wasn't actively unfriendly and got into it. Manfred brought tea and sandwiches on a tray. Pixie went for a shower in the lovely bathroom, bemused to find herself dropped in the midst of such extreme comfort and luxury. Comfy in her shortie pyjamas, she curled up on the bed with her supper and ate.

Apollo had already told Lauren that he had an early start in the morning and that her uninvited visit was inconve-

nient. He had given her wine, made the kind of meaning-
less chit-chat that bored him and sidestepped a blatantly
obvious invitation to have sex. He never brought his lovers back to his various properties. He took them to a hotel
or went to their place because that meant that he could
leave whenever he liked.

'You want me to leave, don't you?' Lauren said in a
whiny little-girl voice that set his teeth on edge.

'Tonight doesn't suit me,' Apollo pointed out without apology. 'I have a busy schedule and I also have a
guest staying.'

'Another woman?' she gasped.

And that was it for Apollo. Lauren had been in his life
exactly two days. He hadn't yet slept with her and now
he knew he never would because her attitude turned him
off. Lauren stalked out in a snit, leaving Apollo free to
indulge in his desire to see Pixie. Of course he wanted to
see her, he reasoned with himself while his brain questioned *why* he would want to see her. But Pixie was very
probably the woman he was going to marry and therefore infinitely more important than a casual hook-up like
Lauren. And in any case he wanted to see if Hector liked
his new hideaway bed.

With a brief knock on Pixie's bedroom door, Apollo
opened it.

He was just in time to catch the look of fear on Pixie's
face and the way she slammed back apprehensively against
the headboard. 'Sorry, did I startle you?' he said, knowing
that 'startled' didn't come near to covering her excessive
reaction and wondering what had caused it.

Pale, Pixie suddenly reddened and unglued her spine
from the headboard to straighten her narrow shoulders.
'It's all right,' she said with forced casualness. 'I thought
you were entertaining?'

'No.' Apollo stared at her. She was wearing pyjamas and there was nothing elegant or alluring about them but, while his rational mind was telling him that, his body was reacting as if she were half naked. The nipples of her small breasts pushed against the thin cotton and her slender crossed legs were exposed yet he only had to look into her flushed and ridiculously appealing face and that bee-stung mouth and he was throbbing, grateful for the suit jacket he still wore as a cover.

'Well, I'm here,' Pixie pointed out nervously. 'Thanks for the bed for Hector.'

Apollo glanced at Hector, who had made himself as small and unnoticeable as possible at the back of the big bed, and a slanting, almost boyish grin flashed across his lean, strong face without warning. 'I thought he might as well hide in comfort.'

He looked amazing when he smiled like that, Pixie ruminated. She hadn't known he could smile like that or that he was a soft touch when it came to dogs, but he so obviously had not been joking when he said he often preferred animals to people. It gave him a more human side, made her a touch less unnerved by him. As for those dazzling, unexpectedly green eyes illuminating his hard dark features, it was a challenge to look away from them. But then of course he had appeal. He was a real player. Young, hot and rich, he was a target for hungry, ambitious and designing women, which was probably why he didn't like women very much. At least that was what she had privately decided about him even though she didn't know if it was true. And why should she care? Why was she even thinking about him in such a way? What Apollo Metraxis was really like shouldn't matter to her, should it?

And the need to stick to business belatedly impressed

her as a very good attitude to take because she did not want to be getting curious about Apollo and wondering what made him tick. Nor did she want to be admiring his stunning male beauty. None of that should matter to her, she told herself urgently.

'Do you mind telling me what you intend to do about my brother's debt?' she pressed tightly.

'If we go ahead and marry he can forget about it because I'll take care of it. If we stay married and you meet my conditions—'

'Getting pregnant?' she interrupted in dismay.

'No, that won't be on the table because it would be unreasonable. You may not conceive and if you don't I can hardly punish you for not doing so,' he conceded. 'As long as you try. That and confidentiality are really all I'm expecting from you. Whether we're successful or otherwise that debt will not come back to haunt your brother.'

'You're paying it off?'

'No, I'm taking over the payments,' Apollo lied without skipping a beat. 'Look on it as my method of ensuring you keep to your side of the bargain throughout our association.'

'It's not necessary to put that kind of pressure on me. I keep my promises,' Pixie argued, unhappy with what he was telling her.

'My tactics work,' Apollo countered levelly, feeling an unexpected stab of discomfiture for not telling her the truth, and the truth was that he already owned the debt in its entirety. After all, there was no way he could have entertained any kind of ongoing arrangement with a thug running an illegal gambling den.

Pixie swallowed hard on the angry, defiant response she wanted to make. When it came to the gambling debt, what he was offering was still much better than anything she could have hoped to achieve on her own. It would take the financial stress off Patrick and his partner and allow them to get on with their lives and concentrate on their coming baby. On the other hand Apollo's decision to maintain the 'carrot and stick' approach towards their marriage would put the weight of expectation squarely on Pixie's shoulders instead and it would worry her constantly that in some field she would fail to please and her loss of freedom and self-will would end up being worthless.

'I think that if you're prepared to marry me, you could be a little more trusting.'

'How can you say that? When I walked in you looked at me as though you expected me to attack you!' Apollo grated in condemnation. 'You don't trust me either.'

'It's nothing personal. I don't trust men generally.' Pixie lifted her chin. 'And why do I have to see a doctor?'

'Health check. Obviously there's no point in us marrying if it turns out that you may not be able to conceive.'

'So, presumably,' Pixie framed, 'you're being tested as well?'

'No.'

'Forty per cent of infertility problems are *male*,' Pixie pointed out. 'Not much point getting me tested if you're not going to get tested too.'

Apollo hadn't thought of that angle and for some inexplicable reason he realised that the suggestion that he might not be fertile really annoyed him. He opened the door. 'I'll see you tomorrow. By the way, *wear* the outfit I had put in the wardrobe for you.'

'Outfit?' she gasped, sliding off the bed and opening the wardrobe to see the blue dress and jacket that hung there in a garment bag and the silvery designer shoes and bag stowed beneath. 'What gives you the idea that you can tell me what to wear?'

'It's another milestone on the road to becoming my wife. Naturally I want you to look your best,' Apollo fielded, dragging his glittering gaze from his perusal of her slender thighs to jerk open the bedroom door again. Maybe he should've taken Lauren to bed, he reflected in annoyance, because he was deeply uneasy about the strength of Pixie's appeal. *Thee mou,* what was the matter with him? She wasn't a beauty but she was exceptionally pretty and there was something remarkably sexy about her as well, something that drew him on a level he didn't understand. Was it her expressive face? Those interestingly perky breasts? The tight bottom? The so touchable thighs and small, slender feet?

Did he feel sorry for her? Was that the source of her strange appeal? He didn't require a therapist to tell him that she suffered from low self-esteem. In the act of shutting the door, he turned and caught the filthy look she was shooting him while thinking herself unobserved and he strode down the corridor to his own bedroom laughing and feeling surprisingly upbeat for the first time since his father's death. No, he didn't feel sorry for Pixie, he *liked* that gutsy irreverent streak of hers even though he was out of necessity being forced to ensure that she reined it in. She really wasn't impressed by him. Or by his wealth. And when had he ever met with that attitude before in a woman? In truth it was a real first for him. The women he was accustomed to would have snatched the outfit out to check that it was designer and would then have praised his generosity with loads of gratitude and flattery to ensure that he did it again.

Pixie? *Not impressed.* Apollo grinned.

* * *

Pixie woke at seven to be greeted by Manfred drawing back the curtains and setting her breakfast down on a table by the window and stepping out through the patio doors to set down a dog dish for Hector. 'Mr Metraxis asks that you be ready for nine,' he told her quietly.

Pixie breakfasted like a king. She loved her food and had always had a healthy appetite. Staying in Apollo's palatial apartment was even better, she imagined, than staying in an exclusive hotel. After a shower, she dried her hair and took special care with her make-up before getting dressed.

She walked uncertainly into the huge main reception room and Apollo stared.

'Turn round,' he told her thickly, turning his fingers to emphasise the order.

Apollo was rapt. She was so incredibly dainty and feminine in that blue dress with the high heels accentuating her delicate ankles that he wanted to lift her off her feet and spin her round, and it was a weird prompting that bewildered him. She had the figure a model would kill for without the height.

'I like the dress,' he said, which wasn't surprising since he had personally selected it.

'It's elegant but I'm not used to wearing skirts or heels,' she complained. 'I'm more of a tomboy than a fashion queen.'

He took her to see a private gynaecologist. She was questioned, examined and scanned and blood tests were taken. The results would be in by the following morning. As she emerged she saw Apollo standing talking urgently into his phone. 'Did you have any idea? Well, no, I didn't think it through either…it's *not* funny, Vito. It was gross.'

Apollo finished the call and strode towards her with

all the eagerness of a male who could not get out of the plush surgery fast enough. 'Ready to go?'

Pixie was trying not to laugh because he had honestly sounded so shocked by what being tested had entailed and she thought it served him right after the process she had undergone without complaint. Evidently he did listen occasionally to a voice other than his own and he was playing fair at least.

'Where to now?' she prompted.

'My lawyers, after which you go shopping.'

'Oh? For what?'

'For a wedding dress obviously and all the rest of it. I'm putting you in the charge of a professional buyer and fashion stylist. She knows what you need as per my instructions. All you have to do is act like a mannequin.'

'But you haven't got the test results back yet.'

'Think positive…' Apollo bent down, his stubbled jaw line grazing her cheek a tiny bit, and every nerve in her body tightened like a string pulled taut. 'And I saw you smiling when you heard me talking to Vito,' he murmured huskily. 'No, I didn't enjoy being handed a porn mag but *ne*…yes, I had a fantasy and it was about you.'

As Apollo pressed her back into the limo, Pixie twisted her head back to gape at him. *'Me?'* she repeated in disbelief.

Green eyes roamed over her burning face with dark satisfaction. 'You, *koukla mou.*'

Luminous eyes taking on a faint bluish cast from the dress she wore, Pixie stared at him in astonishment. 'You're kidding?'

'Why would I be kidding? If I couldn't be attracted to you, how could we do this?'

It was a fair point but the idea that Apollo, all rippling male-muscle perfection and stunningly beautiful, could consider her attractive still stupefied Pixie. And while she stared, frozen to her seat, Apollo moved, scooping her off the seat and settling her down into his lap at a speed that thoroughly unnerved her. But then his mouth traced very gently over hers and that instinctive kick of fear that generally made her back away from men was soothed by that subtle approach, which seemed ridiculously unthreatening. Of course, it didn't dawn on her just at that moment that Apollo had an unequalled sensual skill set that allowed him to read women very easily.

The tip of his tongue traced her upper lip and something deep down inside just melted in Pixie. He followed that tactic up with a nibble at her full lower lip and she shivered, her whole body prickling with awareness to an almost painful degree. No man had ever made her feel anything like that before and she found it wildly seductive not to feel afraid. He teased her lips open and darted his tongue in lightly and a ball of erotic heat exploded in her pelvis and one of her hands flew up into his hair, feathering through the luxuriant strands to cup his well-shaped skull. She felt hot all over and curiously energised, almost as if someone had told her she could fly when all her life she had felt grounded and awkward.

His mouth was hard and yet his lips were soft and she was exploring every sensation with her brain and her body. He tasted so good, like water after a drought, like food after a famine. His mouth claimed hers with increasing pressure and her breasts ached inside her bra, liquid heat pushing between her thighs.

He was so warm she wanted to press into his lean, muscular frame and somehow meld with him. He framed her face with his hands and kissed her with steadily escalating passion and the hungry demand she recognised was thrilling rather than scary. She tipped her head back, allowing him all the access he wanted, jerking at each erotic plunge of his tongue and on fire for the next, which was why it was such a shock when without the smallest warning his hands dropped to her waist and he propelled her back into the seat he had snatched her off.

Blinking with disconcertion and sensual intoxication, Pixie looked at him with a frown of incomprehension as to why he had so abruptly stopped.

'For such a small woman you pack a hell of a punch!' Apollo growled accusingly, because he had been within an inch of ripping off her panties and bringing her down on his aching body, satisfying the raw need that had come at him out of nowhere. And he didn't like it, he didn't like it one bit because he had never been that close to losing control with a woman since he was a teen, and remembering that time when he had been little more than a boy toy for a mature woman's gratification brought him out in a cold sweat of revulsion.

'It was only a kiss,' she framed shakily between tingling lips, even though her body was telling her different and reacting in all sorts of disappointed ways to that sudden severance from his.

'I was ready to have you right here, right now!' Apollo grated through clenched white teeth, his jaw line rigid because he was so furious that for a few wildly exciting moments he had forgotten who he was and who she was and that the very last thing he had been thinking of was the bottom line.

And the bottom line was business, he reminded himself grimly, the business of satisfying his father's will and making the best he could out of being blackmailed into marriage and fatherhood.

'Here in the car?' Pixie gasped, looking ridiculously shocked by the concept. 'Would you have done that?'

And the very slight widening of his gorgeous green eyes fringed by those outrageously lush black lashes of his told her that he would have and indeed had probably had sex in a limo before. That brought her down to earth again with a timely thump. She was a virgin and he was a man whore and of course he had greater expectations and fewer boundaries than the average person. She wondered how often a first kiss had led into full sex for him and a shudder of distaste rippled through her, chasing off the last of the sexual heat he had evoked.

Aware that he had overreacted and exposed a certain sensitivity he had never ever exposed to anyone before, particularly not a woman, Apollo forced himself to shrug a careless shoulder. 'I suspect that you're likely to find living with me rather shocking. I like sex and I like a lot of it. Considering our current situation it's very positive that we light a fire together.'

Pixie shifted almost imperceptibly away from him to widen the gap between them. *I like sex and I like a lot of it.* It was quite an intimidating announcement for an inexperienced woman to absorb. Pixie's biggest secret, kept even from Holly, was that she had never actually *wanted* a man before. She had always been too wary around men to shake off that inhibition by the time she grew up. Usually the minute a man started touching her she wanted him to stop and feared how far he would try to go. But somehow that instinctive recoil, that fear, had been absent with Apollo and that worried her even while she told herself that it was just as well because there was no way on earth that she could somehow avoid consummating a marriage in which she had to try and conceive a child.

They arrived at a very fancy modern glass office building and, before they got out of the limo, Apollo turned to her to say, 'To all intents and purposes this has to seem like we're planning a normal marriage,' he warned her. 'You must *not* mention your brother's debt or anything of that nature.'

'OK,' Pixie muttered uncertainly.

'All you have to sign is a pre-nuptial agreement with a confidentiality clause included,' he revealed. 'You will have your own legal team to advise you.'

'My...*own*?' she whispered shakily, her eyes wide.

'To advise you of your best interests. You must've had access to legal advice to make the agreement stand up in court,' he explained. 'I know a lot about the subject because every one of my father's wives signed one of these agreements and half of them tried to wriggle out of it during the divorce negotiations.'

'I won't be wriggling anywhere,' Pixie mumbled.

'So, act like a girlfriend, not someone I hired!' Apollo advised in a warning aside.

'How would a girlfriend behave?' she whispered.

'I don't know. I've never had one, only sexual partners,' Apollo admitted, grasping her hand to urge her out of the limo.

'Never?' Pixie repeated incredulously.

'Just think about how a real bride-to-be would behave for this and behave accordingly.'

And an hour later, seated at a large conference table where the two sets of lawyers argued, often employing terms she didn't understand, Pixie took Apollo's advice and acted accordingly and accidentally brought the table to a standstill of silence.

'You mean...' she finally grasped '... I get financially punished if I'm unfaithful but Apollo *doesn't*? How is that fair? I won't accept that.'

That was the instant when Apollo appreciated once

again that Pixie could take advice too literally and that characteristically she was seizing on something none of his father's wives had even picked up on. Not only had he underestimated her intelligence, he had also seemingly overlooked what appeared to be a very moral take on infidelity and his heart sank because he had never planned to be faithful during his marriage. He had planned to be very discreet but *not* faithful because only once in his life had he been faithful to a woman and it brought back appalling memories of betrayal and stupidity.

'Fidelity isn't a negotiable concept,' Pixie declared with even greater clarity.

And every man at the table studied Pixie as though she had landed on it wearing wings and carrying a flaming sword of justice.

'If Apollo is unfaithful he has to suffer for it,' Pixie completed with satisfaction, wondering why Apollo wasn't looking impressed that she had finally spoken up and behaved as a real bride-to-be surely would have done.

Apollo compressed his firm sensual mouth and studied the table. In point of fact billionaires who married penniless women didn't expect to suffer in *any* way when they finally got bored, least of all financially. Was this Pixie's clever way of trying to increase her divorce settlement? It had to be the money she was thinking about, the profit, he reasoned and then he glanced up and Pixie nailed him with grey eyes like volcanic rock and he realised that the issue of actual fidelity was one he had completely forgotten to discuss. Breathing in deep, he suggested a break for coffee.

Shown into an empty office, he studied Pixie. 'I wasn't planning to be faithful,' he admitted bluntly.

'Then this arrangement dies now. I'm not willing to

have sex with a man at the same time as he is having sex with other women!' Pixie declared in a wrathful under-tone of ringing disgust.

'You're forgetting that this is a business arrangement.'

'Business arrangements don't normally include sex!' Pixie shot back at him defensively.

A faint line of colour accentuated Apollo's supermodel cheekbones. 'We have an *extraordinary* arrangement.'

'But you don't get to sleep with other women and me at the same time!' Pixie told him doggedly. 'That's im-moral and I refuse to be part of it.'

It was what was called an impasse and Apollo had very rarely met with anything similar. Just when he was within an ace of making the first move towards his goal of regaining his birthright too! He gritted his teeth. 'I'll *try* to be faithful,' he framed in a roughened undertone of frustration.

But Pixie was seriously disappointed in Apollo. She hated cheats and had even less time for married men who played away. And Apollo might not love her and she might not love him but it was not unreasonable for her to expect him to treat her with respect.

'It's not going to look much like a real marriage if you're still acting like the biggest man whore in Europe!' Pixie flashed back at him, watching temper flare like burning flames in Apollo's green eyes and watching him bite it back. And why had he bitten it back? Because she had only stated the truth, she suspected.

And eventually they signed the pre-nuptial agreement with an addendum that stated that the bridegroom would 'endeavour' to remain faithful but relations were strained right round the table, both legal teams well aware that wedding fever was at a low ebb just at that moment. Apollo was merely relieved by the knowledge that he was flying out to Athens that evening. He was also reluctantly recalling that Vito had warned him that Pixie could be hot-headed and difficult and wondering if only his haste had persuaded him to overlook that distinct drawback. What else could it have been?

But how could she be so naïve and unreasonable as to demand fidelity from him? He knew what he was, hell, even *she* knew what he was! But he had promised to try and he would try because he stuck to his word, even if it choked him. And on some strange level he was conscious that her stance had made him respect her. She had standards and nothing he could offer would sway her from them.

CHAPTER FIVE

PIXIE TWIRLED IN front of the full-length mirror and smiled hesitantly because her glossy reflection was unfamiliar. Having enjoyed the attentions of a make-up artist and a grooming day at a salon recommended by Holly, Pixie had never before enjoyed such a level of sophisticated presentation.

'I really did think you'd choose to wear white,' Holly confided.

'White would be wasted on Apollo,' Pixie replied, wrinkling her nose and making Holly laugh. 'If I ever get to have a *real* wedding, I'll wear white.'

'I still can't believe you're marrying him. I was really shocked when Vito told me.'

Pixie sat down on the end of the bed and studied her linked hands. 'There's still stuff you don't know about the deal I made with Apollo,' she admitted uncomfortably because she could not bring herself to admit that sex and conception were involved, fearing that Holly would think badly of her for being so desperate that she would agree to a demand of that nature.

Yet while remaining fearful of the judgement of others, Pixie had made peace with that condition on her own behalf. She had always planned to become a mother some day, to have a child who was absolutely her own to love and nurture and protect. To fulfil that longing while married and to be assured of a future income with which to raise that child might yet prove to be the best chance she would ever get to have a baby and give it the happy childhood she had personally missed out on.

After all, she was no great shakes at dating, she acknowledged ruefully. She had always had to force herself out of the door to even socialise with men and the few she had taken the risk of spending time with had turned her off the notion entirely. Consequently she had decided that, left to her own devices, it was perfectly possible that she would've stayed single and alone and would never have had the opportunity to settle down with a partner and have a family. On that basis, she had decided that her agreement with Apollo Metraxis might well have advantages she had initially overlooked because, however briefly, she would get to experience being a wife and, hopefully, a mother.

Apollo had shared the test results that had come back on one of his calls from Athens. They were both healthy and normal as far as the entry-level testing they had had could establish. There was no obvious reason why they shouldn't conceive as a couple. He was still rather cool and clipped with her in tone because she had not seen him since they had parted at odds after that legal meeting, but Pixie had no regrets on that score. His fidelity while they were trying to conceive, as far as she was concerned, was non-negotiable. It wasn't much to ask, she reflected with faint bitterness and resentment; shouldn't it be a simple question of respect and decency? Apollo couldn't escape every moral obligation by throwing the 'business arrangement' label at her. But how hard would he 'endeavour' to meet her expectations? As a promise, it might well not be worth the paper it was written on.

'Well, you've finally told me about Patrick and there can't be anything worse than the mess he's got himself into, so I fully understand *why* you're doing this,' Holly said, squeezing her friend's shoulder soothingly. 'But you should've come to me for help.'

'Patrick's my problem, *not* yours,' Pixie pointed out with a hint of fierceness because her friend's desire to be generous with her money seriously embarrassed her. 'And this way I won't owe anyone anything. Apollo needs me as much as I need him and I prefer it like that.'

'It's a pity he's so…*so*…' Holly struggled to find a word, her cheeks colouring because it was occurring to her that now Pixie was marrying Apollo, even though it wouldn't be a proper marriage, possibly a little tact was required.

'He's been very good to Hector,' Pixie murmured thoughtfully. 'You know, rich or not, I don't think Apollo had it easy growing up either. Five stepmothers…what must that have been like for a little boy?'

'He's strong. He survived just like us. I suppose what I really wanted to ask is…how will you cope with his women?'

Pixie reddened and her pretty pearlised nails dug into the fabric of her wedding gown.

'Don't go falling for him, Pixie,' Holly warned her anxiously. 'He dumps women the instant they get clingy or needy and he seems to have the sexual attention span of a firefly.'

'Oh, I don't think I'm in any danger of making *that* particular mistake,' Pixie responded in a more relaxed tone of quiet confidence.

She lusted after Apollo and that was all and, as he himself had commented, that was a positive in their situation. The truth that he could make a single kiss that irresistible had been very persuasive. For the first time ever Pixie wasn't in fear at the prospect of having sex. Until he had opened his big mouth and referred to having sex in the limousine Apollo had made sex seem warm and intimate rather than sleazy, potentially painful and scary. He had also made it incredibly exciting.

Pixie's thoughts drifted much the way her dreams had throughout the week leading up to her wedding day, dreams filled with humiliating X-rated images that disturbed her sleep and woke her up hot and breathless and feeling quite unlike her usual sensible self.

Manfred arrived to tell them that the limo had arrived. Her foster mother, Sylvia Ware, was meeting them at the hotel where the civil ceremony would be staged because Holly had arranged transportation for the older woman. But Holly, Vito and Sylvia, as well as Pixie's brother and his partner, would be the only guests because it was to be a very small, quiet wedding, appropriate for a male who not only abhorred publicity but had also recently buried his father. Apollo had initially said no to her brother's attendance but had surprised her by giving way after she had argued that she had to somehow explain why she was leaving the UK. She had agreed not to tell Patrick the truth though.

Before she went into the private function room where the celebrant was staging the ceremony, Pixie paused to twitch her hair straight in a convenient mirror and breathed in very deep. On every level the step she was about to take daunted her because every aspect of living with Apollo Metraxis would be frighteningly new to her and Pixie only ever felt safe with what was familiar and harmless. Sadly, Apollo didn't fit into either category. But, true to her nature, Pixie lifted her head high, straightened her spine and her eyes glittered with determination as Holly opened the door for her to enter the function room. Whatever she felt on the inside, however, Pixie would conceal. Showing nerves and insecurities in Apollo's radius would be like bleeding in the water near a killer shark.

Apollo's rampant impatience lifted when the door opened. She was five minutes late and for all of those five minutes he had wondered if she had got cold feet. Now with the opening of that door his natural cynicism reasserted its hold on him. Pixie was being very well rewarded for marrying him and when had he ever known a woman to turn her back on an opportunity to enrich herself? In his experience, money talked much louder than anything else. And then Pixie came into view.

And all such thoughts vanished at amazing speed from Apollo's mind. She was wearing bright pink, not white, and a short dress rather than a full-length one. And she looked exactly like a tiny, very elaborate porcelain doll in dainty heels. He stopped breathing, shimmering green eyes locked to her delicate face beneath the feathery, distinctly un-bridal fascinator crowning her golden head. For all her lack of height she looked ridiculously regal with her hair swept up, her skin glowing, silvery eyes wide and bright, bee-stung lips as pink as the gown. And in only a few more minutes she would be *his* woman, he reflected with a sudden deep satisfaction that was new to him. *His* in a way no other woman ever had been or would be in the future because there would be no more marriages ahead of him. He had learned from his father's mistakes that there was no perfect wife out there waiting if only you could find her, at least not if you were a Metraxis and richer than sin. But still Apollo could not look away from the vision his bride presented.

Pixie collided with emerald-green eyes that glittered like jewels below the thick black lashes longer than her own. Riveting. Powerful. *Hungry.* And she suffered a heady instant of disbelief that she could have that effect on Apollo, the notorious womaniser accustomed to females more beautiful than she could ever hope to be. She had tried so hard not to think of that aspect for comparisons of that nature were fruitless and would merely feed her anxieties in bed and out of bed with him. Colour ran riot up over her face because she had quite deliberately avoided reflecting on the end result of marrying Apollo... the wedding *night.* Would it be good or would her inexperience and his emotional detachment make it a disaster?

She reached his side and was dismayed to register that she was trembling. She had travelled in the space of seconds from telling herself that she was calm and composed to a jangling state of nerves that appalled her. As the celebrant began to read the wedding service, she forced herself to look up and encountered a searching look from Vito, who was smiling. Unnerved, she looked down again, her heart thumping very fast while Apollo threaded a ring onto her finger, his hand as warm and steady as hers was cold and shaky. *Lighten up, it's a business arrangement,* she reminded herself when the man and wife bit was pronounced and it was over and she believed she could relax again. At least she believed that for as long as it took Apollo to swing her round, his other arm sliding below her hips to lift her in what could only have been described as a caveman kiss.

He hauled her up to his level and his mouth crashed down on hers with passionate force. There was no warning, verbal or physical, simply that positively primeval public claiming that shocked Pixie anew. She had sensed the volatile nature pent up beneath the surface when Apollo had kissed her in his limousine but this kiss was a whole different experience. Before he had asked, this time he literally *took*, disdaining any preliminaries, both strong arms enclosed round her to keep her off the ground and raise her to his level. It took her breath away, it sent her heart thumping like a road drill, it stripped away every illusion that she had any form of control over him or herself. She could *taste* his sexual hunger and it speared through her like a heat-seeking missile, awakening every skin cell to raw new sensation.

It was wild and erotic and exciting but it was also ultimately terrifying for Pixie to feel unmanageable and wanton. For a frightening second, as he began lowering her back to the ground on legs that didn't feel they could possibly support her, she wanted to cling to his wide shoulders and stay exactly where she was. Instead she slid slowly down his big muscular body and not even his suit jacket could conceal the reality that he was as aroused as she was.

Shaken, she found her feet again, and Apollo closed a supportive arm round her lithe body. *His*, body and soul, whether she liked it or not. And he knew, he knew she wouldn't like it at all, and Apollo smiled with sudden blinding brilliance, raising a brow a little at his friend Vito's questioning appraisal and Holly's state of apparent incredulity. Pixie was his wife now and what happened between them was entirely his business and nothing to do with anyone else, he reflected with satisfaction.

Pixie glimpsed that smile and the colour already mantling her cheeks rocketed even higher, a pulse jumping at her collarbone because angry discomfiture was not far behind. With that kiss he had blown her cover story with Holly and she could see that even Vito was taken aback by Apollo's enthusiasm. In fact the only people not staring were Patrick, Maria and Sylvia, none of whom saw anything amiss with a passionate wedding kiss between the newly-weds. Pixie pulled away from Apollo to greet her foster mother, Sylvia, and thank her for her attendance, noting as she did that her brother was looking unusually stiff and troubled in comparison to his more usual carefree self.

Patrick kissed her cheek. 'What's wrong?' she whispered.

Holly tugged her away with an insistent hand on her arm. 'What haven't you told me?' she pressed in an undertone.

'Better you don't know,' Pixie whispered. 'Any idea what's up with my brother?'

'Vito said Apollo gave him a good talking to when he arrived,' her friend revealed. 'Not before time in my opinion. I think he frightened the life out of him about gambling.'

Fury shot through Pixie because she had always acted to the best of her ability as her brother's protector. It had hurt when they had ended up in separate foster homes, seeing each other only through occasional visits often set months apart. What did Apollo know about Patrick's life and what he had suffered? Or how proud Pixie was that her sibling had always had a job when so many other children who had been through the foster system ended up on the scrapheap of opportunity before they had even finished growing up? Yes, Patrick had got into trouble, and serious trouble at that, but that had happened two years ago and he had been paying for it ever since!

Apollo closed a big hand over hers and slotted a glass of wine into her other hand. 'We're eating now and then this nonsense will be over,' he framed with unhidden relief.

'What gave you the right to speak to my brother about his gambling?'

'He almost got you and himself killed the night you fell down those stairs,' Apollo countered with unblemished assurance. 'It was time someone showed him his boundaries.'

'That was not your right or your business,' Pixie hissed up at him like a stinging wasp, her anger unabated.

Apollo dealt her an unfathomable appraisal, his striking green eyes veiled. 'For as long as you remain my wife, everything that is your business will also be *mine*.'

'No, it isn't!' Pixie practically spat back at him in her ire.

'It's too late now to complain, *koukla mou*. That ring on your finger says very different,' Apollo spelt out without hesitation, and he swung round to stride back to Vito's side and laugh about something his friend was saying.

'Oh, dear,' Holly pronounced at her elbow. 'You're already fighting.'

Pixie was so enraged that she could hardly breathe and with difficulty she opened her mouth to say, 'Apparently, he regards a wedding ring on a woman's finger as something very like a slave collar.'

Holly giggled. 'That's only wishful thinking!'

And Pixie remembered her manners and asked after Holly's son, Angelo, who had remained in Italy with his nanny because his parents were only making a day trip to London. By the time that conversation concluded it was time to take their seats at the table and be served with the wedding breakfast. As time went on, Patrick's spirits picked up and he began to relax a little although his sister noticed he was visibly too scared to even look in Apollo's direction, never mind address him.

Sylvia insisted on making a very short speech, which

recounted a couple of tales about Holly and Pixie as teenagers, which made everybody laugh. Vito wished them well, showing no sign of being tempted to make an attack on the bride as Apollo had done with his speech on his friend's wedding day.

'Watch yourself with Apollo's temper,' Holly whispered anxiously over the coffee. 'Vito says he can be very volatile.'

'Think I already know that,' Pixie muttered. 'As well as dictatorial, manipulative and sexist. I could go right through the alphabet with him and not one word would be kind, but then right now I'm angry.'

'When he saw you in that dress he stared at you as if you'd jumped naked out of a Christmas cracker. It was quite funny.'

Obviously, he hated the dress. Well, Pixie didn't care about that. She had gone shopping with her official personal stylist and had overridden her to make her own selections because, had Apollo's recommendations ruled, she would have ended up dressed like a middle-aged lady without fashion sense. Evidently, he didn't want her wearing normal *young* clothes, he wanted her tricked out in longer skirts and high necks. Well, he could just go jump off the nearest cliff with that wish, Pixie thought resentfully.

Why should he think he had the right to dictate the very clothes she wore? Wasn't she already surrendering enough with her freedom and her control over her own body? She was her own person and always had been and marrying Apollo Metraxis was not about to change that reality...

CHAPTER SIX

As Pixie prepared to clamber dizzily out of the helicopter, Apollo vaulted out and took her by surprise by swinging back and scooping her off her feet and carrying her off the helipad.

'I can walk!' Pixie snapped freezingly, feeling like an idiot as the yacht crew hanging around the helipad stared in apparent surprise at what was happening before their eyes.

'If I put you down you have to take your shoes off and walk barefoot. No heels on the decks,' Apollo delivered unapologetically.

'If I take my shoes off, I shrink into something pocket-sized!' Pixie hissed in a most un-bridal manner between gritted teeth.

Apollo shrugged a very broad shoulder. 'That's the rule. Blame your parents for your genes, not me.'

Pixie breathed in so deep to restrain her temper that she was slightly surprised she didn't spontaneously combust like a balloon overfilled with air. 'Put me down, Apollo.'

Holding her up with one arm as if to emphasise how strong he was, he flipped off her six-inch shoes with the other hand and carefully lowered her to the polished perfection of the deck surface. Pixie shrank alarmingly in stature and flexed angry bare toes on the sun-warmed wood. 'You're a dictator insisting on bare feet,' she condemned.

'Some things aren't up for negotiation,' he pointed out quite unnecessarily, striding past her to greet his yacht captain and shake hands, responding in a flood of his native Greek with a wide smile.

Feeling not remotely bridal, Pixie had a bouquet thrust in her arms and managed a beamingly polite smile while Apollo translated the captain's good wishes on what she privately termed their matrimonial nightmare.

What else could she call it when Apollo seemed to be racing off the rails in his resolve to do exactly as he liked regardless of how she might feel about it? She was still furious that he had confronted her brother about a matter she considered to be none of Apollo's business. Having that source of resentment followed by a very long flight in a helicopter that made her feel sick to board Apollo's giant yacht, *Circe*, in the Mediterranean had not improved her outlook. The ring on her wedding finger already felt very much like the slave collar she had mocked.

Long brown fingers guided her by her shoulder in the direction she was expected to go and she wanted to jump up and down and scream in frustration. Apollo was making her feel like a glove puppet. Go here, sit there, *do that*! It was as if he had swallowed the manual of *How to be a Control Freak with your Wife* at the same moment he was told he was married. She had seriously underestimated how very forceful and domineering he could be unless you did *exactly* as you were told. And there was no room for complaint, which he ignored.

'We need to clear the air about your brother,' Apollo announced, urging her into a room fitted out like an office with built-in cabinets, shelves and a very large desk.

'I will only tell you this one more time…' Pixie framed quite shakily but loudly in her rage. 'My brother is none of your business!'

Once again, Apollo ignored that statement. He extracted a slim file from a drawer in the desk and tossed it across the desk. 'Patrick is *still* gambling. Small card games with low stakes but he has a problem and it needs to be dealt with.'

'That's a complete lie and very unjust!' Pixie exclaimed.

'Pixie, there's sibling loyalty and then there's complete stupidity. Show me that you understand the difference and read the file.'

Her face flaming red with angry embarrassment, Pixie grabbed the file and retreated to a chair.

Apollo studied her with an air of exasperation. Why couldn't she understand that it was *his* job as a husband to protect her? That was all he was doing, as well as sorting out a problem that would only get worse if it was ignored. He had no personal axe to grind when it came to his brother-in-law. But it was obvious that Patrick was weak and in need of firm guidance. That had to be sorted out before Pixie's brother got himself into an even bigger mess because Apollo would refuse to settle the younger man's gambling losses if he got into trouble again.

Pixie's shoulders hunched as she read the investigation report, which stated that Patrick often played card games in the evening after he finished work. Her heart sank to her toes, the colour draining from her face to leave her stiff and pale. Her brother had lied to her and she was hugely hurt by that reality. He had *sworn* he would never gamble again, he had *sworn* he was not addicted but the evidence in the file proved otherwise and it was a total slap in the face for her to have to learn that fact from Apollo, who had all the sensitivity of a hammer blow.

'I had him investigated only as a precaution. I will not allow Patrick's difficulties to cause trouble between us. I tackled him today—in a *private* location, by the way—for your benefit and that of his partner,' Apollo informed her on a pious note that made his bride's teeth grit. 'Your brother has agreed to see an addiction counsellor and after her assessment he will follow the advice he receives. Otherwise his gambling debts will come back to haunt him—'

Pixie leapt upright in consternation. 'No, but you promised *me*!'

'The carrot and the stick approach *work*, Pixie,' Apollo cut in very drily. 'He needs a reason to reform and the child on the way is an excellent source of pressure on him to change his ways.'

'Holding that debt over him is so cruel, Apollo,' Pixie framed unevenly, grey eyes wide with stinging tears and accusation.

'He needs professional treatment and support. You are his sister, *not* his mother,' Apollo pronounced with finality. 'I won't change my mind about this, so don't waste your energy arguing about it.'

But Pixie already knew that she was unlikely to get anywhere arguing. Apollo was a steamroller, who travelled in a dead straight line and it was simply your bad luck if you lay in his path because he wouldn't deviate from his course.

Unhappily, his comment about her being Patrick's sister and not his mother lingered longest with Pixie, stirring up memories she would have sooner left buried. From an early age Pixie had been urged to look after her little brother. Her mother had *loved* Patrick in a way she had not seemed able to love her older child and that had stayed true right to the end of the older woman's life when she'd begged her daughter to always support her younger sibling.

As a child, Patrick had got treats, praise, affection and smiles from their mother while Pixie had been denied all of those things and left wondering what it was about her that made her less loveable. As she'd matured, however, she had come to suspect that her mother had been one of those women who would always have idolised her son in preference to her daughter, indeed who saw something almost magical in the mother-son bond from which she jealously excluded everyone else.

A knock on the door sounded and Apollo yanked it open and four little furry feet surged across the floor to boisterously attack Pixie's ankles. Damp-eyed, she bent down and lifted Hector, who was crazy happy to be reunited with her after a twenty-four-hour absence. He planted excited doggy kisses over her chin and made her reluctantly laugh as she petted him to calm him down.

'You need to get changed for dinner now,' Apollo informed her, gratified to have scored a coup by reintroducing the dog at the optimum moment. But then Apollo very rarely left anything to chance. He had planned that reunion as a soother almost as soon as he'd discovered that Patrick Robinson was still gambling because he had known that he had to confront his bride-to-be with the realities of the situation.

If you knew how to handle women, you could avoid conflict. Apollo had been smoothly and cleverly handling women since he was a child because his comfort had depended on the relationship he had established with his stepmothers. He avoided dramas with lovers in much the same style. An expensive piece of jewellery or a new wardrobe could work a miracle with an angry, resentful woman. Pixie, however, so far seemed infuriatingly indifferent to her new clothes and lifestyle but he had not yet had the chance to test her in that line. She could simply be faking her lack of interest, striving to impress him. He studied her tear-streaked face, the grey eyes soft now as she petted the tatty little dog she undoubtedly loved. He liked that she liked animals. It was the first time in a very long time that Apollo had actively *liked* anything about a woman and it shook him.

'You deliberately let me think that Hector and I were going to be apart for weeks,' Pixie condemned. 'Why did you do that? The carrot and the stick approach with me as well?'

Apollo shrugged. 'I dislike arguments. I knew you would be upset about your brother. Hector's your reward for accepting that I'm doing right by Patrick.'

Pixie's delicate frame went rigid. 'Stop trying to manipulate me, Apollo. If you want me to do something just face me with it. Try being honest for a change.'

Even barefoot she contrived to stalk out of the office to join the yacht steward waiting outside for her to show her to the master suite. On the trek there she was shown the gym, the medical centre, the sauna and steam room and the cinema. *Circe* was a massive vessel with four decks and seemed to contain everything Apollo might require to live on it on a permanent basis. He hadn't offered to give her a grand tour as she had somehow expected and now she scolded herself for imagining he might want to do something that normal. He didn't care what she thought of his yacht. He had to know that she had never been on a yacht before and was already utterly overwhelmed by the sheer opulence of her surroundings.

The huge stateroom with the massive bed, private deck and en-suite intimidated her but not as much as the stewardess who greeted her in perfect English as

'*Mrs* Metraxis' and asked her what she intended to wear. From the closets, Pixie picked out a black silky catsuit. So, she had to change for dinner now. Strange the traditions Apollo took for granted, she reflected helplessly as she tried not to let her gaze linger on the giant bed.

She was a bag of nerves but a couple of drinks would steady her, she told herself urgently. This was not the time to fall apart. Apollo wasn't going to hurt her. He wasn't going to attack her. In addition, he might be detached and she might only be a means to an end but he wasn't tactless enough to wrestle her out of her bra and then ask in a disappointed tone where her boobs had gone, as had once happened to Pixie. That experience, added to the guy who had told her that her lack of curves just didn't rev his engine, had been sufficient to kill Pixie's desire to get naked with a man simply to experiment. If truth be known she had envied Holly for the greater sexual confidence that had allowed her friend to sleep with Vito the first day she met him because Pixie knew that in the same circumstances she would have panicked and ended up saying no.

Only no wasn't quite an option with a wedding ring on her finger on their wedding night, particularly not with a male programmed to try and get her pregnant as fast as possible. She practised smiling in the mirror as she renewed her make-up and straightened her hair. She breathed in deep and strong as she dressed and tried not to fret at the trailing hems of the pant legs, which she had expected to wear with six-inch heels. The stewardess provided her with deck shoes and she thrust her feet moodily into them to be escorted to the dining saloon.

And there was Apollo awaiting her, resplendent in a tailored white dinner jacket and narrow black trousers that moulded long, powerful thighs, long black hair flaring round his lean, darkly handsome bronzed face. Gorgeous as a movie star and very, very sexy, she told herself bracingly, but complex as an algebraic equation to someone who had never got the hang of algebra.

She looked like a kid in the trailing pantsuit, Apollo reflected with hidden amusement. Why hadn't it occurred to her to wear something short? Her starlight eyes flickered with nervous tension over him and moved away hurriedly and he wondered why she was on edge because a woman expecting to share his bed had never been on edge with Apollo before. In fact most were enthusiastic, sparkling and downright impatient because he had a reputation for never sending a woman away dissatisfied.

He could see her nipples through the fine fabric because she wasn't wearing a bra and the tiny pouting shape of her breasts made him unexpectedly so hard that he ached, and he was forced to shift position to ease his discomfort while the wine was poured.

'How long will we be on the yacht for?' Pixie asked tautly.

Apollo shrugged, striking green eyes veiled. 'For as long as it takes us to get bored. I set up *Circe* to enable me to work wherever I am. We'll go to Nexos when we leave the yacht.'

'Nexos?'

'The Greek island my grandfather bought for the Metraxis family,' he extended. 'Of course, he had six children, of whom my father was the eldest, and the family was much bigger in his day. My father only had me. I have hundreds of cousins.'

'Didn't your father want any more children?'

'It wasn't an option. He eventually discovered that cancer treatment he had in his thirties had left him sterile. Had he had a check sooner, all his wives wouldn't have wasted their time pursuing fertility treatment,' Apollo admitted wryly. 'That's why I had the check.'

Pixie finished her first glass of wine and watched it being refilled by the silent waiter attending them. It unnerved her having a conversation with staff around but Apollo contrived to act as though they were alone.

The food was out of this world but Pixie felt that for all the enjoyment it was giving her she might as well have been eating sawdust. As the waiter left the saloon to fetch the dessert course, Apollo dealt her a frown. 'That's your fourth glass of wine.'

'You're counting?' she gasped in dismay.

'Should you be drinking at all with the project we have in mind?'

'I didn't think of that.' Pixie set her glass down. 'I don't know.'

'We have a doctor on board. I'll ask him. Aside of that aspect, I'm not having sex with you if you're drunk. That's something I would never ever do, regardless of whether or not we are married,' Apollo declared grimly.

Pixie reddened as if she had been slapped. 'I'm just a little nervous.'

Apollo stared at her with clear incomprehension. 'Why would you be?'

And Pixie knew that it was her moment to tell him the truth. After all, hadn't she urged him simply to be honest with her? Yet here she was covering up something very basic about her. But how could she tell a legendary womaniser that she was a virgin? He would think she was a freak or that no man had ever asked. It would be horribly humiliating. But worst of all, it would give Apollo a glimpse of her most intimate insecurities about herself and that was what Pixie couldn't bear. He would see her fear, her weakness, and he was ruthless and cold and he would use it against her, she thought wretchedly.

'Are you still hungry?' Apollo prompted softly.

'No,' she told him truthfully.

In a split second, Apollo rose from his chair and strode down to scoop her up out of hers, depriving her so thoroughly of breath and brain power that she merely stared up at him in astonishment. 'Time to make a start on that project, *koukla mou*,' he teased.

'You can put me down to walk.'

'I don't want you tripping and breaking a leg.'

'Of course…that would interfere with the project,' Pixie voiced for herself.

'I'm not that cold-blooded,' Apollo parried with a sudden husky laugh, glancing down at her with brilliantly striking green eyes. 'At this moment all I'm thinking about is that you're my wife and I *want* you.'

Pixie didn't believe that and an edge of panic infiltrated her. 'I'm not that experienced,' she told him abruptly.

Apollo smiled down at her, his wide sensual mouth tilting. 'How many guys?'

'A few,' she lied hastily, her face colouring, eyes veiling. 'I'm kind of fussy.'

Apollo liked being told that and rationalised that far from liberated thought with the reminder that she was his wife and naturally he didn't want a wife who had anything like his own track record. He knew that was sexist but it was the way he felt and it was a knee-jerk reaction that took him by surprise.

It was beginning to bother him that Pixie inspired such uncharacteristic urges. She was his wife but not a proper wife, he reasoned, merely the wife he had never thought he would have in the matrimonial step he had sworn never to take. And she was only with him in the first place because he had saved Patrick from the thugs her cowardly little brother had chosen to tangle with. It was a timely reminder but something visceral inside him denied that reminder because all of a sudden he discovered that he didn't like that either. He liked it much more when he looked down into Pixie's luminous grey eyes and read the same hunger that he was experiencing.

As he settled her down on the huge bed Pixie studied him, loving the strong angle of his jaw line, the starkness of his well-defined cheekbones and the classic jut of his nose, not to mention the lush black velvet sweep of his lashes shadowing those riveting emerald-green eyes. Looking at Apollo had the strangest intoxicating effect on her and her lips tingled as if in recollection of the kiss they had shared earlier.

He backed off a step and shed his jacket, embarked on his shirt and her heart started beating very, very fast inside her ribcage as he exposed the hard slab of his stomach and the incredibly defined muscles indenting his broad chest. He was drop-dead beautiful to her wide gaze. The shirt went flying. There was nothing inhibited about the speed with which he was stripping and she tried and failed to swallow as the trousers were unzipped and Apollo got down to boxers that revealed almost more than they concealed. He was already aroused, which shook and surprised her, indicating as it did that he did want her as he had declared he did.

But then, he clearly suffered from a high libido, she reminded herself, and possibly he was merely in the mood for sex and she was the only woman available. Yes, that made more sense to her. She would just be another nick on a bedpost already so full of nicks that hers would vanish into the woodwork. She tugged at the sleeves of her catsuit but he forestalled her, lifting her up in an infuriatingly controlling way to turn her round and unzip the garment, sliding it off her stiff shoulders, tugging it down with all the smooth expertise of a male who could have stripped a woman out of the most intricate clothing in the dark without breaking a sweat.

Pixie trembled. He had even blocked her attempt to get a little tipsy. She was way more sober than she had planned to be, having assumed that the alcohol would make her less nervous. As it was she only felt the very slightest buzz from the wine she had imbibed before he made sobriety sound like her bounden duty.

Apollo was both disconcerted and enthralled by her sudden silence and submissive attitude for it was not at all what he had dimly expected from her. 'I'm not remotely kinky in bed if that's what you're worrying about,' he told her with amusement.

Pixie gulped. 'I'm not the slightest bit worried,' she assured him.

'Then why can't you relax and trust me?' Apollo enquired lazily, his dark deep drawl having already dropped in pitch and the vowel sounds roughened.

In mortification, Pixie closed her eyes. 'I'd really prefer the lights out…'

'Not my preference but if that's what it takes, *koukla mou*.' Apollo reached up to stab a button above the headboard and the stateroom was plunged into darkness although soft light emanated from the lights still illuminating the private deck beyond the windows.

His wicked mouth descended on the slope of her neck and she shivered, a different kind of tension entering her now that he no longer had an alarmingly bright view of her physical deficiencies. She quivered as long fingers expertly teased her straining nipples.

'I'm very small there,' she pointed out, unable to resist a ridiculous urge to draw his attention to the obvious.

'I like it,' Apollo growled next to her ear, nipping at her ear lobe, sending another shot of uncontrolled response darting through her.

'Men always want more, not less.'

Apollo arched his hips and ground his pelvis against her thigh. 'Does that feel like I'm low on sexual interest?' he asked silkily. 'Now, be quiet.'

And Pixie shut her mouth because she was embarrassed by the inappropriate comments spilling from her lips. He rested her against the soft pillows and employed his mouth on her breasts, sending increasingly powerful streams of sensation down into her pelvis. Her hips rocked of their own volition and that shocked her. She could feel herself getting hot and damp there and that shocked her almost as much as her sudden desire to join in and explore him. Of course, she didn't have the nerve. She lay there like a felled statue, settling for being hugely grateful not to be on the edge of a panic attack.

Apollo was wheeling out his entire repertory of foreplay in an attempt to win the fireworks response he had craved from their first kiss. He had never gone so slowly in his life with a woman. He had never had to because usually they were all over him, egging him on to the final act as if afraid he would lose interest if it took too long to get there. He kissed a line down a slender arm and smiled. There was just nothing of her and he would have to be very careful not to crush her. He caressed a tiny foot, flexed the toes, revelling in the novelty of that fragile daintiness. She might be small but everything was in perfect proportion. As he skimmed down her panties he reached up, fingers closing into her golden hair to raise her head and claim her lips again.

A gasp was wrenched from Pixie as he nuzzled her lips with his, brushed them gently apart and then went in for the kill with his tongue and it was as if the top of her head blew off. When Apollo kissed her she literally saw stars and heavenly galaxies. With every caressing, darting plunge of his tongue her temperature rocketed and her still hands finally rose and plunged into the depths of his hair. Finally getting that response energised Apollo's hunger.

There was so much he wanted to do that he didn't know where to begin but he knew he wanted it to be an unforgettable night for her. Why it had to be that way with her he didn't know or care, but then he had always responded very well to a challenge and in many ways Pixie had challenged him right from the start. Unimpressed, cool, indifferent. For the first time in his life Apollo wanted a needy, clingy woman and he didn't understand the desire or where it was coming from.

He spread her legs and shifted down the bed. Pixie froze as if he'd suddenly put the lights back on. He wanted to do *that*?

'I don't think I want that,' she told him hastily.

'You'll be surprised,' Apollo husked, ready to rise to yet another challenge and embarking on the venture with a long daring lick that made her squirm and gasp again. Satisfied, he settled in to drive her crazy. He would be the very best she had ever had in bed or he would die trying. Lack of interest would become craving. Coolness would become heat. Unimpressed would become awed.

Apollo touched her with expert delicacy that she knew she couldn't object to although she couldn't imagine that he could possibly *want* to do what he was doing. He slid a finger into her damp folds and she almost spontaneously combusted in shock and excitement and that was nothing compared to the intense feel of his mouth on the tiny bundle of nerves at the apex of her. All of a sudden control was something she couldn't reclaim because her body had a will of its own. Her hips ground into the mattress below her, her heartbeat thundered and she was breathing so loud she could hear it while the growing tightness deep down inside her was impossible to ignore. She could feel herself, reaching, straining, while the ripples of excitement grew closer and closer together and then an almost terrifying wave of ecstasy gripped her and she was flying and crying out and moaning all at the same time.

'When you come the next time, I want you to say my name,' Apollo growled in her ear while her body still trembled in shock from the sheer immensity of what he had made her experience.

'Never felt like that before,' Pixie mumbled unevenly.

'It will *always* feel like that with me,' Apollo assured her with great satisfaction as he slid over her, tilting her hips up to receive him, and drove down into her with an uninhibited groan of all-male need.

Pixie jerked back in shock from the sharp pain that assailed her and yelped in dismay.

But Apollo had already stopped. He raised himself higher on his arms to instantly withdraw from her again and folded back at her feet, the sheet tangled round him. His lean, darkly handsome face was a mask of disbelief. 'You're kidding me?'

Pixie sat up with a wince because she was sore and way more conscious of that private part of her than she wanted to be. She was still in too much shock to think because she had long dismissed as an old wives' tale the concept of a first sexual experience hurting and had been entirely unprepared to discover otherwise.

'A...*virgin*?' Apollo gritted in much the same tone of

disdain as he might have mentioned a rat on board his superyacht.

Anger began to lace her growing mortification. 'Why did you have to stop?' she gasped, stricken. 'Couldn't you just have got it over with?'

'Like you know so much about it?' Apollo virtually snarled at her as he vaulted off the bed with the air of a man who couldn't get away quickly enough from the scene of a disaster. A little warning voice at the back of Apollo's volatile head was warning him to tone it down but he was genuinely furious with Pixie for wrecking something with her silence that he had been determined to make special. Special...*really*? Where had that goal come from inside him? *Why?* He didn't know but he was still furious about the bombshell she had dealt him when he'd least expected it.

'Maybe I should have warned you,' Pixie framed tightly, recognising that he was sincerely annoyed with her.

'There's no maybe about it!' Apollo thundered back at her. 'I *hurt* you and how do you think that makes me feel? I gave you every opportunity to tell me and you didn't.'

'I thought you'd laugh at me.'

Apollo shot her a narrowed green glance. 'Do I look like I'm laughing?'

Pixie swallowed hard, her face burning at his raw derision. Clutching the sheet to her bare skin, she felt about an inch high while she watched him striding into the bathroom, over six feet of lean golden-skinned enraged male.

What did *he* have to be so annoyed about? She hadn't thought of her body as his business until they got into bed but then suddenly, she registered, it *had* become his business. Discomfiture gripped her. He was accustomed to experienced women and probably feeling out of his depth after she'd yelped cravenly at one small jab of pain. Really, could she possibly have made more of a fuss? Was it any wonder that he was angry?

Guilt stirring, Pixie slid out of bed and pulled on his shirt, because it was the nearest item of clothing that would cover her. She breathed in the scent of him almost unconsciously and sighed because she had screwed up, made a mountain out of what would probably have been a molehill had she simply been a little more frank in advance. But being frank on such a personal topic was something Pixie had never contrived to be, even with Holly.

As she appeared in the doorway Apollo glowered at her from the shower, standing there naked and unconcerned, water streaming from several jets down the length of his big bronzed body. Pixie stared and flushed. 'I'm sorry,' she said grudgingly. 'I should've warned you.'

'But instead of warning me, you actually *lied*!' Apollo condemned emphatically, still struggling to work out why he was so angry when he very rarely got angry about anything. A virgin—very unexpected but scarcely a hanging offence. That she had lied to him annoyed him more because, most ironically, she was the first woman he had ever believed to be more honest than was good for her.

'I said sorry. There's not much more I can do,' Pixie launched back at him a little louder, her temper rising. 'What do you want? Blood?'

'Already had that experience with you,' Apollo derided smooth as polished glass.

And that crack was the last straw for Pixie and she lost it. Her fingernails bit into her palms as her hands fisted and she shot a look of loathing at him that startled him. 'You're just reminding me why I don't like men and *why* I didn't warn you,' she framed jerkily, formerly suppressed emotion surging up through her slight body in a great heady surge.

'And why would that be?' Apollo demanded, switching off the water, grabbing up a towel and stalking out of the shower.

'Because you're threatening and selfish and mean! I put up with far too much of that growing up!' she told him in a screaming surge. '*Men* trying to catch me with my clothes off when I was in the bathroom or the bedroom...*men* trying to touch me places they shouldn't... *men* saying dirty stuff to me...'

Apollo had seemingly frozen where he stood. Not even the towel he had been using to dry himself was moving. 'What men?'

'Care staff in some of the children's homes I stayed in, foster fathers...sometimes the older boys in the homes,' she related shakily, caught up in the frightening memories of what she had endured over the years before she'd reached Sylvia's safe house and then eventually moved towards complete independence. 'So, don't be surprised I was still a virgin! Sex always seemed sleazy to me and I'm not apologising for it. Not everyone's obsessed with sex like you are!'

Listening, Apollo had lost all his natural colour and much of his cavalier attitude. His bone structure was very stark beneath his golden tan. 'You were abused,' he almost whispered the words.

'Not in the strictest sense of the word,' Pixie argued defensively. 'I learned to keep myself safe. I learned that what they were doing was wrong. Nobody ever actually managed to *do* anything but it put me off the physical stuff...'

'Obviously...naturally.' Apollo snatched in an almost ragged breath and veiled green eyes rested on her. 'Go back to bed and try to get some sleep. I won't be disturbing you.'

Taken aback, Pixie stared without comprehension at his tight, shuttered expression.

'I'm sorry I hurt you.'

'It was only a tiny hurt. I just wasn't expecting it,' she muttered awkwardly, but she could see that even that little hurt and the surprise of it had been a complete passion killer as far as he was concerned.

Apollo strode back into the bedroom and she heard him rummaging through the drawers in the dressing room. Moments later he stepped back into view sheathed in tight faded denim jeans and a white linen shirt and, without even pausing to button the shirt, he strode out of the stateroom. So much for their wedding night, Pixie thought wretchedly. Getting into bed he had definitely wanted her, lusted after her, and what had preceded the final act had been fantastic. He had given her an ecstasy she had not known she was capable of feeling. But all too quickly she had blown it...

CHAPTER SEVEN

WHAT WERE THE ODDS? Apollo asked himself as he sat on deck swigging from a bottle of Russian vodka, his black hair blowing back from his lean darkly attractive features, his green eyes very bright. What were the odds that he would end up with a woman who had also been abused? Whose attitude to sex had been inexorably twisted and spoiled by experiences that had happened when she was too young to handle them?

Not only had he hurt her physically, he had also *shouted* at her. Half a bottle further on, Apollo padded barefoot over to the rail. His wife was a virgin and he had acted like an idiot. Why? He was an arrogant jerk proud of his sexual skill and finesse…why not just admit that? He had been so determined to give her the fantasy and it had gone pear-shaped because she hadn't trusted him enough to tell him the truth. And how could he hold that against her when throughout his whole thirty years of life he had never told anyone but his father what had happened to him? He knew about that kind of secret; he *knew* about the shame and the self-doubt and the whole blame game. And even though he had seen slivers of low self-esteem and insecurity and anxiety in Pixie it had not once occurred to him that she too could be something of a victim, just like him.

She had deserved better, much better than he had given her. He had treated her like one of the good-time girls he normally enjoyed, confident and experienced women who wanted fun and thrills in and out of bed and as much luxury and cash as they could wheedle out of him. That had suited him because it left him in complete control at all times. But he wasn't in control with Pixie and that seriously disturbed him. He was clever, he was normally cool and logical and yet instead of being delighted that his wife had never been with another man he had shouted at her.

And paradoxically he *was* delighted because something about Pixie brought out a possessive vibe in him and that vibe of possessiveness had lit up and burned like a naked flame the instant he'd married her. Furthermore, since she had had the courage to tell him something as personal as what she had spilled out in her distress in the bathroom, he really did owe her, didn't he?

Apollo wove his path rather drunkenly back to his stateroom where he tripped over the clothes Pixie had gathered up and left in a heap directly in line with the door. The racket he made hitting the floor and his yell of surprise yanked her out of her miserable thoughts with a vengeance.

Fumbling for the bedside light, Pixie switched it on and stared in wonderment at Apollo sprawled in a heap on the floor. 'What happened to you?'

'I got drunk, 'Apollo informed her with very deliberate diction.

'After a…a crummy night that makes sense.'

'Don't be all English and polite and nice,' Apollo groaned, raking a hand through his tousled black hair. 'I wasn't.'

'But then you're not English,' Pixie parried, marvelling at the vision of her very controlled new husband in such a condition. His green eyes had a reckless glitter that unnerved her a little. Sober, he was a lot to handle. Drunk, he could well be more than she could manage.

'Never been with a virgin before,' he confided. 'I wanted it to be perfect and then it went wrong and I was furious. My ego, my pride, nothing to do with you. I was a...' He uttered a four-letter swear word.

'Pretty much,' she agreed more cheerfully after hearing that he had wanted their wedding night to be perfect, which was a hearteningly unexpected admission when deep down in advance of the bed business she had feared that he would not care a jot. She relaxed her stiff shoulders into the pillows while she studied him and decided that even drunk he was heartbreakingly gorgeous.

'My second stepmother beat me with a belt and left me covered with blood,' Apollo announced out of the blue.

Her jaw dropped. 'How old were you?'

'Six. I hated her.'

'I'm not surprised. What did your dad do?'

'He divorced her because of it. He was very shocked... but then he was sort of naïve about how cruel women can be,' Apollo told her as he drank out of the bottle still clutched in one big bronzed hand, lean muscles rippling to draw her attention to the intricate dragon tattoo adorning his arm. 'He didn't appreciate that *I* was the biggest problem in his remarriages.'

'How?' Pixie asked, wondering if she should try to get the bottle off him or just close her eyes to it. He wasn't acting like himself. He might hate her tomorrow for having seen him in such a vulnerable mood.

'When a woman marries a very rich man *she* wants to be the one who produces his son and heir but I was already there and the apple of my father's eye.'

'By the sound of that beating you got, he wasn't looking after his apple very well.'

Apollo closed his eyes, black lashes almost hitting his cheekbones. 'He married my third stepmother when I was eleven. She was a very beautiful Scandinavian and the only one who seemed to take a genuine interest in me. Never having had a mother, I was probably starved of affection.' His shapely mouth quirked. 'She would come and visit me at school and stuff. My father was very pleased and encouraged her every step of the way.'

'So?' Pixie prodded, sensing the tripwire coming in the savage tension bracketing his beautiful mouth, the warning that all could not have been as cosy as he was making it sound.

'Basically she was grooming me for sex. She liked adolescent boys…'

'You were eleven!' Pixie condemned. 'Surely you weren't capable.'

'By the time she took me to bed I was thirteen. It went on for two years. She took me out of school to city hotels. It was sordid and deviant and I was betraying my own father but…*but* she was my first love and I was fool enough to worship the ground she walked on. I was her *pet*,' he completed in disgust.

Pixie leapt out of bed and darted across the floor to kneel down in front of him. 'You were…what age?'

'Fifteen when I got caught with her.'

'For two years a perverted woman preyed on you.'

'I wasn't even her only one,' Apollo bit out in a slurring undertone. 'She'd been meeting up with the son of a local fisherman on the beach. It was *his* father who went to mine and tipped him off about what she was like.'

Pixie shifted until she was behind him and wrapped

her arms round his rigid shoulders. 'You were just a kid. You didn't know any better.'

'I definitely knew it was wrong to have sex with my father's wife,' Apollo broke in curtly. 'I don't deserve forgiveness for that but he still forgave me.'

'Because he loved you,' Pixie reasoned. 'And he knew his wife was using you for her own warped reasons. I'm so sorry I called you a man whore. You had a really screwed-up adolescence and of course it affected you.'

Apollo reached behind himself to yank her round and tumble her down into his lap. 'I never told anyone about that before…until you told me tonight about growing up in care with men trying to hit on you or spy on you or whatever,' he mumbled into her hair, the words slurring. 'Now I think I need to go to bed before I fall asleep on top of you, *koukla mou*.'

Pixie got up and removed the bottle while he stripped where he stood and, only staggering very slightly, fell like a tree into the bed. He slept almost immediately and she watched him in the half-light for long minutes, thinking how wrong she had been about him once and how much better she now knew him. Yet with what he had revealed he seemed more maddeningly complex than ever and without a doubt the man she had married in a business arrangement absolutely fascinated her. She brushed his tumbled black hair back from his brow and slid into the other side of the bed, hesitating only a moment before edging closer to take advantage of Apollo, whose natural temperature seemed to be the equivalent of a furnace.

She surfaced to dawn very, very slowly, the insistence of her body awakening her to a sweet flood of sensations. It was still so novel for her to feel such things that she knew instantly it was Apollo touching her and just as quickly she relaxed. Her nipples had tightened into needy little buds and the delicate place where his clever fingers were playing was embarrassingly sensitive and wet.

'You awake now?' he prompted gruffly in her ear.

'Yeah…' she framed weakly, her hips moving all on their own because the magical way he touched her made her ache, need and want all over again.

Apollo shifted over her, all rippling muscle and ferocious control. Green eyes glittered down at her, his lean, strong face taut and dark with stubble. She felt him at the heart of her and anxiety screamed that there was too much of him for what little there was of her so it was a struggle to force herself not to stiffen. Fortunately, he went slow—achingly slow—and she gradually stretched around his fullness, tender tissue reacting with unexpected pleasure to the source of that amazing friction. He shifted his hips, moved and a rush of exhilarating feelings engulfed her and her head fell back, eyes wide with surprise.

'Didn't want to give you the chance to get all nervous again,' Apollo admitted. 'Like it was likely to be some sort of punishment.'

'Definitely…*not*…punishment,' she gasped breathlessly, her body rising to meet the gathering power of his, excitement pooling like liquid fire in her pelvis.

'Just sex,' he told her.

And had she still had breath to disagree she would have done but she couldn't breathe against the rising tide of intoxicating excitement. Little undulating tingles of intense arousal were travelling in tightening bands through her trembling length. He was inside her and over her and nothing had ever felt that good or that powerful. Apollo smiled down at her, a smile ablaze with male satisfaction and, for once, she didn't mind his assurance. He gathered up her legs and angled her back, rising higher, thrusting faster, deeper, forcing little moans and cries from her parted lips that she couldn't hold back. The excitement intensified, sensation tumbling on sensation until a sensual explosion detonated deep within her and she went flying high and free on an electrifying surge of pleasure.

Apollo groaned his appreciation into her hair and she wrapped her arms round him. It was automatic, instinctive, something of a shock when he broke immediately free and imposed space between them. His lean, darkly handsome face had shuttered. 'I can't do that stuff,' he muttered semi-apologetically, his beautifully shaped mouth momentarily rigid with tension.

And Pixie forced a smile she didn't feel and shifted back in turn because she got it, she really did get it after what he had explained the night before. A child crying out for maternal affection, initially given it only to discover that it was an evil deception being utilised to gain his trust and love.

She swallowed the thickness in her throat and fought a very strong urge to hug him. He was the only man who had ever had that much power over her and momentarily it scared her. Sometimes Apollo made her want to kick him very hard and then equally suddenly she wanted to put her arms round him instead, even though she knew he didn't want that, couldn't handle that... It wasn't only her body he could make fly out of control: somehow he was reaching her emotions as well, and she knew that was dangerous and she tensed.

Apollo was intensely uncomfortable for a male accustomed to feeling at home in virtually every situation. He very rarely drank to excess and when he did he could still control his tongue, yet inexplicably he had lost control the night before and confided his deepest secrets. He understood that her experiences had reanimated memories he had suppressed and that that had destabilised him but that didn't mean he had to like his own weakness. He really didn't like that sudden feeling of being exposed and vulnerable because it reminded him too much of his lost childhood. For that reason it felt good to have a distraction available.

'I've got something for you,' he told her, reaching into the drawer by the bed to produce the jewellery case he had stashed there several days before. Apollo always thought out everything well in advance, preparing for every eventuality if he could. And she *deserved* a gift much more than the women who usually shared his bed.

The wedding night, after all, had been pretty much disastrous and his getting drunk and telling all in such a girly fashion, Apollo reflected grimly, had crowned the disaster. She had tolerated it all and in spite of everything that had gone wrong she had still lain back trustingly for him to claim her body even though she had feared that consummation.

Taken aback, Pixie stared down in astonishment at the case and then carefully opened it. A breathtaking bracelet ran in a river of glittering diamonds across the velvet inset. 'For me?'

'Wedding present,' Apollo pronounced with relief as he leapt out of bed with alacrity and headed for the shower, convinced that he had done the very best that he could to be thoughtful and decent.

'It's gorgeous and I suppose I need some jewellery to make me look like a proper rich wife,' Pixie murmured uncertainly, battling to rise above hurt feelings she knew she had no right to experience. 'But this was a bad time to give it to me.'

Apollo's long lashes fanned down in disbelief and

he gritted his white teeth before he swung back to her. 'How so?'

Pixie contemplated him as he stood there, buck naked, bronzed and very Greek godlike in his physique. He was without a doubt the most physically beautiful male she would ever be with but, time and time again, he confounded her and wounded her. 'I'm not some whore you have to pay for a one-night stand.'

'I've never been with a professional,' Apollo said icily. 'I gave you a gift. Thanks would have been the appropriate response.'

'It's just the way *this* makes me feel,' Pixie began, struggling to verbalise what she didn't quite understand herself.

'We have a business arrangement,' Apollo shot back at her unapologetically. 'Think of it as business.'

'I can't think of my body as business. I'm not sure what that would make me,' Pixie admitted unhappily. 'But I need more respect than you're giving me if we're going to be stuck together like this for months. I don't think that's too much to ask. Obviously you can't even bring yourself to put your arms round me after sex. I'm not going to turn clingy or needy, Apollo. I'm not about to fall in love with you or the things you can buy me either. I know this marriage isn't real.'

A whine sounded from below the bed.

'Shush, dog,' Apollo groaned in raw frustration. 'You've been walked, you've been fed and watered. Stay out of this…she's enough to handle without your input.'

Pixie had to bite her tongue not to comment on the reality that she had overlooked her beloved pet's needs and Apollo had not. Instead she forced herself to continue. 'Couldn't we try friendship if we can't have anything else that might make you feel threatened?'

Apollo flung back his arrogant dark head and green eyes radiated emerald fire in the sunlight. 'You do *not* make me feel threatened.'

Pixie surrendered and said exactly what was on her mind. 'Don't punish me because you talked too much for your own comfort last night.'

And there it was in a nutshell, what Apollo Metraxis absolutely couldn't *stand* about Pixie. Somehow, *Thee mou*, she saw beyond the surface and saw right *through* him and it was the most unnerving experience he had had in many years. Without another word, Apollo strode into the shower, hit every dial, turned up the pressure and refused to think by blanking out everything, a trick he had learned as a child to stay in control. He held himself straight and taut until the confusion and bewilderment and seething frustration drained fully away with the swirling water.

Suppressing a groan of equal frustration, Pixie tunnelled back down into the bed and made no objection when Hector jumped up to tuck himself in next to her body. Hopefully Apollo would think she was sleeping in. Instead of sleeping, however, she was counting pluses, a habit she had formed as a child to make a grey day look sunnier. Number one, she enumerated, they had done the sex thing and it had been…amazing. Number two, Apollo was damaged but at least he had explained why, even if he did regret it. Number three, he was *trying* to make the marriage work but he hadn't a clue how to meet such a challenge. Female partners who whooped over his financial generosity and who only lasted for a two-week session of nightly sex didn't provide a man with much of an education on how to make a woman feel happy, respected and secure. Was she expecting too much from him? This was supposed to be a business arrangement, she reminded herself ruefully. Maybe *she* was being unreasonable...

Pixie breakfasted alone on the polished deck with Hector at her feet: Apollo was working. He had *phoned* her to make that announcement in a very detached voice that suggested he suspected he could be dealing with a potential screaming shrew. As far as avoidance techniques went, Apollo had nothing whatsoever to learn. When her phone went off again she answered it unhurriedly, assuming there was something he wished to tell her, but this time it wasn't Apollo, it was Holly.

'Vito and I are flying out to join you this afternoon!' Holly exclaimed excitedly. 'What do you think?'

Pixie rolled her eyes. 'The more the merrier,' she quipped, oddly hurt that Apollo had to bring in other people to create yet another barrier between them within a day of the wedding. Was she really that unbearable? She flexed her fingers against her flat stomach and prayed to get pregnant *fast*. The sooner she and Apollo escaped the situation they were in and separated, the better it would be. If they weren't living together and sharing a bed, it would be easier to stick to a businesslike attitude, she reasoned, wondering why her heart now felt as heavy as lead.

'We're all heading to some nightclub on Corfu tonight,' Holly told her. 'Of course, you'll already know that...sorry, I'm talking a mile a minute here.'

Quite unaware that yet another attempt to please Pixie had bombed dismally, Apollo stayed in his office on board until he got word that their guests were arriving.

'I promise not to ask any awkward questions,' Holly whispered as she settled on the end of the bed in Apollo and Pixie's stateroom. 'But you don't look happy and I can't imagine we'd be getting hauled in last minute if you were. Am I allowed to ask about that?'

Pixie grimaced. 'No. I'm sorry.'

'No need to be sorry but you sound attached…and the weird thing is Apollo is sounding attached too—'

'No, that's definitely not happening,' Pixie cut in with confidence.

'Apollo told Vito he wanted us here because he thought it would please you. Vito's never known him to make that much effort for a woman.'

Unimpressed, Pixie shrugged and watched Holly pet Hector while Angelo explored the room in the vain hope of finding something to play with. Bending down, she scooped her godson up intending to get reacquainted with the adorable toddler.

'So, what are you wearing tonight?' Holly prompted, taking the hint.

Relieved by the change of subject, Pixie showed off her outfit.

'My goodness, I'll look so old-fashioned next to you. What time are you getting your hair done?'

'I'm doing my own hair,' Pixie countered in surprise.

'You've got a beauty salon on board and you're *still* going to do it yourself?'

As soon as Holly had realised that Pixie hadn't even known the *Circe* had a full-time grooming parlour for guests and had commented bluntly on Apollo's deficiencies as a husband and a host, the two women set off on an exploration tour designed to satisfy both and entertain Angelo.

Hours later, after a convivial dinner during which Apollo contrived to ignore the reality that he had a wife seated at the same table, which resulted in Pixie going to even more extreme lengths to ignore him, Pixie emerged on the lower deck, fully dressed and ready to board the motor boat waiting to whisk them out to the island of Corfu.

Apollo studied his wife in consternation, his lean dark face taut and cool. 'I don't like the clothing,' he said baldly.

Vito actually flinched and walked Holly over to the deck rail several yards away.

Pixie jerked a narrow bare shoulder in dismissal of the comment. She wore a skintight cerise-pink leather corset and a fitted black pencil skirt with very high heels. It was young and hip and she didn't much care what he thought about it. 'You can command everything else, Apollo, but *not* what I wear. What's your objection anyway?'

His strong jaw line squared. 'You're showing too much of your body.'

'I've heard you've been seen with women who don't even bother with underwear.'

'You're different...you're my wife,' Apollo declared grimly. 'I don't want other men looking at my wife.'

'Tough,' Pixie commented with a combative glint in her grey eyes. 'You're a Neanderthal in a suit.'

'If we didn't have guests, I wouldn't allow you off the boat!' he growled half under his breath.

What a complete hypocrite he was! Pixie thought in wonderment, helpless amusement lacing her defiance. Apollo was a living legend for entertaining women who looked as though they had left half their outfit at home to maximise the exposure of their perfect bodies.

A couple of hours later, amusement had become the last thing on Pixie's mind. She was huddled in the luxury

VIP cloakroom of the club with Holly. 'I'm sorry you've been dragged into this,' she muttered apologetically.

'What? Watching Apollo behave badly? I shouldn't say it but it's his favourite pastime.'

Pixie tossed her head, golden blonde hair dancing round her shoulders, her piquant little face vivid with anger and mortification. 'I can behave badly too…'

Holly pulled a face. 'But provocation is not the road I would take with Apollo.'

Pixie, however, was past being polite and low-key and sensible. Since their arrival at the nightclub Apollo had been swamped by women. He was extremely well-known on the club circuit and he had not made a single attempt to deter the rapacious females trying to pick him up. Pixie had watched in wooden silence while other women pitched themselves onto her husband's lap, danced in front of him in very suggestive ways and squeezed up close to him. He had bought them drinks and chatted to them as if Pixie were the invisible woman and she had had enough of his treatment. She had also learned why he made no effort with her. From what she could see by the over-eager girls surrounding him, Apollo had never *had* to make an effort. He was very hot and very rich and acting like a kid let loose in a candy shop was the norm for him.

Pixie took her cocktail over to the VIP rail and watched the dancers because she loved to dance. Much good it was doing her though, she reflected moodily, wincing at the high-pitched giggling travelling from their crowded table. She wanted to empty entire ice buckets over Apollo and then kick him from one end of *Circe* to the other. Friends, she had suggested mildly, and *this* was the answer he was giving her? And why did she care? Why on earth did she care? She glanced at him out of the corner of her eye and watched a woman run her fingers down his broad chest and her teeth clenched with something that felt very like rage.

'Would you like to dance?' a faintly accented and unfamiliar voice said from behind her.

Pixie spun round and found herself virtually eye to eye with a black-haired good-looking young man with very dark eyes and an Eastern cast of feature and she smiled. Vito had asked her to dance and she had said no, recognising pity when she saw it, and she had said no to Holly too, but a total stranger was a perfectly acceptable substitute for a husband who was ignoring her while simultaneously outraging her sense of decency.

'Yes, thank you…' Pixie acquiesced, noticing how all four of the bodyguards who had accompanied their party from the yacht all rose as one at a nearby table. With determination she smiled to let them know that she was pleased to have company and not in need of rescue.

'I am Saeed,' her companion informed her.

'I'm Pixie,' she said cheerfully, preceding him down the stairs, noting that two of Apollo's bodyguards were now taking up position at the edge of the dance floor alongside two large men of a similar look.

'Where's Pixie?' Apollo asked Holly abruptly.

'Dancing,' Holly announced somewhat smugly.

'With another man?' Apollo demanded with savage incredulity and he flew upright.

Vito sprang up as well and accompanied his friend to the rail that overlooked the floor below. 'You can't thump him. He holds diplomatic status and he's half your size. It would make you look bad.'

At his elbow, Apollo swore wrathfully in four different languages as he finally picked out his wife and her partner from the crowd. He watched Pixie wriggle her diminutive behind while her partner gripped her hips and drew her close. Blinding rage filled him as the other man bent his wife back in a dip that brought their bodies into intimate contact and he strode down the stairs with Vito flying to keep pace with him.

'He's an Arab prince…don't hit him and cause a scene!' Vito warned.

Apollo's powerful hands coiled into fists of fury. What the hell did Pixie think she was playing at? She was his wife and she wasn't allowed to let *any* other man touch her body! He never ever lost his temper, he reminded himself fiercely, but there she was, twitching every inch of that lithe, dainty little body and the Arab Prince wasn't the only one noticing that tight skirt and that fitted little top that showed the slope of her gorgeous breasts. In an almighty storm of rage Apollo acted in what for him was a very diplomatic manner. He stepped up behind Pixie and hauled her off her feet and threw her over his shoulder.

'She's my wife!' he grated down at the startled Prince, who was the same size as Pixie in her heels, which wasn't very tall, and with that clear announcement of his God-given right to interfere Apollo strode off for the exit.

It took several annoying seconds for Pixie to realise what was happening but she instantly recognised Apollo's scent. She pounded his back with clenched fists and screamed at him full volume, 'What the hell do you think you're doing? Put me down right this minute!'

His bodyguards studiously not looking near either of them, Apollo stuffed his wife in the limo that would take them back to the harbour. Like a spitting cat, Pixie launched herself at him to try and get back out of the car again. 'I want to go back and join Vito and Holly!' she yelled.

Apollo drew in a deep shuddering breath and said as mildly as he could, 'You're going back to the yacht and if that's how you intend to behave when I take you out it'll be a long time before you get out again.'

'You can forget that option!' Pixie railed at him, frantically trying to get out of the other side of the car only to be foiled by the automatic locks. 'Let me out!'

'No,' Apollo decreed, temper moderated by the simple fact that he had her back again where she should be. 'You shouldn't have let him touch you like that.'

'Are you for real?' Pixie screamed at him. 'You've had women throwing themselves at you and pawing you all evening!'

Apollo shot her a riveting green glance of near wonderment. 'That approach works on other women…what's wrong with you?'

'What's *right* with me is that I'm not about to let you walk all over me!' Pixie hissed back. 'Anything you can do I can do too and I will. I'll throw myself at every man in my radius if it annoys you enough… I hate you, Apollo… I *hate* you!'

Apollo watched her stalk like a miniature warrior onto the motorboat and sit down as far as she could get from him. Marriage promised to be a great deal more challenging than he had ever appreciated, he conceded, still light-headed from the sheer amount of rage that had flooded him when he'd seen the Prince put his hands on her. How dared he? He gritted his even white teeth while he fought the lingering pulses of fury.

With a flourish intended to convey sarcasm, Pixie whipped off her shoes before she boarded the yacht. 'And we abandoned our guests on our night out,' she remarked in a stinging tone. 'Some hosts we make.'

'If you think Holly and Vito want to come back and find themselves in the middle of a marital spat, you're mental. They'll stay out until dawn,' Apollo forecast, grim-mouthed.

CHAPTER EIGHT

PIXIE SLUNG HER shoes across their stateroom in a gesture of frustrated fury. Apollo had acted like a total ass all evening and then somehow made a fool of her as if *she* were the one in the wrong? How was that fair? How was she supposed to forgive him for that? How was she supposed to cope with being married to such a maniac? So much for the business arrangement!

The door clicked open and Pixie spun. 'I'm not sleeping in here with you tonight.'

Apollo simply depressed the lock and studied her. 'You're not sleeping anyplace else.'

'You've got *ten* guest cabins. What is the matter with you?' Pixie exclaimed furiously. 'What do you want from me?'

Apollo surveyed her steadily, concealing his growing bewilderment at his own actions with difficulty. He had lost his head and he didn't ever do that.

'Are you going to answer me?' Pixie asked impatiently, one hand planted on her hip while her foot tapped cheekily on the floor.

He just wanted her. Somehow she was like a missing puzzle piece he had to have at any price. The sex had been amazing. It was the fireworks and the sex that attracted him. She was having the weirdest effect on him. Problem solved and sorted, he told himself stubbornly.

'Any time soon?' Pixie prodded in frustration. 'Like… tonight?'

Apollo unbuttoned his shirt for want of anything better to do. A knock sounded on the door and he answered it. Hector raced in, paused in horror at the sight of Apollo, gave him a very wide berth and shot trembling below the bed. Apollo locked the door again. 'You're my wife,' he told her finally, and as far as he was concerned at that moment that covered everything he needed to say.

Pixie was perplexed by that response. 'But not a real wife…'

'We're legally married, having sex and I'm trying to get you pregnant. How could it be any *more* real?' Apollo enquired. 'Tonight I felt married.'

Her smooth brow indented, grey eyes shimmering with indignation. 'Well, if that's how you behave when you're married, I wouldn't like to have been around when you were still single.'

'I wasn't expecting you to hit back,' he admitted with startling abruptness, his beautiful wilful mouth curling with a sudden amusement that enraged her even more. 'Clever move, *koukla mou*. Guaranteed to get a rise out of a guy as basic as me.'

Her breasts swelled temptingly over the top of the corset as she breathed in very, very deeply. 'You think it was some kind of strategy to get your attention back?' she shouted at him in disbelief.

'It worked,' Apollo pointed out drily. 'So, presumably it was deliberate?'

'No, it freakin' well wasn't deliberate!' Pixie launched at him, bending to scoop up a shoe and hurl it at him in furious rebuttal of that conviction. 'How dare you be so big-headed that you can think that?'

'I'll let it go this once,' Apollo murmured silkily. 'But if you ever let another guy touch you like that again you'll pay for it.'

'Threatening violence now?' Pixie questioned, scooping the other shoe and holding it like a weapon.

'No, you're rather more violent than I am. You've already punched me once and now you're throwing stuff at me,' Apollo pointed out deadpan.

Pixie threw the second shoe but he was quick on his feet and she missed. Hector started to whine below the bed.

'I can allow you to do a lot of things I haven't allowed a woman to do before, *koukla mou*,' Apollo intoned as he strode forward, 'but I really can't stand by and allow you to frighten that dog!'

Hauling her up into his arms, Apollo sat down on the bed. 'Settle down,' he instructed, pinning an arm round her to stop hers from flailing. 'You've got my full attention.'

'And now I don't *want* it!' Pixie yelled at him, so wound up with emotion she almost felt tearful over her inability to express herself.

'I'm afraid you're stuck with it,' Apollo told her, dropping his arm to frame her face with big controlling hands. 'I want you.'

'No!' Pixie snapped, striving to clamber off him again.

'You want me too, you just won't admit it,' Apollo opined in frustration.

'Do you ever listen to yourself? Marvel at the little megalomaniac remarks you make?'

His beautiful stubborn mouth claimed hers in a scorching kiss and her temperature rose like a rocket.

She felt hot, she felt faint, she spread her hands against his shoulders and, meeting shirt fabric, slid her fingers beneath the parted edges to find warm brown skin. His tongue dipped and plunged and one of her hands delved into his luxuriant black hair. As she knelt over him, he pushed up her skirt and ground her hips down on him. Suddenly she was achingly aware of the long hard thrust of him behind his zip. Liquid warmth surged between her thighs and she gasped, her nipples swelling and tightening. Yanking down the zip on her top, Apollo cast it aside and bent her slender body back over one arm to suck at a pretty pouting nipple, a manoeuvre that dragged an agonised moan from low in her throat.

'I'm not speaking to you!' Pixie exclaimed in consternation.

'Since when was speech required?' Apollo groaned, reaching with difficulty below her skirt to rip at the fragile lace of her panties and then touch her with frighteningly knowing fingers in the exact spot she could least resist.

'Apollo!' Pixie muttered furiously, helpless in the grip of the sensations flooding her and blaming him for the fact.

He met her shaken eyes and he smiled with sudden brilliance. 'I want you much more than I've ever wanted any other woman,' he breathed in a raw and shaken undertone.

Oh, the combination of that smile and those tantalising words, it left Pixie dizzy and without her conscious volition her arms slid round his neck and she leant against him, momentarily hiding her face, her thoughts in a messy whirl. *What's wrong with me? Why do I still want him? What happened to the anger?*

Lifting her head, she clashed with black-lashed gorgeous green and her heart gave a hop, skip and a jump as though he had hit a switch. And she told herself she couldn't *possibly* be falling for him. No, she was too sensible and not at all the type who would build herself up knowing she would only be broken down by the end of the relationship. It was lust, wild, wicked lust, and it was merely hitting her harder because she was a late developer.

Apollo stroked her, teased her tingling core, reducing her defences to forgotten rubble until all she wanted, all she craved, was for the ravaging, greedy hunger to be sated. He tipped her back, removed the tight skirt to the accompaniment of a ripping sound that implied damage, unzipped and came down on her without even undressing. 'Can't wait,' he growled. 'Have to have you now.'

He pushed into her with scant ceremony but that hard, driving fullness was absolutely what her body needed and desired just then. A cry of compliance left her lips, followed by an ecstatic sigh of gratification when he moved. He changed position to hit her at another angle and she jerked and moaned with pleasure, hearing herself, inwardly cringing for herself but wanting him and that feeling so powerfully she couldn't fight her own hunger. The waves of pleasure rolled faster and faster, the sensual power of him overwhelming. Her climax engulfed her like an avalanche driving all before it, emptying her of thought, breaking her down into a blissful bundle of pure satisfaction. In the aftermath she was weighted to the bed by Apollo and she decided she might never want to move again.

He scooped her up and slotted her into bed, kneeling over her to almost frantically wrench himself out of what remained of his clothing. That achieved, he crushed her mouth under his again. 'Hope you're not tired,' he breathed in a driven undertone. 'I think I could go all night...'

They were at peace again. Apollo told himself that that had been his ultimate goal but he already knew that what he craved most was the joy of sinking into her honeyed depths again. There was simply something about her, something that acted on him like an aphrodisiac. He wasn't going to think about it. Why should he? What was the point? Fabulous sex didn't need to be dissected: it simply *was*. Gritting his teeth, he slowly edged an arm round her and she didn't need much of an invitation after that. In fact she scooted across the divide between them and clamped to the side of him like a landmine, doing all the work for him, he conceded in relief.

'Women like hugs,' Vito had told him as if it were some great secret known only to the precious few. Apollo didn't like hugging women but he believed he could learn to pretend that he did...particularly if it encouraged sex, he reflected with a sudden wolfish grin. *Be nice,* Holly had told him without much apparent hope that he could possibly deliver on that suggestion.

But when it came to strategy, Apollo was very much on a level with Vito in business. He had misjudged his audience when he'd waited for Pixie to throw a jealous scene at the club, had actually felt pretty offended when she'd failed to deliver on that front but he wouldn't make that mistake again. No, he would listen and observe and learn until their marriage became much more civilised and both of them got what they wanted out of the arrangement. That was the rational approach and designed to provide the most desirable result, he reasoned with satisfaction.

While Apollo was deliberating with what he believed to be perfect rationality, Pixie was feeling as irrational as a bunch of dandelion seeds left to blow hither and thither in the wind. She had no guidance, no foundation stone for the strong feelings that assailed her when Apollo, apparently quite naturally, wrapped both arms tightly around her. He made her feel safe. He made her feel as if he cared. He made her feel as if she was indeed special. And even though the common sense in her hind brain was already sneering that she was nothing in comparison with the leggy, glamorous underwear models of the type he favoured, she was happy for the first time in a long time, happy instead of just getting through the day...

She decided she wasn't going to waste energy worrying or picking herself apart with self-loathing criticisms. He was right on one thing: she wanted *him*. And if their marriage was to work on any level they had to have that chemistry and use it accordingly. A lean hand smoothed down her spine and she quivered and stopped thinking altogether.

Apollo had already laid the trail and Hector was becoming an old hand at following treat trails.

The scruffy little animal crept out from his roofed hidey hole of a basket and snuffled up the treats, inching half under Apollo's desk while Apollo pretended to ignore his progress. Every week the little terrier dared to move a little closer to the male who terrified him—not that Apollo took that personally. Hector was uniformly terrified of every man that came into his vicinity and considerably more trusting of the female sex. He had first bonded with Pixie in the vet surgery where his injuries had been tended. Pixie had worked next door and, being friendly with the veterinary nurse, had often visited the homeless dogs in their cages. Although Pixie had worked and did not have a garden, the vet had deemed her a good prospective owner because Hector had taken to her immediately.

At least, though, Hector was rather more predictable than Pixie, Apollo conceded with a frown.

He could see that Pixie didn't really trust anything he said. It was as if she was fully convinced that he could never be anything other than a womaniser, as if she believed he carried some genetic flaw that made him unsuitable for any other purpose, and it was quietly driving him crazy. He had never met a woman so resistant to his attempts to change her mind about him. In bed, she was his perfect match, the only woman he had ever met as highly sexed as he was, but beyond that bedroom door she was blind to his best efforts. He tossed a squeaky toy across the desk in Hector's direction. He was expecting the dog to run away from it but Hector took him by surprise and pounced with apparent glee on the toy and pummelled it with his paws, seemingly pleased by the frantic squeaking that resulted.

Pixie stretched a daring toe out of the bed and slowly sat up, checking her newly unreliable body for the roiling wave of sickness that had attacked her on several occasions throughout the week. Even though she stood up equally slowly, that was still when the nausea hit and with a groan she raced for the bathroom. After a shower she got dressed, her stomach restored to normality again. Was she pregnant? If she was, she could only be at a very early stage and she doubted that she could already be suffering from nausea. Her hopes, after all, had been dashed after the first couple of weeks of their marriage passed and her cycle kicked in as normal. It had seemed incredible to her even then that all that sex hadn't led straight to conception. This time, however, her period was a little late but not late enough to risk raising false hopes, so she had said nothing to Apollo as yet.

A false alarm would be embarrassing but what was really bothering her was the disturbing suspicion that even if she *had* conceived she still wouldn't want to rush into telling him. And why would that be?

Pixie coloured as she pulled on shorts and a tee and then dried her hair. No, she still wasn't using the on-board beauty salon for that because she had always liked doing her own hair. She was using it for other services though, she conceded, glancing at her perfectly manicured nails and equally well-groomed brows. Apollo's wealthy lifestyle was slowly but surely overtaking the former ordinary informality of hers. It scared her to accept that she was becoming accustomed to wearing designer clothes and expensive jewellery. Apollo called it 'looking the part' and she had to agree that nobody would take their marriage seriously if she went around dressed like a beggar or a bag lady. But even so, sometimes she felt as though she was losing an essential part of herself and that would have to be her independence.

Of course, everything would change if she *was* pregnant, she told herself unhappily. Apollo would reclaim his previous life and return happily to acting like the biggest man whore in Europe. After all, once a pregnancy was achieved there would be no reason for him to stay with Pixie or settle for having only one woman in his life. There wouldn't even be a reason for him to share a bed with her any longer…it would be the effective end of their supposed marriage.

And there it was. The sad truth that lay at the heart of her anxieties. She was hopelessly in love with a husband who wasn't a real husband. She had learned so much about Apollo over the past six weeks and he was not at all like the playboy he was depicted as in the tabloids and on the gossip sites on the Internet. She had always wondered why he and Vito, who was rather serious in nature, were such close friends when at first glance as men they were so very unalike. And in temperament, family background and outlook they *were* very different but not anything like as different as Pixie had originally assumed.

Apollo supported loads of charities and the main one, she had discovered, was a charity for abused children. But the charitable cause possibly closest to his heart was an abandoned pets' sanctuary he had set up in Athens. On the Metraxis island of Nexos he had also established a therapy centre where the more damaged animals were rehabilitated and she couldn't wait to visit it and possibly pick up a few tips from the professionals there on how best to handle Hector's fear. It was hard facts of that nature that had begun to eradicate Pixie's former hostile distrust of Apollo.

Ever since that evening at the nightclub when they had both lost their tempers, the mood had changed between them. They had not been apart for even a night since then. Pixie's mouth quirked. She wasn't sure Apollo could get by one night without sex. Or that she could. Indeed the stormy fizzing passion they shared in bed thrilled her almost as much as it could still unnerve her. Naturally they still fought on occasion but in every way their relationship seemed so normal that it was a continual battle for Pixie to remember that their marriage wasn't really a marriage at all, but a business arrangement with the ultimate goal of conception and a very firm end date.

Her brother, Patrick, however, wasn't aware of those facts and brother and sister talked regularly on the phone. Since the wedding her brother had become more honest, finally admitting that he did have a problem with gambling. Patrick was now seeing an addiction counsellor and attending Gamblers Anonymous on a regular basis. Although Pixie had been furious when she'd realised that Apollo had confronted her brother about his issues without consulting her, she had changed her mind on that score, deciding that even though she hadn't liked Apollo's methods his approach had been the right one. After all, but for Apollo's intervention she wouldn't even have known that her sibling was still gambling. Furthermore, given advice and support, Patrick now had a much better chance of overcoming his gambling dependency and living a happier and much safer life.

It probably wasn't even slightly surprising that she had fallen so hard for Apollo, Pixie reflected ruefully. He was her first lover, her first *everything* and like any legendary stud he had buckets of charisma when he tried to impress. And that was what she couldn't afford to forget, Pixie reminded herself doggedly: Apollo was *faking* it for her benefit and his. Did he think that she was so stupid that she didn't know that?

Obviously every seemingly concerned or pleasant thing he had done around her was a giant fake!

After all, the stress and strain of a bad relationship could prevent her from getting pregnant while simple strife would keep her out of his bed. So, when she had dived off the top deck of *Circe* to surprise him because she was a very proficient swimmer and diver and Apollo had gone ballistic at the supposed dangerous risk he had deemed her to have taken, his evident concern for what might have happened to her couldn't possibly have been genuine. If she killed herself diving it would be inconvenient for him but with his resources and attraction he would quickly replace her, Pixie thought, miserably melodramatic in the mood she was in.

In the same way, the many trips they had shared, stopping off to swim and picnic in secluded coves and explore enchanting little villages on various Greek islands were not to be taken too seriously. Apollo enjoyed showing off the beauties of his homeland and was a great deal better educated than she had initially appreciated. She had discovered that he could give her chapter and verse on every ancient Greek or Roman site they came on. Her fingers fiddled restively with the little gold and diamond tiger pendant she wore. He had given her that a week after that nightclub scene, telling her that she was much more than a kitten with claws. Since she had scored his back in the heat of passion with her nails the night before he had given it to her she had laughed in appreciation. And that had annoyed Apollo, something she seemed to do sometimes without even meaning to, she acknowledged with regret.

But then, undeniably, Apollo was mercurial and volatile, passionate and outspoken and still in many ways a mystery and a contradiction to Pixie. He was a billionaire with every luxury at his command and yet he could picnic on a beach quite happily with a rough bottle of the village vino, home-baked bread and a salad scattered with the salty local cheese. He clearly loved dogs and could have owned a select pack of pedigreed animals without any need of therapy, but he had not owned a dog since childhood and seemed to prefer to spend his time trying to win Hector's trust. And Hector was the most ordinary of ordinary little terriers with the scrappy stubborn nature of his breed and he was extremely reluctant to change his defensive habits.

The door opened and Pixie scrambled up as her dog trailed after Apollo into the room. Hector wouldn't go *to* Apollo but he was quite happy to follow him at a safe distance. Clad in tailored chino pants and an open-necked black shirt, Apollo slanted her a reproving grin. 'What's with all this sleeping in every morning? You didn't join me for breakfast again,' he complained.

'Maybe you're wearing me out,' Pixie quipped.

His green eyes gleamed like jewels fringed by lush black lashes in his lean, strong face. 'Am I too demanding?' he suddenly asked with a frown.

And Pixie went pink, dismay assailing her because she had been teasing. 'No more than I am,' she muttered, her eyes veiling as she remembered wakening him up at some time of the night and taking thorough advantage of his lean, hard body to satisfy the need that never entirely receded in his radius.

Apollo wrapped a careless arm round her shoulders. 'I do like an honest woman,' he confessed with husky sensual recollection.

'No, what you like is being my only object of desire,' Pixie corrected, her body sliding into the lean, hard embrace of his as if it were programmed to do so.

He bent his dark head and claimed her bee-stung mouth with a hungry thoroughness that tightened her nipples and ran like fire to the heart of her and she trembled against his hard, muscular frame, suddenly weak again in a way she hated. She denied herself the desire to put her arms round him. She didn't want Apollo to know how she felt about him because that would inevitably make their relationship uncomfortable. Hadn't she promised him that she wouldn't turn clingy or needy? And that she had no intention of falling for him? Even worse, she thought painfully, she had truly believed she could deliver on those pledges of faith in his undesirability.

Her incredibly tender breasts ached with a mixture of oversensitivity and swelling desire when he crushed her to him with sudden force and for a split second she knew he could have done anything he wanted with her because she had no resistance and no longer any defences to fall back on to support her.

It was disconcerting when Apollo set her back from him in an uncharacteristic move of restraint. 'No,' he breathed in a fractured undertone. 'I came down to bring you up on deck. I want you to see the island for the first time as we come into harbour.'

And Pixie understood why he had backed off even though it did make her feel a little like an overdose of sugar being rejected by someone who had decided to go on a diet. In truth she had always accepted, she thought ruefully, that Apollo *could* resist her if he chose to do so and naturally that hurt her pride and her heart, but it was also a fact of life she had better learn to live with. After all, if she had already conceived she suspected their actual future as a couple could be measured in days rather than months.

Furthermore, the island of Nexos, the home of the Metraxis family for several generations, was hugely important to Apollo and probably one of the main reasons he had married her. Without a wife and a child he could not securely claim his heritage.

Pixie stood out on deck with the bright blue sky above her and the sun beating down while *Circe* powered more slowly than usual towards the island spread before them. Apollo slid his arms round her from behind and she leant back against him to be more comfortable, her keen and curious gaze scanning the pine trees edging the sandy beach at one end of the island and the rocky cliffs towering at the other. In the middle there was greenery and silvery olive groves and a fair-sized village climbing the hill behind the harbour—little white cube houses stretching in all directions while a little domed stone church presided over the flat land at the water's edge.

'It's beautiful,' she murmured dreamily.

'I didn't properly appreciate Nexos as my home until I thought about losing it,' Apollo intoned grimly. 'If I'd confided more in my father he would not have left that will as his final testament to me.'

'It doesn't matter now, not really,' Pixie reasoned, hopelessly eager to provide comfort when she recognised the emotional undertow of regret in his dark deep drawl. 'Maybe your father simply knew what bait to put on the hook.'

Apollo burst out laughing without the smallest warning and gazed down at the top of her golden head. 'I doubt if he appreciated you would be less than five foot tall and a hairdresser. A talented one though, I must admit, *koukla mou*,' he added, clearly worried that he had hurt her feelings and that she had interpreted that reminder of her more humble beginnings as a put-down. 'As bait you have proved as efficient as a torpedo under the water line.'

Destructive? Was that how he saw her? Was that because he had confided in her about his evil stepmothers? Or because he had shown her that he was as vulnerable as any other human being in childhood? And as amazingly loveable, she conceded wretchedly, worry dragging her down again along with the fear of the separation she saw waiting on the horizon.

CHAPTER NINE

'You SHOULD CHANGE before we disembark,' Apollo urged. 'The press will be waiting at the harbour.'

'The *press*?' Pixie emphasised, eyes flying wide. 'Why would they be waiting?'

'I issued a press release about our marriage last week,' Apollo admitted. 'They'll want a photo since I saw no reason to be that generous.'

'I thought Nexos was a private island,' Pixie admitted tautly, disconcerted at the prospect of camera lenses being trained on her for she had yet to be photographed in Apollo's company. That was undoubtedly because Apollo hated the paparazzi and knew exactly where to go to avoid attracting that kind of attention.

'It is but not as private as it was in my grandfather's day. The islanders need to make a living and my father began letting tourists in twenty years ago. I accelerated that process by building an eco-resort on the other side of the island,' he revealed calmly. 'The years of the locals getting by fishing and farming are long gone. Not unnaturally their children want more.'

'And even if that infringes on your privacy on your island you let them have it,' Pixie remarked in surprise.

'It doesn't infringe. The Metraxis estate is very secure but owning an island with an indigenous population comes with responsibility. The people have to have a future they can count on for their children or the younger generation will leave. My father didn't really grasp that reality.'

Pixie stepped into the motor launch twenty minutes later, clad in print silk trousers with a toning shirt worn over a camisole and a sunhat that she had to hang onto as the launch sped across the gleaming clear turquoise water into the harbour. She tensed when she saw just how many people seemed to be grouped there ready to greet them. It dawned on her that in her guise as Apollo's wife she probably seemed a much more important person to the locals than she actually was.

'Don't answer any questions whatsoever. Ignore the cameras,' Apollo urged, lifting her into his arms to carry her off the launch before she could make for the steps under her own steam.

Flushed and uneasy, Pixie regained her feet and Apollo's bodyguards swung into action to keep the photographers at a careful distance. With the indolent cool of a male accustomed to the press invading his privacy, Apollo dropped an arm round her shoulders and walked her off the marina at an unhurried pace. He exchanged greetings in his own language with several people but he did not once pause in his determined progress towards the four-wheel drive parked in readiness beyond the crush.

Pixie, however, had never been so uneasily conscious of being the centre of attention and she was hopelessly intimidated by the shouted questions and comments in different languages. She felt the wall of stares being directed at her and her tummy gave a sick lurch. She suspected that she had to be a pretty disappointing spectacle for people who had probably expected Apollo to marry an heiress or a model and, at the very least, someone famous, incredibly beautiful and photogenic. Possessing none of those gifts, she felt horribly exposed and all the more aware that she was a fake wife, pregnant or otherwise.

Only when they were inside the car did she breathe again.

'See…that wasn't so bad,' Apollo pointed out with a shrug that perfectly illustrated his indifference to that amount of concentrated interest and speculation.

'I'll take your word for it… I found it tough,' Pixie responded honestly. 'I'm not used to being looked at like that and knowing I am a totally phony wife doesn't add to my confidence.'

'When will you listen to me?' Apollo shot back at her in exasperation. 'You're my *legal* wife!'

Pixie breathed in slow and deep to calm her racing nerves and turned her head to look out of the car windows. Apollo had taught her that a legal wife still wasn't a *real* wife.

'And you will never leave our estate without bodyguards…is that understood? Not even for a walk down into the village,' Apollo specified.

'Is that level of security really necessary?' 'Our' estate, he had said, she noted in surprise, and then wrote it off as either a slip of the tongue or a comment designed to make her feel more relaxed about their living arrangements.

'There's always a risk of paparazzi in the village or even a tourist photographing you to make a profit. My security team are trained to handle all that and ensure that nobody gets to bother you.'

The car was travelling up a steep incline and electric gates whirred back while Pixie gazed at the big white rambling villa at the top of the hill. It was certainly large but it wasn't anywhere near as massive as Vito's giant palazzo in Tuscany and she was relieved. As she stepped out, one of the bodyguards lifted Hector's carrier from the four-wheel drive and set it down to release him. Hector raced out and gambolled round Pixie's ankles, relieved to have escaped his brief imprisonment.

They walked into a grand marble-floored space with staircases sweeping down on either side of the hall and a very opulent chandelier. A housekeeper, dressed in black with a white apron, greeted them and was introduced as Olympia. Apollo spoke to her at length in Greek while Pixie succumbed to curiosity and crossed the hall to peep into rooms. She had never seen so many dead white walls in her life or such bland furnishings. Indeed the interior had the appearance of a house that served as a show home.

Apollo frowned as he examined her expressive face. 'You don't like it? Then you can change it. I had it all stripped, painted and refurnished while my father was ill. Every one of his wives had different decorating ideas and favourite rooms and the house was a mess of clashing colours and styles. When he was well enough to come down for dinner I realised that the décor awakened unfortunate memories so I wiped the slate clean for his benefit.'

'Well, all that white and beige is certainly clean,' Pixie assured him gently, rather touched by his thoughtfulness on his ailing father's behalf.

'I'll show you round,' he proffered, walking her from room to room, and there really was very little to look at in the big colourless rooms. There were no photographs, no ornaments, only an occasional vase of beautiful flowers.

'I thought the house would be much larger,' she confided as he walked her upstairs. 'Holly said you had a lot of relatives.'

'Relatives and friends use the guest cottages behind

the house. My grandfather and my father preferred to have only family members lodge in the actual house. Vito and Holly stayed here with me for the funeral because Vito is the closest thing I have to a brother,' he admitted quietly, his handsome mouth quirking. 'But don't go repeating that or he'll get too big for his boots.'

Pixie laughed as he showed her into a spacious bedroom with a balcony running the entire length. The pale curtains beside the open doors streamed back in the breeze coming in off the ocean. She stepped outside to appreciate the incredible bird's eye view of Nexos and the sea and understood exactly why Apollo's grandfather had chosen that spot to build his family home. 'It is really gorgeous,' she murmured. 'But this place could definitely do with some pictures on the walls and other stuff just to take the bare look away.'

'The canvases are stored in the basement but run it by me before you have anything rehung,' Apollo countered. 'There are portraits of the ex-wives, which I have no desire to see again…and certain artworks fall into the same category,' he completed tight-mouthed.

Pixie rested a tiny hand on his. 'This is your home. The ex-wives are gone now and won't be coming back, so forget about them.'

Apollo bit out an embittered laugh. 'Only if I contrive to produce a child…and who knows whether or not that will be possible?'

Pixie pinned her lips together and stared out to sea and then she couldn't hold the words bubbling on her tongue back any longer. 'There may be a slim chance that this month…well, don't go getting excited yet *but* I am a little late…'

Apollo stared down at her transfixed by even the slender possibility that she had outlined. 'And you didn't even mention it to me until now?' he demanded in seething disbelief.

'Because we don't need to put ourselves through some silly false alarm, do we?' Pixie appealed.

Apollo shook his head as if he couldn't identify with that attitude. His black hair blew back from his lean bronzed features as he leant back against the glass barrier, his green eyes jewel bright in the sunlight. He dug out his phone, stabbed buttons with impatience and started talking in fast Greek while she watched, frowning in bewilderment.

'Dr Floros will come up with a test for us this afternoon.'

'But I'm only a couple of days late,' Pixie protested.

'Even *I* know that that's usually soon enough to tell us one way or the other,' Apollo pronounced. 'Why sit around wondering any longer?'

Well, you chose to open your big mouth and spill, Pixie censured herself unhappily. He would either be very pleased or very disappointed. It was out of her hands now.

'You have to learn the habit of *sharing* these things with me,' Apollo breathed in an almost raw undertone, green eyes veiled and narrowed as he stared down at her.

'Didn't I just do that?'

'Obviously you've been thinking about this on your own for a few days and that's not how I want you to behave, *koukla mou*. The minute anything worries you bring it to me.'

But even as Apollo gazed down at Pixie, his big frame was stiffening and he was losing colour because ill-starred memories were being stirred up by their predicament. He had quite deliberately closed out the awareness that sometimes women died in childbirth: his mother had. More than once his father, Vassilis had discussed that tragedy with his son. Vassilis had idolised Apollo's mother and he had never really come to terms with losing her in such terrible circumstances. At the moment when he should have been happiest with his wife and his newborn child he had been plunged into grief.

'What's wrong?' Pixie asked abruptly, watching sharp tension tighten the sculpted lines of Apollo's lean, hard face.

'Nothing. I forgot,' Apollo said equally abruptly, 'I have a couple of work calls to make. Will you be all right settling in here on your own?'

'Of course I will be.'

Apollo strode down the stairs like a hungry lion in search of prey. If Pixie was pregnant, there would be no home birth, he reasoned with immediate resolve. No, she was going to a fully equipped hospital regardless of how she felt about that decision. He would also engage a standby medical team. He wouldn't take any risks with her because he was too conscious that something quite unexpected could happen during a birth. He wouldn't mention that to Pixie though. He wasn't that stupid. He didn't want her worrying and certainly not to the extent *he* was suddenly worrying.

For a split second he was grudgingly amused by his own attitude. He had married Pixie to have a child and now that there was a chance they might have succeeded at step one, he was suddenly awash with anxiety. She was so small…and the baby could be big as he had been… and now he needed a drink.

By the time Pixie had watched her luggage being unpacked, enjoyed a cup of tea on the shaded terrace alone and even taken Hector for a walk through the meandering gardens with tree-lined paths alone, she had accepted that Apollo was not as excited by the concept of becoming a father as she was excited about becoming a mother. He had vanished like Scotch mist and she felt that they did not have the kind of marriage that empowered her to go looking for him as a normal wife might have done. Looking for Apollo any place struck Pixie as clingy and she refused to act clingy.

Dr Floros arrived, middle-aged and bearded and relentlessly cheerful even in the face of Apollo's grave demeanour. Yes, Apollo had finally reappeared and Pixie could not help but notice that her husband was as grim as a pall-bearer in comparison to the chirpy medical man. Maybe the actual prospect of a child was a little sobering for a playboy, Pixie reasoned uncertainly as she took the test and vanished into the palatial cloakroom on the ground floor. It would be foolish of her to think that he had lost his original enthusiasm for conception. That wasn't possible, was it?

'My wife is very small in size,' Apollo remarked to the doctor while Pixie was absent.

'Nature has a wonderful way of taking such differences into account,' Dr Floros assured him without concern. 'I'll take a blood test as well if the result is positive.'

Pixie watched the test wand change colour, but since the packaging and instructions were in Greek she had no idea what was a positive and what was a negative and had to return in continuing ignorance to the two men.

Dr Floros beamed before she even reached them. 'Congratulations!' he pronounced in English.

Pixie felt a little dizzy at the confirmation that she was going to be a mother and she sat down hurriedly, her attention locked to Apollo's lean, strong face. He froze, betraying nothing, neither smiling nor even wincing in reaction and she wanted to slap him for it. Apollo explained about the blood test and Pixie stood up a little nervously because she didn't like needles. Indeed Dr Floros only got as far as flourishing his syringe before Pixie felt faint, her knees wobbling so obviously that Apollo gripped her to steady her.

'Are you all right?'

And no, she wasn't all right because at that point she fainted and resurfaced lying on a sofa.

'Don't look at the needle…' Apollo urged, quick as always to identify the source of her fear, and he crouched down beside her and held her hand as tightly as if she were drowning.

The test was done. She apologised to the doctor and he said it was probably the combination of the good news and stress that had made her pass out. Dr Floros departed and Apollo reappeared with Olympia carrying a pot of tea.

'You could say something now,' Pixie prompted when they were finally alone.

Apollo frowned. 'About what?'

'Well, it did only take us six weeks…you could look happy, look *pleased*!' Pixie emphasised in annoyance.

'I am pleased,' Apollo assured her unconvincingly. 'But not if it makes you ill and you collapse like that. That was scary.'

'I didn't exactly enjoy it. I hate needles and injections and I felt so dizzy and then everything went dark,' Pixie explained rather curtly. 'I'm not about to be ill. I'm simply pregnant and there are a few symptoms that come with that. Dizziness is one of them. Holly was always getting light-headed.'

'Luckily we have a lift, so you won't have to use the stairs.'

Pixie studied him in wonderment. 'You expect me to use a lift to go up or down one floor? Are you crazy?'

'You could *fall* on the stairs,' Apollo traded with deadly seriousness.

'Thank you, Mr Cheerful.' Pixie rested her head back and tried to imagine becoming a mother. She wasn't about to let Apollo's strange lack of enthusiasm take the edge off her sense of joy and achievement. A baby, a darling, gorgeous little baby who was hers *and* his. She couldn't keep Apollo but she *could* keep their baby. She was happy, really, really happy about that aspect and suspected it would be something of a comfort in the future when Apollo was no longer a constant part of her life.

There would be a divorce first, she reminded herself doggedly. Then she would have to get accustomed to seeing him with other women in tabloid pictures, knowing he was sharing a bed with them while also knowing exactly what he was doing with them there. Doubtless he would phone her to keep up to date with their child's development and from time to time he would visit in person until the child was old enough to go and visit him. It would all be very civilised and polite but she was already painfully aware that losing Apollo would smash her heart to smithereens!

Apollo studied the tears rolling down Pixie's cheeks as she stared up at the ceiling. She wasn't happy about being pregnant and he wondered why he had expected otherwise. She liked kids, he knew she did, but then they weren't having a child in the most ideal circumstances, he reminded himself grimly. She was having a child she would pretty much raise alone and possibly she felt trapped because at her age most women were young, single and free as the air.

A chilling shot of rage assailed Apollo at the image of

Pixie reclaiming her freedom after a divorce and becoming intimate with another man. He had the strangest possessive feelings where she was concerned, he conceded in bemusement. For some reason too he was feeling as exhausted as if he had climbed a mountain. Somehow Pixie being pregnant was incredibly stressful. No, worse than stressful, *frightening*, he adjusted in consternation. For the first time it occurred to him that Vito had been saved from such concerns by only entering his son Angelo's life when the baby was already six months old. Was it normal for a first-time father to feel on the edge of panic? He crushed the reaction and went into denial.

'By the way, we're having a big party here in a few weeks,' Apollo announced in a determined change of subject. 'I organised it last month.'

'Thanks for sharing *after* the event,' Pixie said sarcastically.

'I've invited friends and family here to celebrate our marriage but I didn't fancy a wedding-type event,' Apollo confided with a cynical twist of his mouth. 'I settled on a fancy-dress party for a theme.'

'Oh, joy...' Pixie mumbled sleepily as she turned her face into a cushion, presenting him with her narrow back.

'I've taken care of our outfits,' Apollo told her with pride, relieved she would not be put to the worry of wondering what she should wear and very much hoping that she would appreciate the amount of trouble he had gone to.

'Your way or the highway,' Pixie whispered unappreciatively. 'Don't worry. I knew what a control freak you were the day I married you.'

Apollo surveyed Hector, who was seated on the rug, his little face seemingly anxious. *You and me too, buddy,* Apollo thought wryly while he wondered if it was possible that Pixie could roll off the sofa and hurt herself while she slept. For the first time in his life concern was weighing him down like a big grey cloud closing out the sun. He had never truly had to worry about anyone but his father but now he had a wife and a child on the way. He thought it extraordinary that achieving the pregnancy required to fulfil the terms of his father's will should suddenly and quite inexplicably feel, not like a prize, but more like a poisoned chalice.

Apollo came to bed in the early hours. Having persuaded herself that he might not even choose to still share the same room, Pixie was lying sleepless watching the moon-light glimmer through the shadows. She listened to him in the shower, watched him stride naked towards the bed and sensual heat curled low in her body because she could see that he was aroused.

Apollo slid quietly into bed and lay there, thoroughly irritated by the throbbing at his groin. Pixie was pregnant, fragile and definitely *off-limits*. But it was as if she had lit a fire in him the first time they had had sex. It was a fire only she could seem to cool and that knowledge se-riously disturbed him. Throughout his adult life Apollo had viewed sex as a casual diversion from more impor-tant activities. Sex had always been easily available and his libido had never homed in on one particular woman. His life had been wonderfully simple, he reflected grimly. He would see a woman he wanted, enjoy her for a while and when he got bored move on to the next. And now, for some peculiar reason, he wasn't getting bored any more…and he was feeling urges he had no desire to feel.

Pixie shifted across the bed inch by inch, wishing it weren't quite so big. Her hand settled on the male shoul-der furthest from her and slowly drifted down over Apollo's magnificent torso. She smiled as she felt his hard muscles ripple and tense across his abdomen.

He turned towards her and his eyes glittered in the moonlight. 'We shouldn't,' he breathed with sudden amusement.

'Don't be silly,' Pixie whispered, her tiny hand heading further south to find the long, jutting length of him and stroke. 'I'm pregnant, not breakable.'

Apollo groaned out loud and arched his lean hips while watching her slide below the sheet to administer an even more potent invitation and that fast his once renowned self-control broke like a dam breaking its banks. He tugged Pixie up to him with shuddering impatience and rolled her under him while his hungry mouth tasted hers with heated urgency.

'That's more like it,' Pixie commented a shade smugly as she gazed up at him, her fingers skimming caressingly through his damp, tousled hair. She felt lighter than air at the ego-boosting confirmation that he still wanted her. Intelligence warned her that he was a young healthy male, who was usually in the mood for sex, but she refused to think about that angle, choosing to concentrate instead on the soothing conviction that pregnancy wasn't quite the turn-off she had feared.

'There is only one way this can continue,' Apollo decreed, resting her back against the pillows. 'You lie there... *I* do the work, *koukla mou*.'

And it was amazing, she thought much later, drifting into an exhausted and gratified sleep, but then it always was amazing with Apollo.

Apollo held her while she slept and marvelled at how natural it had become to hold her close. One large hand splayed across her flat stomach. How had he ever believed that he could walk away untouched after conception occurred? How had he credited that he could bring a child into the world and not want to play a full part in his son or daughter's life? The unquestioning arrogance of those selfish assumptions belatedly savaged his view of himself. As fond memories of moments with his own father while he was still a little boy drifted through his mind he finally understood Vassilis Metraxis's almost primitive need to safeguard the continuation of the family line, and he also grasped that walking away at any stage from his own child wasn't an option he would ever be able to live with.

CHAPTER TEN

THREE WEEKS LATER, Pixie blinked sleepily into wakefulness and finally sat up to make a grab for the phone ringing while ruefully contemplating the empty space beside her. It was forty-eight hours since Apollo had flown to London on business. Pixie would have accompanied him had the whole household not been in chaos getting ready for the big party the following day. With the housekeeper, Olympia, presenting Pixie with query after query it had slowly dawned on her that she needed to stay on Nexos to take charge.

'Nonsense,' Apollo had declared without hesitation. 'These matters have been managed without a wife's input for years.'

But during that conversation Pixie had had to race off and be horribly sick, which had driven home hard another drawback. Hours of travel with her current delicate stomach would make her miserable and she was in no hurry to face Apollo with the repugnant downside of pregnancy. She was being ill an awful lot more than she had ever expected because her morning sickness seemed to attack at all times of the day. For that reason she had used the party arrangements as an excuse because she didn't want Apollo to realise just how sick she was. While in her head she knew she should be sharing her suffering with him because he was an adult, it was a struggle to overcome her reluctance. He would fuss and she hated fuss and didn't want to be treated like an invalid. In any case they had arranged for Pixie to have her first scan that very afternoon and she planned to ask the visiting gynaecologist then about her seemingly excessive sickness.

Pixie put the phone to her ear.

'Pixie?' Holly exclaimed before bursting into a mile-a-minute speech that left Pixie, who was still drowsy, none the wiser.

'Sorry, I didn't catch all that,' she confided.

'You've seen that stupid story already, haven't you?' Holly groaned. 'Your voice sounds weird…you've been crying…'

A cold feeling slid down Pixie's spine while she leant back against the pillows, striving to overcome the nausea beginning to creep over her. It would've been easier for her to simply admit that she was pregnant and sick but her best friend would be arriving the next day for the party and she wanted to save her baby news until she saw her in person. 'What story?'

'Vito insists it's untrue…well, with that particular girl.'

'Can I phone you back, Holly?' Pixie gasped, cutting off the call and leaping from the bed in wild haste to charge for the bathroom.

Afterwards, she rested her brow down on the welcome coldness of the marble vanity counter and tried to muster the energy to clean her teeth. Oh, dear, she thought limply, it had not occurred to her that pregnancy would be quite so challenging. Certainly Holly had had a few upsets during her pregnancy but nothing similar to what Pixie was encountering.

And what had Holly been referring to? Some story in a newspaper? About Vito? No, why would she be phoning Pixie if it had been about Vito? And why would Holly think she had been *crying* about something? The chilled feeling of foreboding returned and as Pixie's brain began to function again she reached for the tablet by the bed and put Apollo's name in the search engine. The usual flock of references came up. She knew from experience that if she wanted to she could now access images of herself arriving on Nexos looking like a skinny bird in a very big sun hat that covered her face almost completely…

She sat on the edge of the bed while a tabloid page formed under the title 'Leopards don't change their spots…' And with perspiration breaking out on her clammy skin she read about how the newly married Apollo Metraxis had been pictured entering his apartment building with a very beautiful girl and emerging with her still in tow the following morning. For a few moments she thought she would be sick again but she fought the urge fiercely.

So, what she had always expected to happen *had* happened within only a few months of their wedding. It was no big deal, she told herself squarely and, casting the tablet aside, she went for a shower. Apollo had said he would try to be faithful but the very first time he had had to leave her behind he had found alternative entertainment of the sort he was most accustomed to enjoying. His behaviour sent a powerful message. Clearly, Pixie was no more important or special to him than any other woman he had slept with. How could she ever have thought otherwise?

And Izzy Jerome *was* a very beautiful girl with long corn-blonde hair and endless legs. She was also famous, a fairly recently discovered model/celebrity. Apollo's type in every way. Well, she wasn't about to make a giant scene over Izzy or do anything silly, Pixie warned herself severely. It was time to default to their original marriage setting in which they shared a business arrangement and nothing else. At least she could save face that way, she reasoned in despair, a sudden convulsive sob creeping up on her and squeezing her throat painfully tight.

But she wasn't going to cry over Apollo, Pixie told herself angrily. He wasn't worth her tears. He was selfish and shallow and his betrayal had literally been written in the stars because she had always been well aware that leopards didn't change their spots. The phone was ringing again somewhere in the distance but she ignored it, sitting on the shower seat while the water beat down on her and washed away the shameful tears. A sob escaped her straining lungs and she clenched her teeth in frustration. There was no way she was prepared to greet Apollo with red-rimmed eyes that would tell him just how badly he had hurt her.

And willpower did finally triumph over the tears. She switched off the shower and stepped out to grab a towel but only minutes later found herself throwing up again. Utterly wretched, she curled up on the cold floor for several minutes with Hector nuzzling against her legs. She petted him with a shaking hand. She felt dizzy and sick and dreadful but she wasn't about to show it. Apollo had done her a favour, she reasoned miserably. Her body was already changing. Her breasts had swelled, her waist had thickened and her tummy was no longer perfectly flat. Apollo would soon have lost interest in her anyway and it was better that it happened sooner rather than later.

After all, she had to learn to be independent again and stand on her own feet. Her baby would need her to be strong and brave. She had to cope and rise above the terrible hurt trying to overwhelm her common sense. He didn't love her; he had *never* loved her. The only woman Apollo had ever loved had been the evil stepmother who used him when he was far too young and immature to protect himself and had destroyed his trust and his ability to love. Was it any wonder that he had never had a serious relationship with a woman since then?

Slowly, clumsily, Pixie got herself upright again and began to dry her hair. Apollo would be home in a couple of hours with the gynaecologist he was flying out from London with him and she refused to humiliate herself by behaving like an emotional wreck and letting him appreciate what a fool she had been where he was concerned. Her pride would never recover from such an exposure. And how could she have fallen madly in love with a male programmed from the outset to break her heart? How stupid was that?

And even worse she had that wretched party to get through. As if that was not enough Apollo had contrived to destroy Christmas for her as well for the two of them had been invited to celebrate Christmas with Vito and Holly in Tuscany. Of course she would cry off now. She had no plans to take the shine off the festivities by attending as a betrayed and broken-hearted wife, who had nowhere else to go over Christmas. Apollo would probably take Izzy Jerome with him instead. Of course, Izzy might not still be Apollo's flavour of the month in three weeks' time, she thought wretchedly. His interest in a woman rarely lasted that long.

Squeezing herself into a stretchy skirt, Pixie blinked back fresh tears. Why was she putting on weight so fast? According to what she had read she was supposed to be gaining weight very gradually, not piling it on as though she had been eating for an entire rugby team!

In London, Apollo paced beside his private jet while he spoke to Vito. Who could ever have guessed that marriage could be so stressful? His life pre-Pixie now seemed free as the air, a time of immaturity and egotism. Back then nothing had bothered him very much, not the scandals, not the grasping women, not even the horrendous rumours and gossip about his lifestyle. He hadn't had to explain himself or defend his reputation to anyone because he truthfully hadn't cared what anyone thought about him. It hadn't mattered as long as he knew that he had done no wrong. But now he had Pixie and everything had changed out of all recognition. He had a wife who was pregnant and vulnerable and innately distrustful of him.

'The way the paparazzi follow you around it was bound to happen,' Vito contended. 'And now that you've achieved your objectives and she's pregnant...does it really matter?'

Pure rage slivered through Apollo. 'If it hurts her, it matters,' he breathed in a raw undertone. '*Of course*, it matters!'

'You don't sound quite as detached as you usually do,' his friend commented.

'Look, I'll talk to you tomorrow,' Apollo concluded, ending the call in sheer frustration.

Obviously, he wasn't detached. He was in turmoil. He was thinking things he'd never thought. He was feeling things he had never allowed himself to feel and the result was a state of mind dangerously close to panic. He boarded the jet with the fancy gynaecologist and his small team, yet another source of worry to be dealt with. Dr Floros had suggested that he call in a consultant when Pixie's blood tests had come back with an unexpectedly high count and the result had been forwarded to London. The scan would hopefully reveal whether or not there was any cause for concern. Apollo had persuaded the island doctor not to reveal that fact to Pixie in advance of the scan, lest it upset her, but he knew the older man was planning to share the result with her the following day.

When had his life become so impossibly complicated? An image of Pixie on their wedding day was superimposed over his troubled thoughts. But no, he reasoned, it had started even before then. From the very first day when she'd punched him Pixie had been different. She wasn't impressed by him, she was never impressed by him…except occasionally in bed, he conceded abstractedly, a shadowy smile briefly relaxing the tense line of his sensual mouth.

Unlike other women, Pixie had only ever treated him as an equal. She judged him by the same rules she applied to everyone else. She didn't make excuses for him or handle him with kid gloves. She didn't believe that his vast wealth entitled him to special treatment. In fact she demanded more from him than any woman had ever demanded, only her currency of choice wasn't cash or gifts. Apollo had learnt the hard way that cash or gifts were easy to give while everything else was a challenge demanding more than he was usually prepared to give.

During the flight random memories drifted through his mind. Pixie, grinning with triumph and punching the air after that insane dive she had made from the top deck of *Circe*. Pixie staring dreamily out to sea as the sun went down in splendour, saying, 'You really don't appreciate how lucky you are to see this every day.' Pixie wandering round the picturesque narrow village streets on Nexos, admiring colourful flowerboxes, sleeping cats, starlit eyes wide with interest while she drank lemonade in the café overlooking the harbour and watched the fishermen bringing in their catch. She made everything fresh, Apollo acknowledged in growing bewilderment; she made him see things through less jaded eyes.

Pixie could feel her facial muscles lock as she descended the stairs to welcome the arrivals. She refused to look at Apollo but she was seethingly conscious of him standing back in a stylishly crumpled beige linen suit teamed with a white tee shirt. She showed the doctor, the technician and the nurse into the room where their equipment could be set up and Olympia brought a tray of tea and snacks out to the terrace for them.

'Pixie…' Apollo said then, having demonstrated unusual patience for such an impatient man. 'Could I have a word?'

No, no way, she wanted to scream at him but she couldn't let herself scream. There would be no discussion about Izzy Jerome or about the promise he had given about *trying* to stay faithful. What was done was done and there was really nothing more to say. All she had to do now was draw a line under their marriage as such and default to the useful guidelines printed in her pre-nuptial contract.

'Your office,' she suggested, stealing an involuntary glance at him.

He hadn't shaved and he was still gorgeous. Dark stubble shadowed his strong jaw line and outlined his superbly kissable lips. His black hair was messy, his stunning green eyes glittering warily below his black velvet lashes. He was sexy as sin and a pang of wanton lust pierced her pelvis. Guilty colour washed her pallor away. He had cheated on her with a blonde beauty, so how could she still respond to him on a physical level? Self-loathing inflamed her while she picked her passage through the team of caterers fussing over the chairs that were being carried into the ballroom where the party would be held.

The mere prospect of the party made her grit her teeth. All those people would be attending primarily to see her in her role as the wife of Apollo Metraxis, people who would know he was already playing away with another woman, and yet Pixie would have to pretend that nothing was wrong because that was what she had agreed to do when she chose to marry him. Luckily pretending, however, would allow her to retain a certain dignity, she reminded herself doggedly.

Her visceral reaction was to scream, shout and claw at Apollo and from the curious glances he was angling at her she could see that a major scene was what he expected. But Pixie was determined not to lower herself to that level. Whatever else he was, Apollo was the father of her child and, whether she liked it or not, he would remain a feature of her life for many years in the future. She was determined not to embarrass herself in front of him by revealing that she had made the mistake of becoming emotionally involved.

'I'm relieved that you're giving us the chance to talk before Mr Rollins gives you the scan,' Apollo murmured in an unusually quiet voice.

Was he ashamed? No, Apollo didn't do shame or fidelity when it came to sex, she reasoned painfully. He was probably genuinely grateful that she wasn't making a big scene.

Pixie stationed herself by the window that looked across the sloping gardens and over the top of the trees and out to sea. She steeled her spine. 'I want us to separate—'

'No,' Apollo interrupted immediately.

'It's in the pre-nup agreement,' Pixie reminded him. 'Once I'm pregnant I can if I wish ask to live separately and I would like to return to the UK as soon as it can be arranged.'

Apollo was powerfully knocked off balance by that announcement. Yes, that was in the agreement because before he married her he had assumed that he would want his freedom back as soon as possible. Had ever a man been so bloody stupid and blind? he railed at himself in furious frustration. 'That is exactly what I *don't* want.'

Pixie rested icy grey eyes on his lean bronzed face. 'I don't care what you want.'

'You're not even giving me a chance to explain?'

'No, that kind of discussion would challenge my ability to be civil to you,' Pixie admitted hoarsely, because inside herself where it didn't show she was breaking apart. She hated him and yet she still wanted to be near him. She loathed him for betraying her and yet her weak, wanton body still hummed in direct response to the insanely hot attraction he exuded. The very thought of not seeing Apollo again for months on end threatened to rip her into tiny pieces but she knew the difference between right and wrong and she knew what she had to do to restore the boundaries she needed to feel safe.

And she could never *ever* feel safe with an unfaithful man. It didn't matter that it had only happened once, what mattered was that she had made the mistake of thinking of their marriage as a real marriage and now she was being destroyed because she loved him. But he hadn't asked her for her love or her possessiveness and he had even warned her that fidelity would be a struggle for him. How far in those circumstances could she blame him for what he had done? She had fallen for him and that was her mistake, not his.

'This is crazy...' Apollo breathed with sudden rawness, big brown hands settling over her slight shoulders. 'You won't even look at me!'

'I'm being polite.'

'That isn't you... I don't *know* you like this!' Apollo growled in frustration. 'Shout at me, kick me...whatever!'

'Why would I do that?' Pixie forced a frozen little smile to her lips. 'We've enjoyed a successful business arrangement. My brother is safe and learning how to live without gambling and I'm carrying a baby I want very much. Now you can return to the freewheeling life you prefer.'

Even though his temper was cruelly challenged by that speech, his big hands withdrew from her tense shoulders and dropped away to slowly ball into fists by his sides because he genuinely didn't want to argue with her and upset her. 'Mr Rollins should be ready for you now,' he pronounced with savage quietness.

Pixie chewed at her full lower lip, blaming him for the fact that the scan she had been eager to have had now been horribly overshadowed by his betrayal and her heartbreak. But maybe seeing the shape of her baby on a screen would restore her and cure the agony clawing up inside her. It hurt so much not to have Apollo any more. It hurt not to be able to allow herself to touch him. But a kick, never mind a kiss, would have released the pent-up rage and hurt she was holding back.

She wanted to tell him that she had gone down to the animal rehabilitation centre on the outskirts of the village while he was away and had met the staff and occupants as well as spotting a little dog very similar to Hector. She had wanted to share that with Apollo but then she wanted to share *everything* with Apollo, had in fact got used to treating him like her best friend, and in the wake of his infidelity that was a really terrifying revelation. What had happened to her pride? But now she could feel the new distance forming inside her and she clung to that barrier in desperation.

Having set up the equipment, the nurse and the technician were ready to give Pixie her scan. She got up on the mobile examination table, rested her head back on the pillow and pushed down her skirt to expose her tummy while the consultant talked smoothly about what she could expect to see. He referred to her blood test, which surprised her. Clearly he had consulted the island doctor for that result and she wondered why.

The gel the technician put on her stomach was cool and she shivered, eyes flying wide when Apollo moved forward and closed a hand over her knotted fingers. The amazing racing sound of the baby's heartbeat filled the silence and she smiled in sheer wonder. The wand moved and then the heartbeat surged again.

'Two babies, Mrs Metraxis.'

'*Two?*' she echoed in astonishment.

'Twins. I suspected a multiple pregnancy when I saw the results of your first blood test…'

Shocked, Pixie locked her eyes to the screen while the consultant outlined the shadowy forms of her children. Children, not one child as she had simply assumed. It was an enormous change to get her head around. She wondered if that explained the heavy nausea she was enduring and the physical changes that were already altering her body.

Apollo studied the screen in horror. Two of them? Two babies struggling to make space in Pixie's tiny body? How could that be? That had to make everything more dangerous.

Pixie yanked her hand from Apollo's because he was crushing her fingers. She glanced up at him, reading the raw tension etched in his hard features. He wasn't pleased. But then why would he be? He had only needed one child and two would presumably be more hassle and expense. The nurse wiped off the gel and helped her back to her feet. She took a seat for yet another blood test and shut her eyes tight sooner than see the needle while Apollo took up position behind her and rested his hands down heavily on her shoulders.

She told the consultant about her frequent nausea. He explained that that could occur in a twin pregnancy and that it should settle down by the end of her first trimester, but that if it began to impact on her health she would need support. He mentioned that the twins each had their own placenta, which lessened the chance of complications. The information he gave her was very practical and Pixie was happy to thank him and leave while Apollo demonstrated a dismaying eagerness to stay behind and talk to the medical team.

Apollo's blood had run cold throughout his entire body when the word 'complications' struck him like blow. He felt sick. Mr Rollins informed him unasked that sex was still perfectly fine. Ironically, Apollo had never felt less horny and he was suddenly feeling very guilty. If anything went wrong it would be his fault. He had planned this pregnancy, done everything possible to make it happen and now that he had he was discovering that he had hitched a ride on a rocket that he could no longer control. Not since his troubled childhood had he been made to feel so helpless. By the time the medical team departed on the helicopter to head back to the airport, Apollo was in a seriously sombre mood.

Pixie settled down happily with a pot of tea on the shaded terrace with Hector at her feet. Two babies, my goodness, weren't they going to be a handful? She was in shock but, after hearing her babies' heartbeats, she was excited and pleased as well. She sipped her tea and wondered if the twins would be identical or non-identical and whether they would be boys or girls or even one of each. It was a huge relief to have something other than Apollo to think about.

Apollo strode out onto the terrace and surveyed her. 'I can't let you leave me,' he intoned grimly. 'I *have* to be part of this. They are my children too. I need to be sure you're healthy and looking after yourself.'

'What about what I need?' Pixie countered, eyes narrowing as she looked back at him because he was standing in sunlight, tall and bronzed and muscular as a god in stature and so beautiful he didn't seem quite real to her.

'You need my support.'

'No, I don't. I've been independent all my life,' Pixie traded without hesitation.

Apollo leant back against the low wall separating the terrace from the garden and tossed a squeaky toy at Hector, who bounded after it with glee. 'I don't want you to be independent.'

'Tough. We made a business arrangement,' Pixie reminded him. 'Getting pregnant is my get-out-of-jail-free card and I'm playing it.'

'You're being unreasonable.'

'I love the island. I like my life here but this is *your* house, *your* island and I don't want to live in your house on your island,' Pixie explained without apology.

Apollo breathed in slow and deep and practised a patience that he was in no way accustomed to practising. 'We'll discuss it after the party tomorrow.'

Her life had fallen apart, Pixie thought, suddenly losing the high of finding out that she was carrying two babies. She was about to become a single mum, which most poignantly was something she had once sworn she would never be. But that was life, she told herself, knocking you back on your heels and changing things without warning. And she would be a liar if she argued that she couldn't have foreseen the breakdown of their marriage. After all, that breakdown had been foreseen in the prenuptial agreement she had signed and all the conditions for that breakdown laid out in advance. She had read the terms and she had even read the small print. She knew that she had rights and that Apollo couldn't ignore them.

Apollo crossed the tiles towards her and studied her with gorgeous glittering green eyes. 'I don't want this marriage to end. I don't want a divorce,' he declared. 'I don't want you to leave Nexos either.'

After a noisy pummelling session with his squeaky toy, Hector sneaked across the floor and hovered uneasily near Apollo's feet before he gingerly dropped the toy there. Muttering something shaken in Greek, Apollo stilled and then he bent, scooped it up and threw it and Hector went careening after it. 'He brought the toy to me. He *finally* brought it to me!' he exclaimed in amazement.

'I never said my dog had good taste,' Pixie remarked, in no mood to be captivated.

The following morning, the day of the party, Pixie was following her usual routine of being horrendously sick when Apollo joined her in the bathroom. 'Go away!' she shrieked furiously.

'No, this is my business,' Apollo declared, crouching down to loop her hair out of the way and support her.

'I *hate* you!' Pixie snapped with pure venom because it was the last straw that he should witness her in such a state when all her defences were down, and there were many more such tart exchanges before her stomach settled again.

Having cleaned her up with unblemished cool, Apollo carried her back to bed. 'Do you want me to cancel the party?'

'You can't. Half our guests are already on their way,' she groaned. 'I'll be fine once Holly gets here.'

'I haven't had sex with anyone but you since we got married,' Apollo announced just when she was least expecting any reference to that burning issue.

'Don't believe you,' Pixie gasped, turning over on her side to avoid looking at him. 'Nobody would believe you. I'm not stupid. It's what you do, it's who you are…you probably can't even help it.'

'It's not who I am!' Apollo bit out hotly from between clenched white teeth, his eyes emerald bright and accusing. 'The least you can do is give me the chance to explain.'

Pixie closed her eyes tight and played dead. His sudden anger had unnerved her. She didn't fear him but right then she didn't feel equal to the challenge of such an emotive confrontation. In fact suddenly all she wanted was Holly's reassuringly soothing presence. Tears stung her eyes behind the lowered lids.

'Izzy is Jeremy Slater's kid sister. Vito and I went to school with Jeremy. Although you haven't met him yet, he's a close friend. Izzy was at a dinner I attended. I've met her before and she asked me for a lift because she was visiting someone with an apartment in the same building as my London penthouse. I thought nothing of it,' Apollo admitted grittily. 'I wasn't particularly surprised either when the paparazzi jumped out to photograph us when we arrived because Izzy's every move is currently prime fodder for the tabloid newspapers.'

'So, according to you, you simply gave her a lift,' Pixie recited. 'How does that explain her still being with you the next morning?'

'She spent the night with whoever she was visiting. She phoned me first thing and asked me if I could drop her off on my way into the office. She was waiting for me in the lobby and we left the building together.'

'When you were caught on camera again. Why didn't your bodyguards intervene?'

'Because I suspected that Izzy was using me to raise her own profile and, not having thought through the situation, I saw no harm in it and waved them back,' Apollo ground out angrily.

His explanation covered the facts but his generosity towards Izzy Jerome's craving for publicity when he himself loathed paparazzi attention infuriated her. Since when had Apollo not 'thought through' a situation? He must've realised how the press would present those photos, one taken the night before, the next early the next morning.

'I'm sorry,' she pronounced flatly. 'I don't believe you.'

The door thudded closed on his exit and only then did her tension ease a little yet she had never felt so empty. She had not realised that she could love anyone as much as she loved Apollo and she had not realised that losing someone could hurt so much that it hurt to breathe. And it was a lesson she truly wished she had not had to learn. She had lain awake a long time the night before. Apollo had presumably slept in another room and ironically his absence had distressed her as much as his presence would have done. It was as though she were being ripped slowly apart, divided between wanting him and not wanting him.

Vito and Holly arrived mid-afternoon. As soon as

Pixie heard Holly's bright voice echoing up from the hall she called down to her friend from the upper landing. Apollo and Vito looked up. Pixie reddened and waved to excuse herself for not having gone downstairs to welcome their guests.

'I'm pregnant,' she told Holly baldly. 'And, yes, it was planned.'

'Is that why Apollo is looking a little ragged round the edges?'

'No... I think that was caused by the doctor telling us that we're having twins.'

'*Twins?*' Holly squealed in excitement. 'When are you due?'

As the friends shared due dates, because Holly was expecting her second child, they went downstairs by a service staircase and settled down with cool drinks in the orangery with its tall shady plants and softly playing indoor fountain.

'Vito told me about the will and that you were planning to have a child with Apollo,' Holly confided then.

Pixie sighed heavily.

'And you broke the rules, didn't you?' Holly whispered, anxiously searching Pixie's tense little face and shadowed eyes. 'You went and fell madly in love with his fancy-ass yacht.'

Pixie didn't trust herself to laugh or speak and she jerked her chin down in confirmation.

Holly groaned out loud.

'I wanted a child and because I wasn't very good at... er...dating I thought that Apollo could be my best chance of ever having one,' Pixie admitted very quietly. 'I should tell you now...we are separating after the party.'

'Is it really that cut and dried? I mean, even Vito, who generally assumes the worst of Apollo when women are involved, thinks that there's no way that Apollo would have slept with Izzy Jerome. She's Jeremy's kid sister and sisters are off-limits between friends. And Apollo has *un*invited Izzy from your party,' Holly completed with satisfaction.

'Izzy Jerome was on the guest list?' Pixie gasped in dismay.

'She's not any more,' Holly emphasised. 'I don't think he is involved with her. She's very young, you know, still a teenager.'

'It doesn't matter.' Pixie lifted her head high and sipped at her drink. 'The best way forward for us now is for us to go our separate ways. That was planned from the start.'

Holly shook her head. 'I can't believe you signed up for that. I thought you hated him.'

Pixie said nothing because there was a sour taste in her mouth. Only days had passed since she had planned to tell her friend how very different Apollo was from his public image but recent events had proved her wrong in all her assumptions. In truth she supposed that she had stupidly idealised Apollo to justify the reality that she had fallen in love with him.

'Let me see what you're wearing tonight,' Holly urged in a welcome change of subject.

Pixie took her up to the bedroom to show her the long scarlet dress in its garment bag. 'Apollo had it designed and I don't like it much…it's a wee bit slutty, don't you think? I have no idea what he's wearing.'

Holly skimmed a thoughtful fingertip over the black corset lacing round the bust line. 'Gangster's moll?'

'Well, at least there's no fairy wings included,' Pixie commented flatly. 'But there is a very ornate piece of valuable jewellery which he brought back from London and he evidently expects me to wear it with the costume.'

Pixie opened the worn leather box on the dressing table and listened to Holly ooh and ah over the fabulously flamboyant ruby necklace and drop earrings. She turned her head and glanced back at the red dress again. There was something about it, something eerily familiar but she couldn't pin down what it was.

Dressing for dinner, she donned the costume. She decided it was fortunate that pregnancy had swelled her boobs because the gathered, dipping neckline positively demanded a glimpse of bosom. She tightened the laces, noting with wry appreciation that she finally had the chest she had long dreamt of having. But like her marriage to Apollo, it was an illusion, she thought morosely, for when she had finally delivered her twins she would probably return to being pretty much flat-chested again.

Apollo strode in and she stopped dead to stare at him. He was tricked out like a pirate in tall black boots and fitted breeches with a white ruffled shirt and a sword. And being Apollo and fantastically handsome, he looked spectacular and electrifyingly sexy.

'I gather that I'm a pirate's lady,' Pixie guessed.

'A pirate's treasure,' Apollo quipped. 'You're not wearing the rubies.'

He extracted the necklace from the box and handed her the earrings. 'This set belonged to my mother. It hasn't been worn since she died. I had it cleaned and reset for you in London.'

The eye-catching rubies settled coolly against her skin and she slowly attached the earrings, watching them gleam with inner fire as they swung in the lamp light. 'Thanks,' she said stiltedly.

A very large dinner party awaited them on the ground

floor. With surprising formality Apollo brought his relatives forward one by one to meet Pixie. There were innumerable aunties and uncles and cousins. She marvelled at his calm control under stress and his polished manners. He was essentially behaving like a proud new husband. Nobody could ever have guessed that that dream was already dead and buried. It had been a dream, she reminded herself doggedly, a dream that could never have become reality with Apollo Metraxis in a leading role.

In the ballroom she watched Apollo socialising and frowned. It wasn't fair that she could barely drag her eyes off his tall, powerful physique; it wasn't right or decent that she still felt his magnetic pull. And Apollo dressed up like a pirate was pure perfect fantasy. The arrogant tilt of his dark head, the breadth of his shoulders, his narrow waist and lean, tight hips, the long muscular line of his thighs in skin-tight pants. Her mouth ran dry watching him and her weakness filled her with self-loathing.

Apollo, meanwhile, was in a filthy mood. The planning had gone perfectly but the timing had gone seriously askew. He should have known better; he should have known not to waste his time trying to be something he was not. Since when had he been romantic? What did he even *know* about being romantic? And in any case, she hadn't even *noticed*, which said all that needed to be said. He had taken the cover of her battered romantic paperback and had the outfits copied. Even the costume designer had gazed at him as though he were crazy and he felt like an idiot for going for the pirate theme. Even so, he wasn't going down without a fight.

'I'm no good at slow dances,' Pixie protested when Apollo slowly raised her out of her seat and took her away from Holly, whom she had clung to throughout the evening.

'So, stand on my feet,' Apollo advised, wrapping her slender body into his arms with the kind of strength she couldn't fight without making a scene.

Murderously conscious that their guests were watching them, Pixie pressed her face against his chest and breathed in deep. He smelled so good she wanted to bottle him. Her fingers spread across his powerful shoulders and she drifted in a world of inner pain, wavering wildly between hating and craving and loving. She had missed him so much when he was away from her in London and now she had a whole future of missing him ahead of her.

'I won't agree to a separation,' Apollo breathed softly above her head.

'I don't need your agreement. I'll just leave.'

He went rigid in her arms and missed a step. Pixie was fighting back tears, reminding herself that they were in the middle of a party, that they were the centre of attention as much because she was a new bride as because the bridegroom had been outed as a cheat little more than forty-eight hours previously.

'I'll buy you a house in London…but you stay safe *here* until I have that organised for you.'

'I don't need your help.'

'I'll call you when I've set up the house and you can fly out and give me your opinion.'

Pixie swallowed back a sudden inexplicable sob because, without warning, Apollo had stopped fighting her and had backed off. Instead of feeling relieved, she felt more lost and alone than ever. They really were splitting up. Their marriage was over.

The three weeks that followed were a walking blur for Pixie. Apollo had left Nexos as soon as the last of their guests had departed. He had not attempted to have another serious conversation with her. Those last words exchanged on the dance floor, with her ridiculous threat to just walk out, lingered with her. Yes, she could walk out, she conceded, but she couldn't just walk away from her feelings, the painful feelings that accompanied her everywhere no matter where she was or what she was doing. She couldn't stop thinking about Apollo or fighting off the suspicion that she had condemned him on the basis of his reputation rather than on the evidence.

So preoccupied was she that she barely noticed that her bouts of sickness were fading away. She had to move into maternity clothes rather sooner than she had hoped because most of her fashionable outfits were too fitted to cope with her swollen breasts and vanishing waistline. She purchased new clothes online, loose-cut separates picked for comfort rather than elegance. With Apollo absent she discovered that she didn't care what she looked like. He phoned every week to civilly enquire after her health, and when he asked her if she could join him in London on a certain date her heart sank, because once he showed her the house he expected her to occupy she assumed that the dust would settle on their official separation. Evidently he had accepted that their relationship, their intimacy, was over now.

And wasn't that what she had wanted? How could she move forward without putting their marriage behind her? Apollo had denied infidelity but he hadn't put up much of a fight against her disbelief, had he? But like a sneaky snake in the grass in the back of her mind lurked the dangerous thought that she could, if she wanted, offer him a second chance. She was so ashamed of that indefensible thought that it woke her up at night in a cold sweat. She understood that her brain was struggling to find a solution to her unending grief and sense of deep loss and she knew that the forgiving approach worked for some couples but she knew it would never work for her. Nor would it work for a male like Apollo, who needed strong boundaries and punishing consequences because he wouldn't respect anything else.

Pixie arrived back in London late afternoon in late December with Hector in tow. A limo met her at the airport and whisked her back to the penthouse apartment. Apollo was flying in from LA and had told her that he would not be arriving until shortly before their scheduled meeting. That was why it was a surprise for Pixie to be curled up on a sofa with her dog in front of the television and suddenly be told by Manfred that she had visitors. As she stood up Hector bolted for cover under a chair.

A tall man with prematurely greying dark hair walked in with an oddly self-conscious air but Pixie's attention leapt straight off him towards the highly recognisable youthful blonde accompanying him.

'I'm Jeremy Slater and I apologise for walking in on you like this but my sister has something she has to say to you,' the man told her stiffly. 'Izzy…you have the floor…'

The tall, slender blonde fixed strained blue eyes on Pixie and burst into immediate speech. 'I'm really sorry for what I did. I set Apollo up as cover. I knew he was married but I didn't think about that. I'm afraid I was only thinking about what suited me.'

Pixie was frowning in bewilderment. *'You set Apollo up?'* she repeated blankly.

'I knew that if I was spotted with Apollo, the paps would assume that we were together and that they wouldn't look any more closely into who I was staying with in that building,' she spelled out tautly.

'What my sister *isn't* saying,' Jeremy interposed drily, 'is that she has been involved with a famous actor, who keeps an apartment in Apollo's building. As that man is married, both my sister and he wished to keep their relationship out of the public eye.'

'I didn't intend to cause anyone any trouble,' Izzy said pleadingly.

'But you weren't too concerned when you did cause that trouble,' Pixie pointed out, her stomach churning with shock. 'I can see that I have your brother to thank for this explanation being made.'

'I couldn't stand back and let Apollo take the fall for something he didn't do,' Jeremy declared cheerfully. 'He's been guilty as charged so often and I'm certain that that means that he suffers in the credibility stakes.'

'Yes,' Pixie agreed, her face hot with shame because even she hadn't really listened to Apollo when he'd said he was innocent.

She hadn't asked the relevant questions and she hadn't asked if he could prove his story. In fact she hadn't given him a fair hearing in any way and in retrospect that acknowledgement humbled her. In common with any other bystander she had indeed assumed that he was guilty as charged, but she had had much less excuse than other people because she had lived with Apollo for months and knew that he was something more, something deeper than the heartless womaniser he appeared to be in public.

Jeremy and Izzy departed soon afterwards with Jeremy remarking that he hoped they would soon meet in more sociable circumstances. His sister, however, said nothing, probably guessing that Pixie never wanted to see her again if she could help it.

After that visit, Pixie went to bed but of course she couldn't sleep. She had never trusted Apollo and had essentially regarded her distrust as a trait that strengthened her. Only now was she seeing the downside of that outlook. Looking for the worst and always expecting the worst from a man was not a healthy approach and it was unfair. Even worse, using distrust as a first line of defence had crucially blinded her to what was actually happening in their marriage. She should have recognised how far Apollo had already drifted from his original blueprint for a marriage that was a business arrangement. Time after time he had done things, *said* things that defied that blueprint and she had ignored that reality. After all, *she* had changed—why shouldn't he have changed too?

The next morning it was a struggle for Pixie to eat any breakfast. She had forced a separation on Apollo and had voluntarily given him back his freedom. She had well and truly proved to be her own worst enemy. Pride and distrust had driven her into rejecting the man she loved. Could he forgive her for that? Could he forgive her for misjudging him?

Would her misjudgement and their marriage even matter to him now? After all, his inheritance would soon be fully his because by the time their children were born he would have met the exact terms of his father's will. Nowhere in that will did it state that Apollo had to be still living with his wife.

A limousine collected her at half past nine, wafting her through streets soon to be thronged with Christmas shoppers. Shop windows were bright with decorations and sparkle. Pixie had dressed with care and not in one of her less than flattering maternity outfits. She had put on a green dress. True it was a little tight over her bust but it gave her a shape and her legs were the same as they had always been. In truth, she reflected unhappily as the car drew up outside a smart city town house in a tree-lined Georgian square with a private park, she would never be able to hold a candle to the likes of Izzy Jerome in looks. On board *Circe*, she had marvelled at Apollo's insatiable hunger for her and revelled in it. Now, she had to ask herself if she had anything more substantial to offer a male of his sophistication…

Apollo opened the door of the house himself, which shook her because he almost always had staff around to take care of such tasks.

Pixie stepped over the threshold. She glanced up at him, encountering shimmering green eyes below lashes as rich and dark as black lace, and her heartbeat raced, butterflies unleashed to fly free in her stomach. 'Apollo…' she acknowledged jerkily.

She came to a halt to stare in wide-eyed amazement at the lavish Christmas tree in the hall and the glorious trails of holly festooning the hall fireplace and the stairs. 'Oh, my goodness, this house…it's all decorated for Christmas,' she muttered inanely. 'And it's still furnished.'

'Relax. The furniture and the decorations are mine. This house was rented out for years. My father owned it but he didn't use it and it was too large for me to use while I was still single,' Apollo told her, gently but firmly urging her down into the armchair set by the small crackling fire in the hearth. 'Sit down and stop stressing.'

Pixie sat but she couldn't stop stressing. Apollo was exquisitely well-dressed in a formal navy suit, cuff links glinting at the cuffs of a fine white shirt, and she remembered him dressed like a pirate and every skin cell leapt up in sensual recollection. 'You want me to live in your father's house? I thought I was supposed to live in a house you bought me?'

Apollo dealt her an impassive appraisal that told her nothing about his mood. 'I understand that Jeremy called on you with Izzy last night,' he remarked stiffly.

Pixie flinched and paled, unnerved by that reminder. Of course, it had been foolish of her not to appreciate that his friend would naturally have told him about that visit. 'Yes, I'm so, so sorry. I misjudged you and refused to listen and there's no excuse for that, is there?'

'Perhaps there is,' Apollo conceded, sharply disconcerting her with that measured response. 'Maybe if I'd said more sooner, you *would* have wanted to listen to what I had to say.'

Sick with nerves, Pixie curled her hands tightly together. 'I'm really sorry,' she said shakily again. 'I didn't give you a chance.'

'I have a bad reputation with women,' Apollo allowed reflectively. 'But in one sense it's unjustified. I have always ended one relationship before I embark on another. I don't do crossovers or betrayals. That's a small point but that's how I live. I don't cheat on anyone.'

Her nails dug into her palms because she was so very tense and afraid of saying the wrong thing. She had said she was sorry but she didn't want to keep on saying sorry and she didn't want to crawl either. 'I understand.'

'We were talking about this house,' Apollo reminded her, lounging elegantly back against the marble console table behind him.

'Y-yes,' she stammered.

'I want you to live here with me. With twins on the horizon we definitely need a spacious family house.'

Her smooth brow indented as she struggled to understand. 'Are you saying that you can forgive me for the way I behaved on Nexos?'

'There are still things that you have to forgive me for,' Apollo told her tautly. 'When we first married I pretended that I was still holding your brother's debt over you because I saw that debt as a guarantee that you would do as you were told.'

Her smooth brow furrowed. 'You pretended? In what way?'

'I paid off the debt in its entirety before our marriage. I didn't want any further dealings with the thug your brother owed that money to,' he admitted.

Pixie nodded understanding. 'The carrot and the stick approach again…right? Well, you're good at faking.'

'Thank you,' Apollo murmured wryly. 'I should've been more honest with you though.'

'We both hugged our secrets back then. It takes time to learn to trust someone.'

'You're the first woman I've ever trusted,' Apollo admitted. 'You know the worst of me. You've seen the bad stuff. Give me a chance to show you the good things I can do.'

Pixie unfroze and stared up at him. 'You *are* willing to forgive me for misjudging you,' she suddenly appreciated in wonderment.

His smile slanted into a heart-stopping grin. 'As I can't live without you I don't think I have much choice about that.'

'You can't live,' she began incredulously, '*without* me?'

'I've got remarkably used to having you and Hector around,' Apollo told her almost flippantly.

'H-have you?' Pixie mumbled uncertainly.

'Even though trying to plant an idea in your head is sometimes like drilling through concrete.'

'What idea were you trying to plant?'

'That we could be happy together and stay together and married for ever.'

'You don't do for ever,' Pixie argued, her voice taking on a shrill edge of disbelief.

'But then I met you and ever since then everything I *thought* I knew has been proven wrong,' Apollo admitted gravely. 'That unnerved me...but there it is. You've turned my life upside down and, strangest of all, I've discovered that I *like* it this way.'

Pixie's mouth had run dry. 'I'm not sure I understand.'

Apollo reached down a lean brown hand towards hers and in a sudden movement she grasped it. He tugged her upright. 'I want to show you something and ask you a special question.'

Blinking rapidly, her heart hammering inside her chest, Pixie let him urge her upstairs. He pushed open the door on a bedroom but her attention leapt straight to the garment hanging in front of a wardrobe. 'What's that?' she gasped, for it looked remarkably like a white wedding dress.

Apollo dropped fluidly down on one knee while she stared at him as if he had lost his wits, her grey eyes huge and questioning. 'Pixie...will you marry me?'

'Wh-what?' she stuttered shakily.

'I'm trying to do it right this time. I love you,' Apollo breathed huskily. 'Will you marry me?'

'But we're already married,' she whispered in a small voice. 'You...*love*...me?'

'Much more than I ever thought I could love anyone.'

And the power in Pixie's legs just went and she dropped down on her knees in front of him. 'You mean it...you're not just saying it?'

Apollo flipped open the small jewellery box in his hand and extracted a ruby ring. 'And this is the ruby ring I intended to give you before the fancy dress party but sadly it would have been the wrong time.'

Pixie watched in reverence as he eased the glorious

ring onto her wedding finger. 'Is this an engagement ring?' she whispered.

With an impatient groan, Apollo leapt back upright and bent to scoop Pixie up and plant her at the foot of the bed. 'Yes, it is, and we need to start moving quickly. That is if you're willing to stay married to me?'

'Yes, I am... I'm kind of...' Pixie hesitated and then lifted her bemused head high to look up at him '...attached to you, *so* attached I can't bear having you out of my sight and the last few weeks have been sheer *hell*,' she admitted feelingly. 'I don't know when it happened because I started out convinced I hated you and somewhere along the way I fell madly in love with you.'

Sheer relief rippled through Apollo's lean, powerful frame. '*Thee mou*...you made me wait for that, you little witch. Would you like me to help you put on your wedding gown?'

Another wave of bewilderment rocked Pixie. 'Why would I put on a wedding gown?'

'Because your very romantic husband wants to take you to a church to renew our vows...and this time, we'll mean *every* word and every promise, *koukla mou*. I wanted to see you in a white dress.'

Pixie felt as though her brain had gone on holiday. She was poleaxed by that information.

Apollo lifted her off the bed and unzipped her dress, pushing it off her shoulders until it slid down her arms and dropped to the rug. 'I like the lingerie,' he growled soft and low.

'We're going to renew our vows? You've actually arranged that?' she exclaimed as her brain absorbed that incredible concept. 'Oh, I like that. I *like* that idea very much...'

'And then we're going to fly out to Tuscany to spend Christmas with Vito and Holly.'

All of a sudden, Pixie became a ball of energy. She whirled away from him, a slender vision in white lace underpinnings, and yanked the wedding dress off the wardrobe at speed. 'I hope it fits.'

'I told the designer you were pregnant and she made allowances.'

Pixie wrenched off the bag and dived into the wedding gown as if her life depended on it and indeed at that moment it felt as if her life did depend on it. Apollo was making all her dreams come true at once. He was trying to rewrite their history and she adored him for that piece of unashamed sentimentality. He was, after all, offering her the white wedding dress and the church she had once dreamt of. He loved her. Could she truly believe that? The ruby sparkled enticingly on her finger and she heaved a happy sigh. When Apollo began organising church blessings and getting down on bended knee to propose, it was time to take him very seriously indeed, she thought happily.

It was an exquisitely delicate and elegant lace dress and Apollo was fantastic at doing up hooks. Dainty pearlised shoes completed the ensemble and she dug her feet into them with a sigh. 'You've thought of everything.'

'I had to organise it all in advance even though I was scared you would say no. My first romantic scenario fell very flat,' Apollo pointed out in his own defence. 'Your bouquet is downstairs.'

'What *first* romantic scenario?' she prompted with a frown.

'The one where I had the cover of your bodice-ripping paperback copied for our fancy dress costumes,' Apollo extended. 'The one where I dressed up as a stupid pirate and you were *supposed* to recognise the outfits from the book cover.'

Pixie gasped and her grey eyes widened to their fullest extent. She recalled that sense of familiarity when she had seen the red dress he had had designed for her and she grinned. 'It was the first romance I ever read. I bought it at a church jumble sale…but when I got older, I didn't think it was realistic to believe I could ever meet a man as swoonworthy as the hero…and here you are, Apollo Metraxis, and you're hotter than the fires of hell!'

'Even so, you didn't notice,' he reminded her doggedly.

'I definitely noticed how sexy you looked,' she confided, her cheeks turning pink, and her heart literally sang at the image of Apollo going to so much trouble in an effort to be romantic and please her. 'Breeches and knee boots are a great look on you, so maybe you'll put that on again for me some day and I faithfully promise to demonstrate my appreciation. That night, I'm afraid I was too locked into the hurt of the Izzy business to notice. I'm sorry.'

'And I'm sorry you were hurt,' Apollo confided tenderly as he urged her back down the stairs, grabbed the bridal bouquet out of another room and planted it into her hands. 'Let's get to the church, Mrs Metraxis…'

And the little ceremony was glorious and everything Pixie could have dreamt of it being. She could see the love in Apollo's brilliant green eyes and when he actually paused afterwards on the church steps and posed with his arm round her for the paparazzi, he smiled with even greater brilliance and a level of happiness he had never known before.

'What time are Vito and Holly expecting us?' Pixie whispered as they climbed into the waiting car.

'My social secretary rang them to let them know we

wouldn't be arriving until later,' Apollo revealed. 'I don't want to share you just yet. I want a few hours to privately appreciate my very beautiful, pregnant-with-twins wife.'

'And how do you feel about the babies?'

'Over the moon now that we'll be in London with the best possible medical care on the doorstep,' Apollo told her, drawing her close, the heat of his big frame sending a little pulse of fiery awareness through her. 'I was worrying far too much and your consultant reassured me. You'll be in the best possible hands for the duration of your pregnancy.'

'*Your* hands,' Pixie muttered, pressing his palm against her cheek in a loving gesture. 'You'll look after me… I know you will.'

'You're my whole world and our children are part of us both. I can't believe I ever thought I'd be able to walk away and take a back seat in their lives.'

'Well, you won't be walking away any place now,' Pixie said cheerfully, resting shining eyes on him. 'I love you, Apollo, and there's no escape.'

'And you're the love I didn't believe existed as well as the most amazing woman I've ever met,' he growled, claiming her parted lips with his in a long, deep, hungry kiss of possession that thrilled her right down to her toes. 'Where else will I find a woman insane enough to dive off the top of my yacht? And expect me to be pleased? Or threaten me with a miniature Arab Prince as a rival?'

EPILOGUE

AT SIXTEEN MONTHS OLD, Sofia Metraxis was a force to be reckoned with. She ran over to her brother, Tobias, swiped his toy truck off him and sat back to bat away his attempts to retrieve it.

'That wasn't nice,' Pixie said, scooping up Tobias, who was crying over the loss of his favourite toy.

'You don't do nice, do you, Alpha baby?' Apollo chuckled, lifting his daughter and exchanging the truck for another toy to return it to Tobias.

'She's just cheeky,' Pixie contended.

'And bossy...wonder where she gets that from,' Apollo teased, watching Tobias stop crying to play with his truck. 'I can't get over how different they are.'

And the twins were. Tobias was the quieter twin, clever and thoughtful and methodical even in play. Sofia was all bells and whistles and complaints and needed rather less sleep. Together the two children had transformed their parents' lives, ensuring that Apollo and Pixie spent more time enjoying the wide open spaces and beaches available on Nexos than in their comfortable London town house.

Pixie had spent all of her pregnancy in London. Only after the birth of the twins had Apollo admitted that his own mother had died in childbirth and that that was the main reason he had been so concerned about her. Luckily the twins had been born only a couple of weeks early by a C-section and neither they nor Pixie had had any health concerns. Her brother's little boy had been born in the summer and Patrick and his little family now lived in Scotland where Apollo had found her brother a better-paying job. Patrick was still attending Gamblers Anonymous meetings regularly.

Springing upright, Apollo closed a hand over Pixie's and walked her out to the landing, leaving the twins in the care of their nannies. 'I have a present for you,' he proffered.

'Now? But tomorrow is Christmas Day!' she protested.

'Every day feels like Christmas with you, *agapi mou*,' Apollo traded. 'And Vito and Holly will be arriving in a couple of hours.'

'My goodness, is it that time already?' Pixie asked in an anxious voice. 'I should check the—'

'No,' Apollo stated firmly. 'You don't need to check anything. The house is decked out like a Christmas fair. The gifts are wrapped and our staff have mealtimes covered.'

Pixie gazed down at her gorgeous sparkling Christmas tree in the hall and she slowly smiled. He was right. Everything was done. It had become a tradition that every year the two young families shared Christmas and this year it was Apollo and Pixie who were playing host because Holly was pregnant again with her third child and she wanted to take it easy and be a guest. And although Pixie and Holly didn't compete over who could put on the best festive show, high expectations did add a certain inevitable stress to the preparations. In any case, the whole house was looking marvellous. Holly was good at design and she had put together some colour schemes for the island villa and it was a much more welcoming house now that the bland beiges had been swept away and replaced with clear bright and subtle colours.

'Bed?' Pixie whispered to her husband because the arrival of guests, even if they were best friends, did put certain restrictions on what they could and couldn't do.

'You see, this is why I want to be married to you for ever and ever,' Apollo declared as he swept her up into his arms. 'You think like I do...'

Sometimes he was naïve, Pixie thought fondly. It wasn't that she thought the same way as he did. It was more simply that she could never resist his sex appeal. He was dressed down for the day too in well-washed jeans and a sweater, but her amazing male still took her breath away with one wicked, wolfish smile. He just made her happy. In bed, out of bed, as a husband, as a father, he was all she had ever dreamt of and a couple of years of marriage had only increased his pulling power. His patient approach with Hector had taught her a lot about the man she had married. At heart he was kind and loving and good.

Hector and his little Greek shadow, another terrier called Sausage, followed them upstairs.

Apollo slid a diamond eternity ring onto Pixie's already crowded finger. Her hands sparkled with a plethora of rings and she chose which ones to wear every morning. He liked to buy her stuff and she knew it was because she was rarely out of her husband's thoughts when he was away from her. He kept his business trips brief and, if he could, took them all out on the yacht and did business on *Circe* where he could still have his family around him.

'It's beautiful,' she told him gently, grey eyes silver bright with love and understanding because she had gradually come to see that having his own family meant everything to Apollo. He had longed to have a loving family when he was a child and had been sadly disillusioned by his father's disastrous remarriages. Creating his own family as an adult had given him a kind of rebirth, allowing him to grow into the man he might have become had he had a less dysfunctional childhood.

'No, you're the jewel who outshines every setting,' Apollo insisted, claiming her soft mouth in a hungry, demanding kiss that sent little shivers quivering through her. He pinned her to the bed, gazing down at her with unashamed satisfaction. 'Do you think Vito and Holly are aiming for a football team in the kid department?' he asked curiously.

'I wouldn't be surprised,' she said with a grin. 'But it'll be a year or two before I want another one. Tobias and Sofia are exhausting.'

'Almost as demanding as their mother,' Apollo groaned, intercepting the fingers running along a lean, muscular thigh and carrying her tiny hand to a rather more responsive area. 'But I *love* that about you.'

Pixie looked up into glittering green enticement fringed by black. 'I love you, Apollo.'

'Isn't that fortunate? Because I'm keeping you for ever,' he admitted thickly.

And later when their guests had arrived and every room seemed to be awash with overexcited exploring children and equally excited dogs, the adults settled down with drinks and snacks and Pixie curled comfortably up beneath Apollo's protective arm and admired the sparkling lanterns glowing on the Christmas tree. It promised to be another wonderful Christmas and she was sincerely grateful for the happy ending she had found with the man she loved.

* * * * *